JASON TROCK

ABOUT THE AUTHOR

ISAAC ADAMSON is the author of three previous books starring Billy Chaka: *Tokyo Suckerpunch, Hokkaido Popsicle,* and *Dreaming Pachinko.* He has written for *Time* magazine's Asian edition and recently had his first novel published in Japanese. He plays soccer well, guitar poorly, and lives in Chicago.

ALSO BY ISAAC ADAMSON

Dreaming Pachinko

Hokkaido Popsicle

Tokyo Suckerpunch

Kinki Lullaby

Isaac Adamson

PERENNIAL
DARK
ALLEY

An Imprint of HarperCollinsPublishers

HarperCollins books may be purchased for educational, business, or sales promotional use. For information please write: Special Markets Department, HarperCollins Publishers Inc., 10 East 53rd Street, New York, NY 10022.

FIRST EDITION

Dark Alley is a federally registered trademark of HarperCollins Publishers.

Designed by Jeffrey Pennington

Library of Congress Cataloging-in-Publication Data

Adamson, Isaac.
    Kinki lullaby / by Isaac Adamson.— 1st ed.
        p. cm.
    ISBN 0-06-051624-0
        1. Chaka, Billy (Fictitious character)—Fiction.
    2. Americans—Japan—Fiction. 3. Osaka (Japan)—Fiction.
    4. Journalists—Fiction. 5. Theater—Fiction. I. Title.

PS3551.D39538K56 2004
813'.6—dc22   2004043915

04 05 06 07 08 JTC/RRD 10 9 8 7 6 5 4 3 2 1

Farewell to this world, and to the night farewell.
We who walk the road to death, to what should we be likened?
To the frost by the road which leads to the graveyard,
Vanishing with each step we take ahead:
How sad is this dream of a dream!

—CHIKAMATSU MONZAEMON, *LOVE SUICIDES AT SONEZAKI*

ACT I

Chapter One

The Kinki Foundation

The Royal Ballroom in Osaka's PanCosmo Hotel was one of those rooms you just couldn't trust. Vaulted ceilings, marble floors, ivory columns, a colossal chandelier—all of it luxuriant but suspect, impressive in a way that put you immediately on guard. According to the pamphlet, the room was designed at the height of the bubble eighties and modeled after some long-forgotten Shanghai ballroom from the nineteen twenties, which was itself no doubt based on some vanished piece of nineteenth-century Europe. But there were no signs of age, no traces of history whatsoever. Everything glowed with such a perfect sheen you felt suspended in time, utterly disconnected from the outside world. It was the kind of room where you expected someone to walk in and yell "cut," prompting an army of burly stagehands to emerge from nowhere and begin dismantling the scenery while the well-heeled guests revealed themselves as nothing more than extras in rented suits anxious to check their cell phone messages.

But there were only a few guests left in the Royal Ballroom by the time 1 arrived. Those remaining were clustered in small groups, talking in low tones and exchanging muted smiles. The room lacked the nervous laughter and overdone conviviality of strangers forced to socialize. No one exchanging name cards, no one bowing or shaking hands. Most people weren't even wearing the nametag stickers that came with the information packet. The cocktail kickoff to the Kinki Foundation's annual conference looked less like a meet-and-greet than some solemn reunion to commemorate a fallen comrade long after the cause had been abandoned.

1 ordered a Jack and Coke at the bar and watched an eight-piece band dressed like low-rent Liberaces sleepwalk through some old-timey jazz. Looking around, 1 realized 1 was not only the sole foreigner in the room, but the youngest conference attendee by a good ten or fifteen years. Unlike the other guests, 1 didn't wear a tie or even a coat, just my usual wrinkled white cotton button-down, black slacks, and wing tip shoes. You could've mistaken me for one of the catering staff, except even they were better dressed. And like a dumbass, I'd worn the stupid nametag sticker.

Billy Chaka, it read. *Youth in Asia Magazine.*

1 could've taken the damn thing off, but 1 was too tired to care. My mouth was dry, my eyes stung, and 1 felt like eighteen hours of mass transit. My trip to Osaka had been booked by Chuck, *Youth in Asia* magazine's accountant and

travel agent—a conflict of interest if ever there was one—and he'd sent me on a ridiculous route from Cleveland to Chicago to San Francisco, to Tokyo Narita, where I had to take a bus to Tokyo Haneda before catching my flight to the New Itami Airport and then eventually arriving in Osaka via another bus.

When I finally checked into the PanCosmo Hotel, there wasn't even time for a shower before rushing off to catch the last of the reception. I'd been invited to Japan's second city to accept some kind of award from the Kinki Foundation for "an extraordinarily positive and authoritative" article I'd written nearly eight years ago about a thirteen-year-old Bunraku puppetry prodigy. That's what the fax they sent said, anyway. While the Bunraku theater experience itself wasn't something I'd soon forget, I could barely remember the article and had never heard of the Kinki Foundation. Still, my editor, Sarah, insisted I attend because *Youth in Asia* didn't win many awards. We hadn't taken home any prizes since my old editor was at the helm, and even then it was a second-place bowling trophy.

A quick glance at the event schedule sent by the Kinki Foundation told me what I was in for. "Kinki" was a word used to refer to the Kansai area—Kyoto, Osaka, Kobe, and the surrounding prefectures. It was considered the ancient heart of Japan, center of art, politics, and commerce long before Tokyo started dominating every aspect of Japanese culture. Nowadays, Osaka enjoyed the same kind of one-way, imagined rivalry with Tokyo that Chicago had with New York. The conference's stated purpose was to "celebrate the unique cultural assets, explore the natural wonders, and highlight the commercial advantages of the incomparable Kansai region." This they were doing through a series of guest lectures, presentations, and panel discussions, followed by an awards ceremony to be held on the final night.

I told Sarah that aside from a Pyongyang prison, the last place I needed to be was in a fancy hotel watching veiled infomercials, listening to stultifying speeches, and accepting pointless awards from a group of geriatric regional boosters. As a teen journalist, I needed to be on the streets of Shibuya finding out why golf shoes were all the rage with high school girls, or hanging out in Nagoya discos trying to trace the origins of the *paco paco* dance craze. I needed to be writing about Beijing cybercafés or Korean transsexual pop idols or Balinese cult leaders or anything but the Kinki Foundation.

"You're not going there to write," Sarah said. "You're going to accept an award. It's good PR for the magazine. Have a few drinks, make a nice little acceptance speech thanking the kind people of the Kinki Foundation, and come home. Nothing could be simpler."

"I didn't go into journalism for awards," I said.

"You've made that abundantly clear," said Sarah.

Then she smiled that smile.

One week later, I was in Osaka.

When my whiskey and Coke finally arrived it was mostly Coke and mostly flat. I drank it anyway and was about to order another when I noticed a man eyeing me from across the room.

"Gentleman" was the word that first sprang to mind, for he carried himself with an upright quality that suggested dignity and decorum and all that stuff people had left behind before I was born. He was standing near a group engaged in a slow bout of head nodding, but I couldn't tell if he was actually part of their circle of consent or not. After a few moments, he broke from their orbit and began walking my way.

"Mr. Billy Chaka," he called as he neared. He had a sandpapery voice and was dressed in the standard dark-suit-red-tie combination remarkable only for its unremarkability. I judged by the gray hair swooped back over his squarish head that he was between fifty-five and sixty. "I'm honored you could attend our conference," he said. "We are all of us so very honored." He told me his name was Mr. Oyamada. I told him it was a pleasure to meet him. He said the pleasure was all his. After a moment's hesitation, hc added, "Actually, we've met once before."

I couldn't place him, and was stumbling through one of about fifty stock Japanese apologies I'd picked up over the years when he interrupted with a laugh like an old car failing to start.

"No need to explain," he said. "I'm not surprised you don't remember me. It was some time ago when last we met, though in ways it feels like only yesterday."

"Well, nice to meet you a second time."

I thought he'd hand me his business card next, but he didn't. Instead he took a sip of his champagne. I ordered that second Jack and Coke. When it became apparent he wasn't going to tell me how we'd met previously, I started looking for a graceful exit. None presented itself, so I did the next best thing and stood there grinning like an idiot. At length Oyamada cleared his throat and spoke again.

"I should mention that I am acting executive vice codirector in chief of the Kinki Foundation's Annual Conference Invitation and Awards Subcommittee," he announced. With that, he finally handed me his card. I started to reach for mine and realized I'd left them upstairs in my briefcase, which in Japan is like showing up naked for your mother-in-law's funeral. After apologizing, I followed protocol and gazed at his card as if I were trying to memorize a treasure map. *Daichi Oyamada,* the card read, *Executive Vice Codirector in chief of the Annual Conference Invitations and Awards Subcommittee.* Somehow they'd managed to print his whole title on just one side.

"Must be a big responsibility," I said.

"One I'm perfectly unworthy of," he said. "For a prestigious group like the Kinki Foundation to show such faith in my limited abilities . . . well, it's a tremendous honor."

Mr. Oyamada shot a glance across the room as if suddenly distracted, though there was nothing much going on. I tried again to place him, thinking I would've at least remembered a voice like his. My drink arrived. It tasted a little better than the first one, thanks to the first one.

"Forgive my being presumptuous," Oyamada began. "But perhaps you may remember me after all. They say we remember people in context. You may remember me in relation to a young man named Tetsuo."

The name on his card should've tipped me off right away, but it was only then that I figured out he was Tetsuo's father. Even the name "Tetsuo" would've meant nothing to me a few days ago, but after Sarah delivered the fax I started wondering about the piece on the Bunraku puppeteer that I was being awarded for and decided to go through the back issues of *Youth in Asia* to refresh my memory.

The article was titled "Prince of the Puppets!"—a headline whose giddy exclamation point and general corniness marked it as the work of Ed, the curmudgeonly editor who ran the magazine in the good old days, when Sarah was just an intern happy to pilfer review copies of the latest Melt Banana and Violent Onsen Geisha albums. It was a short piece I'd written about a thirteen-year-old puppeteer named Tetsuo Oyamada, the youngest performer ever given the honor of appearing as a leg operator at the prestigious National Bunraku Theater. The theater was here in Osaka, the birthplace of the art form, and was the only theater in the world devoted exclusively to traditional Japanese puppet drama. As the stringless puppets weighed up to fifty pounds and stood about four feet tall, Bunraku puppeteers worked in teams of three. Only the lead puppeteer was permitted to show his face. The other two were cloaked head to toe in black, wearing hooded masks that recalled both ninjas and medieval executioners. As leg operator, or *ashi-zukai,* Tetsuo Oyamada was the low man on the totem pole. Typically, one had to spend ten years there before moving up to the position of *hidari-zukai,* the left-hand operator, and another ten before being given the honor of *omo-zukai,* the chief manipulator. But Tetsuo was so gifted that many believed he would become a permanent chief manipulator before even reaching twenty-five, an unprecedented feat in the modern history of Bunraku.

There wasn't much more to the article. Just a few quotes, a woefully brief overview of Bunraku, and a picture of mop-headed Tetsuo posing next to an exquisitely costumed puppet of Ohatsu, the doomed courtesan in the three-hundred-year-old play *Love Suicides at Sonezaki.* Not a bad article, but by no means one of my best. Certainly nothing worthy of an award. The fact that the young puppeteer's pop was a ranking member of the Kinki Foundation explained a lot about what I was doing here, though at the time I didn't know just how much.

"So how is your son these days?" I asked him.

Mr. Oyamada grinned and sucked air through his teeth, meaning I'd asked a difficult question. It was a sound I heard so often in Japan I could almost dance to it. For several moments, Oyamada seemed at a loss for words. The crowd was dwindling now. Across the ballroom, the band had stopped playing and looked to be discussing whether it was worth continuing.

"The reception is coming to a close," Mr. Oyamada rasped. "Perhaps you would like to join me for a drink or two? I must confess, I've been looking forward to speaking with you for quite some time."

I tried like hell to decline. Seventeen time zones and two watered-down cocktails had me feeling like an overcooked noodle. All I wanted to do was go to my room, take a hot shower, buy a cold Kirin lager from the vending machine, and turn on the TV to find out if Channel Eight still had the same weathergirl. She had a way of saying "barometric pressure" that put the world into perspective.

But as a representative of *Youth in Asia,* I didn't want to sever any relationships my so-called superiors in Cleveland might be nurturing with these Kinki people and ruin the magazine's shot at good PR, so I found myself agreeing to accompany Mr. Oyamada, even going so far as to say I'd be delighted.

My delight was nothing next to Oyamada's. He nodded enthusiastically, showing a smile like a weathered fence. The band had evidently resolved their dispute, for they now began a creaky rendition of "Somewhere Over the Rainbow." Most of them, anyway. The clarinetist sat with his arms crossed, head dropped against his chin. I couldn't be sure, but it looked like he was sleeping.

I made an excuse to go upstairs and change into some fresh clothes, and Oyamada agreed to meet me in the lobby. In my room on the ninth floor, I put on another pair of black slacks, a clean white T-shirt, and the same white button-down. I'd brought seven of them, one for each day I was staying, but I didn't want to get ahead of schedule. I had a quick shave, too quick, and ended up nicking myself. While I dabbed the cut on my neck with a tissue, I checked myself in the mirror. Jet lag stared back at me, but at least he had a clean shave and a fresh white undershirt.

I walked out of my room and headed down the hall to wait for the elevator. I used to have a phobia about elevators, one I'd mostly conquered, but I still felt a little anxious. The corridor was quiet and empty, with a window down the hall offering a view of anonymous office buildings bisected by a swath of railroad tracks. A light rain was falling, misting the skyline a washed-out gray. I watched black umbrella tops blossom out of buildings, float down the sidewalk, collapse into waiting cabs. A bell sounded and the elevator doors whisked opened.

I stepped inside and the doors were about to close when a hand reached in and stopped them. I hit the "door open" button and the owner of the hand stepped inside.

"Sorry about that," he said. "Thanks for waiting."

Even before he spoke I pegged him right away as American. I can't say why exactly, because it wasn't as if he were chewing bubble gum, wearing flip-flops, and a God Bless America baseball hat. He was a loose-limbed, hawk-faced kid in his early twenties dressed in a wrinkled polo shirt and khaki slacks. The kid had a full head of sandy brown hair and a smile that wouldn't stay put. He punched the lobby button even though it was already lit and backed into the corner.

As we descended, advertisements for hotel restaurants and shops faded in and out on a video screen set in the elevator control panel. The screen was flashing an ad for a hair salon called Viva Diva when my fellow American suddenly spoke.

"So," he said. "Business or pleasure?"

"Business, mostly," I said. "You?"

He gave a one-note laugh. "Long story, I guess you might say."

He rocked back on his heels and that smile started moving around his face again. The guy seemed uncomfortable talking but for some reason felt like he had to, maybe because we were both Americans or maybe because he just didn't like silence. I dabbed the cut on my neck with a tissue. It had pretty much stopped bleeding now. We reached the fourth floor. The doors opened but no one was there waiting.

"First spell in Japan?" he asked.

The doors shut, we continued down.

I shook my head. "Only my second time in Osaka, though."

"You here for a symposium or something like that?"

I was about to ask him how he knew when I realized I was still wearing my stupid nametag sticker. "Something like that," I said. "It's a conference. Group called the Kinki Foundation, promoting the Kansai region. It's their annual meeting."

"Wow. So you're like a motivational speaker?"

That'd be the day. "I'm a journalist."

"You're doing a story?"

"No. Actually, they're giving me some kind of award."

"No kidding? Wow. That calls for congratulations."

"I guess."

"Congratulations it is. Must be nice being you."

I would've guessed he was trying to wind me up except

he just didn't seem like the type. He had that familiar Midwestern nasal quality to his speech that made everything he said sound like a variant of "gee whiz." I peeled off my nametag sticker and slapped it onto his polo shirt. He wobbled, his grin partially eclipsed.

"There you go," I said. "Have a swell time being me."

It took him a moment to unravel, but then he looked down at the nametag sticker and laughed. I laughed with him. The elevator finally reached the lobby and the doors sprang open. Across the lobby, Mr. Oyamada was already waiting.

Chapter Two

The Woman in the Stairwell

There were six different bars inside the PanCosmo Hotel but apparently none of them were suitable because minutes later Mr. Oyamada and I were in a taxicab headed south across the Daini Neyagawa River. Osaka was a city famous for rivers, though most of them had long ago been paved over, drained, and converted into highways or subway tunnels. The city as such had no single focal point, but was concentrated around the rival nuclei of Umeda in the north and Namba to the south— huge shopping and entertainment districts that exerted the gravitational pull of twin planets. Mr. Oyamada pointed out Osaka Castle rising from the middle of the park on our right, spotlit against a diffused background of office buildings looming in the fog.

"All of this is new," Oyamada said. "Except the castle, and it's still a postwar reconstruction. But most of these other buildings weren't here even ten, twenty years ago. This part of Osaka was slow to develop after the war. Lots of bad feelings, lingering superstitions. Thousands died here during the air raids in 1945. Long before that, countless samurai were killed during various castle sieges. Hideyoshi Toyotomi, you've heard of him? He once had some three thousand enemies beheaded right where that park sits. Many of the older generation still associate this area with death. But now it's being developed because, well, no space, no choice."

Rain painted the night an oily black streaked with jittery neon as we neared the celebrated Dotomborigawa, a manmade canal built in the seventeenth century. Oyamada told me what restaurant used to be here and what shop used to be there five years and ten years ago and when he was a boy. At times, I had difficulty understanding him because he slipped into *kansai-ben,* the regional dialect of the Kyoto-Osaka-Kobe area. *Kansai-ben* wasn't taught in schools and you didn't hear it outside the region except in old *yakuza* movies or TV shows featuring *manzai* comedians. Osaka was famous for these comic duos, and its citizens were said to naturally fall into straight man and goofball roles, conversing in rapid-fire rhythms charged with heightening absurdities and quick-witted reversals. I must not have made a very good counterpoint to Oyamada because he'd lapsed into silence by the time the taxi finally came to a halt on Sakai-suji Avenue just south of the Nipponbashi Bridge.

We got out in front of a two-story building decorated by a fifteen-foot-tall space alien lording over a sign for Deep Boom Karaoke. What aliens had to do with karaoke I didn't know, but I was hoping Mr. Oyamada didn't want to spend the next few hours serenading me. My apprehension must have shown, because as we hurried from the cab Oyamada opened his umbrella and spoke, his voice barely audible above the soft hiss of the rain.

"Don't worry," he said with a smile. "I can't sing."

That's what worried me, I didn't say.

"Doctor's orders," Oyamada rasped. "No singing allowed."

We hustled down the sidewalk while cars splashed by on the street next to us and rumbled over the Hanshin Expressway directly overhead. People came flooding out to the subway entrance while others stood huddled under the covered shopping arcade across the way, waiting for the light to change. Activity swirled all around, but Oyamada was completely oblivious to it. The velocity of Osaka was something you only noticed if you didn't live there.

"It's this polyp," Oyamada continued, putting a hand to his throat. "Developed it several years ago. I've had it removed from my vocal cords three times, but it always grows back. Brought my career to a premature end, I'm afraid. You probably recall that I used to be a *tayu.*"

Fact was, I didn't remember until he told me. A *tayu* was a Bunraku narrator. As I'd learned researching my article eight years ago, Bunraku consisted of three elements—the narrator, the puppeteers, and the shamisen players. The *tayu* was considered the intellectual of Bunraku and was the star of any production, as he did each character's voice and chanted, sang, or sobbed for hours on end as the text called for. Not a gig for someone with a ruined voice, though hard-core Bunraku aficionados would likely argue that spirit and stamina and interpretive ability and all kinds of intangible qualities were more important than functional vocal cords. I told Mr. Oyamada I was sorry to hear about his polyp and thought to myself it had been a long eight years.

After a couple twists and turns we came to Hozenji Yokocho, a narrow cobblestone street where the neon gave way to giant paper lanterns and darkened wooden doorways. I'd read about the place, but had never been inside any of the tiny restaurants or drinking establishments. Most Osakans in my age group and income bracket probably hadn't, either. They were the kind of exclusive joints where hostesses were on a name basis with an aging clientele that often numbered in the single digits. Curtained entrances acted as discreet barriers to the uninitiated, and the prices did the rest. A gas leak explosion had recently destroyed a nearby theater with roots in the seventeenth century and razed nineteen bars and restaurants, prompting the government to propose widening the three-meter lane to keep fires from spreading as quickly. Celebrities and Osaka elites who patronized Hozenji Yokocho reacted by spearheading a drive to restore the lane to its original constricted condition, fire dangers be damned. I was glad it was raining.

Oyamada motioned me through the entrance of a place called Kagekiyo's Cave. Six empty stools stood at a short counter and a mute audience of wooden puppet heads gazed down from the bar's perimeter. There must have been almost fifty of them hung ear to ear like shrunken skulls in a cannibal hut, some creepily lifelike in their animated expressions, others like death masks with their Kabuki-white blankness. There were three low tables a short distance from the bar. Everything in this place was a short distance from the bar.

"Oyamada-sama!" The mama-san beamed as we

stepped inside. Her rumpled hair rose in parrotish tufts and she wore a baggy green-checked blouse and purple slacks over her thin frame. It was the kind of outfit no woman would be caught dead wearing in Tokyo but in Osaka hardly raised an eyebrow. Behind her, an array of bottles twinkled under the amber lights.

"Making any money?" Oyamada said.

"Bochi bochi denna," answered the woman with a shrug. Then she asked how Oyamada's son was doing. Mr. Oyamada's only response was the tooth-sucking sound he'd given me earlier.

"You should have brought him along," the woman chided. "I read in the *Osaka Bunraku Hyōbanki* recently that he premiered as chief operator during a touring production of scenes from *Love Suicides at Imamiya*. Or am I mistaken? Was it *Love Suicides at Amajima?*"

"Actually—"

"Love Suicides at the Sunken Well? No, that wasn't it. *Love Suicides on the Eve of the Kôshin Festival?* Now that I think about it, it had to be *Love Suicides in Midsummer with an Icy Blade*. Or *Love Suicides and Double-folded Picture Books*. Or *Love Suicides and the Double-brocaded Obi*. Or was it—"

"Actually—"

"Love Suicides at the Women's Temple?"

"Actually, it was *The Uprooted Pine*," said Oyamada.

"Ah!" The hostess clapped her hands. "I knew it!"

"Just a temporary promotion," said Oyamada. "The great Master Toyomatsu was undergoing a gall bladder operation, and so the honor fell to my clumsy son. Just a collection of minor scenes in a single matinee. Nothing so special."

"But he performed the *michiyuki?"*

Oyamada blushed, scratched his head. "Well, yes, but—"

"Do you know the *michiyuki?*" she asked me excitedly. Before I could answer she told me the *michiyuki* was a traveling scene. There were all kinds of *michiyuki,* she said, but in a love-suicide play, it was the part where doomed lovers make their final journey into the night before dying together at daybreak. "It's the very essence of any double love suicide play," she went on. "The most beautiful literary passages come from the *michiyuki,* and well, it's a very important scene, isn't it so, Mr. Oyamada?"

"Every scene is important," Oyamada said.

"He's being modest," she told me in a stage whisper. "The *michiyuki* is heartbreaking when performed with the skill of someone like Mr. Oyamada's son. Not that Mr. Oyamada himself was any slouch. Ask anyone, they'll tell you he was one of the best chanters of his generation. Not a dry eye in the house when the great Oyamada was at the lectern."

"Bored them to tears," Oyamada said, though the smile on his face said he was flattered. "Mr. Chaka, I'd like you to meet my old friend Ogawa-san. Mr. Chaka is a writer."

"Nice to meet you," I said.

"Oh, my! He really does speak Japanese!" She laughed and daintily clapped a hand over her mouth, giving Mr. Oyamada such a surprised look you'd think I'd just walked on the ceiling. "So you're a writer? How exciting! What do you write?"

"Articles for a teen magazine in America. *Youth in Asia.*"

"How exciting," Ms. Ogawa repeated, somewhat less excitedly. "Welcome to Kagekiyo's. You're probably wondering about the puppet heads. My late husband was once apprentice to the chief head carver of the National Theater. But as one look around will tell you, my husband had no talent."

"Nonsense," said Oyamada.

"It's true," Ogawa trumpeted. "He'd start making the face of a beautiful young woman and by the time he finished it was an ugly old man. He gave it up as a career, but still carved as a hobby. Kept at it for years, but blind old Kagekiyo was the only one he could ever get right."

As she spoke, she pointed at the puppet heads hanging around the bar's perimeter. I was no expert, but I could see what she meant. The collection was riddled with lumpy noses and misaligned eyes, crooked mouths and cracked finishes. Some heads were too pointed, others almost square. Interspersed were several versions of a gaunt old man with bushy white hair, sunken cheeks, and blind eyes that seemed to peer in every direction at once. I guessed he must've been Kagekiyo.

After some more good-humored banter Ms. Ogawa fetched a half-empty bottle of Johnnie Walker Blue and two glasses. Oyamada and I took our seats at a table all of six feet away, neither of us speaking as he poured my drink and I poured his while Ogawa busied herself wiping down glasses and the puppet heads looked on in silence. I thought about the weathergirl on Channel Eight, wondered what she would be wearing tonight. Probably a red blazer. She must've had the world's largest collection of red blazers.

"Journalism must be a fascinating field," Oyamada began.

"Beats scrubbing toilets," I agreed.

Oyamada nodded solemnly and pawed his glass from hand to hand. Ever since he approached me inside the Royal Ballroom it was clear he had something on his mind, and I was beginning to wonder how much longer he was going to talk around it. "Still, you must meet some interesting people," said Oyamada. "After you've written a piece, do you ever find yourself thinking about the subject at some later time? Wondering what became of them?"

"Depends on which subject," I said.

"Of course," wheezed Oyamada. "But take my son, just for example. Do you remember him well?"

Tetsuo Oyamada, I thought. Bamboo skinny, tall for thirteen, proud owner of an unruly mop of jet-black hair. Spent half our interview pushing the bangs out of his eyes and the other half letting them fall over his face like a veil. An intense kid, always fidgeting with nervous energy. Answered questions in a matter-of-fact, polite way but didn't seem comfortable with the whole idea of conversing with an adult. Not so different from a lot of kids his age in that regard. Not so different from a lot of kids in most regards, until you put a puppet in his hands.

"I remember him pretty well," I said.

Oyamada nodded, holding a paper smile in place.

"He seemed like a good kid," I added.

"He's useless." Oyamada chuckled. "But your article was quite flattering. You wrote of him, 'one can't help but notice the relaxed gleam in his eye just before he slips on the black hooded robe of the Bunraku puppeteer. It is the look of a young man discovering his place in the world, the look of someone who has found home.'"

"Sometimes I lay it on pretty thick."

Oyamada shook his head. "No, no, I know precisely the expression you described, saw this look on his face countless times when he was growing up. I've often found solace in your words over the years, whenever my idiot son was faced with some new hurdle. Such a tremendous honor, your article."

I squirmed in my seat and mumbled some kind of thank-you.

"A tremendous honor," Oyamada repeated.

"Yeah, well. What's he up to these days?"

No tooth sucking this time. After a quick glance to confirm that proprietress Ogawa was out of earshot, Oyamada hunched forward, bringing his face within inches of my own. "Things," he said, "could be better. Difficulties have recently developed. Perhaps I should just come out and say it. There's no easy way to put this—frankly, I don't even know how to begin. But yes, I suppose the right thing is just to come out and say it."

Instead, he sighed wearily, leaned back in his chair and closed his eyes. He placed his palms flat against the table as if to keep it from floating away and took a few deep breaths. When he opened his eyes again, he hunkered over the table and spoke in a throaty growl intended as a whisper.

"My son is no longer with the National Bunraku Theater."

Oyamada stared at me for a moment, allowing the full weight to sink in before he slumped back into his chair, the pronouncement taking his every ounce of strength.

"That's a drag," I said.

Mr. Oyamada shook his head. "Tetsuo was the only third-generation performer in the entire company. Now that I have retired, he is all that is left of the Oyamada legacy."

"Well, you know how it goes. Times change."

"My father was a diligent chanter. What he lacked in ability he made up for with discipline. He once famously borrowed a palanquin and ferried passengers all the way from Umeda to the Imamiya Shrine, just to study the rhythm of a palanquin man's breathing so that he might more accurately portray a passing moment in *The Couriers of Hell*."

A method chanter, I thought. A man ahead of his time.

"The war ended his career," said Oyamada, crossing his arms. "And so it was up to me. I had no talent whatsoever. Took me thirteen years to learn the art of weeping, but through hard work even I managed not to make a complete fool of myself. And this was during the darkest days of Bunraku. After the Occupation, when audiences turned their backs on classical culture, condemned anything traditional as backward, even militaristic. We suffered factional in-fighting, union problems, financial insolvency. Tetsuo has no idea how difficult it was then, no appreciation of the sacrifices we all made to keep Bunraku alive, much less keep food on the table. Do you have children, Mr. Chaka?"

I shook my head.

"Being a parent is a duck's work," Mr. Oyamada said. "You're furiously kicking your feet underwater, struggling just to stay afloat, but all the kid ever sees is you moving effortlessly across the surface of the pond. A duck's work."

He nodded to himself and took another sip of his drink.

"I came to accept that Tetsuo wouldn't become a chanter," he said. "Kids are always first intrigued by the dolls, and you saw it yourself, the way he moves with the puppets as if they were an extension of his body, their arms and legs no different from his own. It's the one area in his life where he's demonstrated a modest ability. Getting himself thrown out of the company is simply unacceptable."

"He got thrown out?"

"Unacceptable," Oyamada repeated. His grip tightened around his whiskey glass, his knuckles going white while his face went red. I started to take another sip of my whiskey, but if I took another sip my glass would be empty and Oyamada would refill it. As long as I finished my glass he'd refill it again and again until we stumbled out of the bar in search of the last train home. Osaka is not for the faint of liver.

"There was an incident in Sapporo," Mr. Oyamada said after a time. "Just as the company was finishing up their fall tour. Apparently, Tetsuo and another young puppeteer had some kind of disagreement. A very serious disagreement."

"Like a shouting match or fistfight or—"

"I don't know," said Oyamada. "Master Toyomatsu, honorable director of the puppeteers, would only tell me that this Sapporo incident was very serious. Both Tetsuo and the other young man were dismissed. Tetsuo won't tell me anything about what happened. He claims he did nothing wrong and refuses to apologize."

"I'm sorry to hear it."

"It's a terrible situation. But maybe you can help."

I didn't see how.

"Master Toyomatsu remembers you," Oyamada explained. "We've had many a lively discussion about your article over the years. Though he contested certain aspects of your work, even he was forced to concede that for a non-Kansai native you displayed a rudimentary understanding of the core essence of Bunraku."

I didn't know if it was a compliment or not, and for roughly the tenth time that night I had no idea what to say. My article had been just a few hundred words, a human-interest puff piece containing nothing about Bunraku you couldn't find in a decent encyclopedia. The thought of two lifelong professionals debating my meager offering was even more laughable than the Kinki Foundation giving me an award for it.

"Will you speak with Master Toyomatsu?" Oyamada pleaded. "I realize it's a terrible imposition. Especially on one who has already done so much. But I've exhausted every other course of action."

"Let me get this straight," I said. "You want me to meet Master Toyomatsu and ask him to take your son back into the company? And you think he'll listen to me because of this article I wrote eight years ago?"

"I'm pleased you understand."

"I don't think I do."

"You're an outsider," Oyamada said. "Not part of the Bunraku world, nor Osaka, nor even Japan. You're someone with an objective viewpoint. Journalists are supposed to be objective, no? Neutral. You have nothing to gain or lose in seeing my son back in the theater. You are a completely disinterested party."

He had the last part right.

"I'm at my wit's end," Oyamada said. "I've prayed at the Ikudama Shrine in desperation, and even as I stood in front of the altar I could not see the Buddha's face, obscured as it was behind the clouds of my own discontent."

He lingered over the last line, delivering it syllable by syllable. Maybe being a chanter for so many years had affected his speech pattern or he was quoting from some play or other, but either way I knew I was witnessing a performance of some sort.

"If you could just meet with Master Toyomatsu," he continued, "I've no doubt your mere presence will gently remind him of my son's limited abilities. This problem threatens to destroy my family."

Sounded a little melodramatic, but I could tell that he was intensely proud of his son. Calling him useless and foolish and idiotic was pretty much standard in a place where no one openly bragged about their kids. And though it's a well-worn cliché that the Japanese tend to define themselves based on the various groups to which they belong, it's one I'd found was often true with men of Oyamada's generation. And there was no more traditionally Japanese a group than Bunraku performers, proud guardians of a national cultural heritage, living links to an idealized and rapidly disappearing past. I could understand how when Tetsuo got kicked out of the theater, Mr. Oyamada might've felt he'd lost a part of his own identity, but I couldn't help wondering how Tetsuo himself felt about it.

"What if Tetsuo doesn't want to go back?" I said.

"Bunraku flows through his blood," Oyamada said. "You wrote as much yourself. In the theater, you said, he had the look of someone 'discovering their place in this world, the look of someone who has found home.' My son is a little lost right now. I am confident you will help him find home again."

It wasn't a confidence I shared. I took another sip of my whiskey and tried again to formulate some sort of polite refusal. In the process, I accidentally finished off the drink. Mr. Oyamada smiled gleefully and poured me another.

"To the New Year," he toasted.

"To the New Year," I repeated.

"May it bring good fortune."

"To good fortune."

"May friendships be forged and ties strengthened," he said, eyes gleaming. I repeated the strange toast and wondered if, in uttering it, I'd somehow just agreed to help his son. Oyamada downed his drink in one gulp as if to seal the deal. There was nothing to do but refill his glass. He next proposed a toast to the future of *Young Asian* magazine. I didn't bother correcting him on the title, but just raised my glass and drank, feeling a little like a puppet myself.

*H*ours later the rain had subsided into an icy drizzle, but the taxi driver still insisted on shielding me under his umbrella as he shuttled me to the entrance of the PanCosmo Hotel. Inside, the lobby was bright, expansive, and completely deserted. I had no idea how late it was—my watch was still on Cleveland time and I was too tired to do the math. I listened to my wing tips squeak across the tiled floor, the sound amplified in the emptiness as I walked across the lobby, past the elevators. I decided I'd combated my elevator phobia enough for one day and headed up the stairs.

If the hotel lobby resembled a cathedral hall with its high ceilings, robust columns, and big picture windows, the stairwell was like the passage leading to the bell tower. Narrow and poorly lit, the kind of place you'd expect to find cobwebs, flickering torches, bats. As I trudged up the stairs I wondered just what the hell I would say to Master Toyomatsu tomorrow. And as for coming to Tetsuo's aid, he was a nice kid but one I hadn't seen in eight years. Who knew what kind of adult he'd become? Master Toyomatsu could've had very good reasons for throwing him out. Mr. Oyamada claimed he didn't have the full story, but he must've known more about the Sapporo incident than he was letting on.

It was too late to get out of it now. Mr. Oyamada had given me the address of the National Bunraku Theater and said that Master Toyomatsu would be expecting me after the first performance tomorrow afternoon. Even though I'd been to the theater before, Oyamada insisted on drawing me a little map and explaining in detail how to transfer from the JR Loop train to the Tanimachi subway line. That was the last thing he did before we stumbled out of Kagekiyo's Cave and went our separate ways, he in one cab and I in another, both of us half-asleep and more than half-drunk.

As I rounded the corner leading to the sixth floor, I suddenly became aware of a presence on the landing above. Through the dark I could just make out a figure looming low to the ground. At first I thought it wasn't a person at all, just a shadow, a trick of diminished light and eighty-proof liquor. I took two cautious steps forward. It wasn't a shadow. A woman was lying on the floor, curled up with her hands over her stomach. She wasn't moving.

"Hello?" I called. No answer.

I took a deep breath and moved in for a closer look. The woman had short hair, gelled and fastened haphazardly with a series of metal clips. Her skin was the color of old pearls and her body almost childishly small. She was dressed in a raincoat with a midnight-blue cocktail dress peeking out beneath her unbuttoned collar. I noted the coat was dry, meaning she'd been headed out of the hotel rather than up to her room.

She wasn't dead and didn't appear to be injured. I figured she was probably drunk. Maybe she'd had a few too many at one of the bars in the hotel, Club Myopic on the ninth floor maybe, or Molotov Cocktail on floor twelve. I pictured her dizzily reeling down the stairs, sitting for a moment to get the spins under control before they took over, and she pitched forward, passed out cold. I leaned in to sniff her breath.

Suddenly she bolted upright.

She stared right through me, eyes gone wide, mouth

agape, her throat trembling as if she were trying to scream but couldn't. Her eyes stayed on me as she crabbed backward across the floor until she'd wedged herself against the wall. The movement brought her to her senses. She was no longer frightened, just confused, staring up at me with the look of someone woken from a nightmare. But there was something else in her eyes. Before I knew anything about her past and everything she'd been through, I like to think that even then I recognized a certain sadness there. But I've conjured her image so many times, taken that moment apart and put it back together in so many different ways, that I'll never know exactly what I saw that first night. Maybe I didn't notice anything special at all about the woman in the stairwell, except that she was beautiful.

"You alright?" I finally managed.

She blinked several times and looked around at the barren walls on either side of her. I heard the sound of water trickling down some unseen pipe encased in the walls. Still sitting, she ran a hand over the back of her skull and blinked her eyes. She had no idea where she was.

"Do you need help?"

"I fell asleep," she said. "I'm okay, I just . . . I was asleep."

"Funny place for a nap."

"It's happened before," she said, rising now to stand. Even with high heels, the top of her head came only to my chin. She picked her purse up from the floor and dusted off her raincoat. Nothing in her speech or movements suggested she was drunk. I asked if she needed help down the stairs. She shook her head.

"You sure you're okay?" I asked.

She hesitated as if she were about to say something more but instead she stepped past me and went rattling down the stairs without a word. I stood there on the landing, listening to the clicking of her heels as she descended. I figured she was hurrying away so fast because she was embarrassed, but when she didn't slow her pace after a few floors I began to wonder. I was still wondering when I heard her footsteps stop at the exit six stories below. After a moment's pause, the door to the lobby opened. It closed with a loud thud that echoed through the stairwell and then everything was silent.

Chapter Three

Toka Ebisu and Tibetan Yaks

*T*he National Bunraku Theater was an almost window-
less five-story charcoal-gray box of concrete
and reinforced steel hunkered beneath an
expressway overpass near Dotombori, the
very neighborhood where the art form first
took root some three hundred years ago.
Aside from a few classical flourishes like the
upturned eaves over the entrance and the
vertical latticework running around the first
floor's perimeter, the building was stark
twentieth-century pragmatism, making me
wonder if the architects chose gray to match
the Osaka skyline or because the exterior
would eventually be stained by car exhaust
fumes anyway. Brightly colored banners fluttering in the morning breeze and lanterns
hung above the front doors helped offset the

structure's poker-faced austerity, but overall the exterior offered little indication of the colorful spectacles presented inside.

I arrived at about three P.M. and found the lobby completely packed, mostly with well-dressed men and women on the other side of fifty. Some sort of ceremony was taking place on a makeshift stage in the corner. Several lipsticked young women in white robes and golden hats shaped like giant toes clutched bamboo branches and stood next to a pyramid of wooden sake cups while an older man in a business suit stood in front of a microphone, making a speech. To his left sat a giant sake cask and an oversized wooden mallet.

"Excuse me," a woman in a dark blue blazer called out as I stepped inside. "You're here to see Master Toyomatsu, yes? You are Mr. Billy Chaka?"

I nodded. She smiled above and beyond the call of duty and introduced herself as Kozue. Kozue guided me to a rear entrance manned by a security guard and a bank of video monitors. She spoke near perfect English and worried about my lack of an umbrella and the forecasted rain as we got into the elevator. When the door opened and I motioned her out first, she giggled to cover her embarrassment. I was always forgetting there was no such thing as ladies first in Japan.

The sound of Kozue's heels as we walked down the hall had me flashing back to last night. I thought about the way the woman looked curled on the cold concrete, her shocked expression as she'd suddenly bolted upright, the staccato sound of her descent. It was a sound that had echoed in my head as I lay half-awake into the morning hours, jet lag keeping me semiconscious to more fully enjoy my hangover.

We passed a young guy carrying an armload of what looked to be lacquered hatboxes. Just to break the silence, I asked Kozue what they were for.

"Those are head inspection boxes," she said. "In Japanese drama, there is lots of identity-switching, disguises, playing tricks. Especially in Bunraku, where puppets can transform themselves in ways a real actor couldn't. In some plays, a character is ordered to kill the child of their master. Only sometimes the person substitutes their own child out of loyalty to their retainer. The head inspection box is used to present evidence of the deed. In old Japan, there were craftsmen famous for making beautiful head inspection boxes."

"Nice work if you can get it."

Kozue wrinkled her nose but didn't smile. Then she told me that the forecasters were saying it might rain tomorrow, too. Before she could tell me what the weather was supposed to be like on Sunday, we came to a door at the end of the hall. She knocked and announced my presence. We went inside, took off our shoes, and changed into tan slippers.

The small room was lined with metal shelves bursting with all manner of tools and materials. I remembered the place from my tour, back when I'd first come to write about Tetsuo. Every aspect of the productions, from sewing the costumes to building the props, was handled on-site and subject to centuries of tradition. The dressmaker assembled the puppets' costumes from fine silk that was increasingly hard to come by, making the dolls' kimonos often more costly than the real thing. Rather than use string or wire for the toggles that controlled a puppet's eyes and mouth, a certain type of whale whisker was employed, just as it had been for generations. Aside from perhaps the lights, you could find nothing onstage that didn't exist two or three hundred years ago, and though rehearsals and performances were often videotaped for study, a puppeteer's backstage existence was much the same as it had been for centuries.

Given the emphasis on tradition, it shouldn't have surprised me that the room hadn't changed. On the left side, the head carver sat on the floor, eyes narrowed in concentration as he applied a layer of gesso to a puppet head about the size of a coconut. The heads were reused over and over, caked with new layers of a powdered seashell mix for each new performance until they were nearly twice their original size. When they got too big they were wrapped in wet towels and the gesso peeled off like skin, leaving behind only the original wooden skulls. All were carved of cypress from Nagoya, and some used for more than two hundred years.

But the wigs, the head carver had explained, were made afresh for each production, attached to copper plates, which were nailed to the puppet heads. The same kindly old wigmaster was sitting cross-legged in the exact spot I'd seen him last, looking as if he'd never once left the room during the intervening years. While he painstakingly styled the doll's hair using wire-thin cords of paper, a younger woman to his left sat at a loom making a new wig one labor-intensive hair at a time. In a high corner hung the same framed snapshot of a shaggy Tibetan yak. All the wigs were made from yak's hair. When last I visited, the wigmaster explained that they used to use human hair, but modern shampoos and conditioners and dyes had made them lusterless, unsuitable for the stage. "If the yaks start dyeing their hair," he'd joked, "we're doomed."

And at the center of the room was Master Toyomatsu,

the man I'd come to see. He'd been talking with the wig-master when I arrived, discussing whether a certain char-acter would have a chestnut burr or tea whisk hairdo, but when he saw me he rose, bowed, and made introductions. In an Osaka drawl as thick and sweet as bean paste, he wel-comed me back to the theater, told me how much he en-joyed my article, and how he hoped I would one day again use my talents to help educate people about the inimitable art of Bunraku. Lots of smiling and bowing, but for all that, he didn't seem truly happy to see me.

*M*aster Toyomatsu must've been almost seventy and looked like he'd labored every day of it. His black robe hung loose over his spidery frame, a spare structure that belied the strength and flexibility he'd developed through over half a century of puppeteering. The tight ge-ography of his face was locked in an expression of droll tenacity, as if he were issuing a constant challenge to the world at large, gleefully daring it to cross him. Toyomatsu had been trained to waste as little movement as possible and it showed as we walked down the hall toward his of-fice. For a guy his age, he still had a commanding, almost intimidating physical presence.

When last we'd met, Toyomatsu boasted that pup-peteers had the shortest life spans of anyone in Bunraku. It was a physically demanding art, one requiring the strength of a sumo wrestler and the grace of a geisha. Though there were three puppeteers in a team, as chief manipulator the *omo-zukai* supported the full weight of the puppet throughout most of the performance. What made it even more grueling was that, in order for the puppets to be seen above the horizontal partition used to hide the lower half of the puppeteers' bodies, the chief manipulator had to perform in eight- to eleven-inch clogs made from wood and straw. And because Bunraku developed as a working-class entertainment, the dramas were full of intricately choreographed fisticuffs, swordplay, and full-out battle scenes. At the end of a performance the puppeteers were exhausted and drenched in sweat.

For all that, puppeteering was a comparatively thankless art. Critical praise of a Bunraku performance traditionally went to the narrator, partly because in old Japan puppeteers were often illiterates from Osaka's lower classes and even the untouchable *burakumin* caste. Things had changed in modern times, but I couldn't help thinking the art itself was rigged against the men in black. By design, the audience wasn't supposed to appreciate the puppeteers—nowadays, the audience was allowed to see the *omozukai*'s face, but in the early centuries even the chief puppeteer was hidden behind a black hooded mask. More importantly, the puppet's movements were ideally executed with such fluid precision that for long periods you hardly noticed the puppeteers at all, much less realized they were heaving around fifty pounds of wood, whale whiskers, rope, yak hair, and silk while clomping about on giant platformed sandals and trying not to trip over each other and the unseen prop boys constantly scurrying around the stage to deliver the swords, pipes, fans, umbrellas, and whatever else the character required at any given moment. Bunraku was an art form that simultaneously strove for realism while inherently rejecting it, creating a paradox whereby appreciating a puppeteer's skill meant learning to ignore the puppeteer.

Master Toyomatsu's office looked much like any other. His desk was awash with papers, there were a couple of

framed certificates on his walls. Aside from a few domi-
neering photographs of stern men in formal Bunraku
robes, no doubt Toyomatsu's predecessors, you'd never
know you were in the office of a guy many believed would
soon be named a Living National Treasure. As Toyomatsu
lowered himself into the chair behind his desk, the bottom
of his robe crept up and I noticed his right ankle was bandaged. I wondered how much longer he'd be able to endure
the rigors of the theater, and by the troubled look in his eye
he might have been wondering the same.

"So," he began, "did you see the *Ebessan Musume?*"

"The girls downstairs in the golden hats?" I said.

"Very beautiful, no?" Toyomatsu said. "Today is the second day of the Toka Ebisu festival. Ebisu is the Japanese god
of good fortune and commerce, which makes him an especially popular god here in Osaka. Osaka is a merchant's
town, you know, always been about taking care of business.
The girls are from Imamiya Ebisu Shrine. Being chosen as an
Ebessan Musume is something they compete for all year
long. Anyway, I'm sorry I missed them. We don't get many
women around here, especially young and pretty ones."

He laughed quietly, but what he said was true enough.
Like most Japanese traditions, Bunraku was a male-
dominated world, one where women might work as ticket
sellers or costume makers or even hold high positions in
the front office, but were unofficially forbidden from setting foot onstage.

"Speaking of business," Toyomatsu said, "I agreed to this
meeting as a favor to Mr. Oyamada, but you must promise
me this is all off the record. Oyamada assured me no harm
would come to the Bunraku theater as a result of our meeting, but I need your word that you won't use our discussion
as the basis for some article or other in your magazine."

"I'm just here as a favor to Mr. Oyamada. Same as you."

"Good enough," he said. "As you know, I worked with Oyamada for many years. He was a great chanter. Real shame what became of his voice." Toyomatsu scratched his head, tapped a finger against his desk. "As you can see, I don't have Mr. Oyamada's gift for words. Me, I'm a man who works with his hands. So let's get right down to it. I know why you're here."

That makes one of us, I thought.

"I know why you're here," Toyomatsu repeated, "but there's nothing I can do. I've been mentoring Tetsuo since he was no bigger than a puppet himself, and always figured he'd be my successor. What I'm saying is no one hated to see Tetsuo go more than me. We're like a family here, and losing him was like losing my own son. Not that I have a son, but if I did."

"I appreciate your candor," I said. "But I think what really troubles Mr. Oyamada is that he doesn't understand the circumstances of Tetsuo's dismissal. Tetsuo won't give him any details about this disagreement in Sapporo."

"The Sapporo incident," Toyomatsu said, elongating the last word into a sigh. "Mr. Chaka, I'll share something I'm sure Mr. Oyamada can well appreciate. There are eighty-four members in this company. Every single one of us, from the second shamisen player to the propmaster to the chanter's assistant, all must work in harmony. And nowhere is harmony as important as among the puppeteers. I'm senior director of this bunch. Thirty-one people, more than a third of the whole company, fall under my direct supervision. My job is to make us breathe as one."

He started coughing and pounded a fist against his chest. "There's no room for grudges," he continued, clearing his throat. "Every puppeteer must work with every other puppeteer or the character's spirit will never come to life. Without harmony there's no Bunraku. And the people here, we *are* Bunraku. If I allow discord, I risk the art form itself. Bunraku has survived wars, famines, natural disasters. Movies, television, video games—even this recession. But do you know where the real threat to Bunraku lies?"

I shook my head.

"In the theater itself," Toyomatsu said. "I'm talking about the lowering of standards. Leniency, casual modern attitudes. Lack of discipline. Someday, Bunraku may fall victim to these forces. But not on my watch, Mr. Chaka. Not as long as my eyes are still black."

Toyomatsu then erupted in a rattling cough. As he hacked away, I realized that his long speech hadn't told me anything at all about the events in Sapporo. For a guy who worked with his hands, he could circumlocute with the best of them.

"You alright?" I asked when he'd stopped coughing.

"A cold," he grumbled. "Same cold I get every January. Too many New Year's parties. Anyway, please continue."

I hadn't been saying anything to continue, but I explained again that Mr. Oyamada was frustrated because he didn't know the details of the Sapporo incident. Maybe if he understood what happened it would put his mind at rest.

"Not likely," Toyomatsu said. "In all my years here, I've never seen anything like it. Unspeakable. I'm afraid Mr. Oyamada will just have to accept that his son no longer has a place here. I don't expect him to be happy about it, but he must understand there is really nothing I can do."

"Maybe you can tell me what happened," I said.

Master Toyomatsu said nothing for a moment. I suppose he'd figured I was there to put in an appearance for duty's sake and then be on my merry way, or maybe he thought I'd take the term "unspeakable" literally. But the more he didn't say about that night in Sapporo, the harder my reporterly instincts kicked me in the gut. When people don't talk, it means they have something to say. My job was getting them to say it, and if I was lucky, once in a while I even got the truth.

"Tetsuo assaulted one of the leg operators," Master Toyomatsu finally said, an expression on his face as if the words themselves had a bad taste. "So we asked him to leave."

"You're saying they had a fight?"

"Not exactly," said Toyomatsu. "More like Tetsuo beat him senseless. In the middle of the night. Out of nowhere. They were sharing a hotel room after our fall tour performance in Sapporo, and Tetsuo dragged him out of bed while he was sleeping and slammed his face against the wall. Repeatedly."

So much for breathing as one. "Was the guy badly hurt?"

"He'll recover," Toyomatsu said quietly. "But his nose was broken. He lost two of his teeth, fractured his left orbital lobe, and lacerations on his chin and forehead required nineteen stitches. The doctors said a bone shard from his nose was millimeters from piercing his brain, and just last week, we got a bill from the hotel for recarpeting because the blood wouldn't wash. *That* is what happened in Sapporo. And that is why Mr. Oyamada's son is no longer with the National Bunraku Theater."

The story didn't jibe with the shy, quiet thirteen-year-old moppet I'd met a few years back, but a personality can completely unravel between the ages of thirteen and twenty. Hell, it can unravel between twenty-nine and thirty, between Memorial Day and Labor Day, almost any time at all. I could see why Toyomatsu hadn't wanted to tell Mr. Oyamada about Sapporo. Mr. Oyamada had told me the incident was some sort of disagreement, but this wasn't a disagreement, wasn't even a fight. This was a beating, plain and brutally simple.

"Why did he do it?" I asked.

Toyomatsu tugged at the sleeves of his robe. "He wouldn't say. Even tried to suggest Seisuke had done it all to himself."

"Seisuke. That's the other kid's name?"

"At twenty-seven he's not much of a kid anymore. And Seisuke is his assigned stage name. Seisuke Toyomatsu. All the puppeteers are given one of three stage surnames: Yoshida, Kiritake, or Toyomatsu. Their first name is created using the first character from their master's stage name—I'm Seijiro Toyomatsu, so my apprentices are Seitomo Toyomatsu, Seisuke Toyomatsu, Seijo Toyomatsu . . ." He rattled off about five more names, but I was already lost. "Always been the tradition. I only know Tetsuo's real name because his father and I happen to be friends. But this Seisuke, I couldn't tell you his real name offhand."

"Has he been with the company long?"

"Maybe a year," Toyomatsu said. "He was a graduate of the academy. Not bad for one of the *tentori-mushi*. Bookworms—that's what I call the academy graduates. They don't grow up in the theater like Tetsuo did—like everybody did in my day. The bookworms take Bunraku courses here or at the Tokyo school for a couple of years. Fill their heads with all kinds of ridiculous theories. Too much learning with the brain, not enough with the belly. But Seisuke was enthusiastic, respectful. Clumsy, but not a total waste. Still, we had to let him go after what happened in Sapporo."

"Doesn't sound like it was his fault."

"It's complicated," Toyomatsu said, pitch rising before he began coughing again. I got the feeling Toyomatsu regretted telling me as much as he had, was looking for a way out of the conversation. When I didn't offer him one, he was forced to continue.

"Seisuke was of two minds," he said at last. "First he said Tetsuo had attacked him. Then he said he couldn't be sure, that he didn't remember anything. For whatever reason, Seisuke couldn't bring himself to point the finger at Tetsuo. Luckily, I suppose—it would've been a terrible scandal for the theater if he'd filed charges. Still, his refusal to answer our questions gave us no choice but to expel him."

The whole episode sounded increasingly strange. If a guy beat me up while I was sleeping, I wouldn't go out of my way to get him off the hook, especially if it put my livelihood in jeopardy. Not a lot of job openings for out-of-work puppeteers, after all. I asked Toyomatsu why the kid would've wanted to protect Tetsuo.

Toyomatsu frowned and studied the surface of his desk, then asked if I wanted tea. I declined. He picked up the phone, and moments later one of his teenage apprentices arrived with two steaming cups of green tea. Toyomatsu thanked him and the kid left. He put the cup to his lips, then lowered it back onto his desk.

"Seisuke was a homosexual," he said. "Homosexuality is very rare among Japanese men. Rarer than in most countries. It's been more or less scientifically proven. Has to do with the unique shape of Japanese brains."

I beat back a smile. "That a fact."

"Don't misunderstand me," he hastened to add. "I've nothing against homosexuals. Couldn't last long in the theater world if I did. My point is that I wasn't the only one to notice Seisuke seemed to have developed a special affection for Tetsuo. I think maybe Seisuke made unwanted advances. That night in Sapporo, in the hotel room they shared."

"And you think that's why Tetsuo beat him up?"

Toyomatsu considered his next words carefully, making several false starts before they fell into place. "Maybe it was something else. Who knows? The problem is that Seisuke refuses to say, and keeping him under the circumstances would've disrupted the harmony of the group. Nobody blames Seisuke for what happened, but everyone knew Tetsuo was the future of the National Bunraku Theater. At least as far as the puppeteers are concerned. The kid had something you can't teach."

It struck me that Master Toyomatsu always used the past tense when speaking of Tetsuo, as if being expelled from the theater was the same as being dead and gone. Toyomatsu had been here so long, in his mind it probably was.

"You can teach people to place their hips in line with the head puppeteer," he resumed. "You can teach them to focus their eyes at the back of the puppet's head. Drawing a sword in rage, pouring tea like an eighteenth-century low-level courtesan—all of these skills can be learned. But you can't teach someone how to reveal a character's inner nature, how to bring their spirits to life. Studying the texts, watching the masters—this isn't enough. You have to live, taste life's joys and sorrows. That's why most puppeteers are never any good until they're maybe fifty-five, sixty."

Toyomatsu leaned back in his chair, and for several moments said nothing further. I thought I could hear the shamisen players tuning their instruments in some distant corner of the building.

"Puppeteering is hard work," he said. "Plain and simple. Not that I haven't looked for shortcuts. When I was younger, I even secretly read books about Western methods of acting. Mind you, we weren't even allowed to see Kabuki back in the old days, lest it influence our style. Had my masters known the nonsense I was reading they would have made my life hell, and rightly so. Bunraku doesn't come from books."

As he spoke, I glanced over his shoulder at the portraits hung upon the wall. The trio of grim faces staring back at me looked like the type of old-school disciplinarians who believed a whack with a stick was worth a thousand words. The rigors Toyomatsu had no doubt undergone were part of a culture that no longer existed, even inside these walls.

Toyomatsu sipped from his tea and considered. "But I found certain Western concepts helpful. Like the idea of the subconscious. I don't know how to put this without sounding like one of the bookworms myself, but with Tetsuo, it was as if his subconscious, or his spirit, or whatever you want to call it, was very near the surface. He had an uncanny ability to tap into this feeling and transfer it through the puppet into the hearts and minds of the audience. To reach them on almost a subconscious level. Does that make any sense?"

I said I thought it did.

"You can't will yourself to make that connection," he said. "If you consciously try, you'll inevitably fail. And you can't be thinking about your movements or what happens next in the play or who's in the audience or anything like that. You have to be operating on another plane. And then it's like an electrical current opens, passing through the puppet, connecting you with the audience. It's something you can't control, but when it happens, it's incredibly powerful."

Toyomatsu had a troubled, vaguely irritated expression on his face, as if the right phrase lay just out of reach. "Of course, he still had much to learn," he said, suddenly sobering. "His spirit was strong but undeveloped. His movements at times raw, uncalibrated. But all this talking doesn't matter now. I hear Tetsuo has moved on. Starring in some little company across the river."

"Really? Mr. Oyamada didn't mention that."

"The Nocturne Theater," he said. "They've got some show running called *The Whimpering Goat*. Or *The Goat Whisker*—something with a goat. It's a little black box company that puts on puppet dramas. Modernized Bunraku, so I'm told."

"You haven't seen them?"

"I'd sooner watch the monkeys at Tennoji Zoo."

"What about the other guy? Seisuke. What's he doing?"

Toyomatsu shrugged. "I've got thirty-one other puppeteers to worry about now." He glanced at his watch and coughed. I thanked him for being so generous with his time, wished him luck with the new production, and was standing to leave when he asked how much of what I'd learned I planned to share with Mr. Oyamada.

"I don't want to hold out false promises," Toyomatsu said. "But it's possible one day Tetsuo will be welcomed back into our family. Accepting him again would be unprecedented, but sometimes you have to sacrifice small traditions to protect larger ones. Of course, Tetsuo would have to want to return. And of course, he'd have to apologize with the proper level of sincerity."

"I'll pass it on to Mr. Oyamada."

"Please do," Toyomatsu said. "But I'd appreciate it if you spare Oyamada the uglier details of what happened in Sapporo. No reason he needs to know everything. Mr. Oyamada is a good man, and he's had a tougher life than you realize."

I took a sip from my tea only to find it had gone cold. Moments later, my guide Kozue arrived to escort me out of the building. Just before we reached the street, she gave me an umbrella. I tried to refuse it, but I was never any good at refusing anything from pretty young women. I thanked her and walked off toward the train station. It never did end up raining that day.

Chapter Four

Detective Imanishi

Roughly fifteen minutes later I was underground in
Namba station, trying to choose between
about twenty different energy drinks with
names like Guts, Yunker, and Vaam, all of
them promising to kill my hangover, boost
my productivity, restore my virility, and do
everything short of pad my bank account.
One of them boasted ingredients that included stomach juices from giant hornets,
another contained seal testicles. I opted for
an old-fashioned Mr. Black canned coffee
and picked through the *Asahi Shimbun* while
waiting for the next train to Osakajokoen.
Reading the Japanese dailies gave me the
feeling I was caught in a recurring nightmare.
New politicians starring in old scandals,
more banks embroiled in the bad-loans im-

broglio. Homelessness on the rise, violent crime on the rise, violent crimes against the homeless on the rise. The debate over booting out U.S. forces in Okinawa raging afresh thanks to another rape by off-base Marines, Japan mulling over its role should America decide to attack Iraq, North Korean saber-rattling making everyone nervous, a local sportswriter wondering if this would be the year the Hanshin Tigers finally won the pennant again, a feat they hadn't achieved since 1985. I wondered why they bothered writing new stories at all—seemed like it would've been easier just to reprint random editions from the last ten or fifteen years.

When I got bored with the paper I thumbed through a magazine called *Weekly Jetter* that someone had left behind on the train. It was the usual fare. Gossip about which movie starlets were reputedly still virgins, an exposé about the use of substandard concrete in public works projects, a photo essay illustrating the evolution of the brassiere.

The only piece that captured my interest was an article on the Komoriuta-kai, one of the big three organized *yakuza* crime syndicates in Japan. According to the government's own figures, they had at least thirty-five hundred members nationwide, most of them concentrated in the Kansai region. If you bet on a bicycle race, visited a massage parlor, bought amphetamines, or dealt with loan sharks anywhere from Fukui to Wakayama, you were likely feeding the coffers of the Komoriuta-kai. Their shining moment came when the Great Hanshin earthquake struck Kobe in 1995 and the gangsters embarrassed the government by providing emergency food and water supplies while local officials and Tokyo bureaucrats were still sifting through their own red tape. Though hardly Robin Hoods, they'd enjoyed some measure of popularity in the afterglow.

But the afterglow had faded in recent years. Fewer corporate entertainment accounts meant less money from the water trade, declining stock prices meant threats to disrupt company shareholder meetings fell on deaf ears, lower profits meant fewer subscriptions to the worthless and ridiculously expensive so-called trade journals the *yakuza* intimidated small businesses into purchasing. The Kansai region was especially hard hit when the bubble burst and *yakuza* were consolidating, downsizing, concentrating their efforts in Tokyo just like everyone else. Chinese gangs were moving in on their turf and recruiting was down because even the *yakuza* didn't understand today's youth. Many older thugs felt the younger generation was spoiled, disrespectful of the traditional *sempai-kohei* relationship between juniors and seniors, and generally lacking the moral fortitude to become hardworking criminals.

Good news was that gambling was still popular and the loan shark business was bigger than ever, thanks mostly to rising unemployment. Business-to-business crime was hardly finished, according to the writer, but Japan was in the grips of a desperate new era where gangs were focusing their efforts on the individual consumer like never before.

All of this was just background, a writer padding his word count before getting around to the occasion of the piece, which was that among the Komoriuta-kai's other troubles, a succession problem was looming. Seventy-two-year-old Tadamitsu Noguchi, Osaka native and longtime leader of the Komoriuta-kai, had recently suffered a debilitating stroke. His number two man had just been convicted of weapons violations and was serving a lengthy sentence in Hokkaido's Abashiri prison, and the number three guy had been gunned down two months ago while attending a funeral in Tokyo. Frail old Mr. Noguchi was still officially at the helm, but unnamed sources suggested the gang was actually being run by a *kuro maku* —literally a "black curtain," someone exercising authority from behind the scenes. The perceived power vacuum left the Komoriuta-kai vulnerable. The streets might be calm now, the author wrote, but a great storm was gathering. It was only a matter of time until Noguchi died, and certainly by the summer shots would thunder and bullets rain from the sky, as his would-be successors jockeyed for position and rival gangs tried to cut into the action. The writer's breathless prose made it sound as though he was looking forward to it. I guessed following summer gang wars beat watching the Tigers squander another season.

The photo accompanying the article revealed Noguchi as a broad-shouldered, flinty-eyed man with stony features set in a recalcitrant expression that practically radiated power. Noguchi would've been in his fifties when the picture was taken back in 1981, at the funeral for a former Komoriuta-kai leader. Celebrities and politicians were in attendance, and it was the biggest funeral Tokyo would see until the emperor died eight years later. If you believed the official police stats, there were probably more *yakuza* at the funeral than were left in all of Japan. If you believed the official stats.

No bullets or anything else raining from the sky when I got off the train. I walked into the lobby of the PanCosmo and nodded and smiled to a quintet of women in smart matching green outfits whose job was to stand in formation, looking pretty and efficient while bowing and smiling to anyone who came in the door. They were remarkably good at their jobs.

When I approached the desk to get my key, a red-faced concierge named Mr. Tanaka apologized about ten times and asked if I wouldn't mind moving to a different room. When I asked him why, he issued five more apologies and told me there was a problem with the television. I told him I didn't watch much TV. Nevertheless, he said, surely I'd want to watch television at some point, and the hotel thought it prudent to address the problem now, before it arose. How the PanCosmo Hotel even knew there was suddenly a problem with the TV in my room was a mystery. I hadn't complained, hadn't even turned the thing on yet.

"We're terribly sorry," Concierge Tanaka said, "and sincerely hope moving won't present you with insurmountable difficulties." Several of his coworkers looked on fretfully as he spoke, stealing surreptitious glances from their various posts behind the front desk and peeking out from behind back office doors, as if they'd all placed bets on my response.

"No problem," I said. "Just give me a moment to pack."

My reply only seemed to heighten the tension. The man behind the desk looked away and I thought I heard someone gasp from the back office. "Actually," stammered Concierge Tanaka, "we've already taken the liberty of transporting your possessions. So as not to bring further difficulty upon you."

"No problem," I said. "Do I need a new key?"

A palpable sense of relief descended upon the lobby as the concierge handed over the key card. Then everyone went back to doing whatever they were doing, looking so thoroughly unperturbed I started wondering if I'd imagined their previous concern. As I walked across the lobby toward the stairs, the elevator doors opened and a trio of uniformed policemen stepped out. They gave me a once-over and looked at each other but said nothing. Something told me they weren't here for the Kinki conference.

*M*y suitcase lay open on the bed, just as I'd left it in my previous room. They'd even hung my white button-downs and black slacks up in the closet. I turned on the TV just to make sure it worked and it did so I turned it off. The weathergirl on Channel Eight wouldn't be on for another nine hours. Right now she'd probably just be getting into the studio, having her makeup done and going over print-outs of the latest barometric pressure reports.

Room 1142 was identical to my room two floors below, right down to the beach-scene watercolors hanging on the cream-colored walls. The rooms were nothing like the closet-sized business-hotel accommodations tightfisted Chuck usually booked. In fact, the PanCosmo seemed less a hotel than a country club built inside a shopping mall. The hotel boasted a heated Olympic-sized swimming pool, three indoor tennis courts, a fully equipped weight room, even a rooftop driving range. If you wanted to do a few laps around Osaka Castle, they provided a warm-up suit and jogging shoes. Eight restaurants and six bars were scattered throughout the hotel's forty-seven stories, and should none of those be suitable, the hotel offered free delivery from a host of top restaurants in Kitashinchi. The ground floor was home to a hairstylist, a manicurist, a travel agency, three women's clothiers, and one for men. You could get a massage, have your shoes polished, and your pants taken in without leaving your room, each of which came with its own fax machine. There was a dataport for Internet usage and if you forgot your laptop at home you could rent one from the front desk. International guests were provided with a complimentary cell phone complete with a built-in camera, and they were test-marketing a new service whereby calls to your room could be automatically relayed to the cell if you were out and about. The hotel would probably do your taxes, too, if you asked nice enough.

I had a look at the schedule of events given to me by the Kinki Foundation to see what I'd missed while visiting Master Toyomatsu. Today's theme was "Arts of the Kansai" and several activities had already taken place. A slide show on the work of Pritzker-winning architect Tadao Ando, a debate over whether *manga* should be eligible for the prestigious Naoki literary prize, a video retrospective on the works of early *manzai* comedian Achaka Hanabishi. The speaker for today's "Outlook Kansai" lecture series was the VP of Yoshimoto Kogyo Ltd., the firm who'd managed every famous Japanese comedian for as long as anyone could remember. In about five minutes, he was giving a speech titled "Bringing Laughter into the Twenty-first Century." After my meeting with Master Toyomatsu, I figured I could use a few twenty-first-century chuckles.

I was just about to head downstairs when the phone rang. I picked it up and was greeted by the rattling voice of Mr. Oyamada, so clear and loud it sounded like he was right beside me, hand cupped to my ear.

"Good afternoon," he said. "I tried calling your old room but they told me you'd moved. Makes sense, I suppose. Terrible business, just terrible. We're all shocked beyond words. I hope your new room is okay. Do you still have a view of Osaka Castle?"

"Room is fine," I told him. "But what terrible—"

"Master Toyomatsu said you visited this morning," he interrupted. "Thank you again. I am grateful beyond measure. I'm eager to hear all about your meeting, but of course it will have to wait. As you can imagine, all of us at the foundation are completely in shock. Nothing in our history has prepared us for this sort of occurrence. We're all shocked beyond measure."

"What sort of occurrence?"

The other end fell momentarily silent. "You haven't heard?"

"No. What happened?"

"There's been, that is, last night there was . . ." Oyamada trailed off, sucking at his teeth. "It appears a tragedy has taken place inside the hotel. One involving an American man named Richard Gale. They found him this morning. He was staying on the same floor you were, as it happens. He appears to have died. Violently."

"He was murdered?"

"It's a horrible turn of events."

Somehow I knew right away the dead man was the gangly, awkward twenty-something I'd spoken with in the elevator, the one I'd given my nametag to. His death explained why they'd moved me to a different room, and why everyone on the hotel staff was acting so jumpy. The ninth floor was probably crawling with cops, a PR nightmare for a high-class joint like the PanCosmo Hotel.

"Do the police have any suspects?"

"They aren't saying," Oyamada said. "But you can be certain they'll get to the bottom of it. The Osaka Municipal Police Department have a reputation for excellence that extends beyond our national boundaries. You may remember even the notorious British hooligans avoided tangling with Osaka's finest during the recent World Cup."

"I don't really follow cricket."

Oyamada cleared his throat, or tried to. "At any rate,

thank you again for visiting Master Toyomatsu. I'd have shown my gratitude in person but for present circumstances. Of course, it goes without saying the conference events have been canceled for the afternoon in light of this tragedy. Please accept my sympathies and the sympathies of the entire Kinki Foundation on the death of your compatriot, the honorable Richard Gale."

Then we said our good-byes and hung up. I'd absent-mindedly written "Richard Gale" on a scratch pad by the phone. I pictured that twitchy smile and wondered what had happened to the guy. Compatriot or not, I didn't feel much of anything special. I don't even know why I wrote the name down. He was just some dude I shared an elevator with.

I tore the page from the scratch pad and tossed it in the trash, then opened the curtains to bring in some light. The view of Osaka Castle Park was the same one I had before, only two floors higher. A thin mist was draped over the surrounding high-rises, dissolving them in the low sky. I tried to formulate just how I was going to break the bad news to Mr. Oyamada about the Sapporo incident. Problem was, I only had Toyomatsu's version, and it had more holes than a Cambodian minefield. I reluctantly decided I needed to go down to the Nocturne Theater and talk to Tetsuo, to get his side of the story. I wasn't confident he'd give it to me, but it was worth a shot. Nothing else to do now that the conference was canceled for the rest of the day. I was looking to see if there was a phone book in my room when I heard a knock at the door.

Fisheyed in the peephole was a slope-shouldered slip of a man with hard eyes and skin the color of sour milk. His shirtsleeves were rolled to expose broom-handle forearms and he wore a loosely knotted burgundy necktie that practically dragged on the floor. Right away I pegged him as either a cop or gangster, except he wasn't dressed dumb enough to be a gangster and was too skinny to be much of a cop.

I pulled open the door.

"My name is Imanishi," the guy said. His voice was disarmingly soft and melodious, almost feminine despite its low timbre. A voice made for self-help tapes. You could almost hear gentle waves and New Age keyboards washing in behind it.

"Billy Chaka," I said, bowing.

"Please excuse the intrusion. May I come in?"

I motioned him inside. He stepped in and closed the door like he was handling a Ming vase. I asked if he wanted water, tea, Pocari Sweat, or anything else from the well-stocked minibar. He declined in a whisper. There was something off kilter about his features, out of balance somehow, but I couldn't put my finger on it. We both took seats at a round table wedged in the corner of the room, near the window. I started wondering just what a guy like him did for a living. As if reading my thoughts, Imanishi handed me his card and started speaking.

"My name is Imanishi," he repeated in the same velvety hush. "I'm the house detective for the PanCosmo Hotel. I used to be a member of the Osaka Municipal Police, but now I work for the hotel. As you may know, we had a little problem last night. A guest was found dead."

"Murdered, I hear."

"We don't like making assumptions," he said. "Especially while there is still evidence to be gathered. True, early indications suggest foul play. The victim was discovered in bed. The fatal wound was likely the eight-inch gash in his throat, but there were thirty-two additional lacerations about his face and neck area."

"Doesn't sound like a shaving accident."

"We haven't ruled anything out," he said. "All manner of odds and ends must be unraveled and restitched before we have anything whole. However, no cuts were found on his hands or arms, injuries we commonly refer to as resistance wounds, so we believe he must have been taken quite by surprise, the mortal wound perhaps delivered as he slept. We found a weapon lying on the bathroom counter, still covered in blood. And we found this in the victim's pocket."

He placed a plastic bag on the table. Inside was a small piece of rumpled white paper bordered in blue, one that had been balled up and later smoothed out. *Billy Chaka,* it read. *Youth in Asia Magazine.*

"Billy Chaka is your name, correct?" he asked.

I nodded.

"Can you explain how this came into the man's possession?"

I started to tell him about the elevator ride, but he stopped me. He took out a silver Aiwa handheld tape recorder and placed it on the glass tabletop, right next to the plastic bag containing the sticker. "Do you object to this conversation being recorded?" Imanishi asked.

I said it didn't bother me.

"I'm no longer a policeman," he said. "And you haven't officially been named a suspect. You're not even a proper witness yet. We'll call you a suspected witness, for the sake of convenience. You've every right to refuse if you don't wish to be recorded, and if you don't wish to speak at all, silence is completely within your privileges as a guest of the PanCosmo Hotel. I'm told you speak fluent Japanese, but I should inform you the hotel has an interpreter on staff should you require her services. You'll find her exceedingly capable."

I wondered if she was exceedingly single, but thought better of asking. I told Imanishi no interpreter was necessary. He fumbled with the recorder for a moment before finding the record button. The little wheels squeaked as they turned. "Now then," he said, his voice a notch louder to be heard over the recorder. "If you could start by telling me about your relationship with the man in room 944."

"Is he the one who was murdered?"

"He is the guest we discovered this morning, yes."

So I told Imanishi about the elevator ride we'd shared. How I'd told the guy about the conference and the award, how the man had quipped it must be nice to be me, how I'd given him my nametag as a kind of joke. Turned out it was the kind of joke Imanishi didn't get. He asked me to explain it again, and suddenly I didn't get the joke, either. But as I repeated the story, something he'd said earlier suddenly struck me.

"Did you just say the guy was found in room 944?"

Imanishi nodded.

"That was right next door to me," I said.

This was true, Imanishi said. That being the case, it was imperative I remember if I'd heard any strange sounds the night before. I explained that I'd been out most of the evening, in Hozenji Yokocho at some tiny bar decorated with puppet heads. As I spoke, Imanishi stared down at the whiny tape recorder as if afraid the device would stop working if not closely supervised. Should've bought a Sony. He asked me if I went to the bar alone and I told him I was there with Mr. Oyamada, a member of the Kinki Foundation. Something about the arrangement of Imanishi's features was still bothering me.

"When you returned that night, did you see or hear anything suspicious in the hallways? Did you share an elevator with anyone? Perhaps you heard water running next door? Anything at all you can remember . . ."

And then 1 got it.

His left ear. It was smaller than his right one and the skin tone didn't quite match. Hell, it was about half the size and two shades lighter. 1 became so transfixed scrutinizing the little ear that several moments passed before 1 even re-alized that of course 1 *had* seen someone. The woman sleeping in the stairwell. Suddenly the frightened look on her face and her hurried descent offered a dark new range of possibilities.

Imanishi clicked off the tape recorder.

"Thank you for your cooperation," he said. "Is there any-thing else you'd like to tell me? Anything you may have overlooked?"

1 wavered a moment, then shook my head.

"Maybe there's something you'd like to ask me?"

1 said no. Imanishi stared at me for several moments.

"It's a replica," he said finally.

"I'm sorry?"

"My left ear. It's not real." His lips twisted into a consol-ing smile and 1 half-expected him to reach across the table and pat my hand. "It's a prosthetic, a fake. Don't worry, people often stare. I've grown accustomed to it over the years. The staring, that is. I've never quite grown accus-tomed to the ear itself."

1 tried to simultaneously tell him the ear didn't look fake and 1 didn't notice it and 1 certainly didn't mean to stare and hoped he wasn't offended, but it all came out an awk-ward jumble. Maybe 1 could've used an interpreter after all.

"Curiosity is natural," he said. "Please, take a closer look."

Before 1 could decline, he reached up and gripped the

tiny thing between his thumb and forefinger, grimacing as he wrenched the ear off the side of his head. Then he placed it on the table, right between the tape recorder and the plastic bag.

"You can touch it if you wish," he said. "It's perfectly clean. Cleaner than your own ears, I'm certain. It's made of polyurethane. I wash it each night and soak it in an antibacterial solution. Each morning, I affix it to my head using low-resin epoxy. I used to use a much stronger adhesive, but it gave me a rash. I use makeup to cover the seam. Is there anything else you'd like to know?"

"No, thanks," I said. "I'm sorry if—"

"People usually ask what happened to my real ear," he said. "It got severed in the line of duty, back when I was a police officer. After it happened, some members of the force started calling me van Gogh. But Vincent van Gogh only severed a portion of his ear, you know. Just part of the lobe. Little more than a sliver, really."

"Huh. I didn't know that."

"And it was all his idea," said Imanishi, his voice rising. "He removed it himself, completely of his own volition. Cutting off my ear wasn't my idea. Not my idea at all! I explained to my fellow officers how my situation, upon close examination, bore little resemblance to that of the distinguished painter. Perhaps, I added, this nickname was not so clever as they imagined. Do you find this nickname clever?"

I shook my head.

"Not so clever," agreed Imanishi. He fell silent and his eyes moved aimlessly about the room before he resumed in a flattened tone. "Well, now you know all there is to know about the ear."

With that, Imanishi lifted the sculpted polyurethane

from the table and began reattaching it to the side of his head. Just before he did, I got a glimpse of what remained of his original ear. A black, snail-shaped hole rimmed with purplish scar tissue. He pressed the prosthetic in place, smoothing the edge where it met his skull, then produced a small cylinder of Shiseido makeup and applied a layer over the seam with his forefinger. I looked out the window, saw the tiny figures of kids playing baseball in the dusty park below. Funny that among the infinite possibilities the universe presented, my reality was to be sitting in a hotel room in Osaka, trying not to stare as an ex-cop turned hotel detective who came to grill me about a guy I'd met in an elevator covered up his fake ear. There was a lot not to like about the world, but you couldn't accuse it of being predictable.

"Please don't hesitate to call me if you remember anything else," Imanishi said, looking somewhat sheepish as he slipped the tape recorder and the plastic bag into his pocket and rose to his feet. Now that I was aware of the fake ear, it looked hopelessly phony, a malformed chunk of clay blindly lumped to the side of his head. "My former colleagues in the police department are hard at work on the case, but I must do everything possible to expedite matters. They wouldn't approve of me sharing details of the investigation, but I think our guests have a right to be informed. Conversely, it would please me if you didn't speak with the police without sharing information with me first. I like to think of the PanCosmo Hotel as my jurisdiction."

I told him I had no information to share, but if I thought of anything I'd be sure to let him know. We bowed to each other and I wished him the best with the investigation. As he left, he lingered a moment at the open door.

"Please don't worry for your safety," he said. "The hotel is taking every precaution and the perpetrator, assuming there is one, will no doubt be apprehended soon. If it was a murder, I can assure you that any killer who leaves behind the murder weapon subconsciously wishes to get caught, even craves punishment. By the way, you may wish to take advantage of our pay-per-view television service. We're proud to offer an excellent selection of American films. We also carry adult titles. Domestic releases mostly, and a few from Sweden."

Imanishi the hotel detective then bowed and stepped into the hall and closed the door so gently I couldn't even hear the bolt click. I thought about the woman in the stairwell, how frightened she'd seemed when I woke her, the way she ran down six flights of stairs. I went to my briefcase, pulled out my address book, and picked up the phone. It was time to see what I could learn about the man who'd died with my name in his pocket.

Chapter Five

Curry, Chrysanthemum Clubbers, the Chin-chin Limousine

At around six P.M. I popped out of Higashi-Umeda station in north Osaka, only a few blocks from the Ikudama Shrine where a courtesan named Ohatsu and a soy-sauce merchant named Tokubei met before ending their lives some three hundred years ago, inspiring Chika-matsu Monzaemon's *Love Suicides at Sonezaki*. The lovers could never have envi-sioned what the place looked like today, but I doubt they imagined their fleeting moment of death would be reenacted by puppets for hundreds of years, either. Their spirits were probably somewhere in the afterworld wish-ing they'd hired a good entertainment lawyer.

I headed north, navigating the crush of pedestrians pouring out from the six train and subway stations that converged within a two-hundred-meter radius, and dodging bicyclists that wove fearlessly in and out of the crowds by all the big stores of Umeda. One look at the place and you knew Osaka was still a merchant's town at heart, built on buying and selling. Almost anywhere you stood in the northern city center, a giant department store rose overhead and a subterranean shopping arcade bustled beneath your feet. Osaka had no time for subtlety, and the modern merchants of the city were going to ever more inventive lengths to attract shoppers, whether it be outfitting the mall with a rooftop Ferris wheel at the HEP5 building or installing a gaudy European atrium fountain underground at the Diamor Osaka. My favorite gimmick was at the Matsushita IMP Building near my hotel, where designers had created a "restrooms of the world" theme. Bathrooms on each floor were modeled on authentic restrooms from thirteen different countries, right down to the types of urinal cakes used. So far I'd only had time to visit France. C'est la vie.

After wandering around for ten minutes or so I made my way down Hankyu Higashidori Street, an endless covered lane packed with yet more shops, until I found a little storefront jammed between a *pachinko* parlor and a discount drugstore where every product had pastel packaging. I pushed open the door and the smell was so strong the air was nearly saffron colored, so I knew I was at the right place. I figured all I had to do was wait for my guy to show up, but I was wrong. My guy was already there.

Kenneth "Curry" Balderton was at the counter, sitting on a little stool and shoveling curry rice into his mouth as fast as he could wash it down with Asahi Super Dry. Curry had to be the only foreigner I knew who actually gained weight in Japan. His naked cranium shone under the fluorescent bulbs, and as I walked up behind him I thought of lots of dumb things I could say, but in the end just plopped down two stools over and didn't say a word. Curry was so into his curry he didn't notice me until he'd almost finished the plate. When he finally glanced up he nearly inhaled his spoon. He wiped the sauce off his chin, some of it anyway, and let loose a wrecked smile that established his nationality as surely as his passport.

"Fuck me," he said. "Billy Chaka."

enneth Balderton had lived in Japan nearly six years and swore he was going back to England every one of them. Unemployed at age twenty-three, he'd answered a classified ad in a London nightlife and entertainment magazine and one month later found himself in a podunk town outside Nagoya peddling some version of English in a conversational-school franchise famous for bad pay and nonexistent hiring standards. He worked his way through several similarly unglamorous teaching posts before landing a job here in Osaka as a low-level translator for a *manga* company called Koiwazurai Entertainment that specialized in erotic comic books. Their best-selling title, *Hentai Galaxy Girls*, had recently found distribution overseas, so Curry spent most of his time filling the speech bubbles of the big-eyed, bigger-breasted schoolgirls repeatedly forced to save their hometown from alien invasion by offering themselves to a variety of lascivious space creatures endowed with otherworldly genitalia. I'm not sure how he spun it on his résumé, but the gig had given him a highly specialized Japanese vocabulary.

Like a lot of terminal expats, Curry lived in a limbo between two cultures; as a six-foot-four, 250-pound bald Brit, he'd never quite fit into Japanese society. As a West Ender who'd spent the last six years about as Far East as you can get, he'd never again belong on the terraces at Stamford Bridge or in dusky Chelsea pubs, either. Maybe he never really belonged anywhere, except exactly where we'd agreed to meet. Had curry shops not been popular in Japan, he might have taken himself back to dear old Blighty all those years ago just like he always threatened.

Our beers came and he lifted his glass in a toast. "Here's to that geezer Zola, eh? You see him slot it home against Fulham? Now that Inamoto is with the Cottagers, the premiership is massive here. Thanks to him and that poof Beckham, I suppose. Here's to hoping a Japanese signs with the Rhinos so they'll start putting the Super League on the Nippon telly, as well!"

I raised my glass and took a swig, though I had only the foggiest idea what I was drinking to. We chatted about this and that and he asked what I was doing in Osaka. When I told him about the Bunraku article and Kinki Foundation, his face went sour.

"How's that, then?" he said. "Here I am laboring over comic nasties, and now the bleeding kinky foundation have seen fit to give *you* an award? I suppose muppets are a bit kinky, fair enough, but still—"

"Kinki," I said. "With an *i*. As in the—"

"Kansai." Curry chuckled. "Just having a go, mate."

He brought me up to date on the whereabouts of mutual acquaintances, expats we knew in Tokyo and elsewhere. Most of them had gone back overseas to Australia, Canada, the United States. Some had gone to Hong Kong, which now had more foreigners than the whole of Japan, others to mainland China. We were into our second tall Asahi when I brought up the death of

Richard Gale. Curry said he'd heard the news and shifted uneasily on his stool.

"He a mate of yours, then?" Curry asked.

"He was staying in the hotel room next to mine."

"They must've got the wrong chap then, eh?"

"Funny," I said, though the thought had struck me before. Could someone have seen the nametag and mistaken Richard for me? We were both *gaijin*, but I had probably ten years on him and hadn't spent enough time in Osaka to make enemies. I had my share in Tokyo, only a few hours away by train, but for the time being I decided to assume whoever killed Gale got the right man.

"So did you know the guy?" I asked.

Curry nodded, as I'd hoped he would. He seemed to know every foreigner who'd spent more than six days in Osaka—that's why I was here. Expats in Japan could be an insular bunch. The worst seized the earliest opportunity to tell you how many years they'd spent here, announcing the number like it was a military rank, and lived to correct other foreigners on the kinds of minor grammatical errors the Japanese themselves would overlook without a thought.

The majority of Westerners outside of Tokyo worked in the booming English trade. Every school kid in Japan was required to study English for a minimum of six years, but it was taught in such a rigorously grammatical fashion that almost nobody learned to actually speak the language, which was where the private sector took over. With employment prospects worse than they'd been in fifty years, job seekers were looking for every advantage they could get. Whether or not they actually learned enough to manage an everyday exchange like purchasing a handgun at Wal-Mart, extra English on the résumé still made a nice accessory to the identical suits every job seeker donned during March recruiting season. But for most, English was just a hobby, a self-improvement scheme undertaken in hopes of becoming more worldly and sophisticated.

The foreign white-collar professionals often looked down their noses at the language peddlers, seeing them as a collection of Peace Corps rejects and skilless misfits whose only job qualification was competence in their own native tongue. The hierarchy was more relaxed in Osaka than in Tokyo because there were fewer foreigners around to resent each other and Osaka was just a more down-to-earth place. Still, Curry was one of the few people I knew who moved freely not just among various Japanese social circles, but among the ridiculous expat stratifications, a far more impressive achievement.

"Saw Dickie Gale about here and there," Curry said. "Not to speak ill of the dead and all that bollocks, but he struck me as a bit daft."

"You met him here in Osaka, I take it?"

"Yeah," Curry said. "As I remember it, he lived in Tokyo for a while but it didn't take. Said he moved to the Kansai to discover the *real* Japan, whatever that it is. Never mind like twenty million Japanese live in Tokyo. I guess the Japanese there weren't *real* enough for him."

"Sounds like the two of you didn't hit it off."

"It's not that," Curry said. "It's just—well, here's an example. Last time I saw him was on a subway platform in Tennoji. Walked up to him and tried to be friendly, you know, just take the piss out of him a bit. As I'm talking he holds up a hand and says, 'I'd appreciate it if you would address me in Japanese from now on.' Like he couldn't stomach the fucking English language, right? Him, a bleeding English teacher! It's one thing if you're in mixed company and you don't want to seem like you're leaving people out or whatever—but we were on a train platform! Did he think if I spoke Japanese at him nobody would know he was a foreigner? Daft bastard was a card-carrying chrysanthemum clubber if ever there was one."

"That a flower-arranging group or something?"

"May as well be." Curry laughed. "There's a type of bloke comes to Japan and just goes mental, yeah? Fucking plane's barely touched down and they're like running about in kimonos and learning the bloody tea ceremony. They have this notion that Japan is all about samurai and geisha and fucking Zen meditation. That's your chrysanthemum clubber. And it's the hardcore chrysanthemum clubbers what always wind up Japan bashers in the end. Three years on, you find them at the Pig and Whistle crying into their Guinness about the barmy school system and how all the kids are nihilist monsters and the men are imperious children and the women are empty-headed vipers and everything here is fucked six ways to Sunday."

"So which camp are you in?"

"Me? I'm neutral, mate. I'm fucking Switzerland." He laughed and took another swig of his beer. "You go through phases, like. The first year everything is new and exciting and a bit scary and you learn heaps. The second year you find out everything you learned the first was half-wrong. You make a few mates and soon the Japanese are no longer, like, 'the Japanese' right? They're not these faceless masses packed into trains or whatever."

I nodded and took a sip from my beer.

"Just people being people," he said. "Maybe a bit different from back home, but not so different after all. Not every bloke dreams of being a salaryman, and not every bird's life's ambition is getting married by twenty-five. You find out the average person cares fuck-all about Kabuki or haiku or the Book of Five bloody Rings. Neither is everyone obsessed with comic books and karaoke and naughty pictures of schoolgirls. I mean, it's the blokes what cling to all these silly notions about Japan that end up coming off as wankers. End up like Dickie Gale."

"Meaning dead?"

He tilted back his glass, downing a healthy swallow, then shook his head. "Not what I meant, the poor daft bastard. He was one of those blokes that's just cockeyed, you know, a bit off. I'd wager he didn't amount to much back home in Kansas or wherever. Some expats are like that. They come to Japan and get a bit of attention because they're different, exotic. Guys who couldn't get the time from a clock hop on a plane and suddenly they're pulling birds like they're Mick fucking Jagger."

"So Gale had a lot of women friends?"

"Dunno if he did or didn't," he said. "I'm just saying he fit into the general category. One look at him and you know there's no way he could've married a girl back home like the one he did here. Inoue, her last name was. Kaori Inoue. Our Dickie must've had some monstrous tackle, because I'll be fucked if she married him for his charm and good looks, God rest his soul."

"How long ago he get married?"

"Maybe a year," said Curry. "I was invited to the wedding, God knows why, but was in Thailand on holiday. Heard it was real flash. The Inoues are old money, heaps of it. Descendants of some famous merchant clan like the Koyabashis or the Konoikes or whoever. Of course, nobody ever claims their ancestors were pig butchers or day laborers from the Airin slums, so who knows? But I can't help but wonder if Kaori's old man was overjoyed with her choice of husbands."

"Meaning because he was an American?"

Curry grinned and shook his head. "It's not as if we're living in the Tokugawa era, mate. Conservative types wouldn't approve, maybe, but lots of Japanese marry foreigners. It's just that not many Yanks marry into a family like the Inoues. Not twenty-three-year-old conversation teachers, at any rate. He's what someone like Mr. Inoue would call *uma no hone*. Horsebones, a nobody."

Twenty-three. He was even younger than I'd thought.

"So this Inoue family is pretty well off?" I asked.

"You could say that," Curry said. "Kaori's old man runs Inoue Development. Decent-sized real estate company. Made a fortune before the bubble burst, then took a drubbing like everyone else. Judging from the wedding he'd set aside some rainy-day funds. My mates said there were a few obvious *yakuza* sorts at the wedding, too. Komoriuta-kai. Heard of that lot?"

"Just read something about them this morning."

"Tattooed media darlings of the Kansai." Curry snorted. "What else? Oh, right—strange bit was no one from Gale's side was at the wedding. None of his family, that is."

"Wonder if they'll make the funeral."

Curry sighed. "God rest his poor bastard soul."

"So Gale and his wife lived here in Osaka?"

"Yeah, Tezukayama, down south. Posh neighborhood, that. Big old houses—well, big for here—security cameras, Mercedes-Benzes crawling the streets. People call the trolley that runs there the *chin-chin* limousine."

Curry jammed an elbow in my ribs and laughed. When I didn't join him he pantomimed a conductor ringing a bell, explaining that *chin-chin* was onomatopoeic for the sound. "Also means prick," he said with a grin. "The prick limousine. And they say Japanese have no class consciousness!

Not many foreigners living in Tezukayama, that's certain. Christ, took me four years to get a decent flat here. Even had some old wench tell me she couldn't rent to me because her place was designed specially for a Japanese. What's that mean then, I asked, specially designed for a Japanese? Eventually she said she was afraid the floorboards wouldn't support a fat bastard like me!" -

Curry roared and slapped his hand on the counter. Given the way it shook when his paw came down, maybe the old landlady's fears were justified. I let him catch his breath before turning back to the dead American.

"Where did Gale teach English?" I asked.

"English conversation," Curry corrected. "World of difference, mate. Teaching English is teaching English, but English conversation—that whole industry is dodgy. And it's a massive industry, make no mistake. At most *eikaiwa* language schools you're not hired on as a *sensei* in any professional sense but as a chattering pet foreigner. They tell you all sorts of porky pies about bonuses and profit sharing when you sign on, but you sort out the real story soon enough. No training, no vacations, no health insurance. Work like a slave, live in company housing, abide by all kinds of idiotic rules meant to keep you isolated and ignorant. And as much as they exploit their foreign labor, it's worse what they do to their Japanese customers. Fucking criminal is what it is."

"Okay, so English *conversation*," I said. "Where did he teach?"

"Fucking criminal," he said. Trying to get Curry off a rant was like trying to catch a charging elephant with a butterfly net. "They just prey upon people's insecurities. Japanese tend to be shy about speaking English, yeah? Terrified of making mistakes. These *eikaiwa* pound it into their heads that they'll never be able to travel or make foreign friends or even shop on the Internet unless they go down to the local *eikaiwa* for some expert instruction. Then they trick customers into buying big blocks of tickets for thousands of yen, good for a year's worth of lessons. But the Japanese are a busy people, yeah, and the *eikaiwa* bank on this. They know most people will never get round to going to all their lessons, and they do such a poor job quote-unquote teaching that those who do show eventually get discouraged and drop out. And of course there's a no-refund policy, so at year's end they're left holding all these worthless tickets. It's like a massive bait-and-switch game where the key word is 'turnover.' "

"Gotcha. So where did Richard teach again?"

"The Gamma Academy," he said. "Gigantic national chain. You know, the 'Hiya there howdy' people? Turn on the telly you're sure to see their adverts, always starring Hollywood's latest blow-dried wanker slumming it for yen. If the Gamma Academy spent one-tenth of what they spend on advertising hiring and training competent teachers, this whole country would sound like presenters on the BBC. Mind you, it's probably better our Mr. Gale didn't actually teach English. Wouldn't want all the birds in Osaka sounding like that tosser you elected president, would we?"

I would've explained that Midwestern and Texas accents were totally different or quipped that all his former students probably sounded like football hooligans, but while Curry laughed at his own joke something that had been chewing at the back of my mind gnawed its way to the front. Curry put down his beer, giving me a concerned scowl.

"Don't look hard done by," he said. "Just having a go."

"Why would a guy rent a hotel room in his own city?"

Curry belched, missing the question. "How's that, then?"

"The PanCosmo Hotel," I said. "Richard Gale was staying at the same hotel I was, up by Osaka Business Park. Why would he be staying in a hotel when he lived, what, maybe half an hour away?"

Curry winked. "A bird. No mystery there."

Maybe not, but if Gale was cheating on his wife, it would've made more sense to meet her at a love hotel, Japan's high-glitz version of the no-tell motel. Clustered near every big train station or highway exit, love hotels were unmistakable with their fantastical architecture and animated neon signs advertising names like the Venice Nights Hotel, the Hotel Wedding Bell, J-Hearts Hotel, Tra La La Leisure Hotel. They were cheap fun and offered privacy and anonymity in a land-starved country where people lived in close proximity to their neighbors. A big city like Osaka had hundreds of love hotels, and the Kansai region was still the only place in Japan where you could rent for a single hour rather than the minimum three or four required in more conservative quarters. With all this going for them, I didn't understand why Richard Gale wouldn't have used one for his illicit affair, assuming he was having one.

"Dunno," said Curry when I voiced my doubts. "Me, I quite fancy love hotels. Rotating beds, aquariums in the ceiling, and all that? Wish they had them in the UK. I was in one once had moan-activated lights, right? Like the more noise you made, the more colored lights would flash. Brilliant! Like shagging inside a pinball machine."

"Sounds romantic."

"Anyway, maybe Gale wanted to show his class by taking her to a posh place like the PanCosmo. Or maybe he's afraid of love hotels, what with all the stories in the weeklies about *yakuza* scams."

"What is it this week?"

"New variation, old theme," Curry said. "Gangsters videotape people's vehicles as they enter love-hotel car parks. They look up the license plate info at the local transport office, then ring up the unlucky sods and try to blackmail them. Can't happen very often, but the stories sell magazines. Better than running another exposé on some Diet scandal nobody cares about."

I doubted *yakuza* paranoia was why Gale chose the PanCosmo Hotel, though it would've been ironic if he wound up murdered because he was afraid of being blackmailed. I remembered how he'd asked if I was there on business or pleasure, and when I turned the question around he'd said it was long story. Funny part was, Richard Gale himself had no idea just how long his story would turn out to be. He'd been dead less than twelve hours and was already emerging as a more complicated figure than the guy I'd met in the PanCosmo Hotel. Over the next few days I'd have to remake my image of him several times, but in some ways I never got beyond envisioning him as anything but the goofy kid in the elevator.

Curry drank down the last of his beer and slapped some yen on the counter. "Nice to see you again, Billy boy. Hate to do a runner, but I'm off to Big Cat. Australian mate of mine is playing a band called the Christ Punchers. Experimental music, he calls it. Bloody racket, I call it, but a mate is a mate. You're welcome to come along if you fancy, but I recommend earplugs."

I said I had other plans, but that it was good to see him again. Bit of good luck that, he replied, since similar encounters would be unlikely as he was almost certainly heading back to England soon. Before we went our separate directions, I asked Curry if he knew anyone who'd want to kill Richard Gale. Curry had to nearly shout to be heard above the metallic rush of *pachinko* balls from the parlor next door.

"He was a bit daft, but 1 don't know anyone would want to snuff him," he said. "Just didn't seem the type to inspire strong feelings one way or another. If he was murdered, it was the most exciting thing ever happened to him. Poor dead daft bastard."

Curry turned to leave and 1 watched his bald head bounce through the crowds until it was swallowed in the sea of pedestrians. 1 walked the other direction, joining the masses funneling into Higashi Umeda station. Downstairs 1 located a row of pay phones and dug through my wallet until 1 found a phone card that still had some yen left on it. 1 punched in a string of numbers and waited. A few seconds later, a machine on the other side of world picked up and Sarah's voice told me to leave a message. 1 wanted to tell her 1 needed information on a guy named Richard Gale: credit report, last known address, parents' names, marital status, criminal records, schools attended, porn sites visited, the works. 1 wanted to tell her to call me back as soon as she got the information, day or night. But 1 couldn't. 1 knew she'd never return the call, and if she did it would only be to tell me 1 was in Osaka to collect an award, not get mixed up in some murder investigation. 1 hung up the phone without leaving a message and made my way further underground to the subway.

Chapter Six

The Nocturne Theater

*T*he Nocturne Theater wasn't mentioned in the Osaka city attractions booklet I'd picked up that morning from the brochure stand at the Pan-Cosmo Hotel. As for the phone book, their theater listings went straight from Namba Grand Kagetsu to the Osaka Nohgaku Kaikan. Concierge Tanaka knew nothing about the place, but insisted on calling information for me. When he hung up the phone, he made a face and told me if I liked theater, *The Lion King* was playing at Osaka MBS Theater about a block away. When that failed to spark my interest, Tanaka said information had given him an address but there was no phone number listed for the Nocturne Theater. Maybe, he added hesitantly, that meant perhaps it isn't such a good theater?

Finding an Osaka address without a map was no easy task. Half the streets either had no name or no street sign, which pretty much amounted to the same thing. And even if you found the right building, if it was a bar, nightclub, or, say, small puppet theater you were looking for, you still had to process the tangle of signs crawling over the building's surface to determine the floor you needed. Compared to the migraine layout of Tokyo, Osaka's grid made perfect sense—at least the aboveground part of it—but I still assumed half the conversations I saw on the streets were people asking each other for directions.

Nobody I asked had ever heard of the Nocturne Theater, so I was left to my own devices in the squeezed streets surrounding the youth ghetto of America-mura, a place that started booming in the 1970s as the epicenter of surf culture and all things young, hip, and American, and never really stopped. In the distance a rooftop replica of the Statue of Liberty looked down through a snarl of telephone wires over streets filled with snowboard shops and trendy secondhand fashion boutiques covered in commissioned graffiti. Rap and reggae blared from every corner and there were more peroxide blondes than you'd find at a Hollywood casting call, but with the dense jumble of repurposed Western iconography Osaka's "America village" revealed itself as unmistakably, even quintessentially, Japanese. Same went for the more sophisticated Europa-mura, an upscale neighborhood no one would ever mistake for Berlin or Prague or Paris, either.

I must've wandered the choked geography surrounding America-mura for nearly an hour that evening, drifting through throngs of baggy hip-hoppers glued to their cell phones and bullhorned, spiky-haired *chimpira* in wide-collared suits trying to drum up business as I widened my circle, hitting Soemoncho and the gorgeously sleazy back-alley lanes running just north of the Dotombori River, home to strip clubs and hostess bars, soaplands and cabarets. After I'd passed the same touts so many times, they gave up trying to hand me fliers and tissue-packet ads, figuring I was literally a lost cause. I had already given up on finding Tetsuo and the Nocturne Theater and was heading back toward Namba station when I spotted a small poster plastered haphazardly on the directory of a grubby building, just to the left of the first-floor entrance to the Lollipop Lounge.

THE WHISPERING GOAT

a puppet drama in three acts
presented by

THE NOCTURNE THEATER

warning: It's not for everyone.
Basement level, entrance around the corner

I walked around the corner into an alleyway. The gap between buildings was only about four feet wide and clogged with bicycles that looked abandoned rather than parked. Halfway between the street and a railing overlooking the river, I found a battered metal door layered in blue paint. No sign, no buzzer. I knocked. Nothing happened. I tested the knob and the door lurched open with a grating sound, metal on metal, to reveal a short flight of stairs leading to a constricted concrete hallway.

I closed the door behind me and made my way down the stairs. As my eyes adjusted to the dark I could make out an old-fashioned ticket booth at the far end of the hall.

From a distance the booth looked empty, but as I neared I could see a form inside. Behind the smoked glass sat a pale woman in a black tuxedo. Her hair was slicked back into a ducktail and she wore a monocle, candy-apple-red lip gloss, and an expression of polished boredom. She didn't smile or say a word as she took my money and pushed my ticket through the slot, just melodramatically raised her arm and pointed a single thin finger toward a pair of worn red velvet curtains. Theater people, wacko the world over.

Parting the curtains revealed a small black-box auditorium consisting of forty or so metal folding chairs arranged in a semicircle on wooden platform risers in front of a small stage. It was completely empty save for a man and woman sitting front-row center, both wearing leather jackets and oversized mirrored sunglasses. I took a seat near the back and listened to some kind of electronic chamber music droning quietly through the loudspeakers, glad to be off my feet, off the noisy streets, and away from their jostling crowds. I sat and stared vacantly at the stage curtain, listening to the soft patter of feet as people behind it scurried back and forth setting up the scenery. Before I knew it, I'd fallen asleep. Sometime later I awoke to find the curtain drawn and the play already in progress.

A large bed with milky white sheets stood stage left while a miniature red leather couch and a black coffee table sat in the foreground. The room had no windows and was lit by two seashell-shaped lamps throwing faint triangles of light against the crimson walls. An impossibly small woman with lustrous black hair and a red cocktail dress was sitting on the couch, smoke uncoiling from the cigarette between her doll-sized fingers. A figure entirely cloaked in black loomed behind her, crouched on the other side of the couch like a monstrous, overgrown shadow. It took me a moment to realize this was the puppet's operator. Like Master Toyomatsu had said, *The Whispering Goat* appeared to be a modernized version of the Bunraku puppet theater.

The sound of a faucet being turned on came over the speakers. Then the water was shut off and a door swung open at stage right. Another puppet, this one a broadshouldered man in a lemon-yellow suit, entered the room trailed by his three black-clad operators. The puppet walked toward the couch, legs slowly churning out of time with its progress across the stage, feet hovering above the ground so it floated like a figure from a dream. The puppet stopped at the edge of the couch and for several moments gazed down at the smoking woman, his expression chiseled into a permanent lopsided smirk. He scratched his head and a male voice came over the speakers. They were using prerecorded dialogue in place of chanters. I wondered what Tetsuo's father would make of that particular innovation.

"You really want to go through with this?" the man said.

The female puppet extinguished her cigarette by gingerly rubbing the end against the ashtray like a child absentmindedly tracing patterns in the sand. Then she angled her head toward the puppet in the yellow suit, catching the light so that her face seemed to change expression, harden somehow.

"Once we do this, Kimiko," the man's voice said, "there's no going back."

The last of the smoke ribboned toward the ceiling.

"It won't be pretty," he added. "There will be blood."

Cymbals crashed as Kimiko sprang from the couch and

swiveled to face the man, thrusting her head defiantly forward. The man scrambled back, cowering like a beaten dog. Kimiko took another step forward and stomped her foot inches above the floor, a movement sonically underscored by the beat of a snare drum. A low industrial buzz churned through the small auditorium.

"I'm not a child!" she shrieked. "I know very well what will happen. I've thought of nothing else for days and nothing you tell me is going to change my mind."

"I'm only saying—"

"You're always only saying," she hissed. "It's time for *doing*. Don't tell me about blood. My dreams are stained with it. When I sleep blood rains from the heavens. Blood pools in the streets, blood chokes the filthy rain gutters, swells the rivers and oceans of this world. You have no idea the blood I've seen."

She turned away, lowering herself back on the couch and folding her hands calmly across her lap. The man puppet watched, thoroughly rebuked, at a loss for what to do next. After a time he strolled to the corner of the room and began searching for something under the bed. The puppet knelt while his operators in black crouched above him, observing his actions as if they were helpers eager to assist. The man couldn't find whatever he was looking for, and began to inch farther and farther beneath the milky white bed. The perspective somehow suddenly shifted, so that the puppeteers now seemed to be actively persecuting him, shoving him beneath as if holding a cat underwater to drown. The puppet's legs kicked and thrashed helplessly, its limp feet knocking against the floor as he tried to resist the puppeteers. Each desperate movement only brought him farther under the bed until he'd disappeared completely. All that was left were the three shadowy figures.

"Hajime?" Kimiko called out.

No answer. She floated from the couch and whirled in a half-circle, her manipulating shadow now dominating her, dwarfing her in the little room. "Hajime, where are you?"

Kimiko looked around the room. She glided across the floor, racing with tiny soundless steps toward the door he'd emerged from earlier. She peeked her head inside, and apparently seeing nothing, withdrew it and closed the door. Then she walked cautiously across the room until only a few feet away from the crouching black figures holding Hajime beneath the bed.

"Hajime?" she called out feebly.

The three crouching puppeteers silently turned their heads to look at Kimiko, even as they held Hajime under the bed. In that moment they seemed no longer passive operators but independent, malevolent forces within the drama. It was creepy in a way difficult to pinpoint and utterly unlike anything I'd seen in traditional Bunraku drama.

All four of the puppet operators onstage looked at each other now, nodding their heads like anonymous gods silently deciding the woman's fate. The audience tensed, waiting for the phantoms in black to snatch Kimiko and shove her asunder like Hajime or tear her limb from limb. Suddenly the three crouching puppeteers sprang to their feet in a single fluid movement, yanking Hajime from beneath the bed to a standing position. Kimiko leaped back in surprise, hand covering her mouth as she gasped and the audience gasped with her. Hajime held a plain black briefcase at the end of his outstretched arm.

"Found it!" he boomed.

Relieved laughter. All at once the puppeteers seemed to shrink into the background, relinquishing their roles as the puppets' spectral tormenters and becoming mute servants once again. Whether the puppeteers intended this effect or how they engineered it I couldn't say.

Onstage, Hajime moved past Kimiko, carrying the briefcase to the coffee table where he set it down and undid the latches as his two operators stooped above him. Kimiko approached the couch with fearful, hesitant steps, and sat down next to him. She crossed her legs and adjusted her dress, a movement accomplished with such natural grace it was hard to believe Kimiko was just a puppet. I guessed the puppeteer operating Kimiko was likely none other than Tetsuo Oyamada.

Hajime reached into the briefcase and withdrew a blond wig. He tossed it to Kimiko in a contemptuous gesture.

"Put it on," Hajime said.

Kimiko caught the wig and turned it over in her hands. After a moment, she reluctantly pulled it over her little head, tucking her own black locks out of sight. The wig cascaded in straight long tresses that fell past her shoulders, instantly transforming her into something icy and remote. Kimiko smoothed her hair as Hajime looked on.

"Remarkable," he said. "You look nothing like you."

Hajime reached back into the briefcase and offered her what looked to be a closed folding fan. She gave him a startled look, edging away from him, but he just grunted and forced the black object into her hands. Kimiko trembled as she held it.

"Open it," Hajime said.

Carefully, Kimiko took it in both hands, hunching over the object so it remained hidden from the audience. A moment later she pulled it open and gradually raised it into view, cupping the thing like an offering. The object was a straight razor. At first she merely stared at the razor as if she'd never seen one before, had no idea of its purpose.

Then the lighting shifted, soaking the stage in red. Kimiko gripped the razor's handle in her right fist and held it aloft. A spotlight caught the silvery blade at its peak, making it flash like a beacon as the rest of the stage faded to black.

Just then a commotion erupted in the row behind me. Chairs moving, people mumbling, a woman saying "excuse me" in a choked voice like she was about to cry. She pushed her way into the aisle and then clattered down the wooden platform in such a hurry I didn't get a very good look at her. But I didn't need one. I didn't need to see her at all. Just the sound of that staccato descent would've been enough. I leaped to my feet and made for the aisle. The curtain fell and the audience started clapping.

She was already out of the building by the time I reached the hallway, but for a second I imagined I could still hear her footfalls echoing in the concrete passageway as I raced past the ticket booth and headed for the exit. I burst outside, head swiveling, the night a blur. A fleeting shape rounded a corner at the end of the alley and I followed.

I kept some distance between us as she hurried through the streets, clutching her winter coat closed across her body. She bumped into several annoyed passersby as she fought through the crowds, racing southward. Several times I nearly lost her as she plunged into a side street or disappeared into a swarming crosswalk and twice I found myself mistaking some other woman for her, realizing at the last moment the person simply had the same color coat or the same short black hair. I got the feeling she knew she was being followed, but she never once looked back, didn't quicken her pace or take any evasive maneuvers.

After crossing the bridge she turned left and headed down Dotombori Street. Couples strolled by, smiling tourists posed for pictures in front of the famous clown statue, cinema-goers flushed out of a movie house, and giant mechanical crabs beckoned above restaurants but she didn't seem aware of any of it, may as well have been walking on the surface of the moon. She recrossed the river at the Ebusibashi Bridge, her form silhouetted against a dazzling wall of neon lights, and then headed down Soe-moncho, ignoring the beckoning pink salons and video arcades and batting cages and god knows what else.

Twenty minutes and a handful of subway entrances had passed and though she was no longer hurrying there was no sign she was nearing her destination. She seemed to have no destination at all, but moved with the purposeless rhythm of a sleepwalker. I had fallen into the same rhythm myself, become so mesmerized I almost didn't notice when she finally turned left into a small storefront.

The sign said it was a twenty-four-hour coffee bar called Café Cesare. I stood off to one side and watched through the window as the woman took a table in the corner, not bothering to remove her coat. A waiter dressed in immaculate white raced to her table, menu in hand. She waved off the menu, said a couple words. He gave her a short bow and raced away. The tables surrounding her were empty. Moments later the guy delivered a cup of coffee to her table. She poured in a container of cream, stirred it absentmindedly with a spoon. I waited for a gap in the pedestrian traffic then fought my way across the lane and took a deep breath and went inside.

The Café Cesare was decorated to look like a sidewalk café in an Italian village but had all the overlit, antiseptic charm of an operating theater. The place was spotlessly clean and customer-free save for the woman I'd just followed. The waiter was working over the espresso steamer with a towel when I entered. He nodded a greeting and went for the menu. The woman didn't even glance up as I came through the door and walked to her table.

"Mind if I sit here?"

The moment our eyes met, I knew she recognized me. Her mouth opened, but before she could speak the waiter materialized to pull out my chair. She lowered her eyes and stirred her coffee. I sat down and the waiter pushed in my chair with a loud squawk. I asked him to bring me a coffee, black. He moved like a bullet train and seconds later there was my coffee, served on a wafer-thin saucer in a cup so exquisitely brittle I thought it would shatter if I so much as breathed on it.

The woman across from me avoided any further eye contact. Her hair was a little different than the last time I'd seen her, boyishly short but dry now, no longer fastened with pins and clips. She had on a thick white sweater with a long black skirt and brown leather boots. She wore lipstick but no other makeup that I could see. It's a mystery what makes one arrangement of features beautiful and another plain, but if I studied her face long enough I got the feeling I just might figure it out. In the meantime, I searched for some easy way to begin the conversation. I didn't find one.

"I was at the theater," I said.

She looked up, a flash of alarm breaking her composure for a moment before she dropped her eyes again and resumed stirring her coffee. Outside the window, a seamless flow of people drifted by, gloved and scarfed, puffing into the cool night air.

"You followed me?" she asked.

"You looked upset. I thought you might want to talk."

Her lips moved through a whisper of a smile. "I'm sorry, but I don't want to talk. Forgive me, but I'd appreciate it if you'd please leave me alone now. It's nothing personal, I just don't feel like talking. I hope you understand."

"I'd move but I just ordered," I said. "If I go now, the waiter might not be able to find me. He'll have to pour perfectly good coffee down the drain. Profits will plummet, they won't make rent, the place will have to shut down. The waiter will be unemployed, and with no espresso machine to polish, his pent-up energy will find an outlet in crime. You might even end up being one of his victims. The situation is really very delicate. Poised on a razor's edge."

She put down her spoon. "Alright, you can sit here if you like. But I won't be forced into a conversation just because you followed me. I don't even know who you are."

"My name is Billy Chaka. Yours?"

She didn't answer.

"My name doesn't impress you, fair enough. Always thought it was a silly name myself. Would've liked something plainer. Something like 'Richard Gale.' "

For a full ten seconds she looked right through me without saying a word. And this time I didn't think I was imagining the sadness in her eyes. She brought the cup to her lips, lowered it, gave it another stir with her spoon. She finished her coffee and ordered another. I did the same. It was past eleven-thirty now, and as we both sat there in abject silence the waiter must've thought we were either happily married or on the worst blind date ever. Traffic increased outside the window as people began the drunken scramble for the last trains home. She drank from her third refill. I was watching her mouth as she put down her cup when all at once I realized she'd started talking.

"My husband is in a coma," she said.

Before I could say anything, she held up a hand to stop me. "You're going to say something polite, offer some words of sympathy. Please don't. Don't speak at all. I just want you to listen. To answer your question, my name is Emiko. My name is Emiko and I haven't spoken to anyone in a long, long time. You followed me here, asked me to talk. Now you're going to have to listen. Maybe sometime we can have a real conversation, but right now you're going to have to sit there and listen and not say a word. Do you understand?"

Chapter Seven

A White Horse

*I*t was two A.M. and 1 was asleep when the phone rang. When 1 picked it up, a man identified himself as officer so-and-so of the police department. He told me that my husband had been injured in a car accident and was being treated at the S—— Hospital. A car would be sent to take me there if 1 wanted to visit, but when 1 asked him for details of the accident the man just paused then said, *I'm very sorry.* When 1 got to the hospital 1 could tell it was serious because the doctors wouldn't let me see him right away. Before allowing me to visit, they wanted to warn me that he'd look *different,* that there was bound to be a lot of swelling with injuries like this. But nothing they could have said would've prepared me for the sight awaiting me. Despite their warnings, when they guided me into the room, my first impulse was to laugh. There had been a mistake. This man was most certainly not my husband.

Except it was my husband.

I couldn't bring myself to look at him all at once, but only in glimpses between closing my eyes or looking away, unable to consider the picture as a whole, to face the totality before me. And so my memories of that first night are like some terrible slide show. *Click.* Bloated head like a discolored pumpkin. *Click.* Eyes misaligned slits lost in green-yellow swells. *Click.* Lips engorged black slugs, no nose at all, just two off-center holes punched in his face.

But it was him, wasn't it?

Click. His head had been shaved and a hole had been drilled in his skull. *Click.* A tube running into the center of his head pulsed with yellowish fluid. *Click.* Straps criss-crossed over his body, fastening him to the hospital bed.

But it really was my husband.

Meanwhile, the doctors were explaining everything they'd done since he arrived, telling me about the various procedures, detailing what each strange apparatus was doing to keep him alive. All the while I thought how only hours ago, I'd kissed my husband good-bye and tousled his hair and reminded him to buy me a present while on his business trip to Kanazawa. Now I was standing in front of a trussed wreckage with tubes running into its throat and wires protruding from its chest and fluid pumping out of its skull and the doctors were telling me he had suffered se-vere head trauma and was in a coma and they were doing everything they could for my husband and there was every reason to hope but the next hours were critical. None of this was real, I thought, it's all a mistake. There had been some kind of cosmic mix-up when the phone rang and I somehow woke up inside someone else's life.

When the doctors left me alone in the room with him that first time, I couldn't bring myself to even touch his hand. I just sat there, eyes unfocused and roving the floor as I listened to the whirs and beeps of all the machines. I could hardly breathe. When the nurse came and told me they had to begin some procedure or other, that I'd have to leave him now, I started to cry. The nurse tried to console me, said I would be able to see him again soon. She didn't realize I was crying from sheer relief.

Difficult as that first night was, in many ways those early days were also the easiest. Shock protected me, prevented me from understanding how completely, how irrevocably, our lives had been transformed. I still believed that despite his appearance, he would recover soon, that it was an injury like other injuries, and that in time everything would heal and he would come home and we could pick up where we left off. There was every reason to hope, though in truth hope is seldom subject to reason. The swelling soon went down, some of the tubes were removed, and he began, at least physically, to resemble some recognizable though damaged version of himself again. I could be with him now for long stretches of time and look upon him without crying. When I held his hand I could close my eyes and feel the shape of it and almost make myself believe he was simply sleeping, that it was Sunday afternoon and he was just recuperating from an exhausting week at the office.

During this time, my husband's recovery became my only focus in life. Against the doctors' advice, I quit my part-time job at the Takashimaya department store so I could spend more time at the hospital. I devoured all the medical information I could get my hands on, learned everything I could about brain injuries and head trauma. More importantly, I learned how to listen to the doctors, how to decode their reports and excavate the truths buried under layers of protective ambiguity.

Those first weeks were full of updates, new diagnoses, new treatment strategies. But soon it became clear that my husband wasn't recovering as hoped. He still wasn't responding to external stimuli, exhibited no reactivity or perceptivity. At first the doctors tried to mollify me with all sorts of contradictory prognoses, but after a month or so, they admitted in so many words that they had no idea what would happen next. He might begin to recover tomorrow, he might not recover for years, he might never recover at all.

And even if he did get better, they cautioned, my husband wouldn't be the same person I married. The literature I'd amassed said the same. He may not recognize me at first, or even truly remember me for some time after he regained full consciousness. He may suddenly have different tastes in food, different tastes in music. He might remember how to compute the interest of a housing loan, but be incapable of tying his shoes. He would probably have a worse temper than before, and would find it difficult to control his emotions and sexual urges. When people come out of prolonged states of unconsciousness, the doctors warned me, these people emerge as someone else.

Around this time the physicians intimated that it would be easier on me, easier on everyone, if I visited only a couple of times a week. They said that my husband and I were both victims of the accident, and that I needed to think about healing myself, too. I was encouraged to begin living my life again, to try to get back into a more normal routine, to socialize.

A few weeks later, the same conversation occurred, this time in somewhat more explicit terms. They also wanted me to join some sort of support group. I declined outright. Talking with a bunch of heartbroken strangers wasn't going to repair the physical damage to my husband's brain, and wasn't that really the issue here? If it were as simple as talking and praying and hoping, then what was the point of hospitals at all? From this moment forward, by tacit agreement, my visits were limited to Fridays.

And so I searched for a way to reenter my old life. All of my friends were terribly kind and very sympathetic. The people at my husband's company treated me well, too, sending small gifts, inquiring about his progress, making sure the insurance company paid all the hospital bills in a timely fashion. Everyone asked after his recovery without being intrusive, and were considerate of my feelings in every way.

Nevertheless, I soon grew weary of them. In their eyes, I was no longer Emiko, but Emiko-with-the-Comatose-Husband. His absence became a presence lingering over every conversation, following me like a shadow everywhere I went. And though my friends tried their best to cope with this invisible presence, I could tell the effort wore on them. How could they understand what I was going through when I didn't understand it myself? And listening to them talk about the new Prada store opening in Umeda and complaining about their children's preschool teachers or the bills their husbands had run up in Kitashinchi, I realized I no longer had any place in their world. They were normal people with normal lives and normal problems, and ever since the phone rang one night I was nothing like them. From the moment of my husband's accident, an invisible wall had been erected between me and the world these people inhabited. And by now that wall was so strong and so high, there was no getting around it, no way to reenter my old life no matter how much my friends and family tried to help.

I gradually stopped talking with people. I would let the phone ring, leave e-mail unchecked, refuse to answer the apartment buzzer. If they somehow did manage to get in contact, I would always have some excuse handy. No doubt I became the subject of hushed conversations and concerned meetings over tea. My friends probably decided this seclusion of mine was a phase, something I needed to work through because soon the phone calls and invitations stopped coming. My world became silent and self-enclosed. Short of visits with my husband, by this time I was no longer speaking with anybody.

Though I was no longer truly part of their world, I soon came to realize I had to be with other people. I couldn't stand to be alone with my thoughts, felt an intense, overwhelming desire to be in the company of human beings. But interacting with people on even the most superficial level left me drained, and something as simple as buying groceries or speaking with a bank teller could reduce me to tears. What I really wanted, I decided, was to become invisible, to always be among people and yet never be subject to their idle chatter, their questions, their condolences. I wanted to be freed from their eyes, freed from their tongues, liberated even from their thoughts.

Rather than shut myself in, I would take endless walks

around the city, moving with all the purpose of a wayward cat as I watched people go about their lives. I'd take long morning strolls down the covered shopping arcades, watching the shopkeepers roll up their metal shutters before opening time, sweep and hose down the streets. I'd take loops around Ogimachi Park where men played soccer on the dusty fields. I'd sit on the benches near Osaka Castle, watching the passing groups of listless junior high students forced to jog laps. I'd watch the homeless emerging from their tarpaulined shelters disheveled and blinking into the morning light and the stone-faced salarymen filing into the office blocks of Honmachi.

On my walks I neither sought out places associated with my past nor avoided them. One location held no more interest for me than another, and I rarely visited the same place twice. My secret belief was that if I studied all these scenes intently, if I just looked hard enough at everyday collections of ordinary moments, something essential would reveal itself. Perhaps on these walks I was looking for some hidden shortcut back into the everyday world, though this didn't really occur to me at the time.

Often I would get so preoccupied by my aimless journeys that I would forget to eat, for I never seemed to be hungry. This loss of appetite combined with hours of walking day after day was transforming my body. I was shedding pounds and could feel my legs growing sinewy and hard. Just as the accident had physically changed my husband, it was now changing me.

I walked for longer and longer periods until soon I was on my feet from sunup until sundown. I never spoke with people during these outings. On the rare occasion strangers tried to talk to me, I'd just push past them, even pretend to be deaf. If I saw someone I knew coming toward me, I'd duck into a store or turn down a side street. Which is how it happened that everything suddenly changed one Friday night.

That night started much like any other. I visited my husband, held his hand, and told him about my week. The doctors said it was important to speak with him when I visited, told me that, often, a patient's break-throughs happen when loved ones are present, that even an apparently unconscious person can recognize different voices and that words spoken with love can help heal the mind. Of course, it's not that simple, they warned, and re-covering from a coma isn't like in the movies. People don't just sit up in bed, yawn, stretch, and ask for a cigarette. Usually, the most you can hope for at first are tiny gestures of recognition and signs of muscle control. A squeeze of the hand, the blink of an eye—these insignificant little movements become the milestones of hope.

By then my outward life didn't consist of much, so I hardly knew what to talk about. Often I found myself re-counting my walks. I would talk about the areas I visited, their physical locations, what types of people lived there. I don't remember what I talked about with him on that par-ticular night, but I remember thinking how strange it was that the old him, the husband I knew, was really in there somewhere, trapped in his immobile flesh, listening to the words I spoke. What would he make of these stories about my purposeless walks through the city? Would he realize what I'd become in his absence, worry that I was slowly dis-integrating? And would this fear draw him out, quicken his healing, or would it make him retreat further into whatever dark place he inhabited?

That night I left the hospital feeling drained and dreading the sight of our lonely apartment. I got off the train in Shinsaibashi to walk around and decided I'd stop at a pharmacy to buy sleeping pills. I'd started having trouble sleeping a couple weeks before, and as the problem worsened I'd started taking pills. I avoided buying them at my local drugstore for fear of becoming the subject of neighborhood gossip, though I'm sure my increasing aloofness had already spawned all manner of stories.

As I was walking, I spotted a girl I knew from high school. I hadn't seen her in years, hardly even recognized her at first. She used to be an awkward girl, bookish, and bespectacled, but she'd grown into a truly stunning young woman. A man was walking beside her, clutching her shopping bags, and they were both smiling and laughing like the happiest couple in the world. Suddenly, the woman saw me. She whispered something to the man and then came rushing toward me, calling my name. Panic came over me. I pretended not to see her and ducked into a side street. It was a dead end, running up against the river. There was nowhere to go, and my only chance of escape was a blue door set in the wall. I had no idea where it led, whether it was the back door to some restaurant or shop, but still I pushed open the door and rushed inside, just as my high school friend and her husband rounded the corner.

I braced my back against the door, catching my breath and taking in my surroundings. There was nothing but a stairway and a darkened corridor. I knew I should stay right where I was, make sure the door remained safely closed behind me, but something drew me down the stairs. At the end of the hall, I could see some sort of ticket booth occupied by a woman in man's clothing.

As if hypnotized, I purchased a ticket and went inside

without a thought. The auditorium was much smaller than any I was accustomed to, and was empty when I arrived. After a while a few people showed up, but they seemed different from the usual theater crowd, more dangerous somehow. I'm sure it was just my state of mind, that they were just your average people, but that night I was convinced I was in the company of rapists and drug addicts, gangsters and petty thieves. My stomach tensed. As the houselights went down someone behind me coughed and I nearly leaped out of my seat.

Then the play started. But it wasn't a normal play. It was a puppet show, some kind of twisted version of Bunraku. I was no great fan of Bunraku, had only seen it once while on an elementary-school field trip, and I didn't pick up a program, so I didn't know the title of the play or any of the puppeteers' names. Despite all this, I found myself engrossed in the production almost from the outset. Sitting there in the dark, silently watching the hidden people and their puppets move around on stage, I felt a strange contentment, as if a burden had been lifted. Suddenly, I realized I'd found my solution, stumbled upon the place I'd been looking for all this time. In the theater, I could finally be *invisible*. I could watch lives unfolding and nothing was expected of me but to buy a ticket and sit there quietly in the dark.

Of course, I knew it wasn't real life. In any theater, you're seeing actors going through a prescribed set of motions, speaking scripted words and generally pretending to be someone they're not. Puppet dramas are even further removed from reality, for realistic as these dolls were, no one would ever mistake one for a living, breathing person. Yet in a deeper sense, I *was* seeing real life, much more than I would watching films or television. Because at that moment, the puppeteers' lives consisted of being onstage, manipulating the dolls, right there in front of me. I was seeing people live out two hours or so of uninterrupted existence. The dramas they acted out were beside the point—I didn't need stories or fantasies or meaning or suspension of disbelief. I just needed to see bodies and hear words and watch physical movement. I could just as well have been sitting in an office building or on a factory floor, but only in the theater was I completely safe from interaction.

All of this came to me much later. That first night, I didn't think about the dynamics of the situation at all, but instead found myself engrossed in the happenings onstage. The play wasn't a very good one. It was an ugly, hopeless story about an unhappy couple named Daisuke and Mariko whose child has just died from a rare form of meningitis. The illness has torn the family apart and brought the couple to the brink of financial ruin. As the play ends the husband suggests to Mariko that maybe they should take a trip, the two of them, to get away from it all. This seems to offer some hope, but as they pack to leave, we see Daisuke put a bottle of poison into his suitcase. Then the phone rings and it's a hotel clerk in Kamikuishiki, a village near the famous suicide forest of Aokigahara. He's called to confirm their reservation for a single night.

As I said, not a great drama by any means, but somehow it resonated within me. I cried at its conclusion, and when the lights came on and I was forced to go back to my dreary apartment, I still couldn't leave the play behind. All night I could think of nothing but the doomed couple and their dead child.

I suppose, given my own circumstances, it was little wonder that I identified with Mariko, the unhappy female character in the play. On the surface, I suppose we had much in common, but I felt a deeper connection. The puppet could hardly be said to look like me, but I recognized myself in her every gesture, felt somehow as if I were watching a smaller version of myself. Not the real me, but a dream version of me. A version of myself at once exaggerated and understated, full of life and yet not living, a me without secrets, where what I felt inside was on display in every gesture, where I spoke my most private thoughts without so much as moving my lips.

To say the least, it was very confusing for me to connect so deeply with a fictional character, especially one embodied by a puppet. I attributed it to the strain I'd so long been under. For though I tried to keep myself safe from troubling thoughts, part of me knew my life was unraveling. I wondered if the insomnia and the pills I used to treat it were destroying my mind.

The next day I went on a long walk as usual, but I was unable to concentrate on my surroundings. That night, I returned to the strange little theater. Initially, I refused to give myself over to the drama, resisting the action of the play so that I might turn a more critical, objective eye on the Mariko character, discover what had drawn me to her. But soon I was once again completely absorbed. Just as before, I cried as the man slipped the poison into his suitcase and the final curtain descended, and if anything my connection with Mariko only intensified.

I returned on Sunday, saw both the matinee and the evening show. There were no performances on Monday, but I attended the other three performances that week. During each I noticed subtle aspects of the performance that had previously eluded me. In one scene, for instance, Mariko is washing dishes when her husband first broaches the idea of taking a trip together. It's a mundane conversation, but I began to appreciate how Mariko's small, almost imperceptible movements betrayed the dawning realization that her husband is proposing they die together, that she understands everything is coming to an end, that she accepts this as her fate.

Other insights were harder to put into words, but each show heightened my awareness, revealed hidden meanings, and made me feel strange, powerful new emotions. Not only the puppeteers, but the theater and the audience itself seemed to disappear, leaving myself and the characters locked together in a secret dialogue. By week's end, I felt no longer invisible. I felt that Mariko could see me, could see right through to the core of my being. I believed she could feel the longing in my heart, that her every tilt of the head or sweep of the arm was a silent message meant only for me, that the world was suspended as long as she and I were together in the dark. As I watched the puppet move around the stage, I often felt my pulse quicken and my mouth grow dry. It wasn't until much later that I realized I'd been experiencing symptoms of sexual arousal.

After each show, I would be so electrified I had even more trouble sleeping than usual, and so I began upping my dosage of pills. During the day as I wandered the city I'd find myself thinking about the play, about poor Mariko, and suddenly forget where I was. Twice I nearly got hit by oncoming cars, and I once became so thoroughly lost that I didn't make it back to my apartment until nearly dawn. In the span of one week, the Nocturne Theater had completely rearranged my senses.

As usual, I visited my husband that Friday. I began to tell

him about how I'd spent my week, but found myself unable to speak about the puppet show. Somehow I knew I had to keep my fascination with Mariko a secret. After all, my husband was somewhere in that body, listening to me, and what would he think to hear me speaking in such terms about a puppet? Talking to my husband was even more difficult than usual that night, for I could hardly recall where I'd traveled or what I'd seen that week. It struck me that for all my life consisted of, I might as well be the one in the coma. And yet, for the first time in months I felt strangely alive, aware of a whole universe of possibilities, energized by a dizzying optimism about the future. I cut my hospital visit short and hurried across town to the Nocturne Theater, anxious to catch the next performance.

But when the curtain went up, an unfamiliar scene greeted me. The unhappy couple's squalid little apartment was gone, replaced by an outdoor setting of lush pinks and emerald greens, some park during cherry blossom season. It slowly dawned on me that this was a new production, a different play entirely. With a growing sickness I realized what this meant; there would be no Mariko. Not on this stage, not anywhere. Like I said, it wasn't a great play, and there was simply no way another company would ever stage it. And even if they did, who else would do the play as a modern puppet show? My Mariko was gone. Lost forever as if she'd never existed, as if she really had gone out to die with her husband in those dark woods.

I felt as though a stranger had walked up and punched me in the stomach, left me crumpled and gasping for breath. I'd been duped, made to believe in a cheap illusion any sane adult should have seen through. I didn't wait for the new play to start, but rushed from the theater on unsteady legs, sweating and dizzy as I fought my way from the building, bile surging in my throat. Somehow I managed not to get sick. Somehow I managed to make it all the way home to my apartment where I threw myself into bed, head throbbing, stomach churning. I took double my usual dosage of sleeping pills but still ended up lying awake all night, helpless and sick, drifting in a state between sleep and wakefulness. In my fevered condition I convinced myself that I couldn't move, that I'd fallen into a coma as a punishment for my obsession with Mariko and I would have to experience for one night the same existence my husband had endured for months.

The next day I got out of bed early, tired and groggy but determined that things must change. I didn't leave to wander the city, but instead cleaned the apartment from top to bottom, aired the futon and swept and dusted and scrubbed like a demon until there was nothing left to clean. And when I was totally exhausted, I took a hot shower then collapsed into a deep sleep.

On Sunday, I didn't even get out of bed, but spent the entire day waking and sleeping, sleeping and waking. Monday morning, I finally arose feeling utterly refreshed, old business forgotten, ready to take on whatever challenges life offered. I made myself a large breakfast and wolfed it down with three cups of coffee, then did all the dishes. I decided to call a few of my friends—surely they must've been worried, must've been wondering about me. I would apologize for being out of touch for so long. I would make myself speak calmly, I would sound rational and upbeat and tell them everything was fine, because wasn't it, really, all things considered?

I tried a few numbers, but no one was in. By the time I finally did reach one of my friends, the sound of her voice so startled me that I found myself unable to speak, and hung up the phone without a word. She called me back immediately, but I didn't answer.

As the day went on I grew anxious. At lunch, I couldn't eat but a few spoonfuls of miso soup. I phoned in an order of Korean food from a local restaurant for dinner, but when the delivery boy came I couldn't bring myself to answer the door. The apartment seemed to shrink as the evening wore on, as if the walls were closing in with each disappearing ray of sunlight and I had to get out before they crushed me.

And so I walked, just as I'd promised myself I wouldn't. And before long I was thinking again about Mariko. Two days had passed now, and though I tried to convince myself the whole puppet infatuation had just been some strange side effect from months of loneliness and worrying, I had to admit it was more than that. And of course, the more I tried not to think about the puppet, the more she was in my thoughts. It was like a joke my father used to play on me as a little girl—he would tell me he'd buy me all the candy in the department store basement if I could sit in a corner for one minute and not imagine a white horse. At the end of the minute he would say, "Emiko, did you imagine a white horse?" And when I said no, he always laughed and told me I was lying, which of course I was.

I walked for hours that night. It was a cold, windy night but I walked and walked, listening to the great deafening buzz of an inaccessible world, hoping that immersing myself in this noisy swamp of buildings and cars and trains and people would quell all the troubling thoughts going through my head. Finally, I stopped in some tiny nowhere of a park. I sat on a bench and wrapped my coat around myself, watching my shadow shivering in the dirt, losing myself in my own black projection. For a moment I imagined myself as Mariko the puppet and my shadow as the hooded puppeteer who controlled me. I wondered what my shadow had in store next, whether it would continue waking me at all hours of the night, whether it would keep forcing me to take endless walks until I was nothing but bones, or whether it would abandon me altogether, leave me a lifeless heap to be bundled in a box or hung inside a closet.

And in that instant, I suddenly realized what had happened to me at the Nocturne Theater. Everything was so simple it bordered on absurd. Here I'd been obsessing over what so drew me to Mariko and worried I was losing my mind only to realize it wasn't about the puppet at all. The truth was more ordinary, closer to the normal world, and yet fantastically, beautifully strange. It wasn't the puppet I was in love with—it was her shadow. A man I had spent night after night with and never even seen.

Chapter Eight

The Tin Man

*I*was relieved. It didn't matter that this man was faceless, anonymous, little more than a silhou-
ette. He was at least a living, breathing
person. Invisible in a sense, the way I tried so
hard to be, but underneath a human being of
flesh and blood. And through his actions onstage, the thoughts and emotions he transferred through the puppet, I believed I could
see the inner him, experience the person behind the hooded black veil. So I returned to
the Nocturne Theater, night after night. And
for a while, this made me happy," Emiko said.
"Or something close to happy."
She stopped talking and sipped from her
fourth coffee of the night. I'd given up coffee
and was on my third or sixth glass of water.
It was past five in the morning and my head

was swimming. Safe to say I'd never seen such a normal-looking woman tell such a whacked-out story. As she'd requested, I hadn't said a word since she'd begun, just listened. The whole time she'd spoken in an even, calm tone, looking me straight in the eye, her body perfectly motionless save for the delicate movements she used to bring the coffee cup to her lips. The fastidious waiter was slumped on a stool behind the counter, fast asleep. Outside the sun was edging over the horizon, but if morning birds were chirping or temple bells ringing or garbage trucks making their rounds I couldn't hear them. Everything seemed eerily still, poised on some invisible border. I felt like I'd been dislodged from reality, like I was standing on some distant shore and watching it drift away without me.

"I'm sure you must find my story a little odd," Emiko said.

I nodded. Any words would be an exercise in understatement.

"But maybe my story isn't so unique," she resumed. "People develop crushes on strangers all the time. On actors, especially. And what is a puppeteer but an actor whose mask is more complete than most? An actor unbound by a face, freed from a voice? I never wished to see what this puppeteer looked like, never wanted to learn his name. I didn't care that I couldn't speak to him or touch him. From the way he handled the puppets, I always knew which character he portrayed no matter what the play, and to be with him for a few hours every night was enough. And I didn't feel any guilt for being with him. Or not much, anyway. It wasn't even really an affair, I told myself. But maybe I was kidding myself about the guilt. Because it was around this time I first started having the dreams, and maybe there is a certain logic to what happened next."

She couldn't expect me not to ask. "What happened next?"

For the first time since she'd started talking, her eyes wandered from mine and her voice faltered. "Circumstances forced me to have a real affair. To sleep with a man. A stranger. For money."

As if on cue, my cell phone started ringing. I gave Emiko an embarrassed grin as I fumbled to dig it out of my pocket. The caller ID said only PanCosmo Hotel, but as all calls were routed through the hotel, it always said that. At this ungodly hour, I knew it could only be Sarah. Maybe she'd got the wordless message I left and was calling to ask what was going on. Maybe asking for some info on Gale was worth a try—I didn't have to tell her the guy was dead, after all. Obviously I couldn't discuss the matter in front of Emiko, but I felt reluctant to get up from the table. For a few seconds I just sat there staring at the ringing phone, wishing it would stop.

"You'd better answer," Emiko said, eyes meeting mine again. "It must be important if someone is phoning at this hour."

"Probably just a wrong number."

"You never know," she said, a faint smile making its way onto her face. I told her I'd be right back, then stood and walked toward the hallway that led to the bathrooms. Just before I ducked out of sight I took one last glimpse of her sitting there at the table, outlined against the pale morning light, the cup raised silently to her lips. Then I rounded the corner, hit the talk button, and put the phone to my ear.

"*Moshi moshi,*" I said.

Silence on the other end. I checked the display screen. Someone had sent me a picture.

I looked at the digitized image for maybe a second, two at most, but that's all it took. A figure sat crooked in bed, arms limp at his sides, head bent at a wrong angle. His jaw sagged open and his half-closed eyes gazed nowhere. The rest of his face was a hackwork smear of featureless viscera. Blood already going black trailed from a gash in his neck, soaked one side of his white T-shirt. Blood spotted the walls, the headboard, the pillows, the bedsheets. The bed was identical to the one I'd awoke in before setting out this morning from the PanCosmo Hotel.

I closed my eyes but opened them before the after-image fully burned in. I turned off the phone and shoved it in my pocket. Then I turned the phone back on and waited a moment to see if whoever saw fit to send me the picture of Richard Gale's corpse would call back. No call came. I took a few deep breaths and tried to clear my head.

When I walked back into the room Emiko was gone.

In her place sat a large man in a silver suit. He had a bullet-shaped head and was hunched forward in his chair as if trying to overwhelm the table with his shimmering bulk. He was clutching the coffee cup Emiko had been holding only moments before, the cup looking like something from a dollhouse in the catcher's mitts he had for hands. I walked up to the table and stood right in front of him. He paid me no attention whatsoever. The man took a sip of the coffee and recoiled as if it had bitten him.

"Hot," he said.

"Where did she go?" I said.

He angled his bullet head to me. "I'm supposed to give you something."

"You the one who just sent the picture?"

"I don't know anything about any picture." The man reached into his jacket and rummaged clumsily through one pocket, then another. I glanced around the room. The waiter was wide awake now, wiping down the espresso machine, rinsing glasses and stacking cups and doing everything possible to avoid looking in my direction. The sun had risen and was blasting through the window, splashing the room orange and sending razors of light off the man's shiny suit. The guy found what he was searching for and tossed a thick envelope on the table.

"It's for you," he said. "You're supposed to take it."

"This is from Emiko?"

He shook his head. "From my boss. But I'm not supposed to get into all that. I'm supposed to give you this money and tell you to mind your own business is all. You're supposed to take the money and go back to America."

"And who are you again?"

"Me?" He looked around, swiveling his thick head as if I could possibly be addressing someone else. "I'm the guy supposed to give you this money. You're supposed to take the money. It's a lot of money. There's a plane to America this afternoon. I don't know which one, but they said it wouldn't matter."

"I'm not taking the money."

That puzzled him. "But it's a lot of money."

"I'm not taking the plane, either."

He stared down at the envelope, waiting for his next thought to coalesce as steam rose from Emiko's coffee cup. Were it not for the lipstick imprint on it she'd left behind, I might have convinced myself I'd dreamt the whole thing. "If you don't take the money," the man finally announced, "they said I'm supposed to break your arm."

There was no menace in his voice, no aggression in his

body language. He looked up at me again, brows crow-
barred across his forehead, eyes flat and hard as he stood
and pushed in his chair. At six foot three or so he was bigger than I'd guessed, and apparently had the mental capacity to figure out how dumbbells worked. I let him come
halfway around the table and relaxed my muscles and concentrated on my breathing and tried to remember if I'd
paid my health insurance premium this month. Standing
fully upright, he looked like a cross between the Tin Man
and the Incredible Hulk.

"I'm going to break your arm now," the man said.

"They tell you which arm to break?"

That stopped him. It was a good question, one that required intense contemplation. While he bent his mind to
the problem, I swooped up the coffee cup from the table
and emptied it across his face. He yelled, stumbling backward against a chair, knocking it to the floor as his hands
shot up to cover his eyes.

"Hot!" he screamed.

No curse words, no threats of retribution, just "hot,"
over and over, "hot," as he tried frantically to wipe off his
face. He was still trying when I lunged around the table and
swung my foot into his groin. No more "hot" from the Tin
Man. His eyes sprang open, a little less hard but just as dull,
then he folded and toppled into the table, bringing it down
in a clatter. I kicked him once in the head. I wanted to keep
on kicking but I didn't.

The waiter stood frozen in place behind the counter,
not saying a word as I raced across the room and out the
door. I'd expected more thugs to come rushing at me just
then, hopping out of cars, encircling me with motorcycles,
emerging from alleyways, popping out of manholes. I ex-

pected lots of shouting, pointed guns, drawn knives, swing-
ing baseball bats. But all that greeted me was a deserted
morning street in a section of Osaka not known for morn-
ings. The air was crisp and cool and Emiko was nowhere in
sight.

Chapter Nine

The Woman with the Auburn Hair

You go to an island across the ocean to accept an award
you don't even want from an organization
you don't even know, and a harmless-looking
gentleman you've met before but can't remember asks you to join him for a drink, and
before you realize it you're following strange
women out of basement puppet theaters, listening to their bizarre stories and being
threatened by stupid men in shiny suits—all
because you once wrote a story about a
thirteen-year-old kid who was really, really
good at the world's most ancient and sophisticated form of playing with dolls. Beats
plucking chickens, 1 guess, but 1 knew the
mess I'd become involved in was only going
to get messier and more involved.

When 1 got back to my hotel room, that

morning's copy of the *Asahi Shimbun* was there waiting. While scanning for news about Richard Gale's death I came across a story about junior high school kids getting banned from a local judo competition because their eyebrows were trimmed too thin—"intimidating their opponents and causing displeasure," according to one of the judges. A cop in the Hyogo Prefecture was arrested for drunkenly assaulting a cab driver, and an article about the changing Japanese language said that *sutureso,* or "stress," was now the most widely used English word in the country.

I finally found Richard Gale's death buried in a one-inch column at the end of the regional news section. The article gave away almost nothing—not the name of the hotel where it happened, not the victim's identity, not even whether police were considering it a homicide. All it said was that an American had been found dead inside a prestigious hotel near Osaka's Business Park and police were investigating possible foul play. Strange, considering murders were still rare enough in Japan to often make the front page. I wondered who was squelching the story—the Inoue family, the police, or the hotel itself.

I was reading an article about bid rigging on an expressway noise-barrier project when I heard a soft, almost apologetic rapping at the door. I opened it to find hotel detective Imanishi doing a good impersonation of a zombie. His ash-gray suit looked slept in, but he couldn't have slept much because the whites of his eyes weren't, and the bags beneath them had bags of their own. He sorried his way into the room and closed the door remorsefully behind him, then wished me good morning and said he hoped everything at the PanCosmo Hotel was meeting my standards. He asked if I knew about the shoeshine service and I told him I did. Pleasantries dispensed with, he popped open a latch on his briefcase. The thing was scuffed and frayed at the edges like it had been passed down generation to generation since the days when Osaka was known as Naniwa.

"Allow me to show you something," Imanishi said. He opened the briefcase and took out a videocassette. Then he went across the room and closed the curtains before walking back and inserting the tape into the VCR. He turned on the TV and the screen came to life, lighting the room blue. A grainy image of the PanCosmo's lobby appeared. The shot was taken from just behind the front desk, a high-angle view looking over the shoulder of Concierge Tanaka, framing him between two decorative columns in the middle ground of the lobby. To the left, the entrance of the hotel. To the right, the elevator bank. A time code ticked in the upper corner.

And for a while that was the show—the concierge just standing there with his back to the camera, leaning on the counter, surveying his empty domain while time did what it does. Then at the far left of the screen, a flicker of movement. A man and woman walked silently into the frame, side by side, making their way toward the front desk. Even without seeing his face, I knew it was Richard Gale. And as they moved closer to the camera, I realized something else.

The woman next to him wasn't Emiko.

She was wearing a raincoat, just as Emiko had been when I found her in the stairwell. She carried a handbag, just like Emiko did, and her face even looked a little like Emiko's, though given the poor image quality it was hard to read much more than its general shape, especially since the woman was wearing sunglasses.

The difference was the hair. Whereas Emiko's was natural black and clipped short, the woman onscreen had dyed dark auburn locks with bangs drawn precisely across her forehead, while the sides came to her jawline, neatly framing her face. Poor Richard should've known any woman who wore sunglasses at night in January was bad news, but then recognizing bad news and avoiding it were two different things. Maybe bad news was exactly what he'd been looking for.

I was relieved the woman wasn't Emiko, but not much. If Emiko wasn't involved, why had the Tin Man shown up and threatened to break my arm less than an hour ago? When I'd asked Emiko if she knew Richard Gale, she could have just said no and told me to take a hike, but she didn't. Either she was incredibly desperate to talk, or her story had been a long preamble to a confession she never got to deliver. And, of course, the big question—who was this new woman with the auburn hair?

Imanishi hit the pause button just as the woman was turning her head, freezing her in a faceless blur. Next to her, Richard Gale had one hand extended to receive the key to the last room he'd ever occupy. The time stamp read 11:33 P.M.

"And so," Imanishi said softly.

"So, indeed." I had no idea what he wanted.

"What's your initial impression of this footage?"

I looked again at the blurry image. "It's no *Seven Samurai*."

Imanishi smoothed his tie between his thin fingers, showing neither amusement nor annoyance. He stared at the unmoving image on screen for several moments before speaking. "On your hotel registration form, you listed your profession as journalist. This information is correct?"

"*Youth in Asia* magazine. It's for teenagers."

"And this *Youth in Asia*—it is a humor magazine? Some sort of lampoonish publication?"

"Not intentionally."

Imanishi nodded to himself and fell silent. After some consideration, he hit the eject button and the room went TV blue again. He took out the tape and walked back over to the table, then stuck the tape in his briefcase and snapped the case shut. Except for his incongruously pale left ear, his face had gone crimson, flushed with ill-concealed embarrassment or half-restrained anger. I couldn't say which, but knew I should apologize even if I wasn't sure why. Maybe this was how it felt to be Japanese.

"I'm sorry," I began. "I just don't know what you—"

"It's quite alright," Imanishi said. "Don't think me such an innocent fellow. In my days with the police, I was exposed to callousness of every shade. And not just from the criminals. Among our ranks, there were men who took great pride in base remarks. I suppose such men exist in all walks of life."

"I'm just confused why you're showing me this tape."

"Is that so?" Imanishi asked. "Perhaps the following story will help alleviate your confusion. I must warn you that you may find this narrative shocking. You may find it repulsive, perhaps even disgusting. Or perhaps you'll merely find it fodder for further jokes."

"Look, don't get the wrong idea. I'm just—"

"The first week I was on the force a prostitute was murdered," Imanishi said quietly. "In February, as I recall, during the coldest week of the year. I remember every detail of that day, right down to the headlines in the papers. Something about airplanes, I believe. But mostly I remember the cold. That morning my partner and I got a call from the dispatcher. A jogger had seen a 'troubling shape' while on her morning run along the riverbank. This shape turned out to be a dead Korean woman lying facedown on the north bank of the Yodogawa River. Or should I say the torso of a dead Korean woman. Her arms had been amputated at the elbow. Hacked off, presumably so we couldn't fingerprint her. The killer had also smashed all her teeth, caved them in with a heavy blunt object. We believed this was done to make dental records useless. When my commanding officer arrived as we were preparing to transport the remains of this woman, he said something I'll never forget. Do you know what he said?"

I shook my head.

"He said, 'Better hurry up and get her to Kuromon. She won't fetch much once she starts to smell.' "

He awaited my reaction.

"Kuromon is a wholesale market," Imanishi added. "They are famous for their fresh seafood selection. My commanding officer was making a joke. He was comparing this woman's lifeless body to that of a dead fish."

"I guess that's not very—"

"A fish!" Imanishi spat. "The others all laughed, laughed in the very presence of this woman, a citizen of the city they were paid to protect. But I did not laugh. Far from it. Risking gross insubordination, I gently reminded my commanding officer that this woman was not a fish, but a human being. That she had once been a little girl, someone's daughter, maybe someone's sister or sweetheart. Perhaps, I ventured, she once enjoyed flying kites, or collecting some sort of collectibles. My passion aroused, I now addressed my comments not simply to the captain, but to all assembled. 'It is a part of us, gentlemen, that has been murdered,' I said. 'A part of each and every one of us that has been violated and fiendishly butchered here on this day, cast into this godforsaken river running through the city we call our domain!' "

By now Imanishi no longer seemed to be present in my room at the PanCosmo Hotel at all, but moored on the clouded banks of the Yodogawa during some distant February morning. For a few moments he said nothing else, but only stood immobile in the center of the room, bathed in the light of the television, posture rigid as if he were bracing himself against a strong wind.

"Perhaps I acted rashly," he finally resumed, the tension slowly leaving his body like air leaking from a bicycle tire. "For my speech certainly did not achieve the desired results. Precisely the opposite, I fear. At any rate, now you know the reason I felt duty bound to share this videotape. And of course, share the photograph I sent to your mobile phone early this morning."

So it was him who sent it. I guess it was sort of a relief.

"I apologize if you found the image upsetting," he said in a tone miles from apology. "And I know it was quite early in the morning for such communication, but the message was intended as a wake-up call of sorts. I hoped such an image would underscore the reality that we live in a world where evil lurks ever present. We can joke about it, or we can combat it. Mr. Chaka, I'm sharing evidence about this case in the hope you will return the favor. I suspect you are privy to certain information you're concealing from me. I have thus far withheld these suspicions from my former colleagues in the police department, but I'm certain they would have plenty of questions for you should I choose to go forward with my evidence."

"What evidence would that be?"

"There is the nametag, to cite but a single example. And the fact that you entered the hotel at roughly the same time the murderer was likely engaged in—"

"The police don't know about the nametag?"

"To cite a single example. There is also circumstantial—"

"But didn't they bag it at the crime scene?"

Imanishi pinched his face into a sour grimace and in-haled deep breaths through his nose. "If you wish to deal with the Osaka authorities, that can certainly be arranged," he sniffed. "You'll find them neither as patient nor as un-derstanding as myself, this I assure you. With that in mind, perhaps there is something you wish to share with me. Some information that will aid us in our mutual struggle on behalf of the good people who patronize this hotel. On be-half of humanity at large."

I bit my lip and shook my head. "Wish I could help."

Imanishi's eyes could've punched holes through steel but his mouth remained closed. Despite everything I'd learned since the last time the hotel detective had ques-tioned me, here we were, both in the same place again, neither of us any closer to finding out what happened to Richard Gale, me keeping Emiko's presence a secret for reasons I didn't fully understand, Imanishi suspicious of me for reasons just as unclear. I kept thinking of my encounter with the Tin Man, wondering who'd sent him. Given what Curry had told me about certain guests at the Inoue wed-ding, I had a hunch. I decided to put the question to the hotel detective.

"How much do you know about the Komoriuta-kai?" I asked.

The words seemed to trigger something in him. His nos-trils twitched and he ran an index figure along the seam of his fake ear before snapping to and giving me a stoical look. "Just what are you insinuating?"

"I wondered if maybe they were involved somehow."

"Involved?"

"Right. In the murder."

"Oh," said Imanishi, looking suddenly embarrassed. He reached up to fiddle with the ear again but caught himself. "For a moment I was under the impression— What makes you think the Komoriuta-kai might be a party to this?"

I told Imanishi that I'd talked to a friend earlier, and he'd mentioned in passing that he knew Gale, that Gale had married Kaori Inoue, and that the Inoue family was rumored to have close ties with the Komoriuta-kai. I didn't bring up Emiko or the Tin Man.

"Pointless and groundless," said Imanishi. "To answer your question, I am more than familiar with the Komoriuta-kai. I'm not one to boast, but in the line of duty I once came face-to-face with the leader of this reprehensible outfit, the notorious Mr. Tadamitsu Noguchi himself. Have you ever had occasion, Mr. Chaka, to gaze upon pure, unmitigated evil?"

I shrugged. "Met an insurance-industry lobbyist once."

Imanishi didn't bat an eye. "A man like Mr. Noguchi has a very broad face, as does Mr. Inoue. That these men may sometimes move in overlapping circles has no immediate bearing upon this case. Unless, that is, you have evidence to the contrary."

I shook my head. "Just a thought."

"To one unschooled in the ways of the criminal mind, this may look like *yakuza* business." Imanishi clasped his hands behind his back like a lecturing professor. "But I've never known a professional killer to use so crude a weapon as a straight razor. And the Komoriuta-kai know better than to commit foul acts in an establishment like the Pan-Cosmo Hotel. Such a high-profile setting would draw unwanted attention."

"Doesn't have the earmarks of a *yakuza* hit, you're saying."

"I beg your pardon?" hissed Imanishi. He took a step forward, eyes shooting daggers, lips clenched into a hard line. "What exactly are you implying?"

"I'm agreeing with you."

"Oh." He blinked several times in rapid succession, his features softening. "Well, then."

The detective let out a quiet sigh and started for the door. Just as he reached it, he turned around to face me. "Several of the hotel's restaurants serve breakfast," he said. "Both Japanese and Western style. The establishment on the third floor is particularly good. I'm told their toast is first-rate."

With that declaration the odd little hotel detective bowed and walked out the door. My thoughts anchored on something he'd said earlier. *Straight razor.* Whether he meant to or not, Imanishi had just leaked the murder weapon. No wonder he hadn't lasted long as a cop. I listened for the sounds of his footsteps receding down the hall, but the thick carpet didn't allow for it. For all I knew he was crouched outside with his good ear cupped to the door when I called the front desk. Fifteen minutes later I was on the Internet, typing the words "Komoriuta-kai Inoue Development Tadamitsu Noguchi" into a search engine on a rented laptop.

The search didn't yield much. Lots of articles about a shoot-out at a funeral for a Komoriuta-kai boss in Tokyo, something about a recent case involving an Osaka prefectural official accused of misappropriating funds. There was a link for the official Inoue Development web page, which provided even less than the usual noninformation you get on corporate web sites. Nothing I found connected Inoue and the gangsters, until I clicked on a link to an article titled "Chayamachi Troubles Put Tee Times in Peril." The article was posted on a message board for golfers, of all places, with a note saying the piece was originally published in 1996 in a now-defunct Japanese weekly called *Shukan Tsunokuni.*

According to the article, Inoue Development was involved in a redevelopment deal gone sour. It all started in Chayamachi, an old neighborhood just northeast of Umeda, one of the few to survive the World War II Allied bombing campaigns intact. Spared the destruction of the war and the frenzy of reconstruction that followed, Chayamachi was about the only place in central Osaka where you could still find tiny wooden row houses and cobblestone streets well into the nineteen-eighties. Then at the height of the bubble, Inoue Development, Oshoku Construction, and a few other unnamed companies began a multimillion-dollar land grab that drove out longtime residents and businesses in the area. Developers reportedly employed members of the Komoriuta-kai to help convince reluctant sellers that getting out of Chayamachi would do wonders for their life expectancy. Old houses were boarded up and left standing while the firms gobbled up the neighborhood block by block. By about 1988, Chayamachi was a ghost town.

The following year, the trendy Loft complex went up, a sign of what lay in store for the area. Ambitious plans were drawn to turn Chayamachi into another massive shopping-and-entertainment compound, when suddenly the bubble burst. Stock prices plummeted and the bottom fell out of the hyperinflated real-estate market. Oshoku Construction, Inoue Development's partner, was heavily invested in Tokyo, where values dropped by as much as fifty percent almost overnight and kept falling. It was the usual story. Oshoku defaulted on loans and was eventually forced to declare bankruptcy, which left Chayamachi plans in the lurch. At the time the article was written, pockets of Chayamachi still remained boarded up and abandoned, while Oshoku Construction and its various partners were under investigation by the Deposit Insurance Corporation of Japan, which was slowly wading through the wreckage of hundreds of collapsed housing loan companies nationwide.

Inoue Development managed to keep afloat through the Chayamachi affair, but in order to survive, they'd done some no doubt obfuscatory restructuring that left their flagship development, Emerald Greens, on indefinite hold and in uncertain hands. Emerald Greens, the article said, was conceived as the premier golf course in the Kansai region, if not all of Japan, and was scheduled to open in 1997 in a suburb near Ibaraki, north of Osaka. Construction was well under way when everything went to hell. The article ended with the author wondering whether the golf course would even be completed before the new century dawned.

Evidently not. A second search I ran on the term "Emerald Greens Golf Course" yielded nothing but File Error 404s. That was the sum total of what the Internet had to offer regarding any ties between Inoue Development and the Komoriuta-kai. An article from a defunct magazine about an unfinished golf course, and a handful of dead links.

I had just typed "Richard Gale" into the search engine and was scrolling through the predictably random results when the phone rang. On the other end someone was offering a more old-fashioned way to go about digging up information.

Chapter Ten

The Joyful Twilight

As the cab moved north over the Ajikawa River I looked
out the window across Osaka Bay, past the
giant Ferris wheel of Tempozan Harbor
slowly churning against the winter sky. For
years Osaka had been creeping westward
into the ocean, and now skyscrapers rose in
the distance from man-made islands that
didn't exist ten or fifteen years ago. An oversized replica of the *Santa Maria* was anchored on the shore of Tempozan like some
ghost ship drifted in from another century.
What Columbus's famous vessel had to do
with Osaka Bay was anybody's guess, but you
learned pretty quickly not to bother guessing. When it came to Japanese tourist attractions, history was a playground, relevance
irrelevant.

The driver took another look at the address I'd given him, then handed the fax back through the partition. I slipped it in the pocket of my black suit jacket. It was the only suit I owned and I hadn't planned on wearing it until the Kinki Foundation's awards ceremony, but I hadn't planned on Curry calling to tell me about an engagement he figured I wouldn't want to miss.

Curry had received Richard Gale's death notice in the mail, which acted as an invitation to the *osōshiki*, the public funeral ceremony the Inoue family were holding. Since I seemed so curious about Gale, Curry thought maybe I'd want to attend in his place. To accommodate Mr. Inoue's vast network of business associates, the family had to rent the second-largest *kaijo* in greater Osaka, a funeral hall called Joyful Twilight on the northern outskirts of the city. Curry referred to the place as the "Twilight Zone" and said I'd understand why when I saw it. He told me I shouldn't worry about crashing the ceremony as there were bound to be loads of people, maybe even a few Yanks.

In my experience funerals weren't the hotbed of leads they were portrayed as in movies. No ominous umbrellaed figures skulking at the edges of rainy cemeteries, no love affairs dramatically revealed or wills publicly fought over, no simmering family tensions erupting into clumsy fistfights. Didn't happen that way, especially in a country famous for its sense of decorum. Any emotional outbursts would've occurred during the *tsuya,* the all-night vigil preceding a funeral in which mourners got blind drunk, sobbing and carrying on so much you might mistake them for particularly stoic Italians. But the *tsuya* was a private event, off limits to everyone but family and very close friends. At the public *osōshiki,* you saw only people numbed by loss, going through the motions with a quiet, sad dignity as they burned incense and traded the same two or three formal condolences with the family and ate and drank and talked small and truly remembered the dead only in those wordless silences that descended from time to time out of nowhere.

Thanks but no thanks, I'd told Curry. I'd hung up the phone and waded through more Richard Gale links. There was a Richard Gale who played for the Bradley and Bradley softball team in Santa Fe, New Mexico, and had a beer gut and a bad mustache. There was a Richard Gale in the UK who was a livestock breeder specializing in Dutch heifers. A Richard Gale was listed in an obituary as the sole surviving heir to Martin and Leslie-Anne Gale, who died in a Colorado plane crash. Another Richard Gale was a bassoonist with the New York City Ballet Orchestra. There was a Richard Gale in Alabama who was in the third grade and wrote a report on the state of Alabama. After about ten minutes, I shut down the rented laptop and called Curry back.

Five minutes after that, he faxed directions to the Joyful Twilight directly to my room. Half an hour later I'd gone to a stationery store on the ground level of the hotel to buy a *bushigi bukuro,* the white envelope tied with a black ribbon in which you stuffed *o-koden,* incense money. Condolence always consisted of new, crisp bills and I didn't have any so I ended up ironing some old ones in my hotel room before I left. I was pretty lousy with an iron, and singed two otherwise fine 1,000-yen bills before producing acceptably stiff cash. The marred bills went to the shoeshine guy in the PanCosmo lobby, the other 5,000 yen went inside the sealed envelope with my name written on the back, as was customary. Of course, I didn't actually write my name, but Kenneth Balderton's, just in case they later checked against the invitation list. Then I called a cab.

During the drive, I kept thinking about Emiko, picturing her sitting across from me at the empty café, her voice quiet and dispassionate, her eyes hardly straying from mine as she spoke, not telling her story so much as letting it unfurl. Of course, I didn't have the entire story yet. My stupid cell phone rang and Emiko had vanished, an unfinished dream chased away by the dawn.

To get my mind off Emiko, I thought about my conversation with hotel detective Imanishi. This didn't prove the best strategy because I kept returning to the revelation Imanishi had casually let slip during the conversation.

Richard Gale had been killed with a straight razor.

Not a knife or a sword or a box cutter or even a regular old razor blade, but a straight razor. Which made me think of the strange play at the Nocturne Theater, the part where the female puppet brandishes the same weapon. Given what Emiko had told me about her troubled life, she could've had a number of reasons for running out of the theater in tears, for running out of practically any place in tears, but with this new information about the razor the timing of her flight called everything back into question.

Could Richard Gale have entered the hotel with one woman only to be killed by another? Was Emiko meant to be found in the stairwell as part of some kind of setup? Or had Emiko, or someone else, been somehow trying to frame the woman on the surveillance tape? With so little to go on, anything was possible.

Suddenly I realized how Imanishi had become so convinced I knew more than I was telling him. The surveillance camera was placed so that it would have captured me entering the lobby after meeting that night with Mr. Oyamada. Moments later, it would have caught Emiko exiting the stairwell. Imanishi had obviously seen the footage, and that's why he was suspicious. Why he didn't just come out and confront me about it, I couldn't say. Maybe it was that stereotypical Japanese avoidance of confrontation, but in Imanishi's case, I doubted it.

I listened to the gentle hum of the taxi engine as we crawled toward the northern suburbs. I closed my eyes but didn't sleep. The car twisted through the hills for about ten minutes until we hit a massive traffic jam and I knew we'd arrived.

Several limos idled in front of the Joyful Twilight while a white-gloved employee of the funeral hall struggled to direct traffic to the parking lot. Few businesses in Osaka could afford space for parking lots, but few were making as much money as funeral halls. The costs of living in Japan were nothing compared to the costs of dying there, and an aging population was making the bereavement business one of the few growth industries in the country. But judging by the crowd outside the Joyful Twilight, the Inoues would more than break even on the event. They'd probably still be counting their condolence cash when their American son-in-law completed his forty-nine-day journey to heaven.

The Joyful Twilight was three stories high, dirty stucco white with large plate-glass windows displaying an orgy of flowers. The canopied entrance was a logjam of women in black dresses fussing with their pearls and men in black suits tugging at their shirt cuffs. There were curt bows of recognition here and there, but nobody said much. Scattered on either side of the entrance, shifty men stood with hands jammed in their pockets, puffing cigarettes and squinting through the smoke. Aside from a portly blond woman in a square-shouldered black business suit and a skinny guy with an ill-advised pompadour, I didn't see many foreigners. Of course, if Gale's family had made the trip, they would certainly already be inside, front and center at a place of honor.

I got my share of once-overs as I hurried from the cab and went to stand in line at the entrance. I wasn't worried about being discovered because people would be at a loss about how to properly address me without knowing my relation to the deceased, and no one would bother asking because they didn't want to seem rude, and chances were I couldn't speak Japanese anyway. As the line slowly snaked inside the building, all I got were a few sad smiles and some sympathetic head nodding and that's all I gave in return.

Inside, a pert receptionist collected my condolence envelope, silently bowing to me before handing the money to a studious-looking guy behind a folding table. He carefully noted my name and the amount I'd given in a ledger, then passed the envelope to a third person sitting next to him. This woman copied my name onto a small envelope of her own and handed it to me. Inside was a formally worded thank-you card from the Inoue family and a packet of purification salt. The Joyful Twilight Funeral Hall had also seen fit to enclose a business card promising ten percent off future services.

After receiving my thank-you card, I made my way into the main hall and was confronted by an island of black suits engulfed by white flowers. There must have been over five hundred folding chairs set out, but they weren't enough. Those who'd arrived late, like me, were forced to stand along the sides or against the rear wall, jostling for position with the jungle of ceremonial wreaths wedged into every available space. The pinwheeled flower bouquets came in three sizes but were otherwise identical, save for the white banners placed on the easel-like stands to publicize who was honoring the departed. From the looks of it, every business headquartered in the Honmachi district had sent floral condolences: Dentsu Advertising, Daiichi, Hankyu, Kusanagi Investigation and Research, NEC, Matsushita Electrical Industries, Daimaru Incorporated. One bouquet was even decorated with a crest I thought I recognized as belonging to the Komoriuta-kai. They must have donated a bundle, too, because their wreath was in prime position, standing proudly to the left of the funeral dais.

All but lost among the flowers lay Richard Gale, his body concealed inside a polished, cream-colored casket draped in some kind of embroidered gold cloth. On either side of the coffin twin beams of white light cut through swaths of incense smoke to spotlight a giant, black-framed death portrait of Gale himself. In the photo, his hair was styled to within an inch of its life. He was wearing a ruffled white tuxedo shirt and a black bow tie, standing in front of a fake tropical sunset. He squinted uneasily at the camera, a hesitant grin on his face like he was trying to figure out whether someone was making fun of him. The photo was undoubtedly taken at his wedding, probably the first, last, and only time most of those gathered in his memory had ever met him.

The hall was buzzing with muted conversations punctuated by the occasional crying baby. Through diligent eavesdropping, I learned that the priest was late, apparently because the funeral fell after a *tombiki* day. *Tombiki* meant something like "friends following" and occurred every sixth day. Superstitions held that if a funeral was given on a *tombiki* day, a friend of the departed would soon follow him to the grave. Accordingly, all the funerals and wakes

normally taking place yesterday had been pushed back,
doubling the priest's workload. In order to keep things running on schedule, the mourners had been forced to pay
their final respects to the dead before the ceremony
started rather than at its conclusion, which explained why
the room was already heavy with sickly sweet incense
fumes when the priest finally arrived.

He was an old, no-nonsense guy trailed by two shaven-
headed monks who looked just out of high school. A hush
fell over the crowd as he marched to the front of the hall,
his ceremonial robe flapping as he walked. He stopped and
kneeled on a cushion before a table in front of the dais. A
microphone was hastily put in place and the monks adjusted the priest's robes before kneeling just behind him.
On the table sat an incense box and two candles. Keeping
his back to the audience, the priest began chanting in a
deep, guttural voice, amplified so it boomed through the
entire hall and mesmerized even the squealing children
into silence. Every so often one of the monks would strike
a small bell and a sustained high note would ring out above
the priest's voice, reverberating for an impossibly long
time before ever so slowly fading away.

I craned my neck hoping to catch a glimpse of Kaori,
Richard Gale's wife, the one Curry said was such a looker.
From my vantage point I couldn't see much of the family
but the backs of their heads, but there were plenty of good-
looking women in the crowd. A group of five or six college
girls were clustered together a few rows in front of me, and
even in their somber black dresses and understated
makeup they looked more like they belonged at the funeral
of some fashion designer. There were a smattering of *gai-
jins* here and there, but still not the turnout I'd expected.
Evidently, the Gale family hadn't made the trip.

The priest continued chanting sutras for nearly thirty minutes and I noticed more than a few heads bobbing, fighting off sleep. At last the priest got to his feet. After a bow and a few words to the Inoue family, he quickly made his way back down the aisle and out of the room, his acolytes trailing behind. In all likelihood, there was a car outside waiting to rush him off to another *osōshiki* across town. A respectful silence lingered in the air but a moment, and then everyone began talking again, moving from their seats, shuffling off toward another large hall where food and drinks would be served.

As people made their way out of the room, I took one final glance at the picture of Gale standing in front of the dopey tropical backdrop and wondered what he would have made of the whole thing. Then I followed the crowd, moving toward a doorway on the left side of the main hall. I was just about to pass through it when I spotted maybe the last person I wanted to spot.

The Tin Man hadn't donned his silver suit this time. In a shiny black number a size too small and with his hair greased back over his bullet-shaped head, he looked like a polished chunk of volcanic rock. When his eyebrows fell and his lower lip dropped I knew he'd spotted me, too. I watched his eyeballs dance in their sockets as his three or four brain cells huddled together to decide if I was really that mean man who'd thrown the hot black stuff in his face. I didn't wait for their verdict.

I spun and weaved back down the passageway toward the main hall. I could hear the Tin Man muttering clumsy apologies as he lumbered through the crowd in pursuit. There was nowhere to hide, and if I made a run for the exit he'd surely see me. I was quicker than him, but something told me he wasn't alone this time. I thought about the shifty-eyed characters smoking outside the entrance and figured they were probably Komoriuta-kai. With nowhere else to go, I tried a door on the left side of the hallway.

It opened onto a darkened room. I stepped inside and locked the door behind me, listening for the Tin Man's footsteps, waiting for him to try the knob. Nothing to hear but the sound of shuffling feet and muddled conversations. Then I heard someone sigh. The sound came from behind me, only a few yards away.

*T*he woman's face emerged from the shadows at the far side of the room, disembodied as she brought the lit match to the tip of her cigarette. Her eyes met mine for a moment and then she closed them and exhaled a gray cloud of smoke.

"Who are you?" the woman asked.

I almost blurted out my real name before I thought better of it. Not knowing who this woman was, I figured I'd better not use Curry's name, either.

"Name's Randy," I said. "Randy Chance."

"Randy Chance," she repeated, rolling the name around her mouth like she was tasting it, deciding whether to spit it out. Even in the darkness I could feel her eyes moving over me.

"*Hajimemashite,*" I began. "*Dozo yori—*"

"Likewise," she said. "Turn on the light, huh?"

I found the switch and the room was suddenly flooded in white. A confusion of wreaths lay scattered across the small room, some on wire stands, others stacked or strewn haphazardly over the floor. I figured it must have been some kind of storage area, a place to put all the extra flowers they couldn't fit in the main hall. The woman was sitting atop a table, her slender legs scissored at the knee. She didn't look much older than twenty, had long dark hair and lots of makeup and was clutching a bottle of red wine. She'd worn the compulsory black dress and optional pearl strand and her neckline plunged a little low for a funeral but I wasn't complaining. I doubted she got many complaints from men about much of anything.

"Quite a turnout," I said. She shrugged, took a swig from the bottle. I tried again. "They'll need a semi truck to take all these flowers home."

"Who will what?" she said.

"The Inoue family. To take home the flowers."

"The Inoue family," said the woman, exhaling smoke. "Don't get me started. Anyway, the flowers belong to the funeral parlor. They're rented. After the service, they just take off the banners, put on new ones. Use the same wreaths for the next funeral and the next funeral and so on. Ugh, this thing is driving me crazy."

She put down her wine and reached up and grabbed a fistful of hair. Squinting her eyes, she gave her scalp a hard tug. The wig came off and her real hair tumbled out from beneath it. It was auburn red, bangs straight, sides meeting her jawline—a helluva lot like a hairstyle I'd recently seen in a surveillance video. I tried to hide my surprise by staring at my wing tips. The PanCosmo man had given them such a fantastic shine I could see my dopey face staring right back up at me.

"My mother insisted on this," the woman said, examining the wig. "Said it would be bad taste to show up at the funeral with red hair because red is the color of celebration. Like my hair is even really red, you know?"

"So what color do you call it?"

"Arson Climax," she said. "That's what it said on the bottle, anyway. My mom wanted me to dye my hair back to normal, but I said forget it. I'm sure Richard wouldn't have cared. He liked my hair the way it was."

That she used his first name told me she must have known Gale pretty well. I decided to ask how well. As soon as the words came out of my mouth I knew I'd made a mistake. Instead of answering, she dropped her cigarette on the floor, letting it smolder as she tossed the wig on the table and picked up the bottle of wine. She took a long swig then wiped her mouth with the back of her hand.

"They say it tastes even better in a glass," I said.

"Were you at the wedding, Mr. Randy Chance?"

I shook my head.

"Didn't think so. I would've remembered you. So just what is your relationship with the deceased?"

"No fair," I said. "I asked you first."

"Whoever said I play fair?"

"If you don't play fair, no one will play with you."

"Finding new playmates has never been a problem."

"What's your secret?"

"Should be obvious to a guy like you."

"Guys like me can be pretty dumb."

"See? You knew my secret all along." She gave me a victor's smile and offered me a sip from her bottle by way of consolation. I declined. "Now I believe you were about to tell me how you knew Richard Gale," she said.

I suspected the question might be put to me at some point so I'd come with a story all prepared. Randy Chance knew Richard Gale from back when they taught together in Tokyo, during those first months Richard had lived in Japan, before he moved to Osaka. Like all good lies, it was mundane, fleshless, as boring as possible. She nodded impatiently as I spoke, not bothering to feign interest.

"You speak Japanese pretty well," she said.

"Thanks, anyway."

"Really, you speak a lot better than Richard," she said. "Richard talked like a woman. Not his fault, he was always surrounded by women. You know, teaching his classes and everything. I guess it's no surprise that he ended up speaking feminine Japanese. But you? You sound masculine."

"I taught boys."

"In Tokyo?"

I nodded.

"So did you come to Japan to find a wife?" she asked.

"Is that why Richard said he was here?"

"I'm asking about you," she said. "I can't imagine why else an American would willingly live here. I figure they're either here to find a wife or to sleep around. Or both. So which is it?"

"Neither."

"You don't like Japanese girls?"

"I like all kinds of women."

"Foreign men have funny ideas about Japanese women."

"Men have funny ideas about women, period. And vice versa."

"Maybe," she said.

"So are you going to answer my question?"

"Which question was that?"

"The one about how well you knew Richard Gale."

She dug a fresh cigarette from her handbag, pinning it to the corner of her mouth as she spoke. "I guess I knew him pretty well. Or thought I did. I was married to him, after all."

This I hadn't expected. "You're Kaori Inoue?"

"Yes," she said. "The tragic widow, at your service."

"I'm sorry, I didn't realize—"

"Forget it," she said. "People have been tiptoeing around me all day. It's exhausting. Things are hard enough without having to deal with my father's cronies on top of everything else. Most of these people never even knew Richard. Most of these people barely even know *me*. The whole thing is a big show. Everyone playacting, everyone in costume . . ."

As if to underscore the point, Kaori tossed her black wig through the air. I caught it, felt the hair brush against my hands, strands of fiber fall through my fingers. For some reason I was thinking of the wigmaster back at the National Bunraku Theater and his picture of the Tibetan yak, when someone thumped at the door.

"You in there?" a guy shouted. He pounded against the door again, the sound echoing in the room. "You're in there, aren't you? Unlock the door. I'm supposed to come get you."

I recognized the voice—syrupy thick and as confused as ever. It was the Tin Man. He'd found me. Before I could decide what to do, Kaori hopped up from the table. She groaned and pushed past me.

"Go away!" she yelled at the door.

"Everyone is looking for you," the Tin Man said.

"They can stop looking now."

"Everyone is waiting," the Tin Man pleaded.

"Let them wait."

"But that's what they told me," said the Tin Man. "They said to find Kaori and tell her everyone is waiting. They're almost ready to read the telegrams. Everyone is looking for you. They said the appointment for the crematorium—"

Kaori rolled her eyes. "Go away. I'll be out in a minute."

"But I'm supposed to—"

"I'll be out in a minute!"

Silence on the other side of the door. Kaori walked back

to the table and grabbed her purse. She let her cigarette drop from her mouth and ground it into the floor with her heel, then tilted the bottle one more time. Her face should have been the same shade of red as her hair by now, but despite all she'd drunk she looked unfazed. She slung her bag over her shoulder and headed for the door, turning to face me just as she reached it.

"Nice meeting you," she said.

"I'm very sorry about your husband."

"Uh-huh. Sorry about your friend, too."

"Can I see you again?" I said. "I mean, once things have calmed down a little. I know this must be a difficult time, but I'd like to talk with you."

"You always make passes at funerals?"

"I just want to talk."

"That's how it usually starts."

In the dining hall, someone was talking on the PA, thanking everyone for coming. The flower petals vibrated with the volume. Kaori looked at me for what felt like a long time, arms crossed over her chest, head tilted slightly to the left. For the first time I noticed the unnaturally perfect crease of her eyelids and wondered if she'd had surgery to make her eyes look bigger, more Western. Lots of women were doing it these days.

"Tonight," she said. "You know where Crysta Nagahori is? Meet me underground, near the Shinsaibashi station exit around ten o'clock. If I'm not there, it means I've come to my senses."

"I appreciate it," I said. "Don't forget your hair."

I tossed her the wig. She caught it and pulled it onto her head, her fingers expertly tucking errant red locks under the less celebratory disguise. Watching felt intrusive, like spying on a stranger undressing in a distant window. I was only dimly aware that I'd just met the woman who might've killed Richard Gale.

"By the way," she said. "If you want to pretend you taught with Richard in Tokyo, you should take into account that he worked at an all-girls school. Meaning you couldn't have taught boys there."

"I knew there was something funny about those boys."

"Better work on your story before tonight."

Then Kaori turned and walked out the door. A moment later an employee of the funeral parlor came into the room with an armload of flowers and a perplexed look on his face. Before he could ask what I was doing there I gave him a dumb grin and mispronounced the word for restroom. He smiled and walked me all the way down the hall, through the main room, where the Joyful Twilight staff were packing away the folding chairs and dismantling the flower stands. Richard Gale grinned down from his death portrait but the casket had already been whisked away.

Chapter Eleven

The Rainbo Leisure Hotel

*N*ow that the cops were no longer crawling the hotel, the
Kinki Foundation conference was back in full
swing. I checked out the guide to see what
was in store. That day's theme was "Kansai
Firsts—Inventions, Innovations, and Discov-
eries." In the morning, free canned coffee
courtesy of UCC Ueshima, inventors of the
beverage in 1969. That was followed by a
presentation called "The Instant Ramen
Story," which segued into a lunch banquet
featuring the nine most popular instant noodle flavors in the nine Kansai prefectures. I'd
already missed those offerings, but if I hurried down to the fifth-floor conference room
I could still catch "Origin of the Mosquito
Coil," or a presentation on the development
of the groundbreaking Yagi-Uda TV antenna

competing for attention in the adjacent conference room. I decided to hold out for a four P.M. lecture being given by a chemical engineer from Asahi Home Products on the technological evolution of Saran Wrap.

In the meantime, I tried to catch up on the shut-eye I'd missed listening to Emiko's strange story. It was Sunday afternoon and I hadn't slept more than about three hours since the plane touched down Friday night. I stripped down to boxers and a T-shirt, flopped onto the bed and stared at the ceiling, waiting for sleep. I forced my eyes closed. Sleep still didn't come. Sleep wanted absolutely nothing to do with me.

I drank a beer from the minibar, turned on the TV to some feudal samurai drama, and counted the close-ups. A Japanese director I once knew told me rural Japan was so overrun with power cables that most period pieces had to be shot in Korea. You could always tell which were actually filmed in Japan, he'd said, by the lack of wide-angle or establishing shots. Sure enough, almost all the scenes were interiors, and as soon as the loyal retainers ventured outside the camera glued itself to their faces, conveying their historic journey across the majestic Kanto plain by cutaways of clomping horse hooves and tight shots of fluttering banners and tall grass swaying in the breeze. I wondered how long it would be until they had to film the grass abroad, too.

Sleep was finally making its first tentative advances when the ringing phone chased it away. I picked up and heard someone scraping their nails across a chalkboard. Actually, it was the voice of Mr. Oyamada apologizing for not getting in touch earlier. He'd been wanting to talk, but the Kinki Foundation had been running him ragged. Mr. Oyamada then asked if I was planning on attending the singing contest tonight in celebration of the invention of karaoke, another proud Kinki first.

"Think I'll skip that one," I said.

"I can't sing," he said. "Doctor's orders. I developed a polyp on my vocal cords and, well, I believe I've already told you about that. At any rate, seeing as how we're both free, I was hoping maybe we could get together and discuss Sapporo?"

"Tonight would be difficult," I said. Difficult because I was planning to meet Gale's widow, Kaori Inoue, I didn't say. Instead I told him the first excuse that popped into my head. "To tell you the truth, I wanted to get Tetsuo's side of the story before I talked with you. There are a few things about Sapporo that aren't entirely clear from Master Toyomatsu's account."

Like everything, I didn't say.

Oyamada made uncertain grumbling noises. "How were you planning on contacting my son?"

I wasn't, I didn't say. "I was hoping you could arrange it."

More inarticulate mumbling.

"That would be complicated," he managed.

As was everything with Mr. Oyamada, also unsaid.

"My son and I aren't exactly on speaking terms," said Mr. Oyamada. "Tetsuo moved out after this Sapporo trouble. I know where he's staying, of course, but he doesn't know that I know. I couldn't contact him without causing embarrassment. It would be a mistake at this stage."

"Where can I find him?"

"A friend of the family owns a hotel," he said. "It's temporarily closed for renovation, but they're allowing him to stay in one of the rooms while work goes on. It's in Tennoji. A placed called the Rainbo Leisure Hotel."

Like "fashion" hotel or "boutique" hotel, "leisure" hotel

was a euphemism love hotels used to appear less sleazy. Not that anyone even cared to be fooled. I asked Mr. Oyamada to fax me a map, said I'd drop by Tetsuo's new digs unannounced. If Tetsuo asked how I found him, I'd just lie and tell him someone from the Nocturne Theater told me where he lived.

"The what theater?" asked Oyamada.

Whoops. Apparently Oyamada didn't know.

"Never mind," I said. "Can you meet tomorrow night?"

Grumbling noises, followed by an agreement to meet in the lobby of the PanCosmo Hotel tomorrow night after a slide show he was attending on the natural wonders of the Hyogo Prefecture. I hung up the phone, and waited for the next wave of sleep to come along and carry me off.

The wave was just reaching a crest when the fax machine across the room chattered to life and spit out a hand-drawn map to the Rainbo Leisure Hotel. Oyamada had written that I could find his son in room 410. Seeing as how he'd gone to the trouble, I gave up on sleep and got dressed. Outside, lean clouds stretched across the city like they were being pulled apart by unseen hands.

The sun was just starting to go down when I arrived in Tennoji, a neighborhood in south-central Osaka preserved in a kind of perpetual twilight. Like Namba and Umeda, Tennoji was a hub where subway and JR trains converged, but it didn't have much else in common with its richer cousins. Aside from a few newer buildings like the space-age Abeno Lucias, Tennoji was free of the high-tech glitz and brand-name glamour you'd find in the other big neighborhoods, instead acting mostly as a refuge for blue-collar pensioners who weren't afraid to wear funky tweed jackets and green sweatpants at the same time. The nearby park was one of the biggest in Osaka, home to a rundown zoo and botanical gardens that didn't offer much in January. Today, like every Sunday, the path through the park had become a miniature flea market complete with raggedy old-timers drinking cheap beer and belting out *enka* ballads from makeshift karaoke tents, looking happier than about anyone else in the city.

I headed toward the northeast end of the park, where a cluster of love hotels sat a respectable distance from Tannimachi-suji Avenue, replete with rooftop signs announcing names like the Green Gable Anne Hotel and the Hotel K Sera Sera. The lights were switched off at the Rainbo Leisure Hotel but the place was still tough to miss, as any seven-story rainbow-colored building plopped down in Tennoji would be. A sign on the door apologized profusely to the honorable customer for the regrettable fact that the hotel was undergoing extensive renovation so that it might surpass the needs and expectations of Osaka's most discriminating and highly valued clientele. Beneath that it said "Closed."

The glass door was wide open to reveal a darkened, half-disassembled miniature lobby. The carpet was ripped up and bits of chipped plaster littered the concrete floor while a display board showing available fantasy suites was wrapped in protective plastic. The love hotel business was fiercely competitive and trend driven, forcing hotels to change styles and completely remake themselves every two or three years, just like Madonna. I started to go inside when I heard the voice behind me.

"Hotel's closed," it said. I turned to see a hard-hatted fireplug of a man with a jumpsuit tucked into his rubber boots and a badge on his chest that said "Ichiban

Construction." "Remodeling. You're not the jackhammer man, are you?"

I shook my head.

"Didn't think so. Anyway, hotel's closed. Remodeling."

"Maybe you can help me," I said. "I was here a couple months ago and left my watch behind. I was wondering if—"

"You'd have to see the manager," the man said. "I'm just waiting for the jackhammer man. Until the jackhammer man comes, we're all of us just waiting."

"Where can I find the manager?"

"Manager's office," he said, pointing around the corner. I thanked him and stepped through the doorway. The lobby was gloomy and fogged with dust and I'd already taken a few steps inside the room before I noticed several construction workers scattered around the perimeter, smoking cigarettes or simply sitting with their backs against the wall, shirts open to reveal their bellybands, eyes droopy as if fighting off sleep. They must have heard the exchange I'd just had because one of them pointed disinterestedly down a corridor to my left.

I walked a short way down the hall until out of the workers' sights, then ducked into the stairwell and made it up to the fourth floor without encountering sleeping women or anybody else. Nothing much remained of the hallway but the green carpet. Wires twisted from naked wall sockets and gaudy light fixtures were strewn over the floor. The doorknobs to each room had been removed and sat in the hall like shoes left out for an overnight polish. They'd even removed all the room numbers, forcing me to peep through empty doorknob hollows in search of Tetsuo.

The figure I first glimpsed through the enlarged peep-hole bore little resemblance to the kid I'd seen eight years ago. The moppety black locks were gone and his hair was dyed frosty blond and shaved monkishly close to his skull. Bunraku had given him the lithe muscularity of a dancer, every contour suggesting motion while his face was all eyebrows and cheekbones, handsome if a touch severe. Tetsuo was sitting cross-legged on the floor, scribbling away in a notebook. From the overwrought look on his face you'd think he was either writing a suicide note or filling out a loan application.

As if suddenly sensing he was being watched, he stopped writing and looked up. I backed away from the doorknob hole, stood upright and knocked. The force of it swung the door slowly open. When Tetsuo saw me standing there, he didn't have much of a reaction.

"Yes?" he called out.

"Tetsuo Oyamada-san?"

"Yes?"

"Mind if I come in?"

Tetsuo looked me up and down. "Who are you?"

"We met once before," I said. "About eight years ago. I was writing a story about you. I'm a reporter—*Youth in Asia* magazine, from Cleveland. My name is Billy Chaka."

He narrowed his eyes and nodded slowly while he sized me up. "Eight years. That was a long time ago."

"Just think how the Hanshin Tigers must feel."

"I don't follow baseball."

"I don't blame you. Got a moment to chat?"

Tetsuo looked back over his shoulder as if to consult the empty room before unenthusiastically motioning me inside. I took off my shoes and left them in the hall, but I needn't have bothered. No carpet, no tatami mats, just a bare concrete floor and a worn futon. Piles of books stood stacked at the foot of the mattress, others lay strewn open faced as if scattered by a tornado. I glanced at the titles on the spines. *Jungian Archetypes in Modern Drama. Dadaism Made Simple. The Theater of the Absurd. Aesthetics of Decay. The Theater of Pain. The Theater of Absurd Pain.*

As I made my way across the room, Tetsuo dropped his notebook, then rose and motioned me to take a seat on the floor while he fetched a candle next to his bed. There was a tentative clumsiness to his movements, as if he'd borrowed his body from someone else and was still getting used to it. While he tried to light a match I looked out the window behind him, watched the Tsutenkaku Tower blink the Hitachi logo into the darkening sky. The last time I came to this city to interview Tetsuo, I'd been inspired to write a piece about how the Tsutenkaku Tower encapsulated the whole of Japan's twentieth century—built as Asia's tallest structure in the heady modernization rush of the Meiji Restoration, broken down for scrap metal during the desperate war years, reconstructed afterward like everything else, now acting as a giant advertisement for an electronics behemoth. But my piece never ran. Instead, the magazine printed teen pop sensation Yuki Kimura's top five spots to go on a dream date. One was Tokyo Disney and another was Disneyland in L.A. I forget the other three.

Tetsuo finally got the candle lit, then loped across the floor and sat down across from me. I apologized for arriving unannounced. He apologized for not being able to offer me tea or anything else to drink. I apologized for arriving empty-handed. He apologized for not having an extra pair of house slippers for me or chairs to sit in or lights that worked, since they were rewiring the building. I apologized again for arriving unannounced.

"So why are you here?" he asked when we'd both run out of apologies. "Are you doing some kind of follow-up story?"

"Not exactly."

"Because I left the National Bunraku Theater."

"So I hear," I said. "Actually, I saw you at the Nocturne Theater last night."

Maybe it was just the flickering of the candle, but his eyes seemed to come to life. "What did you think? *The Whispering Goat* is one of our more conventional pieces plotwise, reactionary almost, but we tried to instill a menacing undercurrent of anxiety and dread and foreboding. To show how society can, well, that society does stuff to people. That the unstopping, or—no, what's the word? Unrelenting. That the unrelenting global capitalist marketplace creates an atmosphere of foreboding and dread and anxiety. Not to mention there are some pretty radical subversions of the normative puppet-puppeteer dynamic, what we like to call the Fifth Wall, and—well, I could go on, but I'd like to hear what you thought about it."

"I kept waiting for the goat."

"Oh," he said, scratching his chin. "The goat. Right, right, but well, the thing is, there's no actual goat. The whispering goat isn't a real goat. Like with horns and stuff. It's more, how do you say, an *implied* goat. It doesn't appear onstage, but it acts like a symbol."

"So a metaphorical goat?"

"Exactly," he said, clapping his hands together. "It's a completely metaphorical goat, absolutely. To tell you the truth, I wanted to call the play *The Dog-faced Man* but we came to a consensus that a goat was more, what—atavistic? I mean, dogs, sure you can argue there's plenty atavistical about metaphorical dogs, but we went with the goat. You may remember that speech in the third act—"

"I didn't stick around that long."

Tetsuo blinked a few times. "No?"

"Don't get me wrong, I like puppets. They're cute, make me laugh. But I had to leave. Long story. Anyway, you were operating the female puppet, right? I think the character's name was Kimiko."

"How'd you know I was Kimiko? We don't have programs."

"I could just tell."

Tetsuo grinned despite himself and ran his palm over his white-stubbled head. Without a puppet around, he didn't seem to know what to do with his hands and his eyes never stayed in one place for long, either. The guy was crackling with so much manic energy I worried if he sat too close to the candle he might spontaneously combust.

"So how did you know where to find me?" he asked.

"Part of my job is knowing how to find people. As to why I'm here, your father wanted me to talk to you. I also spoke with Master Toyomatsu. Yesterday. You can probably guess the rest."

"Sapporo," he huffed. "I get it now. You're here about the infamous incident in Sapporo. Here to convince me to apologize so I can return to the illustrious National Bunraku Theater. You're wasting your time."

"I guess if I didn't, someone else would."

"Why send you, anyway? What've you got to do with this?"

"Nothing. I'm neutral. A completely disinterested party."

"Neutral," Tetsuo huffed. "That's perfect. That's so them. Well, you can tell them there's no room in theater for 'neutral.' Neutrality leads to things staying in a state of not changing. To what's it called? Stasis. Neutrality leads to stasis. Stasis leads to death. You go ahead and tell them I said that."

I struggled to keep a straight face, trying to remember

what it was like to be young and self-assured, bursting with energy and ideals and hell-bent on changing the world. These days I knew the precise market value of my ideals and used most of my energy just trying to keep the world from changing me. Part of me was grateful not to be Tetsuo's age anymore. The other part would've traded places in a second.

"Neutrality, stasis, death," I said. "Anything else?"

"Look, I don't know what they told you." Tetsuo's hands fidgeted between his knees as he spoke. I noticed the first two fingers of his right hand were larger than those of his left, thick with calluses from years of working the toggles and strings that controlled the puppets' eyes and mouth. "But I'm not interested in rehashing Sapporo again and again. Getting out of the National Theater is the best thing to happen to me as an artist. There's no way you can understand."

"Yeah, you're probably right."

"My problem isn't with Bunraku," he started, shoulders inching up as he spoke, muscles tensing into knotted ropes. "But the National Theater is a museum. They've made the art into a relic, turned Bunraku into this neutered thing for tourists and old people. It's no longer a living, breathing theater, hasn't been for generations. I mean, it's hard for me to explain to someone outside the Bunraku world—and that's just it. The Bunraku world is so small. Small and protected, like you can't breathe? Suffocating—that's the word. I was suffocating there and didn't even realize it. But now I'm free. An artist needs freedom. The freedom to subvert conventional aesthetic paradigms. Freedom to challenge the, well, everything. To criticize society and taboos and stuff."

Funny to think that last time I saw him I could hardly get

a peep out of him, and now here he was talking about par- adigms. In the blink of eye he'd gone from the stereotypical shy, sensitive teenager to stereotypical angry young man— granted, that blink lasted eight years and maybe the shy, sensitive kids always become the angry young men. I won- dered what became of disaffected thirty-somethings but didn't want to think about it.

"So you've no plans to go back?" I asked.

Tetsuo's face took on a pinched expression in the dark, eyebrows furrowed so deep it looked as if they were trying to trade places. "Here's the thing—I've nothing against Master Toyomatsu. An apprentice puppeteer couldn't ask for a better teacher. He taught my mind discipline, in- grained the fundamental principles of puppetry into my body. He showed me the importance of studying the texts, bringing out the spirit of the character."

"But?"

"But if I stayed there, I'd become a zombie," he said. "Ten years from now I'd still be doing scenes from *Love Sui- cides at Sonezaki* for crying old *obasans.* People my age— they couldn't care less about Bunraku. Why should they? Bunraku doesn't speak to them, doesn't even use their lan- guage. Even most older Japanese don't understand the ar- chaic dialect these things are written in. You know why *Love Suicides at Sonezaki* was so popular in its day? Be- cause it was about *real people.* The events Monzaemon wrote about in that play happened only a month before the production. Ohatsu and Tokubei weren't lofty historical figures or cultural archetypes from like a million years ago. They were flesh-and-blood Osakans, people just like those in the audience. But that's all been lost now. There's noth- ing contemporary, nothing regular people can relate to."

"Fair enough," I said.

He seemed disappointed I didn't contradict him, but I wasn't there to debate the merits of Bunraku. "If you wanted to play devil's advocate," he said, "you could bring up all that universal stuff. Love and beauty and sadness and death. Social obligation versus personal feelings and so on. You could say that nobody talks Shakespearean English, but he's still popular in the West and throughout the world. You could beat that universal horse for hours."

"Thanks for the offer, but—"

"Big themes, okay, they're timeless," he went on. "Good point, no argument from me. But the structures they're locked in are a product of a specific time and place, right, and that world is dead and gone. Today's reality is broken. Not broken, but what? Fragmented. Fragmented and chaotic. But Bunraku is all about preserving the old ways, about doing everything as it was done two, three hundred years ago. Well, I don't live two hundred years ago, and neither does the audience. It's become nostalgia masquerading as art. And nostalgia is just a way of shielding our eyes from the truth of what this country—hell, this world—has become. I mean, do people even stop and think about what this world has become?"

"I think about it at least once a week," I said. "Usually happens while I'm shaving, but I can't vouch for everybody. Anyway, what does any of this have to do with you beating up some guy while he was sleeping?"

Tetsuo gave me a wounded look and slid his eyes to the floor. As I watched the candlelight cast shadows over his features, I found myself wondering what Emiko would make of the unmasked Tetsuo. Was this manic, pontificating puppet prodigy the sort of guy she'd actually fall for if they'd met in a bar? Or would seeing the person underneath the hood ruin the mystique and render him powerless? As with all things Emiko, I had no idea what the answers were.

"Let's talk about Sapporo," I prompted.

A dry laugh from Tetsuo. "It's the past. Dead and gone."

"The past doesn't die that quickly," I said. "If you're happier outside the National Theater, okay. You don't want to apologize, fine. I could care less what happened in Sapporo, except for one thing. I somehow accidentally promised your old man I'd get to the bottom of it. It was a stupid promise but one I plan on keeping. You tell me what went down, we can both get back to our regularly scheduled lives."

"Our regularly scheduled lives," he slowly repeated. "Just a sec. I like that. Just a sec." Then he uncapped a pen and fumbled after the thick blue notebook on the floor. He opened to a random page and scribbled feverishly in the margin, muttering the words to himself as he wrote. " 'Our regularly scheduled lives.' You don't mind if I use that, do you? It would be perfect for a scene I'm working on."

"You're writing plays now?"

"Our productions are collaborative," he said. "Designating puppeteers, playwrights, set designers—that's an outdated division-of-labor thing used to preserve the, oh, what is the phrase? Like chickens, when they're eating? The pecking order. An outdated division of labor used to preserve the pecking order of capitalist production models. At the Nocturne, we all peck the music, I mean *pick* the music, create the sound effects, record the dialogue—"

"But don't you mostly work the puppets?"

"Well, yeah," he said. "But the point is I'm free to contribute in other ways, including writing scripts. Like for instance, certain imagery from *The Whispering Goat* is from this dream I keep having. A recurring dream, I guess you'd call it. I've been journaling. At the Nocturne Theater, everyone is encouraged to keep a diary of their dreams. It's part of our manifesto—'truth resides in the ambiguities of the subconscious.' "

He closed the notebook and showed me the cover. *Ambiguities of the Subconscious* was scrawled in big black Magic Marker letters. The cover was scuffed, the pages well-worn. Looked like he'd been doing a diligent job of inking his dreams. I tried to remember the last dream I remembered, but could only recall that it was something about mowing the lawn. I turned the conversation back to Sapporo.

"Sapporo," Tetsuo echoed. He shook his head and blinked his eyes and scratched his chin at the same time, as if his body were governed by a triumvirate. "Okay, Sapporo. Here's what happened, and this is the truth—I didn't do anything to Kiyoshi. Never so much as touched the guy."

"You're claiming there was no fight?"

"Nothing like that at all. Kiyoshi was cool. Kind of a square, you know, a little uptight. But he was cool. We'd been roommates for the whole tour and never fought. We never even really argued. I considered the guy my friend."

"Kiyoshi—that's Seisuke's real name?"

"Right," he said. "Kiyoshi Hasegawa. Seisuke Toyomatsu is just a stage name. Everybody has a stage name. Mine was Seishiro Toyomatsu. We had like ten Toyomatsus at one point—Seiji, Seijo, Seijiro, Seitaro . . ."

As he made a dizzying rundown of the stage names I suddenly wondered if Richard Gale had been given one of those florid Buddhist death monikers, the kind always written in obscure characters no one could actually read. Somehow I couldn't imagine Kaori mustering up the lofty sentiments, but neither could I imagine the Inoues allowing their family burial plot to be defaced by *katakana,* a script reserved for foreign names, loan words, and advertisements. It struck me that the body of a U.S. citizen would normally be sent back to America for burial, but I remembered the Tin Man mentioning an appointment at the crematorium when trying to coax Kaori out of the flower room during the funeral. I didn't know what to make of this thought, so I was forced to release it on its own recognizance, with a stern warning not to leave town.

"... Seitomo, Seigoro, Seizaburo," Tetsuo finished. "Anyway, Kiyoshi and I always called each other by our real names when we weren't at the theater. Like I said, we kinda got to be friends."

"So if you didn't beat him up, what happened?"

Tetsuo waited for words. When they didn't come he hopped to his feet and began prowling the darkened room as if to scare them out of hiding. I watched his shadow move over the walls, steep and angular, limbs exaggerated into grotesque shapes.

"I was asleep," he said, still pacing. "And I must have heard the sound because I suddenly opened my eyes and Kiyoshi was standing in the corner, like ten feet away, kind of wavering." Tetsuo rocked back and forth on his heels, his shadow blurring in and out of focus with the movement. "He still had his night robe on and I couldn't understand what was happening at first. It was like when you wake up but you're still dreaming. And then *wham!*" Tetsuo lunged forward, bending at the waist, his foot slapping against the concrete. "His head goes into the wall."

He stopped pacing now and stood half-turned to face the wall, regarding his shadow as if it were an unwelcome guest. For several moments he stared at his own shape projected before him, a mounting anxiety evident in the subtle shifts in his posture, shoulders tensing, hands balling into fists.

Suddenly he broke from his shadow and resumed speaking, voice little more than a whisper. "By the time I realized what was happening, he must have done it four or five times. I yelled at him, but he didn't seem to hear me. It was like he was still sleeping. I got out of bed, ran over to him, grabbed him by the shoulders. Then he stopped, sort of wobbled. That's when I noticed the blood on the wall. Lots of it. I called his name again and he turned to face me. His face was just . . . it didn't look like him. And it wasn't just the blood. He had this dazed, far-off expression. Then he just fell over, collapsed on the floor. That's when I ran to get help."

Tetsuo took one final look at his shadow, then turned a half-circle and sat down again opposite me, drawing his knees to his chest and keeping his eyes focused on the candle flame. His story was like something culled from a horror movie, but at the same time I didn't exactly think he was lying. I knew at that moment that if I were ever to get to the bottom of Sapporo, I'd have to visit Kiyoshi himself, though I half-suspected his account wouldn't add up, either. I was starting to feel like I was trapped in a bad version of *Rashomon*. Outside the night sky was a shiftless black, as close to real darkness as it ever got in the city. I checked my watch, mindful that I had a meeting with the widow Kaori.

"Master Toyomatsu thinks Kiyoshi is homosexual," I said.

A hollow laugh from Tetsuo. "And what, homosexuals like bashing their heads into walls?"

"He thought maybe Kiyoshi had a crush on you, made some kind of advance. You didn't like it, so the two of you got into a fight. That's his theory."

"Master Toyomatsu never lacks for theories." Tetsuo

chuckled. "Especially for a guy who talks so much about thinking with the belly. Look, everyone knows Kiyoshi is gay. So what? If he had something for me, he kept it to himself. And even if he had made a pass, that means I'm gonna beat him up? It's ridiculous. Even though I was higher in rank, Kiyoshi was like a big brother to me. After we both got kicked out, I wanted him to come join the Nocturne Theater. Use his skills to help revolutionize the puppet theater, bring it to a serious international audience. But he wouldn't return my calls."

"What is he doing now?"

"From what I hear, he just spends all day at some bird sanctuary in Nanko," Tetsuo said. "Trying to get his head together or whatever. I don't know what happened to him, but the Kiyoshi everyone knew isn't there anymore. He just, the way he looked that night, I don't know. It's like part of him was somewhere else. Maybe he's still waiting for that part to come back."

I made a mental note about the bird sanctuary and asked Tetsuo if there was anything else he wanted to tell me about Sapporo. Tetsuo gave me a wan smile and said he hadn't wanted to tell me anything in the first place. Then he rose and loped across the floor and grabbed a sheet of paper lying near his futon, accidentally knocking over a pile of books in the process.

"This is our manifesto," he said, handing me a sheet of paper. "If you want to write about something kids might actually be interested in, you should do a piece on the Nocturne Theater. We're the future of puppetry. And look, I know I said a lot of harsh things about Bunraku, but it's nothing against the people there. I mean, I would like to have left under different circumstances, but maybe what happened in Sapporo was fate."

I thanked him for speaking with me, then folded the manifesto and slipped it in my pocket. Tetsuo gave me a funny look, like something had just occurred to him. He opened his mouth to speak when suddenly the building rumbled, drowning out his voice. The jackhammer man had arrived.

Chapter Twelve

Scenic Views of Scotland

*T*he Crysta Nagahori shopping center was so bright and
clean you could forget you were inside what
amounted to a big hole in the ground. Osaka
gave a whole new meaning to the term "underground economy," and while I waited for
Kaori Inoue, I thought about how you could
spend entire weeks riding the subways from
one subterranean shopping arcade to the
next, never seeing the sun or the moon, living like a mole with a credit card.

Kaori showed up late. She was dressed in
a red wool coat and black mittens and the
same Burberry scarf and Louis Vuitton handbag I must've seen on half the women in
Osaka, but somehow she managed to make
the ensemble look entirely her own. I'd expected her to be a hungover mess given the

way she was gulping down wine at the funeral, but she looked fine. Better than fine. Lipstick and eyeliner just so, her dyed auburn hair styled to a perfect sheen, eyes alive and twinkling in the night. The way she radiated vitality as she came down the marble staircase, I started to understand why older women hate younger ones so much.

She didn't say hello or apologize for being late. And I don't know why she insisted on meeting at Crysta Nagahori, because as soon as she came down the stairs she had me follow her back to street level. She asked if I'd eaten yet. When I told her I hadn't, she asked if I'd ever had *okonomiyaki*. The last time I was in Osaka, everybody insisted I try the local dish, so I'd ended up eating *okonomiyaki* almost every night. Playing a good guest, I shrugged and asked Kaori what *okonomiyaki* was. To my surprise, she answered in English.

"It's like omelet or pancake," she said. "With seafood or meat or what you fancy. Vegetables, too. It's cooked on the table and you sauce it with mayonnaise and teriyaki. Osaka is famous for *okonomiyaki*. I'd be a bad host person if you go home without testing *okonomiyaki*."

So that's what she was now—my host. Across the wide avenue, the entrance to Shinsaibashi lane was ablaze with light. A minor-key jingle came out of nowhere, signaling pedestrians to cross the street. Behind me a bicycle bell dinged and I all but leaped aside as I stepped off the curb. The other pedestrians made only slight, instinctive adjustments, creating just enough room for the cyclist to weave his way through. I'd once read that Osakans walk faster than anyone in the world. I didn't know if that was true, but I was beginning to appreciate that pedestrianism was a local specialty, an acquired skill like navigating the freeways in L.A. or swearing at total strangers in New York.

We reached the other side of the street and moved under the covered walkway of Shinsaibashi-suji, hemmed in by rows of brightly lit shops and restaurants that seemed to go on forever. After a few moments, she took me by the elbow and steered me through a doorway to our left. The instant we stepped into the restaurant every employee from the waiters to the cooks hollered a volley of greetings to us as if we were long-lost relatives returned from some distant land. No matter how many times I visited Japan, I could never get used to these routine courtesies. Even McDonald's was staffed by well-scrubbed kids who smiled and greeted you politely and hustled after your French fries. It was a fantasy vision of fast-food service, one you could only find in the States on TV commercials.

Seconds later we were seated in a dark wooden booth. A waiter wearing a *hanimachi* headband and an open happi coat over a black T-shirt took our order. Kaori ordered a tall Asahi for me and a lime *shochu* for herself and *okonomiyaki* with the works for both of us. The waiter dashed away and Kaori started talking. I wondered if she was speaking English just to show she could, or because she didn't want people to know what we were talking about.

"After we talked, you went away," she said.

"Funerals aren't really my scene."

"What's your true name?"

"My true name?"

"I read the list," she said. "The one from the funeral place where it's saying who gave incense money gifts. There was no Randy Chance written. But maybe you didn't bring a gift? Maybe you are meager?"

"My name is Billy Chaka."

"What is your work?"

"I'm a writer."

"Really! You don't get payment by the word, I think."

"What makes you say so?"

"Mmmm. I don't know how to say. You have a hard mouth?"

"Kuchi ga katai." She was saying I was tight-lipped.

"Yes! What do you write? Novels, plays, newspaper stories—"

"Features and a monthly magazine column."

"Did maybe I read something from you?"

"Only if you read *Youth in Asia*."

"I don't know this magazine."

"It's for teenagers. Young people."

"Is it quite fashionable for young people?"

"It's popular with a few of them."

"Do you enjoy your work?"

"Never thought much about it," I lied. Just then our drinks arrived. She poured my beer and we raised our glasses and, lacking anything to toast, just said *kompai* and left it at that. She fished a cigarette from her purse and lit it.

"I'm very sorry maybe I was strange earlier," she said.

"No need to apologize. I'm sure it's a very difficult time. How are you holding up?"

"How am I holding . . . ?"

"Are you doing alright? Are you finding it difficult to cope with everything?"

"It's okay," she said. "But my family, they're unbelievable people. Being with them just makes me crazy feeling. But you aren't a sincere person, I think. You told me a wrong name, said a lie that you were taught with Richard in Tokyo. But okay, I think maybe you are still an interesting person for me. A mystery guy. So how much did you know Richard?"

"I didn't actually know him that well."

"No? What do you mean?"

"I met him once in an elevator."

"You first knew him in the elevator?"

"First and only time I met him was in an elevator. The night he was killed. We were at the same hotel. He was staying in the room next door."

"This is all you know from him?"

I nodded.

"And now you're being a detective person?"

"Well, something like that."

She turned her head and exhaled a stream of smoke. I couldn't decide whether my playing detective amused or annoyed her. She had a face that didn't give much away, but it was clear she wasn't comfortable with the whole setup. What could I tell her? That I had to find out who killed Richard Gale because I didn't want to believe it was a woman I'd encountered sleeping in the stairwell? That based on some grainy video surveillance footage being withheld from the police, I suspected it might even have been Kaori herself that killed him? I wanted to reassure her my motives were good, but I wasn't even sure what my motives were.

Luckily I was spared saying anything further when the cook came by and poured a floury egg mixture chock-full of octopus, diced scallops, vegetables, and who knows what else onto the flattop grill built into our table. He let it sizzle then folded and shaped it with a metal spatula. Kaori put out her cigarette. She gave the okonomiyaki a generous dousing of teriyaki sauce and mayonnaise, then chopped it into bite-sized cubes.

"*Itadakimasu,*" she said quietly, not looking at me.

I repeated the standard premeal utterance and we dug in, picking pieces off the grill with our chopsticks. The *okonomiyaki* was hot and thick and even better than I remembered, almost enough to take my mind off everything else. Here I was in the city known as the kitchen of Japan, and I'd been so busy questioning ex-communicated puppeteers, being grilled by hotel detectives, and running from silver-suited gangsters that I hadn't even had a proper meal yet. Then again, being too busy for a proper meal was an Osaka tradition itself. This was the birthplace of conveyor-belt sushi and instant ramen, after all, a city where inexpensive snack foods like grilled octopus doughballs were often eaten standing up or rushing off to the next money-making opportunity.

"Do you fancy?" Kaori asked.

"*Oishii,*" I said. Delicious.

She nodded and we continued eating. It almost felt like a date, and I had to remind myself that I was dining with the dead man's wife, the woman who may have killed him. As I looked at her now, she didn't seem like the type to slit her husband's throat. Then again, who ever does? I wondered just what her relationship was with the Tin Man, and had purposely sat facing the door just in case he should wander in. I even thought about ordering a coffee just so I'd have something hot to throw in his face.

"So tell to me, detective, you know who killed my husband?"

"The police still haven't—"

"Maybe I am a suspect in the investigation by you?"

"It's not like that," I said, not knowing what else to say. "Look, you've every right to be wary of me, to be suspicious. Especially after what I said at the funeral. But I'm not the police. I'm not trying to interfere in your business or—"

"So what is your purpose?"

"It's hard to explain," I said. "I guess I'm trying to get some idea of what Richard's life was like because I want to understand why this happened. Tell me if I'm wrong, but the picture I'm getting so far is that Richard wasn't the type anyone had anything to gain by murdering."

She lit another cigarette and stared across the table at me, her gaze penetrating the smoke. "And you are knowing this from your elevator ride?"

"I've learned a few things since then."

"Of course," said Kaori. From the look on her face she was seconds away from standing up and walking out the door. Instead she picked up her drink and gave the ice cubes a shake. "But maybe you're wrong," she said in a subdued voice. "Richard was not the person of your imagination."

Just then the restaurant staff hollered greetings to a group of salarymen who slinked in. Used to be guys like that would swagger into places like this as if they owned the restaurant and everyone in it, but these men looked timid and worn-out, fugitives on the verge of surrender. I took a sip of my beer. It had gone warm and flat.

"There were secrets of Richard," she resumed. "Secrets that maybe people found. If secrets had part to do with his death, I don't know. Richard was a good person at heart, but he wasn't the person he pretended. I think nobody is the person they pretend. What do you know of my family?"

I told her what Curry had told me. That the Inoues were wealthy descendants of a respected merchant clan, that Kaori's father was a successful real-estate developer. I told her that I knew she and Richard had been married for about a year and were living together in Tezukayama, that Richard taught English at a conversation school. I didn't mention her father's alleged coziness with the *yakuza*, the Chayamachi land deal, the Emerald Greens golf course fiasco, nor where I'd learned any of it.

"Everything is maybe one-half true," Kaori said when I'd finished. "For example, my marriage. It's true I got married one year ago. But this is not the same as I've been married for one year. Richard and I aren't living together since July. We were finished for a couple."

"He'd been living at the PanCosmo for the last six months?"

She nodded. "For most of it, I think."

The cost must have been staggering. "Why did you separate?"

"There is more than one reason maybe."

"Give me as many as you like."

Kaori tapped ashes into the ashtray and let out a sigh. "When we are getting married, Richard said we can move to America when his teaching contract is finished. But then he made a new contract. He must teach another year. So Richard lied to me. And I don't like being given lies. So I left."

"Just like that?"

"Yes, like that."

"Did you file for divorce?"

She shook her head.

"Then you were still hoping to reconcile?"

"Maybe for a time," she said. "But I think we both had no feeling soon. We didn't talk so much. Divorce is a trouble, and we both just are maybe thinking we will do it later. Also, if we had a divorce, Richard is afraid he will lose his marriage visa and so his residence becomes a danger."

Retaining a spousal visa seemed a minor concern when he could've just got a work visa. After all, Kaori said he'd signed a contract for another year at the Gamma Academy, which should have made it easy enough. Of course, since I never stayed in the country longer than a few weeks at a time, I didn't know the ins and outs of the immigration bureaucracy. I voiced my thoughts and Kaori gave me a flimsy smile.

"Except Richard was sacked," she said. "They dismissed Richard. Not so long after we are apart. Richard wouldn't tell me why, only that he was, mmmm, that he was put on the train tracks?"

It took a moment to untangle. "He said he was railroaded?"

"Yes! He was railroaded. Richard was very angry feeling at the Gamma Academy people, and I didn't want to make difficulties in his life. I think Richard's purpose was to become a Japanese citizen. You must understand, he very much fancied this country." She smirked as she said this, as if the notion struck her as comical.

"But you wanted to move to America?"

"Yes. Or also Scotland."

"Scotland?"

"My father went on a golf vacation there when I was a girl," she said. "He brought a picture book for me. *Scenic Views of Scotland.* I remember looking at it for many hours. The sheep, the moors, castles. And so much green! I think maybe Scotland is kind of fairy-tale feeling place for me. America, it's more practical maybe. But sometimes it's a gray feeling here. It's not so gray in America, is it?"

I shrugged. "Where I live it's mostly brown."

I thought about what Curry had said regarding the so-called chrysanthemum club and Gale moving to the Kansai to experience the real Japan. Funny that he should arrive only to marry a woman who wanted to get out. Funny too because Kaori's life in Osaka didn't seem so bad. Her family was rich and well connected, she had a posh house in Tezukayama, it was pretty obvious she didn't need to work for a living. Then again, wealth wasn't the same thing as happiness, or so the rich constantly reassure us lest we take up pitchforks. As delicately as I could, I wondered aloud why she'd want to leave Japan when she seemed to be doing comparatively well. She blinked several times and gave me a smile as big as it was uncomfortable.

"If you want this investigations to be good," she said, "you can't decide because of the surface. My family is not so rich as you maybe think. They're not so rich as maybe *they* think. My father won't understand that his business difficulties aren't a simple trouble that will go away soon, won't make himself know the situation of his partners. My parents, they both have an idea today is nineteen eighty-five. They have always cheerful feeling, believe everything is okay. Making them understand the new truth is a great difficulty. And when I am in Osaka, people always know me for Mr. Inoue's daughter. But when the name Inoue isn't important soon, then what will I become? So you understand, maybe this is not such a good place for me."

Her forthright manner left me both impressed and suspicious. However open she seemed, she must've had reasons for telling me as much as she did, especially about her family. Kaori didn't strike me as the type of woman who'd say whatever popped into her head, and something about the whole encounter felt calculated. I'd been surprised she agreed to see me so soon after Gale's death, but maybe I shouldn't have been. I was beginning to think I fit into some kind of agenda for her, even if I didn't know just what that agenda was. And I also got the feeling that speaking English might be her way of hiding, of filtering her words to make sure she didn't say anything she shouldn't, of masking any resentful tones that might otherwise emerge in her native tongue. All of which made me feel less shy about asking questions like the one I put to her next.

"Was Richard seeing anyone else?"

"I suppose maybe," she said, unfazed. "It's difficult for me to think of, but okay. He was a kind of odd person, you know? Many people maybe think of him as *henna gaijin*. Strange foreign person. One time he asked if my grandmother ever made her teeth black. Or he wants to know can a foreign person truly understand the Japanese soul feeling, if I could teach to him *wabi-sabi*. He had many strange notions. But he was a heartful person."

I nodded. "Just not the person he pretended to be."

Kaori nodded and said nothing further. The waiter strolled by and she asked for the bill, then tucked her cigarettes back into her handbag and zipped it up like she'd just remembered she had somewhere better to be. She insisted I was a guest in her home city and there was no talking her out of paying. Back to playing the host again. I told her the next time was on me. She made a point of telling me there would be no next time.

We left the restaurant and I walked her to the Shinsaibashi subway station, where I asked her one final question.

"Who did your premarriage investigation?"

"Why do you think there is one?"

"Your parents sound pretty conservative," I said. "I figured before they let their daughter marry they'd want to be sure her future spouse was on the up-and-up."

"Because they wanted a reason to stop me?"

"Maybe."

"Because Richard isn't a Japanese person?"

"Maybe that, too."

She thought a moment. "So many questions."

"Occupational hazard."

Maybe she didn't understand what an occupational hazard was, because she suddenly switched into Japanese. "Be careful," she said. "I'm talking to you because you're the only one who seems to care what really happened. And I want to know too, for my own reasons. But some people might not like the questions you're asking."

"Anybody specific?"

Kaori wasn't taking the bait. "A man named Kusanagi did the marriage investigation. A friend of the family who's worked for my father on all kinds of things. His office is on Midosuji, not far from here. And it's true my parents were against the marriage at first. But after the investigation didn't turn up any dirt, I guess they figured there was no point standing in my way. I can be pretty headstrong when I want something."

I didn't doubt it. The name Kusanagi rang a bell but I couldn't place it immediately. Then I remembered. Kusanagi Investigations and Research. I'd seen the company name displayed on one of the many wreaths at Gale's funeral. There was another potential friend of Mr. Inoue's at the funeral I wanted to ask about.

"Last question," I said. "The big guy who came looking for you, the one banging on the door—I'm guessing he's another friend of the family. I'm guessing he runs with an outfit called the Komoriuta-kai."

"That doesn't sound like a question."

"So I'm right?"

She smiled and adjusted her scarf. "Good night, Mr. Chance, Mr. Chaka, whoever you really are. It was a pleasure to meet you. Enjoy the rest of your stay in Osaka." Then she turned, headed down the stairs and vanished into the crowd.

Chapter Thirteen

The Nanko Bird Sanctuary

*M*onday morning I woke early, brain three steps ahead of
my body. It was like my mind had risen hours
before and was chomping at the bit to tell me
all the great things it had been up to while I
slept. And now that I had returned to consciousness, the thing was rambling a mile a
minute, headed in so many directions I felt
like going to sleep again just so I didn't have
to follow it. Emiko was the hot topic, and
there was lots of noise about Kaori Inoue, as
well. My brain thought maybe Kaori Inoue
really did kill her estranged husband, because most murders are committed by
someone close to the victim, and besides,
the videotape captured her entering the
hotel and she didn't seem exactly broken up
about his death, even going out for

okonomiyaki with a strange man the very night of her estranged husband's funeral. She was obviously attractive, if
you're into the obvious type, but there was something cold
about her, an edge of expediency, and her prominent family had friends in low places. My brain thinking no, maybe
Emiko was the one who actually did it, because hadn't I
found her that night in the stairwell, and hadn't she freaked
out at the Nocturne Theater when a straight razor appeared in the puppet show, and hadn't Richard Gale been
killed by a straight razor, and besides, wasn't it clear Emiko
had some psychological weirdness going on and that she
was beautiful, yes, beautiful in a way I found arresting and
difficult to pinpoint, but was also about as far from a
healthy, well-adjusted woman as you could get. And didn't
she have a husband in a coma and wasn't she already smit-
ten with an anonymous puppeteer, not that either had anything to do with anything, and hadn't the Tin Man
threatened to break my arm when I was in her company?
My brain thinking finally that both Emiko and Kaori were in
on it somehow, which was where it hit a dead end and
started looping back. For all my brain's feverish urgency it
didn't really have anything new to say. Mostly it just im-
peded my progress out the door.

I tried to quell my thoughts, but Emiko stayed in my
head all the way to the train station. Was she now also
outside, walking the streets just as I was? Was she thinking
about her husband, or the nameless puppeteer I knew was
Tetsuo? Or was she maybe even thinking about the strange
man who'd followed her from the theater, the man who'd
listened to her story inside the coffee shop in Shinsaibashi?

Emiko was the person I really needed to speak to, but
until the Nocturne Theater opened I had no idea where to

find her. In the meantime, I decided to head to the Nanko Bird Sanctuary at Sakishima Island to see if I couldn't find Tetsuo's former roommate/friend/admirer/apparent victim Seisuke aka Kiyoshi. The idea was that getting to the bottom of the Sapporo Incident once and for all would allow me to concentrate on getting to the bottom of Richard Gale's undoing, which would allow me to concentrate on picking up my award from the Kinki Foundation and getting back to Cleveland, where I had nothing worth concentrating on.

Before leaving the hotel, I'd called Kusanagi Research and Investigations and made an appointment to speak with Mr. Kusanagi himself. It's no easy task talking your way into an appointment in Japan without a third-party introduction, but I said I was doing a story on Japan's escalating divorce rate, and thought a private investigator might have an interesting perspective on the matter. My plan was to steer the conversation to premarriage investigations in hopes I might be able to learn something. I doubted I'd get much, but it beat sitting around the hotel dodging Mr. Oyamada's calls.

The ride southwest to Sakishima Island was a long one, the train virtually empty for a Monday morning. Lots of families on the train, too. Young guys in conservative suits, a shocking number of girls in kimonos. I thought I was witnessing the birth of some ultraretro fashion trend until I realized that today was Coming of Age Day, a time when all kids turning twenty that year publicly celebrated their transition to adulthood. Those on my train were likely headed to a big assembly being held at the Osaka Dome, one of thousands of civic ceremonies happening all over the country. In recent years, participation in Coming of Age ceremonies had been declining, a trend organizers were trying to combat by holding events at places like Tokyo Disney and having pop stars perform. Increasingly, kids wanted nothing to do with Coming of Age Day and were more or less bribed into attending by their parents' offers to buy them a suit or kimono. Suits were expensive and kimonos even more so—a decent one cost anywhere from two to five thousand dollars, and for many women, Coming of Age Day would probably be the first and only time they wore a kimono in their entire lives.

Coming of Age Day was also a media favorite, because it provided a convenient opportunity to pillory today's youth for their lack of decorum. In recent years, ceremonies had been marred by ringing cell phones, kids chatting through speeches by government officials, even setting off firecrackers. From an American perspective, the furor over these transgressions seemed almost quaint, given that any mass adolescent gathering in the United States would require metal detectors, if not fully equipped riot police.

The new adults and almost everyone else had exited the train by Awaza station. With no kimonos to look at, I busied myself reading all the advertisements dangling from the ceiling of the train. In my car alone, I counted four different ads for four different English conversation schools, including one for the Gamma Academy that featured a smiling cartoon starburst character with big blue eyes. He was giving the thumbs-up sign while the speech bubble next to him said *"Hiya there howdy! Do you like ice-cream?"* I was wondering if Gale had done something to get himself fired or if he'd been railroaded like he claimed and how an unemployed guy could afford to stay at the Pan-Cosmo, when the subway rocketed out of the earth over a bridge spanning Osaka Port. A cloudless expanse of blue above and shimmering sea below as the train pulled soundlessly into Cosmosquare station, last stop, end of the line.

A reclaimed piece of land roughly one-third the size of downtown Cleveland, Sakishima was the largest of three artificial islands built in the Port of Osaka with a fourth on the way. Conceived as two parts business, one part leisure, Sakishima's multimillion-dollar Cosmosquare development boasted the highest skyscraper in Western Japan, a huge exhibition center, and a bunch of other high-gloss commercial buildings all huddled together at the center of the island like they'd been marooned and were awaiting rescue. Six massive red and white construction cranes bent over the skeletons of more new office towers rising in the distance on nearby Yumeshima Island. No matter how bad the economy fared, politicians and industrial bigwigs made sure construction was booming throughout Japan, building new train lines nobody needed, new highways nobody used, redundant bridges laced across the country's vanishing waterways like so many sutures over a wound. Environmentalists saw Osaka's ocean expansion as just another example of construction run amok, but you couldn't walk a piece of geography that didn't exist twenty years ago without admitting it was a damned impressive piece of engineering, something like Atlantis in reverse.

The Nanko Bird Sanctuary was about a fifteen-minute stroll from Cosmosquare, no people and nothing to look at save rows of colossal steel cargo containers on one side and the ocean on the other. I could smell the sea and as I walked toward the bird sanctuary, I heard something I hadn't in days.

Silence.

No cars, no rumbling trains, no bicycle bells, blaring *pachinko* parlors or high-pitched advertising jingles, not even the twenty-four-hour hushed roar of a multilayered city in constant motion. Maybe I was starting to think like a true Osakan because, national holiday or not, I couldn't help but think all this silence meant somebody was losing a lot of money.

I had no idea what Kiyoshi Hasegawa, the ex-puppeteer, looked like, but hoped I'd recognize him anyway as I headed to a wooden observational hut near the entrance to the bird sanctuary. Inside, five or six men aimed high-powered cameras out the windows toward a marshy pond. The guys wore hats, gloves, coats so thick you'd think they were on an Arctic expedition, even though they were indoors and it was heated. They were all too old to be Kiyoshi.

Walking back outside, I took a dirt path that wound through a forest of scraggly trees and bushes. Along the way posted signs indicated what types of birds might be found, but in the dead of winter there were no birds in sight, just occasional rustling noises in the undergrowth. A few minutes later I passed under a canopy of trees that opened onto an expanse of brown grass and suddenly he was there.

I don't know how I knew this was my man, but something about his stooped posture made me sure of it. He was sitting alone on a log bench at the top of the hill, hands in his coat pockets, back bent and knees drawn together like he was trying to crawl inside himself. It was just cold enough that I could see his breath emerge and dissipate in the morning air as I made my way up the hill, once again confronted with starting a conversation without a natural starting point.

"Excuse me," I said as I neared. "But are you Hasegawa-san?"

He nodded, unsure what to make of me. I'd remembered to bring my cards this time, so I handed him one and introduced myself. Kiyoshi Hasegawa's hair jutted in greasy, windblown tufts, he needed a shave, and a jagged pink scar cut across the bridge of his nose. Another bisected his left eyebrow and the largest formed a half-moon on the underside of his chin. They were new scars but you could tell they would last. Even so, the scars would never make him look tough. Kiyoshi looked more like one of those guys destined to live with his parents through middle age, pursuing harmless but vaguely creepy hobbies in his bedroom.

I told him in so many words why I was there.

"Tetsuo knew I'd be here?" Kiyoshi asked, a hesitant smile revealing where his teeth had been chipped. I nodded. He pocketed my card and gestured me to take a seat on the log bench next to him.

"We came here once in the summer," he said. "Me and Tetsuo and some other people in the company, back when I first joined. Birds everywhere, every kind you can think of. No birds in the winter, but I still like it here. It's quiet and I can think. Just listen to how quiet it is."

We both listened to how quiet it was.

"This place reminds me of something I once read," Kiyoshi started. "A story about an old hermit in the mountains who collected wounded birds. He'd find these crows and keep them in little wooden cages. Feed them, mend their wings, nurse them back to health. And while they convalesced, the old man would paint them. He'd paint these crazy designs on them using all sorts of brilliant colors—pinks, yellows, oranges."

"Cousin of mine used to collect beer cans," I said.

Kiyoshi frowned. "I'm sorry?"

"He collected beer cans," I said. "Never painted them or anything like that. Just stacked them in pyramids on top of his stereo speakers. I never saw the point. Anyway, sorry to interrupt. Go on."

"Right," Kiyoshi said. "So the old man, he'd paint these birds. And when a bird was all healed, he'd release it. The painted crow would try to return to his old life, to rejoin his family. But his fellow crows, they no longer recognized him. The radiant colors and the bold markings confused them, frightened them. So the crows would gang up and attack the painted bird. A group instinct, couldn't be helped. The painted bird would try to fly off, but there was no escaping. The other crows worked themselves into a fury—screaming, diving, tearing the painted bird apart in midair. Meanwhile the old man watched from below. He'd watch and smile to himself as the bird plummeted from the sky, dead before it even hit the ground. Then he'd walk back to his hut, where more wounded birds were waiting to be painted."

Kiyoshi looked away, shoving his hands back into his coat pockets. He looked away a lot during our conversation, and I'd wager the beating he'd taken in Sapporo wasn't his first. Japan's public schools were even more hellish than most for people who didn't fit in, and Kiyoshi struck me as the type who unconsciously evoked predatory instincts in adolescent sociopaths. A bird of a different feather, so to speak, which I figured was the whole point of his little story. I figured only half-right.

"Tetsuo is like a painted bird," Kiyoshi declared. "He's always going to have a tough time because he's different. I know what that's like, to be different, but things are harder for him."

He broke eye contact again and pushed a clump of dead grass around with his shoe. Out at sea, a huge freighter moved imperceptibly across the horizon. When you were in the city proper, you could forget Osaka was a harbor town, an outpost bordered by a vast stretch of deep blue wilderness. You could forget there was any such thing as wilderness or an ocean at all.

"Tetsuo is under tremendous pressure," Kiyoshi continued. "Has been from a very young age. Everybody knows he's special. And I think that deep down, what Tetsuo has frightens people. Maybe even Master Toyomatsu. Maybe especially him."

"What makes you say so?"

"Toyomatsu is sixty-three years old," Kiyoshi said. "Been in Bunraku his whole life, seen all there is to see. Then along comes a guy like Tetsuo. This inexperienced upstart, a mere kid in the Bunraku world. But there's nothing left for Master Toyomatsu to teach him. Sure, Master Toyomatsu will be awarded National Living Treasure status. And he deserves it—no doubt about it, he's the finest puppeteer of his generation. But he's also enough of an artist to know the relative worth of government awards."

"So you think he's jealous of Tetsuo's talent?"

"Not exactly," Kiyoshi said. "I'm not trying to say anything against Master Toyomatsu, though I suspect he never cared much for me. He resents those of us who didn't grow up in the Bunraku theater like he did. Which is to say almost everybody who came on since the seventies! He thinks we've had it too easy."

I nodded, recalling Toyomatsu's quip about "book-worms."

"He only put up with me because my mother was born in Awaji, same as his," Kiyoshi continued. "Figures anyone with Awaji blood has to know something about puppetry. Anyway, the pressure he puts on Tetsuo is nothing compared to the pressure Tetsuo puts on himself. He's consumed by the idea of greatness, haunted by it. Tetsuo is about the unhappiest person I know. Nothing he does is ever good enough. I'll tell you something funny I learned while we were roommates on tour, something I think says a lot about Tetsuo. He jumps into his pants."

"He does what?"

"When he's getting dressed, he jumps into his pants," Kiyoshi said, showing me his crooked smile. "Holds them out in front of him about waist high, then hops and lands with both legs through. Apparently, as a little kid he was a big fan of some pro wrestler called the Crusher. One day he's going on and on to his dad about how great the Crusher is, and his dad is getting annoyed. So finally his dad says, 'Great as you think he is, the Crusher still puts his pants on one leg at a time, just like everybody else.' Well, right then and there, Tetsuo decides no one was ever going to say that about him. So at seven years old, he began training himself to put his pants on both legs at a time. And he still does this, doesn't even see anything odd about it."

Kiyoshi's whole face seemed to brighten, only to fade with whatever thought came next. As we sat there in the middle of the deserted bird sanctuary, I got the feeling that, like Emiko, he hadn't spoken to anyone in a long time. I needed to find out about Sapporo sooner or later, but I wasn't pushing the subject because the more Kiyoshi talked the more I came to realize he was operating under

an entirely different definition of need. A guy doesn't sit in
a birdless bird sanctuary for days on end for fun, after all.
Kiyoshi had exiled himself to the edge of the world—or as
close to it as you could get on the Chuo line.

"So what did Master Toyomatsu tell you?" Kiyoshi
asked.

I gave him a sanitized version, telling him how Master
Toyomatsu said Kiyoshi refused to stick to one version of
the events, that he suspected Kiyoshi was somehow complicit, may have said something that led to the fight. I mentioned that Master Toyomatsu suspected him of having
some kind of crush on Tetsuo.

" 'Crush' isn't the word," Kiyoshi said. "Though I don't
know what the word is. It isn't 'love.' I understand that
much now." He drew a sharp breath, considering. "It was
more like I was under a spell. Though I'm told love is like
that, too. I can't explain it. There was just this electricity."

"Did Tetsuo know how you felt about him?"

Kiyoshi studied the ground again, his face reddening.
"He's in his own world so much of the time it's hard to
know what filters in and what doesn't. Sometimes, I decide
that he must've known. Other times, I think he couldn't
have. But when you feel a connection that strong, you can't
bear to think you're just imagining it."

"But you never said anything to him?"

Kiyoshi shook his head. "I tried to make my feelings
known in small ways. Little gestures I now realize weren't
so bold after all. I know that Tetsuo didn't hate me, though.
I think he even liked me in his own way. Even with Sapporo,
I know Tetsuo never hated me."

Dry leaves rustled behind us as an unseen bird hopped
through the undergrowth. When talking with Master Toyomatsu and Tetsuo, the beating in Sapporo had seemed ab-

stract, historical to the point it had grown capitals, become the "Sapporo Incident." Only talking here now with Kiyoshi did the events of that night seem in any way real. Even without the scars, you could measure the violence by his face.

"Funny," he said, "but when I think 'Sapporo' the first thing that comes to mind is still my forearm. I'm an *ashi-zukai,* a leg operator. Or was. Not sure how much you know about Bunraku, but unlike the male puppets, the females have no legs. The *ashi-zukai* simulates walking and what-not by moving his arms under the puppet's kimono. Well, there was one scene where my character was sitting, listening to a *kudoki* by another character. You know what the *kudoki* is?"

I shook my head.

"It's like a soliloquy," he said. "One given by the female lead character. It's a big highlight in lots of plays. Anyway, my job was to fill out the lower part of the character's kimono, make it look as if she is kneeling. We do this by holding a forearm against the inside of the fabric, simulating the outline of her knees."

He demonstrated by leaning forward, his arm extended about shoulder height and bent ninety degrees at his elbow, forearm parallel to the ground.

"Looks easy enough, right?" he said. "But try holding this position for eight, ten minutes. For some reason the *kudoki* seemed to go on forever that day. It was like the narrator and the shamisen player were conspiring against me—filling the speech with dramatic pauses, stretching out the music. My arm was trembling, burning with pain. Even after everything else, it's this pain I remember most clearly."

Kiyoshi had been rubbing his forearm as he told the

story, but now he stopped. "Later that night we drank a couple beers and watched TV," he said. "Tetsuo fell asleep but I stayed up a while longer. The TV was still on, but I wasn't really watching it. I was watching Tetsuo as he slept. Just looking at his face, following the slow rise and fall of his chest. Not really thinking about anything. It was kind of a routine I had, staying up while he slept. I know it probably sounds strange."

I shook my head, told him to continue.

"It was the last night of the tour, the last night we would be rooming together," said Kiyoshi. "I didn't let myself display any emotion in front of Tetsuo, but I couldn't help experiencing certain feelings. He was a great guy and we'd had a lot of fun on tour. Of course, my true feelings ran much deeper than that. But I limited my thinking to those terms. 'Great guy, lot of fun.' Because I understood he could never feel what I felt. And though I knew I'd be seeing him back in Osaka when we began new rehearsals in a week, I couldn't shake the sensation that everything was coming to an end."

I sat there picturing the scene. Kiyoshi watching Tetsuo, drinking beer from a can, the light from the TV playing over his face. I'd experienced the loneliness of cheap hotels enough to fill in the rest. Nicotine-yellow curtains, glasses sheathed in plastic, muffled sounds from the room next door, a smell that was never quite right. A lumpy mattress and twenty channels of nothing on TV.

"Eventually I tried to sleep," Kiyoshi continued. "It must have been around one o'clock in the morning. I guess I drifted off, because sometime later I woke to the sound of Tetsuo moaning and rolling around on his bed. He was grinding his teeth and his legs were twitching. This wasn't the first time I'd seen him having nightmares. I thought about waking him, but decided not to. After a while, his breathing grew regular, his face muscles relaxed. I went back to sleep."

Kiyoshi trailed off, closing his eyes. He slipped his hands back into his coat pockets and sighed. When he opened his eyes again, he kept them trained at the withered grass below.

"The next thing I know Tetsuo is calling my name," he said. "And I can feel his hands on my shoulders. Only when I turn around the room has gone cloudy and he looks very far away. But I can see he's got this weird expression on his face. I want to ask him what's wrong but I can't talk. Something is pouring from my forehead, getting in my eyes, and there's a thick taste in my mouth. I put my hand to my face and that's when I see the blood. And then the pain just comes flooding in, all at once. Four directions, eight directions, an unbelievable pain. Next thing I'm on the ground. I can see more blood smeared on the walls, but I don't realize it's mine, don't really even realize it's blood, you know? I remember people rushing in and out after that, lots of yelling. The next day I woke up in the hospital."

Kiyoshi shrugged and bit his lip. Except for a few details, his story seemed to mesh with Tetsuo's, meaning it still didn't make any sense. I suppose it was possible that Kiyoshi sleepwalked into the wall, but I didn't think he could've smacked into it over and over again. I was pretty much back where I'd started.

"And that's all you remember?" I asked.

"Well, one other thing," he said. "It's stupid, but I remember I was having this dream. I didn't really think about it until days later, when I was back in Osaka. In the dream I was onstage, performing. Not at the National Bunraku Theater but in some giant place in front of thousands of people, like at a rock festival or something. In the dream I realize I can't move. There's this invisible wall around me, like I'm trapped inside a giant glass jar. I can't move and I can't breathe and I'm starting to panic. That's all I remember. And the dream was in color. I can't recall ever dreaming in color before. Like I said, just a stupid thing I remember."

"What did you tell Master Toyomatsu?"

"Less than I just told you," he said. "He asked a lot of questions at the hospital. *Did Tetsuo do this to you?* I don't know, I said. *Well, he was the only one in the room, wasn't he?* Yes, I said. *And you'd hardly do something like this to yourself, would you?* No. But no matter how much I tried, I couldn't remember anything else. So I can't say for sure it was Tetsuo."

"But do you *think* Tetsuo did it?"

Kiyoshi considered a moment and shook his head.

"Then you think you did it to yourself?"

Kiyoshi shrugged like he just wanted to forget the whole thing. But getting beat up, fired, and having your romantic fantasies utterly destroyed in one fell swoop is a lot to forget. I asked what his plans were, what he was going to do next. For the second time that afternoon, Kiyoshi surprised me.

"My plans are simple," he declared, unconsciously running his pinky finger over the scar on his eyebrow. "I'm going to get Tetsuo back into the National Bunraku Theater."

Now it was me who had to look away.

"You know, Tetsuo has already—"

"The Nocturne Theater," Kiyoshi said, echoing Master Toyomatsu's dismissive tone. "Interesting but hopeless. Let's face it, nobody is clamoring for experimental puppet theater. And what they're doing isn't even anything that radical. Tetsuo only thinks they're so groundbreaking because he's never been exposed to anything outside of Bunraku. Ask him about Brecht or Beckett or even *butoh* and you'll get a blank stare. In his mind, this is the biggest split in the puppet world since the Takemoto-za and Toyomatsu-za rivalry of the eighteenth century. But the Nocturne Theater is doomed to fail."

"He seems to enjoy it."

"As a novelty, maybe," said Kiyoshi. "But their whole style—to the extent they even have one—it just doesn't suit him. They're more the *higashi* type. Hard, fast, more masculine movements. He's always been better at the *nishi* style—soft, subtle, feminine. Their puppetry is not Bunraku and Bunraku is the only chance Tetsuo has of finding any kind of satisfaction in this world. With his mouth closed, the guy is a genius. But he's not very smart about himself. I can see things about him that he can't. Without Bunraku, Tetsuo will never survive."

"What if Master Toyomatsu won't take him back?"

"But he will!" Kiyoshi exclaimed. "He will. Believe me, I've thought about it from every angle. I know what I must look like, and you can think whatever you want, but it's not like I've been sitting out here day after day wallowing in self-pity."

"No one said you were." Not out loud, anyway.

"What I've been doing is thinking," he stressed, tracing his chin scar. "Strategizing. And things are getting clearer every day. Master Toyomatsu will take Tetsuo back because Tetsuo is his legacy, and Toyomatsu genuinely wants what's best for Bunraku. The problem is Tetsuo's pride and his new fixation on this so-called freedom. He doesn't realize freedom is the rope he'll hang himself with. I don't intend to sit by and watch that happen."

His throat tightened around the words until they were half-strangled. Rather than dull his feelings for Tetsuo, the Sapporo Incident had clearly honed and sharpened them. The way he kept unconsciously caressing his scars like cherished keepsakes made me think Kiyoshi needed to get the hell off this little island before he went nuts. Problem was, I didn't know any nice way to tell him and it was none of my business anyway. None of this was.

"What are you going to tell his dad, anyway?" Kiyoshi asked.

I shrugged. "Master Toyomatsu asked me the same question. He said to break it gently because Oyamada has had a tough life."

"His other son," Kiyoshi said, nodding solemnly.

"What other son?"

"Tetsuo had a twin brother," Kiyoshi said. "It isn't something he likes to talk about. His brother died in an accident when he was six years old. Really bizarre."

This was news to me. "What happened?"

"Got mauled by a dog," Kiyoshi said. "The Oyamadas were on a family vacation at a mountain inn on the Izu Peninsula and Tetsuo and his twin brother were playing *kakurenbo*. It was Tetsuo's turn to count, and I guess his brother went off to hide in the woods when this dog happened upon him. Someone had abandoned the thing weeks before and it was half-crazed with starvation or rabies or something. Tetsuo was the one who discovered the body."

"Tetsuo told you this?" I asked.

Kiyoshi nodded. "We were doing performances in Yokohama and had two days off, so some of us were talking about going to a hot spring in Atami. Tetsuo didn't want to go, was acting all weird about it. I pestered him until finally he told me why. I think it explains a lot about the crazy energy he has, the intensity. It's like since his brother died, he's trying to live for two."

Severed ears, husbands in comas, people bashing their heads into walls or getting their heads bashed into walls, having their throats slit in bed, getting attacked by starving dogs. What the world needed was a people sanctuary. But I suppose as soon as it was built, people would move in and make it into just another city, another place to get away from. I left Kiyoshi huddled and staring out toward the sea, a pained expression on his face like he was looking for a secret way out.

Chapter Fourteen

Dead Wet Leaves

It looks much nicer in spring," the woman said. She was
an office lady at Kusanagi Investigations and
Research, a trim twenty-something with a
button nose and a smile like a derailed train.
I was in the reception area, sitting on a fancy
designer couch and looking out the window
at the barren trees lined up on either side of
Midosuji Avenue six stories below. "And in
the fall it's simply gorgeous. The whole avenue turns gold from the ginkgo leaves. It's
really a breathtaking sight."

She smiled and told me the unique thing
about Japan was that it had four seasons—
winter, spring, summer, and fall—which she
counted out on her fingers. I smiled back,
marveling how I could never spend four days
in Japan without being told about the four

seasons at least once. *You're very lucky to be Japanese,* I imagined a teacher telling impressionable first-graders. *Most countries have only three seasons, poor ones just two. But in Japan, we have four. Now then, before we begin our lesson on asymptotic formulas, let's refresh our memory with a quick recitation of all prime integers between one and three thousand. Ryou-san, if you would be so kind . . .*

A few moments later another woman came in, bowed, and said Mr. Kusanagi was ready to see me. I followed her down the hall and wondered if the office ladies were really getting younger and prettier every year, or if I was just getting older and more easily impressed. Mr. Kusanagi was a jovial man somewhere in his forties and looked more like one of those round-bellied raccoon *tanuki* statues than the head of a thriving metropolitan detective agency. His office wasn't much, a row of file cabinets, a desk, a window. No picture of his wife or kids on display, which wasn't unusual, just a framed photograph of a mangy German shepherd next to his computer, which was. The office lady went to fetch tea. I handed Kusanagi my card and was taking a seat when I heard the sound of rattling chains behind me.

"Down, boy," Mr. Kusanagi said.

I turned around and nearly catapulted out of my seat. I was face-to-face with the German shepherd in the picture, and he was even bigger and uglier in the fur. His ears flattened and his lip curled in a silent snarl to show me yellow teeth and pinkish-gray gums glistening with saliva. His eyes were all but lost in the black smudge of his face.

"Don't you worry, he's harmless," Kusanagi said. I didn't know if he was addressing me or the dog. "Down, Totoya."

The dog looked up at Kusanagi, considered, then lowered his head and slumped back to the floor. His collar was attached to a thin chain bolted to the wall. I thought about Tetsuo's dead twin and wondered which would give first if the dog got serious—the chain, the bolt, or the wall itself.

"That there's my dog," Kusanagi explained, nodding toward the photograph of the dog rather than the dog itself as he settled in behind his desk. "Some people think it's peculiar, me keeping an animal in the office. Way I see it, a dog humanizes people. Lot of folks get nervous first time they visit a private detective. Come in here expecting to find me downing whiskey, wearing one of them hats. Totoya helps show them I'm just a regular guy. Type of fella might just own himself a dog."

Having a massive German shepherd crouched within leaping distance of my jugular didn't make me think Kusanagi was all that normal, but I thanked him for agreeing to see me on such short notice and explained again why I was there. When I'd called him that morning, he told me in the thickest Kansai-ben I'd heard yet that he was just god-awful busy as all hell this week but was curious to know who had put me in touch with his firm. I told him I'd asked the concierge at my hotel who was the finest detective agency in the city, and he'd answered Kusanagi Research and Investigations before I could finish the sentence. Mr. Kusanagi had immediately switched to standard Eastern Japanese, and asked if two-thirty would work. Right now it was going on three and he'd slipped back into his own glad-hand version of the local dialect.

"I should tell you our firm don't specialize in divorce work," Kusanagi said, folding his hands on the desk. I took out a notebook I'd bought on the way, acting like I was really on assignment. "Our bread and butter is still pre-marriage investigations, least on the consumer front. Making sure educational and employment backgrounds check out, looking into family registries, medical records, that sort of thing. Divorce jobs is just gravy. But we're swimming in gravy now, no question. See that file cabinet there? All divorce jobs."

"What exactly is a 'divorce job'?" I asked. "Besides gravy."

"Glad you asked it," Kusanagi said. "First off, has anyone explained to you how divorce works in this country?"

Not exactly, I told him.

"Because it ain't like where you come from," he said. "Nephew of mine lives in Los Angeles and so I know a little something about your divorce laws. Not as much as that randy little fool does, though." He leaned back in his chair and laughed, then suddenly hunched forward over the desk. "Say, I wonder if you could see your way to not mentioning my nephew in your article?"

"Not a problem," I said.

"I am still his uncle, after all."

"Understood."

"Could you . . ." He made an erasing motion with his hand. I obliged and pretended to scratch out words I hadn't actually written. If only television producers could get this guy and hotel detective Imanishi together. One fat guy, one skinny one. One with his *kinki* colloquialisms, the other with his uptight NHK Japanese. One with a big dog, the other with a fake ear, the two of them constantly getting on each other's nerves while they managed to outwit the police, solve Osaka's most puzzling crimes, and put the bad guys behind bars. I figured maybe I'd go to the Channel Eight building and pitch the show myself, try to get my favorite weather lady to sign on as coproducer. Surely reading the weather must get old. Meanwhile, back in reality, Mr. Kusanagi rambled on.

"Things are different here in Japan. Most divorces are settled in more or less amicable fashion between the two parties concerned. They just fill out a 'Notification of Divorce' form, attach their personal seals, and drop it by their ward office. This is what's called *kyō gi rikon*."

Meaning "divorce by consent." He spelled it out for me, one syllable at a time, then continued. "Now this is the most common, easiest way to go about the business. But let's say there is a child custody issue, or one party or the other don't want a divorce, well then the couple they go to what we call family court. *Katei-saibansho*."

"And this is where you get involved?"

"Now just you hold on a minute," he said. "Not even lawyers are involved yet, just court-appointed mediators. Mostly they're retired folks and housewives. They meet with the couple three or four times, hear both sides of the story. Usually they try and persuade the couple to stay together, especially if there's kids. If that don't work, well then they issue a judgment calling for 'Divorce by Mediation.' *CHO-TE-I-RI-KO-N*."

"Gotcha," I said. "And then your firm—"

"Just you bear with me here," Kusanagi said. "Now, if one side don't accept the family court's ruling, they can appeal to the district court to obtain what they call a Divorce by Judicial Judgment. But this here is a long and expensive proposition we're talking about. With the divorce rate climbing the whole court system is like a backed-up toilet, pardon the expression. For one thing, we don't have many lawyers in Japan."

"Count your blessings."

"Bank does that for me," said Kusanagi, giving me a wink. "See, this whole mess is great for my business. Because before a party goes to all this fuss—weeks of family court mediation, hiring an expensive lawyer, and going through the backed-up shitter torture of this judicial-type divorce—they're going to make damn certain they got a solid case. Meaning evidence of a tangible nature. See, in Japan, unless a split is mutually agreed upon, you gotta show just cause for divorce. Something vague, like what you call your irreconcilable differences, that just don't cut it. Which is where my company comes in."

I wrote it all down for show. Mr. Kusanagi was one big congenial smile, clearly relishing his role as the expert sharing his knowledge with the eager American visitor. I figured I'd ask a few more divorce questions for appearance's sake, then try to swing the conversation back to pre-marriage investigations. I'd ask how he went about it when one party was a foreigner, and from there just hope he'd let something drop about the Richard Gale investigation. That he was the talkative type meant my job was already half-finished.

"So you try to establish just cause for the client?"

"That's the idea," Kusanagi said. "Especially when a client is after some kind of alimony. Now my nephew in California, he claims that in your country, a woman gets divorced is automatically entitled to half a man's assets and salary, whether she has kids or can show she's been mistreated. That a fact?"

"More or less. It depends."

"I'll be damned!" laughed Kusanagi. "And I thought that dumbass nephew of mine was just too cheap to get proper counsel. In Japan, alimony is by no means a given. It's usually a lump sum, maybe one or two years' salary, and payment is awarded only when one party is seriously at fault. If a guy is, how shall we say, chronically fucking someone ain't his wife, or maybe if he smacks the old lady around a little too much. That's most of our divorce jobs right there—beaters and cheaters."

"So you try to catch them in the act, or—?"

"And catch them we do," he said. "Surveillance jobs. Tailing people, taking pictures through windows. Just like in the movies except the people usually ain't so pretty to look at. And despite what TV may have you believe, no reputable firms do *wakaresaseya* work anymore. You make sure and write that down, capital letters and exclamation points. No *wakaresaseya*."

That I wasn't familiar with the term surprised Kusanagi.

"I guess this show ain't on in America," he said. "Couple years back, there was a hit TV series about an agency that specialized in breaking up couples. Since then, the practice has spread like wildfire. Say party number one wants to end a relationship but don't know how. They hire a third party, a *wakaresaseya*—some pretty young thing to lure party number two into an affair. But we don't do that. Absolutely not. The Kinki Detectives Association banned the practice just last month. Of course, we still get requests. I tell folks there's plenty of freelancers handing out cards in Shinsaibashi, you want that sort of thing. I won't dirty my hands with them *wakaresaseya*."

"How much do people charge for something like that?"

"I wouldn't know," he said adamantly. "Kusanagi Investigations and Research simply don't engage—it's just nonsense is what it is. Go ahead and forget I even brought it up."

He grew silent for a moment and took another furtive glance at his desktop photo of Totoya. Funny, but now that I thought about it, he hadn't once looked at the actual dog, just the dog's picture. Kusanagi looked out the window and said, "A little cold, huh?"

"It's warm compared to Cleveland."

"I mean conversationally speaking," he said. "When a conversation gets awkward, we say it's a little cold. Osakans are a warm, friendly people. Not like them snobs in Tokyo. Tokyo, you could have a heart attack and fall down in the street and people just step right over you. In Osaka, people will stop and say, 'Hey buddy, you alright? What's that you're doing down there? You need a glass of water or something?' We're a big city, but we're just regular folks."

With the millions in Osaka, there had to be regular folks somewhere—people who didn't bash their heads into walls, or threaten to break my arm, or fall asleep in hotel stairwells, or keep big dogs in their office. People who gave you a glass of water with your heart attack. But either I didn't know how to find them or I needed to broaden my definition of "regular." All I said to Mr. Kusanagi was, yep, I sure had met a lot of nice, regular folks here in Osaka. He smiled and bobbed his head.

"So fifty percent for nothing, huh?" he said.

"I'm sorry?"

"In America. Alimony."

"Oh, right," I said. "It all depends."

"Better keep quiet about it." He chuckled. "You tell any Japanese girls and you'll be facing an invasion. All you American fellas will find yourselves hitched and divorced faster than you can holler 'shark attack.' Used to be a mistress here and there was no big deal, but women are different now. Sometimes I think this whole country is going to hell. Actually, don't write that about me saying the country is going to hell. I guess be careful is all I'm saying."

"I'm not looking to get married."

"Don't matter," he said. "By the time they're done, these women will have you thinking the whole thing was your idea all along. You're still young enough, healthy in the manly sense, I take it. You've got a decent job, you're a foreigner. There's a type of girl goes for foreigners, you know. They'd see you as quite a catch."

"I'm a lot of work for fifty percent of not much."

"They'll take it just the same," he said, shaking his head. "My line of work, I oughta know. And not just younger women. Hell, more and more young people don't even bother with marriage. That would mean moving out of their parents' house, contributing to society instead of just being goddamn parasites. It's the older folks surprise me. Women who've been married twenty, thirty years. Husband retires or gets laid off and starts puttering around the house, and they decide they don't actually need the old fella that much after all. Call their husbands *nureochiba*— you know what that is?"

I shook my head and made a show of readying my pen.

"Dead wet leaves," he said. "You know, them kind cling to your pant legs and such? Salarymen are getting wise, putting a little something away in secret accounts to hide from the Minister of Finance at home. Which just means another service yours truly can offer as part of our divorce package—comprehensive asset investigation."

Mr. Kusanagi laughed, belly straining at the buttons of his shirt. I stole a glance at the file cabinets behind him. According to the labels the files were arranged alphabetically by client but could just as well have been sorted by human flaw. Lust in one drawer, jealousy in another, greed with an entire cabinet of its own. Every case folder representing some insolvent happiness, a partnership dissolved in a carefully documented series of betrayals that inevitably rendered misery into currency, because finally money is the only thing any of us really understands. I didn't blame Mr. Kusanagi for laughing.

The phone rang and chains jangled behind me as the dog scuttled to his feet. Kusanagi excused himself and took the call. I felt the dog's hot breath on the back on my neck and tried to ignore it while Kusanagi grunted over and over into the phone. I counted thirteen grunts before he hung up. As soon as the phone hit the cradle it rang again. This time he just grunted twice.

"Sorry about that," he said. "Looks like my three o'clock has arrived. No holidays in my business. This here fella, he's a salesman pushing a new kinda spray that can detect traces of jism in undershorts. Makes it glow green."

Kusanagi grinned and leaned back in his chair, a far-off look in his eye like he was reminiscing about the good old days of lipstick on shirt collars. "You know, I've changed my mind," he drawled. "You go ahead and write I said this country is going to hell. Somebody has to say it. Anyway, was there anything else you wanted to ask? Sure do hate to give you the bum's rush, but—"

"Just one quick question."

"Shoot."

"You said you mostly work on premarriage investigations?"

"That's right."

"My article is going to appear in an English-language publication," I said. "So the audience will mostly be foreigners. As such, my readers might be interested to know how you go about one of these premarriage inquiries when one of the parties has lived most of their life outside Japan. Isn't it hard to track down the records you need from foreign countries and such?"

Concern flitted across Kusanagi's features before he chased it off with a smile. "It's a little more difficult," he said. "Takes a little longer usually."

I scratched out a few words and closed my notebook. I hadn't really learned anything about Richard Gale or his premarriage investigation, but I could tell my last question bothered the detective. Besides, between hopeless Kiyoshi and his bird sanctuary and Mr. Kusanagi's lecture on the marketplace of marital collapse, I figured I'd had enough of other people's misery for one day. I just thanked the detective for his time, and promised I'd send a copy of the article once I finished it.

"Looking forward to it," he said, rising to guide me to the door. "By the way, which hotel was it you were staying at again? Wanted to thank the concierge who recommended me. See if I can send a little business his way."

"I'm at the New Otani."

"One by the castle or by Shin-Osaka station?"

"The castle," I said.

"Damn nice hotel."

We shook hands and bowed then cantered sideways toward the door. Even I knew there was no Hotel New Otani by Shin-Osaka station. Kusanagi was suspicious, and if he got suspicious enough he could check his phone records and see that I'd called from the PanCosmo Hotel, the same place where a foreigner he'd done a premarriage investigation on had recently been found dead. Wouldn't take much of a detective to figure things out from there.

As we neared the door the dog rose, growling and giving me another look at those teeth. Kusanagi told him to sit down, be a good boy. The dog probably heard him say it ten times a day, and he looked like he was sick of it.

Chapter Fifteen

The Scarecrow

Hiya there howdy! Isn't this a fun day?
I pondered the question posed by the
giant Gamma Academy billboard outside
Namba station while I spent the rest of the
afternoon killing time riding the escalators of
the Takashimaya department store where
Emiko once worked. As I watched the shop-
girls I tried to imagine Emiko among them,
calling out cheerful greetings to customers,
endlessly refolding sweaters on the winter
clearance tables, rushing back and forth to
make change, wrap purchases. She must've
been an entirely different person just a few
short months ago to work here.
I kept thinking of Emiko as I walked
around Dotombori and through Sennichimae, down Shinsaibashi-suji and up Soemon-

cho, crossing and recrossing various bridges over the canal while I tried to retrace the route Emiko had taken after fleeing from the theater that night. The area was a glittering circus of light and sound, a nonstop electric extravaganza featuring nearly every form of amusement humanity had dreamt up over the last few hundred years. I stuck to people-watching because it was still the cheapest. I was watching a pair of Beastie Boys look-alikes strike out with one group of pretty girls after another on the Ebisubashi Bridge when a maniacal-looking dude approached and asked in heavily accented English, "Baseball?" then grinned and shoved a flyer in my hand.

The flyer urged me to call the governor's office and demand that he clean up the polluted Dotombori Canal. Not out of environmental concerns, but in hopes of finding a statue of Colonel Sanders that had been missing for nearly twenty years. The story was a local legend—last time the Hanshin Tigers had won the Japan Series, people celebrated by jumping into the river. Someone got carried away and tossed in a statue of the Colonel stolen from a nearby KFC. The statue was never recovered, and the Tigers had been cursed ever since. The flyer said I should remind the governor that a Hanshin pennant would help boost the local economy.

As I wandered I recognized several intersections but somehow never managed to find Café Cesare. All I was left with from that night was Emiko's strange story and scenes of the waiter zipping back and forth with endless cups of coffee, blurred pedestrians outside the window thinning and finally disappearing in the empty streets as the moon arced and faded across the awakening sky and the stars blinked off one by one and we sat there, unmoving figures in the center of an overlit café. One of the most mysterious nights of my life and all I could do was render it in time-lapse imagery lifted from some arty TV commercial.

Finding the Nocturne Theater proved to be no easier the second time around. I still ended up drifting through the streets surrounding America-mura for nearly half an hour before I finally spotted that crude little sign tacked up near the entrance of the Lullaby Lounge. Once again the blue metal door was unlocked. Once again the strange woman in the tuxedo took my money and gave me a ticket, and once again there were only a few people in the theater. Emiko wasn't here yet, but I knew she couldn't keep herself away even if she'd wanted to. While I waited, I read the document Tetsuo had given me when I'd visited him yesterday at the Rainbo Leisure Hotel.

The Nocturne Theater Manifesto

Our aim is to reimagine the puppet theater for the twenty-first century. The Nocturne Theater is envisioned as a place where dreams and reality collide in beautiful and sometimes terrifying revelations on a nightly basis, except on Mondays. We have no target audience save the world at large, though we're often told our shows are not for everyone. The following precepts are a few of the ever-changing and sometimes contradictory philosophies and practices that shape our work. Above all else, we believe the truth lies in the ambiguities of the subconscious.

1. All puppeteers, including the omozukai, *are to have their faces covered at all times, as was done during the early days of the traditional Japanese Bunraku theater. Their identities shall remain unknown to the audience.*

We do not wish to make celebrities of our artists, nor do we see them as personalities or performers in any traditional sense. Rather, they are to be dramatic forces rendered half-visible, faceless and anonymous, spirits trapped in the material world. Pay no attention to the man behind the curtain.

2. No narrator shall preside over the plays. Having one voice act as the central authority of any work prevents the audience from fully engaging in the drama and dissuades them from creating their own interpretations of onstage events. All plays are written and performed according to a collaborative, democratic process. Though as in all democracies, not all voices count equally and some aren't heard at all.

3. Puppets are to be constructed using modern techniques and materials. Handcrafted cypress and fine silk embroidery shall be no more a part of our stage than they are a part of contemporary life. Latex, plastics, silicon, materials manufactured by machines and third-world wage slaves—this is the stuff of our waking life and so the stuff of our dreams and our dramas. Embracing mass-produced artificiality is the only way to engage contemporary reality in any meaningful sense.

4. The Nocturne Theater shall print no programs or playbills. The names of Nocturne Theater personnel shall not be made available to the audience or the media. No scripts, synopses, transcriptions, or other details about a work shall be published, excepting the title. Productions shall be presented as much as possible as if in a void, unfettered by critical commentary or scholarly

interpretation. All plays will be original productions, and no performance run shall extend beyond two weeks. When you lie down to sleep, you know not what dreams await.

5. Ticket prices shall vary between 500 and 2,000 yen. The figure for each night shall be arrived at using a formula involving the Nikkei index, the day's average temperature in Botswana, and the score of a simulated game of table tennis on PlayStation II. We do this because we believe the world is governed by seemingly random forces. We do this also to combat accusations that we are humorless. We're not humorless.

6. We make no claim that any of these precepts are new ideas or that concepts written herein or presented on-stage originate with the Nocturne Theater itself. In fact, we're suspicious of anyone making a claim to originality in this day and age. The world is an old place and has seen so much already.

I couldn't decide which parts were serious and which weren't, as I'm sure the writers intended. I folded the manifesto up and stuck it back in my pocket, right next to the Colonel Sanders flyer. Then I watched the entrance and consulted my watch every five minutes while somber music pulsed quietly through the speakers and muted footfalls echoed from behind the curtain. Once again I managed to fall asleep before the show even started.

ou look nothing like you," the man's voice said as I blinked awake. Onstage, the yellow-suited Hajime puppet opened his briefcase. Both he and the blond-wigged Kimiko were still in the same red room, the stage so dark I could barely make out the puppeteers looming behind them. Hajime took out the razor and handed it to Kimiko, just as before, and she held it up under the spotlight. I studied Tetsuo's hooded form as he put Kimiko through a series of subtle movements, making her examine the blade with a growing fascination. Tetsuo was so controlled, so dexterous and sparing in his movements, it was hard to believe the guy onstage was the same fidgety perpetual motion machine I'd met yesterday. Onstage, Kimiko slowly lowered the blade and the spotlight faded out. The curtains fell and there was a smattering of applause, but the houselights never came on. Someone coughed, a chair leg squeaked across the floor. I looked around the theater for Emiko, but it was so dark I couldn't see the end of my nose.

Moments later the curtain rose onto a scene submerged in deep blue light. It looked to be another hotel room, almost the negative image of the one in the previous scene. All the furniture was the same, but placed opposite where it had been before. The colors were inverted too, with only the bed remaining the same opaque white. On the far right of the stage, a puppet leaned against a closed door while three puppeteers stood behind him, making the man scratch his neck and shake his head. He was a smaller puppet than Hajime and wore a mauve suit, glasses, and a terminal frown. The puppet knocked twice on the door, but there was no answer.

"This isn't like you at all," he said, facing the door. Still no reply. He left the door, walking to the front of the stage, where a can of beer and a glass were resting on the coffee table. With a series of deft movements, the puppeteers made the man open the beer and pour it. Muted sounds of appreciation echoed through the audience, and a few people even applauded when the puppeteers made the puppet drain half the glass without spilling a single drop. The man lit a cigarette and exhaled a puff of smoke. Obviously a puppet with bad habits.

"You're being childish," he called back over his shoulder. "You know that, don't you? If I wanted this nonsense I could've gone home to my wife. Wouldn't have come to this miserable little room. A little room which is not free, by the way." No answer from the other side of the door. The man heaved a sigh, then froze as if something had suddenly occurred to him. He clapped his hands together, head bobbing with silent laughter, then rose and plunged a hand into his jacket pocket. He withdrew a mobile phone and dialed. Seconds later, the sound of another phone rang from behind the door. The ringing stopped.

"Tricked you," the man said into the phone. "Look, don't hang up. I'm sorry, alright? Will you please come out of there already?" Behind the door, a muddled, high-pitched flurry of unintelligible speech. The puppet rolled his eyes. "No. No, I didn't mean it that way. I'm here with you now, aren't I? Don't be so touchy. There are lots of places I could be, but I'm standing here on the other side of this door. Doesn't that count for something?"

More unhappy sounds from behind the door.

The man angrily stomped his foot. "You know what this is! You've known all along. We're not kids, so don't talk like you're nineteen."

Suddenly, the sound of glass shattering. The audience gasped, the man spun around to face the door. "You're killing me here." He sighed into the phone. "Is that what this has come to? Locking yourself in the bathroom, breaking things? You're really killing me. Shiomi . . . Shiomi?"

But apparently Shiomi hung up.

"She's killing me," the puppet mumbled, dropping his cigarette into the beer can, where it went out with a hiss. He put his phone back into his jacket pocket and stood motionless for several moments. No sounds from Shiomi behind the bathroom door. "Now would be a good time for a soliloquy," the male puppet said, puffing up his chest as he addressed the audience. He scratched his head, thought for a moment. "I'm tired," he announced. "Why am I always so tired? All I want is to sleep. To sleep, perchance to dream. Thank you all. You're too kind. Have a wonderful evening."

The puppet performed a mock bow. As he turned and walked toward the bed, the shadowy puppeteers seemed to impede his movement across the floor, as if reluctant to let him rest, fighting to keep him on his feet. After much struggle, he finally wrestled himself into the bed, lying in a prone position with one puppeteer crouched on either side of him and a third above him, looking down from behind the headboard.

"Stay in there all night if you like," he called to Shiomi. "You'll get no attention from me. I'm done with drama. I'm doing what a sensible person would do and going to sleep. When I wake, you'd better not still be in there or I will break down that door and drag you out by that pretty black hair of yours. Sweet dreams."

He flopped over onto his side and shut off the bedside lamp. The lights dimmed until his form on the bed resembled a blot of ink spilled across a blank white page. Behind the door, Shiomi began crying. With the aid of the puppeteers, the man grabbed a pillow and put it over his head to muffle the sound.

Nothing happened for a while. Nothing happened for a

long while. The audience began shifting uneasily in its seats. Shiomi's crying came in fits and starts, building and receding, then sputtering out entirely only to start anew. Listening to someone crying for a long time in a play proved very much like listening to someone crying for a long time in real life. It was becoming unbearable when a door at the opposite end of the stage slowly opened.

The figure of Kimiko came gradually into view, her face a limpid pallor hovering in the murky darkness as she peeked in from behind the door. She floated onstage to the accompaniment of faint bells meant to represent her footfalls as she moved into the room. Kimiko was wearing the blond wig and a shapeless black dress that merged with the forms of the puppeteers carrying her, making her look like nothing more than arms and a head. Unseen Shiomi was still crying from the bathroom, quieter now, the sound drowned out by a passing train. Kimiko stopped near the edge of the bed and studied the figure of the sleeping man, his face still covered by the pillow. She raised her left hand, previously hidden from the audience, and the straight razor once again caught the light, throwing silvery needles across the blackened auditorium as she lifted it high overhead and took another step toward the man. The sound of the train grew louder and the woman wailed from the bathroom and the figure on the bed stirred and Kimiko hesitated but a moment and then she was upon him.

In a single movement Kimiko slashed his throat.

She leaped back as he bolted upright, pillow falling off the bed, his hand slapping his neck as if he'd just been bitten by a mosquito. A dark stain slowly spread across his chest. Kimiko dropped the razor and clamped her hands over her mouth while the man blinked his eyes, regarding the shuddering woman before him.

"Who the hell are you?" he asked.

A stream of blood sprayed a pattern on the white bed. Kimiko stumbled backward. The man looked at his hand, looked again at Kimiko and tried to rise. Blood jetted from his neck, arcing into the air with each amplified beat of his heart.

"Now wait just a goddamn . . ." The last words were drowned in a thick blackish sludge that spilled from his mouth. He slumped back against the headboard, gagging and coughing and covering the bedspread in a red mist. His eyes rolled back and his efforts to draw a breath produced only a wet sucking sound. "You'll get no more drama from me," he sputtered, the words more liquid than air. Then his head slammed back and he coughed once more and was silent.

Kimiko moved as if on wheels, hands still clamped over her mouth, still trembling as she floated backward out the door and it slammed shut. The sound of the train receded in the distance. Shiomi had stopped crying.

"Ichiro?" she called. "Ichiro, are you still there?"

The three puppeteers operating the man turned their heads to each other. They looked at the bathroom door, at each other again, then nodded in silent agreement. Two of them slipped beneath the bed and disappeared, leaving the man's lifeless body propped awkwardly on the mattress, head cocked back, eyes staring blanks. The third moved stealthily across the stage and took a position by the bathroom door, sliding his back up against the wall and waiting for Shiomi to emerge.

"I'm coming out," said Shiomi. "Ichiro? Please don't be angry with me. I'm sorry. I'll be out in just a second."

She turned on the faucet, water splashed in the sink. The faucet went off and Shiomi inched open the bathroom door. The puppetless puppeteer looked ready to pounce, but the moment she emerged the curtain fell and the houselights came blazing to life. I winced and squinted my eyes. The speakers announced a ten-minute intermission.

When I got to my feet and turned to shuffle down the aisle, I found Emiko standing right behind me, her eyes red and moist as if she'd been crying. She recognized me at once and I started to say something but she shot me a look and muttered through clenched teeth, "Don't speak. He is here. Follow me and don't say a word."

The Nocturne Theater had no lobby, so everyone ended up milling around in the narrow hallway. No one talked or even looked at each other, but instead just stood there smoking cigarettes, checking their cell phone messages, or staring at the floor. A sign on the wall said bathrooms were on the first floor, and several people were making their way to the elevator. Emiko was one of them. I followed her down the hall and got in the elevator car. She glanced at me but said nothing, adjusting her position so she stood directly behind me. The elevator was spacious by local standards, probably big enough to hold half the capacity of the Nocturne Theater. Besides Emiko and myself, there were four people already inside and more on the way. Suddenly Emiko reached out and squeezed my hand.

"*Kakashi,*" she whispered.

The Scarecrow? And then I saw him.

The man who'd just stepped into the elevator was little more than a stick figure, a stiff little arrangement of skin and bones wrapped in a brown gunnysack of a suit. His mouth was like a child's drawing and he had stringy hair the color of uncooked pasta that looked less grown from his head than pasted on it. Scarecrow was probably the kindest nickname he could ever hope for.

He gave Emiko a knowing glance and shuffled up next to me, clearing his throat. More people crowded into the car, wordlessly jostling each other as they fought to make space. I started to sweat, felt my pulse quicken. There must have been about fifteen bodies in the car when the elevator doors finally started to close.

"Now," Emiko whispered. Suddenly she pushed me forward, fists balled against my back, using me like a human steam shovel to plow through the crowd. As we neared the front she squeezed past me and grabbed my wrist and we lunged through the narrow opening of the doors. Annoyed grumbles and muttered insults trailed behind us and the Scarecrow shoved his way forward and was just about through when the doors whisked closed right in his face.

Emiko was off and running down the hall, shoes rattling over the tiled floor. I caught up with her just as she got to the blue door. It didn't open. She put her shoulder into it and the thing barely budged. She banged a fist against it. Several people were staring at us from the far end of the hall. I moved her out of the way and readied to charge.

"Sorry, sorry," came an embarrassed voice on the other side. "Sorry, please excuse me."

The door swung open and we rushed outside.

"Please forgive—" the guy who'd been leaning against the door started to say. Then he stopped. "Don't move. I'm not supposed to let you go anywhere. They said I'm supposed to stay out here and make sure you don't go anywhere."

The Tin Man stepped in front of us, holding up his hand like a traffic cop and blocking the bicycle-strewn alleyway that led to the street, his silver suit shimmering under the

moonlight. "Nobody move. You're not supposed to go anywhere."

"Get out of the way," I said.

"They didn't tell me you'd be here," he said. "You're not
even supposed to be here."

"Change of plans," I said. "You're supposed to let us go."

He shook his big bullet head. "I'm not supposed—"

I charged, running at him hard, coming in low, my
shoulder catching him just below the sternum as my arms
wrapped around him. A good ol' American tackle straight
from the gridiron, technically flawless, executed with
speed and power. Except I may as well have been trying to
tackle an oil tanker. The Tin Man let me bounce off him,
then hoisted me up by the collar.

"Go!" I yelled to Emiko. "Run!"

He didn't waste any time, giving me a hard right that
sent my head buzzing and a left that made me glad I had an
empty stomach. I doubled over and crashed against the bicycles, grabbing hold of one to keep myself from falling.
My eyes were flooded, but I saw that Emiko was still standing frozen and wide-eyed only a few feet away. Behind her,
the Dotombori River moved silently downstream, a black
ribbon strewn with fragments of reflected light.

"Don't move," the Tin Man growled at her. I was still
doubled up. The Tin Man swung a foot toward my gut and
I turned enough to take the impact on my upper arm. Small
consolation. My arm went numb and I scrambled sideways.
The Tin Man took his time now, letting me stumble in a
semicircle before he gave me another kick, this one more
of a shove to send me clattering against the railing. Dumb
as he was, even the Tin Man was smart enough to know he
had me trapped. By now I'd reached that point where you
know you're getting your ass kicked, where the real fight is

over and there's nothing to do but relax, keep your wits, try to minimize the damage and hope your attacker does something stupid. I only wished Emiko would run away already so she didn't have to see me get finished off.

The Tin Man took a deep breath, nostrils flaring as he tried to suck all the air out of Osaka. I tried to at least stand upright, figuring maybe it would look better that way, but my stomach wouldn't unbend. The Tin Man skipped forward and let loose an uppercut to make me kiss the moon.

I moved my head about an inch and heard a rush of air as his fist sailed past my ear. He must've been sure it would connect, because he put everything into it, more than he ever should've. And there it was, the last-chance mistake I'd been looking for. His momentum carried him up and forward, both of his feet leaving the ground. His midsection landed on my shoulder and I forced myself to lunge forward and heave. Simple physics took care of the rest. The Tin Man slid over my shoulder and over the railing. A moment later he splashed into the river below.

For about three seconds Emiko and I looked at each other with the same dumb expression, each wondering who was the more surprised, then we hurried off to lose ourselves in the crowded streets. I imagined the Tin Man thrashing in the water, muttering "cold" over and over to himself.

Onscreen a smiling couple strolled hand in hand down the beach, the man with a yellow sweater tied around his shoulders, the woman barefoot and holding her sandals in one hand, both of them silhouetted against a postcard sunset so gorgeous it made you want to throw up. I tried picturing a world where people with windblown hair and perfect teeth wore clamdiggers and tied sweaters around their shoulders and took sunset strolls on empty beaches, but I needn't have bothered—the video makers had already done it for me. Beneath the couple the words "my heart has endured so many winters" scrolled across the screen while a fancy string arrangement beat me over the head with romance. On the other side of the booth Emiko sipped from her water and moved her eyes from the screen to me like she was trying to figure out why I'd picked the song. In truth, I'd just randomly punched in numbers on the remote. We weren't going to be singing anyway, but Emiko thought we should put on something just to avoid arousing any suspicion on the part of the Worldwide Aria Karaoke staff.

After fleeing the Nocturne Theater, we'd ducked into the karaoke box because it was the first place we thought to duck into. The Scarecrow would no doubt be prowling the neighborhood and The Tin Man had probably managed to pull himself out of the Dotombori River by now, provided his shiny suit didn't stiffen with rust and sink him to the bottom, right next to Colonel Sanders. Neither Emiko nor I wanted to risk being on the streets in case the Cowardly Lion showed up next, so renting a private karaoke box seemed like a good idea at the time. Listening to the music swell to an overblown crescendo while the onscreen couple blew each other kisses, I wondered if maybe we shouldn't have just taken our chances.

I asked Emiko what had happened to her back at the Café Cesare, why she'd suddenly disappeared. She explained that seconds after my cell phone rang, the big guy in the shiny suit had walked in and told her in no uncertain terms to leave. She knew he was in league with the man she called Kakashi.

"So who is this Scarecrow guy?" I asked.

Emiko shrugged. "He didn't exactly give me his card."

"But how do you know him?"

She swirled the straw around her glass and gazed down at the floor. A new song came on now, something called "Lovebeat of My Heart." A giddy bass line reverberated under a toy piano synth melody while three pigtailed girls in Day-Glo cheerleader uniforms did a synchronized dance in front of a rear projection of the Leaning Tower of Pisa. Emiko looked up at me, her face luminous in the dark.

"I don't know where to start," she said.

"Maybe the beginning."

She gave me a tired smile. "I don't know where that is."

"Then let's start where you left off," I said, picking up the remote to turn down the karaoke volume. "Last time we spoke, you mentioned something about an affair. Sleeping with a man for money."

She nodded, dropping her eyes again. The song played out and a new one came on, an old slow number I didn't recognize. When it was over she played it again. By the time she finished her story I'd heard the song another twenty or thirty or fifty times, but I never did figure out what it was called.

Chapter Sixteen

The Man in the Enormous Wheelchair

Mondays were always the hardest. The Nocturne Theater was closed on Monday, so often I would
walk well into the night, returning home exhausted yet unable to sleep. I would lie in bed
with the lights out and wonder if some new
production would greet me on Tuesday.
When I did sleep I would have dreams about
trying to go to the theater but being unable
to find it, or arriving only to discover the auditorium had been transformed into my old
elementary-school classroom. But even the
way I dreamed had started to change at this
point.

I hardly know how to describe these new
dreams, except to say they were nothing like
the dreams I was used to having. My old
dreams had typically been cast from figures

in my waking life. One of my coworkers from Takashimaya would appear perhaps, or a long-forgotten college class-mate, maybe a friend of my parents from when I was a girl. My husband was a frequent visitor. In dreams he appeared as his old self, the man he was before the accident.

But these new dreams were populated by strangers. I scarcely recognized a single face, and even familiar set-tings looked unfamiliar. These new dreams were more vivid, often frightening. I dreamt I was a child wandering a large empty house in the mountains, going room to room, searching for something. I couldn't find whatever it was, and the house kept getting darker and darker until I could barely see. And then with great relief I finally came upon a door at the end of the hall. I opened it and there was an old man sitting upright in bed, his hands trembling as he whis-pered words I couldn't understand. I looked closer and re-alized the old man had a long snout and teeth like a wolf. He began to snarl and foam at the mouth and suddenly the door slammed closed behind me, trapping me in the room.

I'd wake from this dream terribly frightened, but when I tried to figure out what might have inspired it, I was com-pletely at a loss. It seemed unnatural that my dreams should change so radically all of a sudden. Two or three times, I woke to find I wasn't in bed where I'd fallen asleep. Once I woke inside my closet. Another time, I woke to find I had pulled a nylon over my head and was tapping the bathroom mirror with a hairbrush. Once I suddenly dis-covered myself standing in the middle of the street in front of my apartment, still dressed in my nightgown. For some reason, I was carrying one of my husband's shoes.

Sometimes I thought these dreams and the sleepwalk-ing that occasionally accompanied them were triggered by the cumulative stress my husband's condition had caused over these many months. Sometimes I wondered if my passion for the anonymous puppeteer had awakened something dormant in me, heightened my awareness to the point that I was more susceptible to the subconscious currents running through my mind. Sometimes I thought they were simply the byproducts of guilt.

I worried that maybe the sleeping pills were contributing to these dreams, so I stopped taking them. As a result my sleeping patterns became even more erratic, and I forced myself to walk greater and greater distances, exhausting my body in hopes that my mind would follow. But nothing helped. Sleep was difficult and the dreams kept coming.

One particular Monday I had walked myself into a state of utter fatigue and didn't return home until around nine-thirty P.M. All I'd eaten that day was an egg-salad sandwich from a convenience store, and even though I wasn't really hungry I ordered a delivery of Korean food from the usual place. After half an hour the delivery boy arrived and I buzzed him up. I ordered double the amount I usually ate in hopes the meal would make me feel drowsy enough to get at least two or three hours of rest.

But when I answered the door, the usual delivery boy wasn't there. Instead there stood a skinny man with leathery yellow skin and a brown suit coming apart at the seams. I don't know whether it was his thin lips or his straw-colored hair, but the moment I saw this man I thought of him as "the scarecrow." I was so startled by the sight of him I just stood there inside the door, clutching the money I'd intended to hand the delivery boy.

Quite a lot of food for one person, the Scarecrow said. *Are you sure you're not hiding a lion somewhere in there?*

I muttered something or other and tried to pay him for

the food, but he smiled and stepped halfway into the apartment before I could shut the door. The Scarecrow said that to eat this much and look the way I did, I must be very lucky. Except, he said with a chuckle, he knew for a fact I wasn't lucky.

The moment I reached out to take the delivery, he stepped all the way in and shut the door. Besides the smell of the food, I became aware of an unpleasant odor not unlike gasoline. I wondered if any of my neighbors had just seen this man enter, hoped for once those busybodies had been spying through their peepholes and would be listening for trouble, ready to call for help if I screamed. The man kicked off his battered shoes and put on my husband's slippers. The casual disrespect in the gesture so shocked me I couldn't bring myself to say a word.

The Scarecrow told me he was here on behalf of a business associate of my husband's. They were sorry about the accident and realized things must be very difficult for me. I'd heard these words so many times I began my automatic response, but the Scarecrow paid no attention. He walked right by me as if I weren't even there, that sickly gasoline smell trailing as he passed. He went into my living room, stepped out of his slippers, and sat himself under our *kotatsu*—a low heated table of sorts covered by a blanket. I could hardly believe what I was seeing—what possible business could my husband have had with such a man?

The Scarecrow told me he'd already eaten, and besides, Korean food was too spicy. He told me to bring him a beer. And now that he thought about it, he said, a little spicy food wouldn't exactly make him burst into flames. He said to go ahead and bring him a plate, too, so we could have a nice dinner together and discuss my husband.

I was too confused to be truly frightened, so I simply did

as instructed. I found a can of Asahi Super Dry in the fridge, one I must have bought when my husband was still with me, for I didn't drink beer. I brought the Scarecrow a beer and a glass, and even poured it for him, then went back to fetch the plates, chopsticks, the food containers. All the while the Scarecrow sat there quietly drinking my husband's beer. I imagined I could see vapors coming off him.

Just then his phone rang. The Scarecrow answered *moshi moshi* but said nothing more. After a few moments he hung up, then grabbed a piece of barbecued beef and shoved it into his mouth, chewing noisily. He licked the grease from his fingers, then stood and stepped away from the table.

There's been a change in plans, the Scarecrow announced. He told me he'd had this whole evening all arranged but was afraid I'd just have to get the abridged version now. He'd wanted to explain the circumstances better and really was terribly sorry that it had worked out like this. *Amateur hour,* he grumbled.

I just stared at him, not knowing what to say.

The short of it is, the Scarecrow began, *your husband is in a bit of a jam.*

He locked his eyes on mine as he spoke, relaying the story in such a casual tone that I could hardly process one astonishing phrase before he was onto the next. My husband was a gambler, said the Scarecrow. Not a particularly good gambler, but at least an honorable one, one good for his debts. The Scarecrow's friends knew my husband was a reputable man, so they had covered for him when he'd lost a large bet. Only then the accident happened and now these friends were worried. They'd spoken to my husband's doctors and knew his condition wasn't improving. They knew that seventy percent of people in comas for

more than a few days never come out of them. *If there's
one thing my friends understand,* said the Scarecrow, *it's
percentages.* And if my husband never got better, he would
never be able to pay off the loan, which put his friends in a
difficult position. The longer the Scarecrow talked, the
more the gasoline stench grew.

It would be ideal if you could repay this loan, said the
Scarecrow, *but my friends know you haven't got access to
that kind of money.* The Scarecrow said he was here to
arrange a meeting where his friends and I could discuss
how the situation might be resolved. A car would be sent
for me tomorrow night. The Scarecrow said he wished he
could go into greater detail, but I'd just have to wait until
tomorrow. The smell was filling my nostrils and making me
nauseous.

Then he reached into his jacket pocket and withdrew
an envelope. *This next part wasn't my idea,* he said, throwing out his hands. He looked as if he wanted to say more,
but instead dropped the envelope on the table and turned
to leave. I stared at the envelope as he walked out of the
room. I could hear him in the foyer changing back into his
shoes when his phone rang again.

Moments later, the Scarecrow walked back into the living room and announced there had been another change
in plans. The car was coming tonight. Actually, the Scarecrow said, the car was already here. He was sorry but I'd
have to finish eating some other time because his friends
were already outside waiting. *Letting the elephants run the
circus,* he huffed.

As I listened to this vile little man with his shabby suit
and ridiculous yellow hair ordering me around in my own
house, something inside me snapped. I jumped to my feet
and hateful words surged through my mind but when I

opened my mouth nothing would come out. I felt light-headed and thought I might faint.

I can see you're upset, said the Scarecrow, moving toward the door. *I apologize all over myself. I had it all planned out and it wasn't supposed to be like this. These people, it's like herding cats. Take a look inside the envelope. Be in the car downstairs in ten minutes.*

I followed him into the hall, trying to keep a distance as he once again put on his shoes. The Scarecrow left and I shut and locked the door, holding my breath all the while. After I heard his footsteps trail off down the hall, I went to the kitchen cupboard and found an air freshener and sprayed it until the living room was cloaked in a fine mist. Still the smell remained. I threw my food in the garbage and poured out the rest of the beer. Only then did I open the envelope he'd left. Inside was a single Polaroid photograph. I took one look at it, dropped it on the floor, then ran to the bathroom and vomited.

black limousine with lace curtains over the windows sat idling in the center of the narrow road, blocking traffic in front of my apartment building. A uniformed driver held the door open and I got inside. I didn't know where the Scarecrow had gone, but there was no one in the car except the driver. Inside was warm and dark and smelled vaguely of sandalwood. As we pulled away, I could see my neighbors peeking out from behind their curtains, wondering what such a car could possibly be doing in our neighborhood.

The car went west until we merged onto the expressway. I took out the picture the Scarecrow had given me. It was of my husband, propped in his hospital bed. I could tell it was taken recently because the bruises and swelling were gone and his face was now limp and pale, a human face now but still not the face I remembered as his. In the picture, a man's arm entered from the upper corner of the frame, angling downward. In his hand he held a gun. The gun was pointed at my husband's head.

Could my husband hear these men, did he recognize their voices, did he know what they were doing? The picture was clearly intended as a warning that these people would kill him if I didn't cooperate, but the gun was an absurd touch. Nobody needed a gun to kill my husband. Unplug a couple of machines and he'd die all on his own in a matter of minutes.

I tucked the photograph back in the envelope and put the envelope back in my purse. The driver never spoke a word, nor did he put in a CD or turn on the radio. The car was completely soundproofed, blocking out the noises of traffic so all I could hear was the hum of the engine and the soothing whisper of the heater. We seemed hardly to be moving over a road at all, but floating on cushions of air as we traveled past miles of factories belching fumes into the night and through nameless suburbs of rolling hills cluttered with houses. Inside the car everything was warm and quiet. Sleep came so easefully I couldn't resist.

When I awoke the car was traveling over a narrow dirt road. Swirls of yellow dust were illuminated in the headlights and large trees enclosing the road swayed and shook in the wind. The car continued up a short hill until we came to a clearance. A weathered sign overgrown with weeds stood to the side of the road. WELCOME TO EMERALD GREENS, it announced. Ahead, a silver sports car was parked in front of a small concrete building. Beyond it lay a sea of dead grass rippling in the wind. Wherever we were, we weren't in Osaka anymore.

The driver pulled over and cut the engine. The doors opened automatically and I got out and walked along a small dirt path toward the building, wind whipping at my knees, pushing my hair into my face, making my eyes water. A large man in a silver suit was standing in the doorway of the building. He motioned me inside and guided me down the hall. Most of the windows in the building were broken and the place was littered with trash. The man motioned me into a darkened room without a door.

In the center of the room sat an old man in an enormous wheelchair. He was dressed in a stiff black suit and his head rested crooked on his shoulder. The windows had been boarded up, allowing only a few feeble rays of moonlight through the cracks, and it was so dark I could hardly make out the old man's face. Two figures flanked him, one on either side, their faces also hidden in the shadows. A folding chair had been set up in the center of the room. The man in the silver suit bid me sit down, then left the room. It was terribly cold and I wrapped my arms around myself to keep from shivering as I sat.

Do you know who we are? the old man asked. He was using some gadgetry to disguise his voice, making the words alternately run together and fall apart. *My name is Tadamitsu Noguchi. Do you know who that is?*

I shook my head.

I told you so, said the old man to no one in particular. *People are forgetting already. Show her the picture.*

One of the men flanking him stepped forward.

She's already seen the picture, he said.

The other picture, said Noguchi.

He bowed in a hurry and motioned to a second man. The man stepped forward and handed me a photograph. I had to squint hard to make out the details, but I could tell right away the man in the photograph wasn't my husband. The picture was of a grinning man in a white tuxedo standing in front of a tropical sunset. He was a foreigner, a Westerner.

You're going to meet this man, said Mr. Noguchi in his warped low voice. Now that my sight had adjusted to the dark, I could see Mr. Noguchi's eyes were fixed in the distance and one corner of his mouth turned down as if snagged by a fishhook. His lips seemed not to move as he spoke. *You're going to sleep with this man three times. After the third time, your husband's debts will disappear. Like in a fairy tale.*

I said nothing.

Mr. Noguchi sat unmoving, propped like a doll on his gigantic wheelchair. *Keep the photograph,* he said at length. *Remember the man's face. You'll receive a phone call telling you where to meet him.*

Text message, sir, one of the men whispered.

Stand where I can hear you, said old man Noguchi.

We've decided to send a text message, the second man said, stepping forward. *She'll get a message rather than an actual phone call.*

What difference does it make? Noguchi said. His voice boomed but his body remained absolutely motionless. *We'll be in touch again after your first time with this man. We're pleased you're here to make good. We all wish your husband a speedy recovery.*

That Friday I arrived earlier than usual to visit my husband at the hospital. The nurses had just finished turning him on his side, rotating him as they did three times daily to avoid bedsores, one of the many complications his injury left him helpless against. Ulcers, urinary infections, appendicitis, and lung infections were a constant worry and he had to be dressed in special antiembolic stockings to keep the blood from pooling in his legs, while blocky devices on his feet called space boots stabilized his posture to prevent deformities caused by long periods of inertness. His eyes occasionally ratcheted open but he wasn't capable of blinking, so they were regularly moistened and taped shut at night with flesh-colored patches that made it look as if his eyes had been wiped clean off his face, leaving not even empty sockets behind. With everything they made him wear, not to mention the tubes and wires hooked to machines that did the work his brain was incapable of, it was as if the injury came with its very own uniform, one that marked him as an alien form.

While the nurses finished up, I took a seat and tried to think about what I would say to him. Since the Scarecrow's visit I hadn't left my apartment. I hadn't gone on my walks and avoided all thoughts of the Nocturne Theater, feeling somehow that the appearance of the Scarecrow was payback for my "affair" with the puppeteer. I knew this wasn't a rational conclusion, but my world had long since stopped operating according to coherent principles. But for the last few days, I'd tried to reason it all out nevertheless, hoping that careful thinking might reveal some hidden possibility. I'd slept only seven hours in the three days since meeting Mr. Noguchi and the Scarecrow.

I thought first about going to the police. But considering I hadn't spoken more than a few words to a conscious human being for months, I dreaded sitting in some smoky little room and confronting the cops' dead-eyed gazes as they listened, scribbled notes, and constantly interrupted to clarify this or that point. In my condition I simply wouldn't be capable of it—delivering a coherent recollection of making breakfast would have been beyond me.

And even if I didn't go to pieces, what would they make of the story itself? A Scarecrow barging into my house smelling of gasoline? An abandoned building in the middle of nowhere housing an old man in a giant wheelchair? A foreigner I was to meet and sleep with three times, like in a fairy tale? They'd likely dismiss it as some elaborate paranoid fantasy. Even to me the events of that night seemed like a series of unfolding hallucinations.

Of course, I had the pictures to back me up. I could show the police the photograph of my husband with the gun to his head, show them the picture of this grinning tuxedoed foreigner on a fake beach. But what good would it do? The gunman's face wasn't in the first picture, so it provided no tangible lead. And if the photograph convinced the police to at least make a few inquiries for appearance's sake, it would likely cause all sorts of trouble for the hospital. Besides, the police wouldn't be able to protect my husband twenty-four hours a day until he regained consciousness. The photograph was proof that these people had already penetrated the hospital's flimsy security, and I had no doubt they could do it again.

What finally kept me from going to the police was the fact that I'd been allowed to keep the photograph at all. The Scarecrow could've simply shown it to me and taken it away, but he'd purposely left it behind. He knew I wouldn't go to the police with the threatening photograph precisely because of the threat leaving the picture implied. These people weren't afraid of the police, the act warned. Going to the police would only make the picture come true.

And what about these so-called debts of my husband's? Neither Mr. Noguchi nor the Scarecrow had offered me any paperwork, shown a receipt or any other evidence that my husband had borrowed this huge sum to cover his gambling losses. What if I could prove that he hadn't borrowed so much as a mosquito's tear, that he wasn't a gambler like they said, that he was completely innocent and they were trying to manipulate an awful situation for who knows what awful purpose?

But, having already ruled out the police, who was I even hoping to prove this to? To the Scarecrow? Mr. Noguchi? If it was a lie, it was obviously one they'd constructed. For three insomniac days my thinking continually ran up blind alleys and circled back on itself, and by Friday morning I'd concluded what I'd known in my heart all along.

Once the nurses had left I sat down in the same drab pale green chair where I'd spent so many hours by my husband's side, holding his hand as I spoke. Touch is important, said the doctors, and recovered coma victims often claim they could remember experiencing tactile sensations. But today I just couldn't go through with it. Every time I looked at his bloated, eyeless face I pictured that gun to the side of his head.

As I stared at him lying there awkwardly on his side I felt only anger. Anger at these loan-shark criminals for taking advantage of the situation. Anger at myself for feeling so powerless, for forcing myself to come here week after week when it was clear my husband was getting no better. And, most of all, I felt anger at my husband. Anger for the gambling, for the loans, anger that he'd allowed himself to get into a car wreck. I couldn't help feeling that he'd tricked me somehow, that his coma was the playacting of a selfish child, a way for him to escape responsibility. Falling into a coma instead of simply dying was just like him—wishy-washy, irresolute. Once these thoughts started coming, I couldn't stop them. They bubbled up one after another and made me sick to my stomach. I hated him for abandoning me, hated him for remaining so helplessly alive.

I wanted to tell him if he saw one of those glowing white tunnels common to near-death experiences, then he should ignore whatever voices were keeping him here and by all means walk, no, *run* into it as fast as he could. *Nobody is waiting for you here,* I wanted to tell him. *If you've ever felt anything for me at all, make a decision. Come back now or leave me forever.*

Instead, I just sat there stewing in my own nauseated revulsion for nearly an hour. Ten minutes before my scheduled visit was up, I decided I had to say something. And if he was in there, if he did come back, I wanted to make sure he heard. And I wanted him to remember my face as I said it. I ripped off his eye patches and pried his lids open, his eyes beneath jellied and unfocused.

Listen carefully to me, I said, putting my face right up against his. *Tonight I am going to sleep with a stranger in order to save your life. And if you get better, if you recover one day and you wonder, did this really happen, did I really hear Emiko say that, and it eats at you, and for days you think about bringing it up in some offhand way, making some little joke about this really strange memory you have, one you're sure never occurred, one that must have been a dream but is really odd just the same, and you think maybe you should share it with me, just for a laugh, just to see what I'll say—well, don't. Because if you ever mention this, I will leave you. I'll leave you and I'll never speak to you again as long as I live. But I want you to know one thing. It wasn't a dream. It really happened. All of this really happened and it was all your fault.*

With those words, I turned to leave only to find a nurse standing in the doorway. She gave me an embarrassed look and glanced down at my husband. "His eyes . . ." she started. Something in my expression stopped her. I dropped his crumpled eye patches to the floor and pushed past her into the hallway without a word. I was waiting for the train when my cell phone rang. *The Horse of a Different Color,* read the text message. Beneath was an address in Kitashinchi. I was to be there in one hour.

Chapter Seventeen

The Horse of a Different Color

Emiko pushed the straw around the inside of her empty
glass. Onscreen, a single raindrop swelled
and trembled at the end of a radiant green
leaf. At last the drop fell and the camera followed it down until it landed in an impossibly
blue puddle and made a slow-motion splash,
the pool sinking in the middle, then rising,
rippling outward. Then the scene faded out
and a little cartoon Elvis look-alike blinked
from the corner of the screen while the song
reloaded.

"So you went through with it?" I asked.

She sat with her knees drawn together,
leaning forward, one elbow propped on the
table, while I fiddled with the ashtray, nudg-
ing it back and forth across the surface of the
tabletop, the two of us slouched and restless

like teenagers marooned at Denny's on a Saturday night. The song started up again with a delicate keyboard descent that was always a prelude to something awful. Strangely enough, I kind of liked the song, though, gooey keyboard intro and all.

"More or less," she said with a shrug. "I did my part but ever since that night the Scarecrow and his people have been following me. They haven't invaded my home again, they haven't even talked to me, but I know they're watching. That night at the café, when you got the phone call, one of them approached. That man in the silver suit."

I nodded. The Tin Man.

"I panicked. I didn't know what to do, so I ran. But I can't live like this. Let them unplug my husband. If that's what's going to happen, there's nothing I can do to stop it. I'm not going to run anymore. And no matter what they do, I'm not going to be with that man again."

"No chance of that happening."

"It was the most humiliating night of my life."

"At least you're still alive."

Emiko cocked her head. "Where do you fit in all of this?" she finally thought to ask. She didn't seem alarmed, just curious. "When you first followed me out of the Nocturne Theater the other night, I thought you must be with them. Noguchi's bunch. But as soon as you started talking, it was obvious you weren't one of those terrible people. Yet somehow you knew the name Richard Gale. And you knew I was with him. How?"

"I guessed after I saw you that night in the stairwell."

"I don't understand."

"You were there the night he died."

She screwed up her face and peered at me through the dark. "The night who died?"

"Richard Gale."

Emiko's eyes saucered. "He's dead?"

Lots of people will tell you they know how to spot a liar. They'll say there are specific tells, changes in speech patterns or gestural ticks. They'll say that people hold their breath or blink too much. My editor Sarah tells me she can just sense when someone's lying, feel it on a gut level. I believe her, but I've never been so lucky. I'd been lied to and played for a sucker any number of times, probably more than I'll ever know. Only time would tell if this was one of them.

"He's dead?" Emiko repeated.

"Not just dead, murdered," I said. "They found him in bed with his face shredded and his throat slashed. His body was discovered the morning after I came across you sleeping in the stairwell."

"But that means . . ." She trailed off, unable to attach words to the thoughts flooding her head.

"You might have been the last person to see him alive."

Her face drained of color. "I should be a suspect."

"You would be," I said. "Except I haven't told the police or anybody else that I saw you there that night. And surveillance videotapes taken from the lobby show Richard Gale entering the hotel with a woman who had longish red hair. I'm guessing that's who the police are looking for. How is it that he entered the PanCosmo with her and ended up with you? Where did the two of you meet? What—"

I stopped. Emiko had her hands over her face and was shaking her head. I couldn't see the tears but I knew they were falling just the same. There was no point in saying anything further. I just sat there watching karaoke lyrics scroll across the screen, not even bothering to read them.

Emiko stopped crying after a while. She wiped her face with her sleeve then went into her handbag for a tissue. But instead of tissue, she brought out something else, an object she tossed upon the table with an air of resignation. She sniffed and rubbed her eyes with the heels of her palms.

I stared down at the lumpy tangle of red hair on the table. The wig looked like some strange animal, something you hoped was actually dead. Neither of us spoke. We might've gone on like that forever had someone not come knocking on the door.

"Hello, sorry, excuse me," came the tired voice from the other side of the door, followed by another knock. On-screen, an airplane touched down on a runway. This video had everything. "I'm sorry but we're closing now," said the karaoke worker. "Please settle your bill up front. Thank you very much. Good night. Please come again soon."

A moment later the lights came on. Four barren walls, empty glasses on a table, a big TV, a disco ball. Take away those, the place had all the romance of an interrogation room, which is what I'd managed to turn it into. Emiko sat blinking in the light and staring at the wig. The song played through one last time. When it was over, Emiko scooped up the auburn wig and unceremoniously stuffed it back into her purse.

I paid the bill and we walked outside. We'd missed the last train and we both stood there wondering what would happen in the next five minutes. Groups of kids in their twenties streamed by red-faced and reeling, drunk and warm in their thick winter coats, not caring what happened for the next five years.

"Take me to the police," Emiko said, almost to herself. "I can't go there on my own."

"Not sure going to the cops is such a great idea."

"You can't leave me alone right now. Please."

I had no intention of leaving her alone. I would have stayed with her if she planned to do nothing but wander the city all night humming that nameless tune I'd been listening to for the last several hours. I still didn't know what had happened in the time between her meeting Richard Gale and my finding her passed out in the PanCosmo stairwell, but I just couldn't believe she'd killed him. I was already inventing unlikely explanations for the wig, concocting convoluted scenarios involving figures sneaking into Richard's room, razor brandished, just like in the puppet show at the Nocturne Theater. The possibility that the strain of everything had made Emiko crack or that she'd willingly participated in a scheme to off the Kansas kid was something I couldn't bring myself to consider. She wasn't lying to me. Emiko had been set up. She'd been tricked. Someone else killed him. She was innocent, but if she went to the police now, she was as good as gone. Confused and exhausted as she was, they'd have a signed confession in a matter of hours and I'd never see Emiko again except in the papers, on the TV news.

"We're not going to the police," I said. "We're going back to your place. You're going to tell me everything that happened that night with Richard Gale. Everything. And then we'll figure out what to do next."

"But Mr. Noguchi's people will be waiting, they'll—"

"If the Komoriuta-kai come, I'll deal with them."

For the second time that night her face went blank with shock. The look said until now she'd had no idea Mr. Noguchi and his bunch were anything but garden-variety loan sharks, two-bit bogeymen. But even Emiko, lost as she was, knew who the Komoriuta-kai were. They were real and they were dangerous and if they'd wanted, both she and her husband would already be dead. The question was why they'd allowed her to live, knowing as much as she did. The question was how much longer she had left. Now that I was involved, the questions applied to me, too.

We walked to a row of taxis idling on the street outside Shinsaibashi station. We got in and she gave the driver an address in Imazato, on the east side of the city. Along the way I looked out the window and tried not to think too much. We took some expressway that cut through the center of Namba, the city rolling by on all sides, an endless tangle of glass and concrete, wire and steel. We exited the expressway and the signs changed to *hangul* as we passed through Korea town. Sometime later we got out of the cab and walked up the stairs to her second-floor apartment. No Scarecrow, no Tin Man, no flying monkeys.

Emiko's apartment was a modest, low-key affair, fairly spacious for a Japanese apartment but less than half the size of my room at the PanCosmo. There were two rooms, three if you counted the bathroom, with the living room and kitchen separated from the bedroom by a sliding *fusuma* door. Shelves lined every wall, crammed with books, CDs, DVDs, all kinds of Winnie-the-Pooh and Tigger knickknacks. A large home entertainment center took up about half the living room, while the other half consisted of a square *kotatsu* table and a couch draped in a white sheet. The curtains were drawn over a single window facing the street.

Maybe it was because I was looking for them, but signs of her husband seemed to be everywhere. When Emiko hung my coat on a rack in the kitchen, I saw his right there next to it, above three pairs of business shoes and a pair of Puma sneakers lined up on the floor below. His golf clubs leaned against the wall in the living room, his watch sat in a metal tray atop a stereo speaker. A pack of Lark cigarettes and a lighter sat on the kitchen counter, and I hadn't seen Emiko smoke. A pad like this had virtually no storage space so it made sense that his stuff was everywhere, but it seemed like Emiko was trying to preserve his presence, convince herself he'd be home any day now. All the place lacked was a half-eaten sandwich and a note tacked to the fridge saying he'd gone out for cigarettes.

Emiko went into the bedroom to change. Just before she slid the door shut I spied a picture of the couple taken in front of the entrance to Universal Studios Osaka. He was wearing jeans and a red T-shirt and looked like a decent enough guy. Hard to imagine he was the type to run up thousands of dollars in gambling debts, but you can tell only so much from a picture. There weren't any photos around of friends or family, no New Year's cards tacked to walls, nothing to indicate the couple were part of the outside world at all. Made me feel like an intruder violating some cloistered sanctuary built for two. I took a seat on the couch and listened to the blood pounding in my head, afraid to touch anything.

Emiko came out wearing light blue sweatpants and a loose-fitting gray sweatshirt. She asked if I wanted a glass of water and fetched two from the kitchen. Meanwhile, I went to use the bathroom. An empty bottle of sleeping pills, two toothbrushes, and Genet shaving cream sat on the counter.

That and an ivory-handled straight razor.

The sight of it jarred me. I knew it wasn't the murder weapon because Imanishi said the killer had left it behind, but still. Who the hell actually used straight razors anyway? Where did they even sell these things? Were old-fashioned hair-removal instruments part of some new grooming trend sweeping Japan? I picked up the razor and slipped it in my front pocket. I may not have believed Emiko killed Richard Gale, but there was no point leaving around props for a repeat performance in case I was wrong.

When I got back to the living room I found Emiko had pulled aside the curtain and was peering at the street below. She stayed there a moment before turning off the lights, presumably in case anyone was watching. The room went completely dark and I heard her footsteps pad across the floor. She lit a candle and took a seat on the floor, at the foot of the table. I watched the flame dance and tried to think of something to say.

"Nice place," I managed.

"It must seem very small. Americans live in big houses, no?"

"Not me. I live in a place about like this."

"But you're not married," she said. "You live alone?"

"I live by myself."

She smiled. "Is there a difference?"

I shrugged and Emiko took a sip of her water. She tucked her hair behind her ear as the candlelight played over her face, so small and white in the dark. It struck me that I'd never seen her in daylight. It was hard to imagine her as any part of waking reality, as someone buying groceries or riding the train or even checking in at the front desk of the hospital. Making small talk seemed pointless under the circumstances.

"So why the wig?" I asked. "Was it Mr. Noguchi's idea?"

"It's complicated, difficult to explain."

Complicated and difficult, my tireless companions. If I heard the words one more time, I might bash my head into a wall over and over or hack up my own face with a razor. I smiled and asked Emiko to try to explain anyway, complicated and difficult though it may be.

"I wanted to become someone else," said Emiko. "If I was going to sleep with the man in the picture, I would have to convince myself I wasn't Emiko. The wig was a disguise, but not for other people. It was for me, to help me get into character, to hide me from myself. I bought the wig at a shop in Umeda, along with a pair of sunglasses, a new dress, new shoes. I wanted to transform myself. Maybe it was the Nocturne Theater that gave me the idea. Seeing how a puppet can be remade into so many different characters with a change in hairstyles, different clothes."

Forget TV and movies, videogames and comic books, I thought. People could get all the bad ideas they needed from puppet shows.

"So where did you meet Gale?" I asked. I knew she must have met him outside the hotel to appear on the lobby video, though I was still holding some faint hope that the woman on the tape wasn't her, that someone else was involved, maybe Kaori Inoue.

"I met him at a snack bar in Kitashinchi," said Emiko. "A place called the Horse of a Different Color. I found the man sitting at a table in the corner, just like they said I would. I was afraid he wouldn't be able to speak Japanese, but when I asked if I could sit with him, he said he was waiting for somebody. I said I was too, so we might as well wait together. We had a couple of drinks. We talked. I say it like it was some casual encounter, but of course I was a nervous wreck. I've never been the type to approach strangers and strike up a conversation. Well, whoever he was waiting for never showed up. He'd been set up, just like me."

I asked what he was like, what the two of them talked about.

"I can hardly remember," Emiko said. "He was kind of a

strange guy. Not scary strange, just a little out there. He didn't speak like most men I know. He was very polite."

"Kinda feminine almost?"

"A little, now that you mention it," she said. "But it wasn't just the way he talked. The things he said were odd, too. At one point, he told me I had a classically Japanese face. I asked what he meant and he told me my face was perfect for shadows. What kind of compliment is that, I thought, telling a woman her face belongs in the dark? Then he started talking about some essay he'd read about Japanese skin. How Japanese skin is a different white than Western skin, cloudier or something like that. Then he asked if I'd ever seen a traditional Japanese toilet of laquered wood. His Japanese wasn't the best, so it was hard to understand him sometimes. The whole time I tried to push the thought from my mind that I had to sleep with this person, to stop myself from wondering how I was going to get through it. But it never came to that."

"But you accompanied him to the PanCosmo Hotel?"

She nodded, took another sip of water. "We stayed at the Horse of a Different Color for a couple hours. He said the person he was meeting obviously wasn't going to show and he was ready to call it a night, but I suggested we go for one more drink since we were hitting it off so well. Which we weren't, but anyway. We got a cab and went to some place inside his hotel. We had another drink there but the conversation went cold. I started wondering if he was under orders to sleep with me, too. Mostly, I sat there wondering what Mr. Noguchi and his people had to gain from this whole arrangement."

As I listened to Emiko, I was wondering the same thing.

"I purposely missed the last train," she continued. "The man told me getting a cab from the hotel would be easy. I said I couldn't afford a cab. He told me he'd pay. I told him I couldn't accept his money, he offered to get me a room at the hotel. I said I'd rather just stay in his. I could hardly believe the words coming out of my mouth, but I was determined to see it through. I had to practically throw myself at him, but finally he gave in."

"What time was this?"

"Maybe one, one-thirty. So we left the bar, took the elevator down to his room. He was so drunk he could hardly get the key card in the door. We went into his room and he said he was going to take a shower if I didn't mind. I could feel the energy draining from my body and just wanted to get it over with, but if he wanted a shower first, so be it. He went into the bathroom and I sat down on the couch. The room was huge. I'd never been in a hotel room like this before, and thought whatever this odd American did for a living he must have been very successful. My wig was itching so I took it off. I closed my eyes and listened to the sound of the water. Then I must've fallen asleep. The next face I saw was yours."

"You fell asleep in his room, but woke up in the stairwell?"

She nodded. "Like I said, lately I'd had sleepwalking episodes. I don't really remember what happened. One minute I was listening to the sound of the shower, and the next I was in the stairwell."

"That's a tough sell," I said.

"I know." She sighed. "I wouldn't believe it myself, normally. But I'm not part of the normal world anymore, so who am I to judge? You could leap from the couch and strangle me, or turn into a giant butterfly and fly to the moon, and I'd be in no position to say, 'Hey, wait a minute, this just doesn't make any sense.' "

The candle had burned halfway down now, wax spilling over the edges. Emiko rocked slowly back and forth, her knees drawn up under the blanket of the *kotatsu*. I couldn't help but think that Richard Gale was right about at least one thing. Her face had an opaque quality that made it softly radiant in the dark.

"What are you going to do next?" I asked.

"I'm going to sleep," Emiko said. "Right now I'm too tired to think anymore, so tired I might actually be able to sleep the whole night through. What about you? Will you still be here when I wake up?"

I nodded, lacking the energy to line all the words up in my head. After a moment she rose and walked silently into the bedroom annex, then drew the door closed behind her. I sat on the couch and watched the candle flame flicker, thoughts not so much going through my mind as past it, just out of reach. I lay down and listened to Emiko in the next room, her breathing already grown deep. I closed my eyes and told myself everything would make more sense in the light of day.

But I never made it that far. Sometime in the night, I woke with a chill. The candle had gone out and the room was freezing cold. I got up to look for a blanket or just find my coat, but it was so dark I could hardly see. As I felt my way across the room I saw moonlight spilling in from the entryway. The front door was wide open. I rushed back into the main room. The screen to Emiko's room was pulled back to reveal an empty bed.

Act III

Chapter Eighteen

Four Photographs

At this hour of the night, Osaka was another place altogether. Stripped of the noise and the neon and the crowds, the metropolis became a ghostly outline of itself, an empty stage of darkened houses and shuttered stores facing streets where nothing moved. Street lamps buzzed and power cables hummed low overhead, but the loudest sound was my own footsteps as I wandered the residential lanes of Imazato looking for any sign of Emiko. I hoped I'd find her curled under an entryway to some apartment block, maybe sleeping in some tiny park or ambling down the middle of the street, arms outstretched like a B-movie zombie. But she was nowhere in sight. I didn't pass so much as a stray cat.

I was at least a few miles from my hotel.

The local trains wouldn't be running for hours and it wasn't any place you'd find a cab. I thought about stealing a bicycle but didn't want to chance getting hauled into the local *koban.* Foreigners had a bad enough rap without me contributing to their image problem. So I kept walking, heading north along some miserable sludge-filled canal, trying to think of what to do next.

I had an idea, a bad one, one I'd been fighting back all day in hopes that a better one would come along. But time was wasting and dawn would be too late. I finally gave in and took an unlocked bicycle parked outside Imazoto station. Someone else would have to fight *gaijin* stereotypes. The bike looked like something Mary Poppins might have ridden but it worked well enough, getting me across town to the Minami ward as the night began slowly relinquishing its grip over the city.

The ginkgo trees cast angled shadows over the sidewalk as headlights prowled Midosuji Avenue. Even at this hour Osaka's biggest street was alive with cars, most of them vacant cabs on the hunt for one last fare, or maybe the first one. I found the building I was looking for, then ditched the bike in a rack outside some beautician's college and made my way around back. Problem was, the front of the building seemed to have no spatial relationship whatsoever with the rear, and before I knew it I was lost in another one of those back-alley mazes. Eventually I popped out on Midosuji Avenue again and had to start all over.

If finding the rear of the building was harder than expected, breaking in was a lot easier. I found a first-floor window that was unlocked, pushed it open, and climbed in. Judging from the posters on the wall, I was inside a travel agency. I made my way out of the room and into the hallway, keeping an eye out for security personnel or cameras but finding neither. Six flights of stairs and one long corridor later I stood outside Kusanagi Explorations and Research. The door was locked, but it was no match for my trusty Cleveland YMCA membership card.

Moonlight slipped through the blinds, striping the room in blue shadows. Amazing how cheerless an office lobby could look without pretty women running around watering plants and fixing tea. No alarms went off as I moved through the lobby, though I couldn't rule out silent ones. I didn't risk turning on the lights but felt my way down the hall until I found Mr. Kusanagi's office. All those file cabinets filled with secrets and the guy hadn't even bothered to lock the door. It was downright unprofessional. My bad idea was starting to look pretty good after all.

I wasn't sure which file cabinet to look in, so I started at the top left. They were arranged alphabetically, which meant I didn't have to rifle through many to get to INOUE. I had just pulled out a thick manila folder and was considering whether to risk turning on a desk lamp when I heard a sound behind me. A tentative, quiet tinkling followed by a louder rattling noise. I realized what it was before I even turned around. Kusanagi had a security system after all.

The dog had awakened and scrambled to its feet, its claws clattering over the hard tiled floor as it surged forward and the chain caught. The thing was little more than a crouching shadow, an unshaped mass inset with pinprick eyes and teeth that flashed white in the dark. He strained against his leash and gave me a low steady growl that didn't need translation. I stood frozen to the spot, still holding the folder, thinking I'd been right all along. Coming here was a bad idea.

There was no way to get out of the room without passing the dog, and there was no way to pass the dog without leaving behind a hunk of flesh. I tried to remember what the dog was called but it hardly mattered. Not likely the thing was going to roll over and let me rub his tummy just because I knew his name.

I considered removing a ceiling panel and climbing through an air duct. But the ceiling had no panels. Tear up all my clothes and fashion the strips into a crude rope, then push open the window and rapel seven stories to the street below, naked? Maybe if I were a cartoon. The clock on the wall said it was 4:44 A.M. Nothing to do but sit around and wait for Kusanagi to show up in a few hours. If my suspicions were correct, the best I could hope for was that he'd call the police. More likely he'd ring up some goons from the Komoriuta-kai.

But the dog wasn't willing to wait. His snarl changed pitch and he coiled on his haunches, ears flattened against his skull. I'd just remembered the dog's name was Totoya when he sprang. The chain went taut and the dog spun halfway around in the air with a strangled yelp and the ring bolt ripped out of the wall, taking a chunk of plaster with it. My heart surged in my throat and I dropped the folder and hopped behind the desk. That bought me all of half a second, but it was enough.

I reached into my pocket for the straight razor, the one I'd taken from Emiko's bathroom. The dog came around the corner in a blur, hunkered low to the ground, legs sliding out beneath him as he tried to get footing on the hard floor. I just managed to get the razor out and was fumbling to open it when Totoya leaped.

He slammed like a wall against my chest and I saw a flash of teeth as I toppled backward. I'm sure the thing was

barking or snarling and I was probably making all kinds of
panicky noises but I didn't hear a sound. Everything was silence and darkness, the smell of fur and rancid hot breath
against my face, and an immense thrashing weight pinning
me to the floor. I got one arm in front of my throat and the
dog clamped down hard and yanked his massive head and
I emptied my lungs in a scream. The sound broke the spell,
brought me halfway to my senses. I wedged my right hand
underneath the dog's neck, thrust and yanked. Hot liquid
spurted over my face, streaking my vision. The dog yelped
and snapped and came down right on the razor blade,
catching the rubbery corner of his mouth and opening his
snarl half an inch wider. He wrestled forward, fur slick and
damp with the blood issuing from his neck as he fought to
get at mine. I struggled to keep his muzzle back and I felt
the razor bite across my cheek as he writhed and knocked
it from my grip. The weapon clattered across the floor, out
of reach, and then I was back inside that still silent bubble
again, nothing to see and nothing to hear.

I don't know how much time passed before I came out
of it, but the dog seemed to have forgot what he was doing
while I was away. He'd stopped coming at me and was
standing a few feet to one side, shaking his head as if trying
to chase away a circling fly, sending lazy strings of reddish
saliva arcing from his mouth. I edged backward, propping
myself on my elbows, readying to kick if he lunged. Instead
the dog gave me a look like he wondered what I was still
doing there, then turned a half-circle and slumped to the
floor. I watched the slow rise and fall of his rib cage, the
unsteady rhythm of his panting broken as he sputtered and
gagged on the blood filling his mouth. The front of his coat
was a syrupy mat now and a dark pool was slowly spreading over the floor like a hole opening up to swallow him. I

knew he was finished, but I was surprised how long he managed to hang on. His whole body jerked, once, twice, the leash jingling with each shudder, and then everything was still.

When I was sure the dog was dead I got slowly to my feet. My left forearm throbbed and my shirtsleeve was torn to reveal a half-moon of teethmarks on the skin beneath. There was going to be a bump on the back of my head where it met the floor and I was dizzy with nausea. I put a hand to my cheek where the razor had caught me. There was blood alright, plenty of it, but I couldn't be sure how much was mine and how much was the dog's. The smell of him was all over me and I felt the sickness rise like a ball in my throat, buckled over, and grabbed Kusanagi's little plastic trash can.

When I was all emptied out and I'd stopped trembling and the waves of dizziness receded, I wiped the water from my eyes and pushed the trash can away. I tore what was left of the sleeve from my shirt and used it to clean the blood off my face as best I could. The wound on my cheek was superficial, maybe an inch long, not much worse than a nick you might get shaving. I rose and began looking for the Inoue file, hoping it hadn't been ruined. Luckily the file had ended up under the desk during the struggle. A handful of documents and four photographs spilled out from inside. I picked up one of the photographs and clicked on the desklamp to get a better look. Someone noticing a lighted window was the least of my worries now.

The picture was taken inside a bar. Qualitywise, it wasn't much better than the PanCosmo security videos, but it was good enough that I could tell the woman with red hair and sunglasses sitting across from Richard Gale in a corner booth was definitely Emiko. The bar was likely the

Horse of a Different Color, though it could have been the one they'd visited inside the hotel, too. No matter, I now had proof that Kusanagi was part of the setup, and given the name on the folder, my suspicions that the Inoues put him up to it looked to be on the mark, too.

But the other three photographs didn't fit so neatly. In one, Richard Gale was emerging from a love hotel called Christmas Time Chapel with a woman who looked to be Thai. She wore a black leather skirt, stylish knee-high leather boots, and a red vinyl jacket the same voltage as her lipstick. Gale looked shaken. Another photograph showed him with a more conservatively dressed female, albeit one who looked no older than sixteen. They were getting into a cab outside an entrance to Soemoncho. In the third picture, he was with two women in a hotel room. All three of them were naked and passed out, sprawled across the bed like they'd been tossed by a hurricane.

Interesting as they were, the photographs were nothing compared to the papers. The first sheet didn't contain much, just a faxed copy of a short article from the *Wichita Eagle*. It was one I'd come across only a day before on the Web, but I hadn't bothered to click the link.

Corefluxus Founder Dies in Plane Crash

Aspen, CO (AP)—The bodies of Corefluxus Inc. founder Martin Gale, 57, and his wife, Leslie-Ann Gale, 42, were discovered early this morning by rescue workers at the site of a plane crash in a remote mountain area approximately seven miles outside Aspen, Colorado. The couple were reportedly embarking on a holiday ski vacation when the accident occurred.

The private jet, a 1981 Gulfstream III, had left Jeffer-

son County Airport at approximately 4:10 P.M. MST and was en route to the Aspen-Pitkin County airport when it lost radio and radar contact with air traffic controllers. The pilot, Frank Baum, 32, of Kansas, MO, was also killed in the crash. No other passengers were onboard. The wreckage was spotted at approximately 5:54 P.M. MST by the pilot of a Cessna air taxi also bound for Aspen, who noticed a small fire burning on the mountainside. The National Transportation Safety Board is investigating the cause of the accident.

An engineering graduate from the University of Kansas and lifelong resident of the state, Martin G. Gale founded Wichita-based Corefluxus in 1978. In 1992, his company patented a seismic data-processing and 3D image-modeling software application called Stratum. Stratum was wildly successful, and soon became the world standard for use in oil exploration, making Corefluxus the second-largest corporation headquartered in Kansas and an important player in the worldwide energy industry.

Martin Gale and Leslie-Ann Gale are survived by their son, twenty-one-year-old Richard Gale. Leslie-Ann Gale is also survived by her parents, Derek Helmer and Dora Ann Helmer, of Memphis, TN, and her sister Emma Ann Helmer.

I didn't read the other two obituaries, the ones from the *Wall Street Journal* and *Forbes* with Japanese translations attached. I didn't pick through the Corefluxus Annual Report and didn't glance at young Richard Gale's bank statements or his college transcripts, either. I didn't need all that to figure out why the esteemed Inoues didn't have any problem with their only daughter marrying an American horsebones, or how it was an unemployed English teacher could take up residence at the lush PanCosmo. It was a safe bet that Richard Gale was the only English conversation teacher in the Kansai who happened to be the sole heir to a multimillion-dollar fortune back in Kansas.

Outside the sky was getting lighter. In the corner I found an old brown leather satchel bag, one Mr. Kusanagi must've upgraded from years ago. I peeled off my wet shirt and wrapped the bloody razor inside it. The soles of my wing tips were tacky with blood, so I took my shoes off and wrapped them inside the shirt, too, so as not to make tracks through the whole building. After wavering a moment, I took the file and shoved the whole messy package in the satchel. I put on a tan raincoat hanging on a coatrack, then turned off the lamp and climbed gingerly over the desk to avoid the dog and the mess congealing around him. As I shut the door behind me I couldn't help feeling a little bad for Mr. Kusanagi. He was in for one hell of an ugly morning. As it turned out, my day wouldn't win any beauty contests, either.

Chapter Nineteen

A Strand of Modacrylic Fiber

The face in the mirror belonged in the PanCosmo Hotel
like a sewer rat belonged in a flower arrangement. But there it was anyway, surrounded
by sleek designer furniture, plush carpet, a
great view, and everything you could want in
a hotel room except someone to share it
with. I'd done a pretty crummy job cleaning
myself up at Kusanagi's office. The cut on my
cheek didn't look so bad, but the smudges of
dog's blood streaked across my neck and
forehead did. Add to that the caked brown
mess in my hair and the insomniac gleam in
my eye and I felt like calling security to have
myself forceably removed.

Instead I took off the borrowed coat and
tossed the satchel bag in the closet. I walked
to the bathroom and ran a hot shower, let-

ting the room thicken with steam until the mirrors couldn't bring any more bad news. I stripped down and was just stepping into the shower when I heard the knock at the door. Whoever it was could wait. I closed my eyes and let the hot water beat against my neck and realized this might actually be the most perfect shower in the history of the world. But that perfect shower wasn't to be. Whoever it was at the door couldn't wait after all. They knocked two more times. Then they came inside.

When I heard the doorknob click I left the water running and slipped out of the shower. I pulled on my pants one leg at a time and hummed a few bars of the first thing that popped into my head, hoping the intruder would think I was still happily scrubbing away. The first thing that popped into my head turned out to be "Toryanse," that damn tune that droned from every crosswalk in Osaka, the one whose lyrics meant something like "you can enter here." I put on a clean white T-shirt and hoped I could avoid getting this one covered with blood, too.

I pushed the bathroom door open a sliver. From my vantage point I could only see the bedroom. No one there. I stepped out and eased the door closed behind me and listened. Nothing but the sound of a perfect shower being wasted. Just then I saw a flicker of movement, a figure reflected in the mirror hanging above the bedroom dresser. It passed like a shadow and then everything was still again. I waited, debating what to do next, watching the mirror for signs of action in the other room. When I got sick of waiting, I hunched down and crawled on all fours out of the bedroom like a dog, hiding behind the furniture.

Imanishi the hotel detective was sitting with his back to me at the writing desk, gazing out the window. I stood up and cleared my throat. Imanishi turned to face me. He needed sleep even more than I did, seemed to be vanishing by degrees. He wore the same expression of grim fortitude, but his hair looked styled with transmission fluid and his fake ear was only partially affixed, practically dangling off the side of his head. I tried not to stare at the thing as he rose and came toward me.

"I apologize for the intrusion," he began.

"I'll tell your boss you at least apologized. Maybe you'll get severance pay."

"It was urgent that I speak with you."

"My shower was pretty urgent, too."

"Please resume bathing if you wish," Imanishi said. "I am content to wait until you are finished. I trust the maids have provided you with an ample supply of toiletries? The PanCosmo Hotel is proud to offer the finest array of personal hygiene products from the leading cosmetics companies of Europe. Should you be allergic to any of these, we also offer organic—"

"Just tell me what you want."

"Very well," said Imanishi. He wearily reached into his jacket pocket and took out his little silver tape recorder. "Have you any objections to this conversation being recorded?"

"No more than I have to this conversation in general."

"The recording is in no way meant to act as an official document of the exchange, but rather as an aid for my personal memory. During my time at the Osaka Municipal Police—"

"Get to the point."

Imanishi gave up on the tape recorder, slipping it back into his pocket while his other hand pinched the space between his eyes like he was trying to squeeze off a headache. "Mr. Chaka, I'm here to give you one final chance. I know you saw something the night Richard Gale was murdered. Or rather, someone. I know you passed a red-haired woman on the stairwell. The security tapes show her leaving through the front exit only moments after you entered and, as I told you, our elevator logs recorded no activity at this time of night. So she had to have taken the stairs, just as you did."

"I didn't see anybody," I said. "She must have heard me coming and ducked out on one of the floors. Probably listened for my footsteps, waited until I had passed, then went back into the stairwell and continued down. That's how I would've done it."

Imanishi's eyes wandered the room as he thought it through. They stopped for a moment on Kusanagi's satchel bag sitting in the corner and I could see him making the calculations, remembering it wasn't there before, planning on asking the porter how many bags had been delivered to my room when I first checked in.

"The scenario you present is plausible," Imanishi grudgingly concluded, nodding to himself. "And I might indeed believe that's what occurred were I not in possession of information which leads me to deem otherwise. Mr. Chaka, I propose that you not only passed this woman, but that the two of you interacted in some way. Furthermore, I believe that this stairwell encounter was not your only contact with this woman. The latter belief is one I can readily prove."

Imanishi permitted himself a meager smile as he reached into his inner jacket pocket. He produced a stack of snapshots and spread them across the writing table like a magician laying out a card trick. There were eight or nine pictures altogether. A few indoor shots, a couple of underground photos, a series taken outside through a window.

Some were slightly out of focus and some were a little underlit, but Imanishi wasn't a bad photographer. He just hadn't found the right subject matter yet.

"Well?" he said, rocking back on his heels as he awaited my reaction. Anything short of a fainting spell or tearful confession seemed likely to disappoint him.

"I like this one." I pointed at a photo of me and Kaori Inoue eating *okonomiyaki* at the restaurant. "The way the viewer can see your reflection ghosted on the glass. Like you're this wandering spirit forever condemned to be on the outside looking in. Sad, but in a poignant way."

A vein I hadn't seen before rose in Imanishi's neck, tunneling like a blue worm under his skin. Even his prosthetic ear looked like it was turning red.

"You admit you are the man in the pictures?"

I wasn't in all of them. Besides the pictures of Kaori and me eating at the restaurant, there were shots from the funeral. Me entering the door of the little flower storage room at Joyful Twilight. The Tin Man coming by, knocking on the door. Kaori emerging from the same door. Me emerging moments later. Other than that, there were a few of me waiting around at the Crysta Nagahori underground shopping mall and one of Kaori coming down the stairs to meet me. She looked good in the picture. I thought about asking if I could keep it, so one day I could tell everyone at the nursing home she'd been my sweetheart before she suffered one of those mobile-phone brain tumors that claimed so many of her generation.

"Yeah, it's me. So what?"

"Very well," Imanishi said. "I propose the woman accompanying you in these pictures is the same woman you passed on the stairwell the night Richard Gale was murdered. I have independently established the identity of this woman. Her name is Kaori Inoue. There is an acknowledged link between her and Mr. Gale."

"She was his wife," I said.

"Correct," said Imanishi, reaching into his pocket again. He removed a plastic sandwich bag and placed it on the table next to the photos. As far as I could tell, the bag was completely empty. I looked at Imanishi and shrugged.

"Inside is a single red hair," he told me. "One I recovered from the crime scene. Microscopic analysis leads me to conclude that this hair is not of the human variety. Rather, it is a type of modacrylic fiber often used in the construction of inexpensive hairpieces. I thereby assert that Kaori Inoue wore a red hairpiece the night she killed Richard Gale, the same one she is wearing in these photos taken at the underground shopping center and the restaurant. But her real hair is black, as the photographs from the funeral hall attest. Kaori Inoue is therefore the woman captured on surveillance footage from the lobby of our fine hotel. Kaori Inoue killed her husband, Mr. Chaka. And, with all respect due to you as a guest of the PanCosmo Hotel, I am forced to conclude that you are complicit in this crime."

It took superhuman effort to keep from laughing. Detective Imanishi was so right and yet so hopelessly wrong. Given what he had to work with—a few photos, a video, a hair fiber—he'd come to a conclusion I might have reached myself. But I knew things Imanishi didn't, and the reality of what had happened was a multiplicity of absurdities that couldn't have been dreamt up by the worst playwright at the Nocturne Theater. A woman with black hair (Emiko) showed up on videotape as a woman with red hair because she'd worn a wig. And the woman with dyed red hair (Kaori) appeared in the funeral photos as a woman with black hair because she'd also worn a wig. Two women wearing two wigs of different colors at different times. Kaori and Emiko couldn't have made it more confusing if they'd planned it. Detective Imanishi had chosen the simplest solution, and had thus inadvertently merged the two women into one. If anyone ever did get to the bottom of who actually killed Richard Gale, there was a strong case to be made for charging the entire wig industry as an accomplice.

"So what now?" I asked.

"You must tell me everything you know about Kaori Inoue. I need the details of your discussion in the stairwell, as well as at the funeral hall and the restaurant. If you cooperate, perhaps the police will argue for leniency when you are prosecuted."

I shook my head. "Can't talk now."

It wasn't the reply Imanishi was expecting. He blinked and pursed his lips. I watched the pulse in his neck quicken. "You realize being uncooperative will reflect poorly on you during sentencing?"

"I'm not worried."

"In your place, I should think—"

"You aren't going to the police."

Imanishi made a play for the ear, caught himself.

"I have some theories of my own," I said. "Way I see it, you can't mention me or Kaori Inoue or anything else to the cops without betraying the fact that you've been withholding evidence from the moment Richard Gale's body was discovered by the cleaning lady."

"My duties as resident detective for the PanCosmo Hotel—"

"Don't include conducting your own homicide investigation," I said. "Truth is, you haven't been cooperating with the police at all. You haven't shown them the video surveillance footage or these photographs. You haven't told them about me or this so-called woman in the stairwell. I'd even bet you ransacked Richard Gale's room before reporting the body. Bagged all the hair fibers, the nametag, took fingerprints and whatever else before the real police even showed up. I'm guessing there are laws in Japan about tampering with a crime scene?"

Imanishi laughed unconvincingly and gave me a smile a blind man could've seen through. "Why would I behave in so reckless a fashion?" he asked. "I have nothing but professional respect for my former colleagues in the department, and in fact—"

"Maybe you've got a grudge. Something to prove."

"That's the very definition of preposterous."

"Come off it," I said. "Neither one of us has time. A man has been killed in your hotel and you're speaking with the one person who can help you find out who did it. I'm not saying I know everything about the murder, but I know a few things you don't. And I'm gonna help you, but only if you quit bringing up the police every five seconds. And only if you quit following me around and taking pictures and don't come barging into my room while I'm in the shower. You can't afford to get on my nerves, Detective Imanishi-san, because there's nothing to stop me from checking out of this hotel and hopping on a plane back to Cleveland. And if I do that, any chance you have of solving this thing goes with me. I'm sure the Kinki Foundation could always stick my award in the mailbox."

By the time I was finished, Detective Imanishi was staring down at the carpet, head bowed like he was waiting for someone to come along and lop it off. Seeing him in his cheap wrinkled suit looking dead tired and defeated, I couldn't help but feel for him. He'd come in the room full of blustery confidence, sure that I'd fold once he laid out the evidence, and now he looked like a puppet hung in storage, limp and utterly lifeless. Maybe that's why I decided to say what I said next, decided against my better judgment to throw him the bone he nearly choked to death on.

"You're right about a few things," I began. "Richard Gale was definitely set up. And the woman in the stairwell was involved, and I have spoken to her. But the woman in the stairwell isn't who you think she is."

"Without evidence, everything you say is mere—"

"You're not the only one with evidence," I said, nodding to the satchel bag I'd taken from Kusanagi's office. Imanishi pretended he hadn't noticed it before. "But I need to work out exactly what went down that night before anything else bad happens. A young woman's life is at stake and it may already be too late to save her. But I have to try just the same. Which means you're going to have to back off and give me time."

Imanishi thought it through. I didn't see that he had much to think about, but I let him weigh his nonexistent options as I thought through a few things myself. Namely, how the hell I was going to find Emiko. In about an hour, Mr. Kusanagi was going to walk into a bloody mess and it wouldn't take him long to discover a very sensitive file had gone missing. He'd figure out who stole it easily enough. I knew the Komoriuta-kai would be coming for me and I knew the file was the best chance I had of keeping Emiko alive. Provided she was still alive in the first place.

Imanishi sighed. "Exactly what are you proposing?"

"Twenty-four hours," I said. "Give me twenty-four hours and I'll tell you everything I know. I'll turn over all the evidence I've gathered and tell you exactly what happened in your hotel. I'm gonna put all the documents in that safe over there, right under the minibar. You take one key, I'll keep the other. You don't hear from me by this time tomorrow, it's all yours."

"This puts me in a difficult position—"

"And that's another thing—I hear the words 'difficult' or 'complicated' one more time, the whole thing is off. Nothing personal, just a pet peeve of mine. We have a deal?"

The hotel detective closed his eyes, as if he couldn't bear to see himself nodding in agreement. Then he opened them and went about collecting his photos, pocketing them like a traveling salesman gathering his samples after another blown sale. I gave him a key to the room safe and listened to the shower still blasting away in the bathroom. Imanishi paused at the door.

"The PanCosmo Hotel has partnered with Spa Globe, one of the most popular *sento* in Osaka," he said in a hollow voice. "Should you wish to indulge in a hot springs bath. The multistoried facility offers a variety of bathing and relaxation pleasures, including Korean-style skin peels. Transportation is, of course, provided free of charge."

Thanks anyway, I told him. Imanishi shuffled out and closed the door gently behind him. I went to the peephole once he'd gone. Imanishi stood planted in the middle of the hall, arms dropped to his sides, chin on his chest. He was swaying on his feet, not exactly moving but not quite standing still. He stayed like that for a long time.

Sometime later the phone rang. I checked the caller ID, hoping the name Emiko would come up. It didn't. Instead it was Mr. Oyamada, no doubt wanting to find out if I'd talked to his wayward puppeteer of a son and when he could find out what I'd learned about the Sapporo Incident.

I let the phone keep ringing and picked through all the documents in Kusanagi's file, laying them out on the table and reading them one by one. Kusanagi might have been the best private investigator in the Kansai after all—he'd managed to gather a wealth of information during the pre-marriage investigation, though most of it was about Richard's father and his company rather than the Kansas kid himself. There was a copy of the software patent application for what would become Stratum. Articles from oil-industry trade journals about how Stratum had revolutionized oil exploration, streamlining the interpretation of seismic acquisition datasets, geophysical analysis, and hydrocarbon accumulation statistics—whatever that meant—to reduce drilling risks and cycle time. A gushing profile of CEO visionary Martin Gale in *Prairie Entrepreneur,* transcripts of a speech he had given at the Midwestern Regional Symposium on Energy Exploration.

The info on his son was a bit sketchier. A birth certificate dated June 10, 1978, from a St. Francis Hospital in Wichita, Kansas. Copies of Richard's mediocre school report cards, unremarkable SAT test scores, a college transcript from the University of Kansas. Then a gap in the records for the next year and a half. No known address or occupation.

Then suddenly Japan enters the picture, in the form of an acceptance letter congratulating him on his new position as teacher's assistant at Seisen International High School in Tokyo. Next, a copy of a letter informing him Seisen International had regrettably decided not to renew his contract and wishing him success in his future endeavors. Then a copy of another acceptance letter, this one from the less than prestigious Gamma Conversation Academy cheerfully welcoming him aboard, followed by a curt letter of dismissal written four months ago.

Nothing to suggest why some Kansas millionaire with an undergraduate degree in media studies would suddenly decide to move to Japan and teach people how to say "good morning" and "do you like ice cream?" The only link he had to the place was an Introduction to Japanese Literature class his junior year in college. He got a C minus.

The rest of the story I had to fill in myself. He met Kaori, fell for her, got hitched far too quickly and probably much too young. I assumed that he didn't let on about his money, kept it a carefully guarded secret. I decided it was possible Kaori herself might not even have known about it. Could be both of them married an exotic, half-formed fantasy and found the reality underneath a little wanting, she deciding he wasn't much like Leonardo Di Caprio or David Beckham after all, he discovering she was no demure geisha content to mince three steps behind him. Then again, it was hard to believe either of them was actually that stupid, especially Kaori. Maybe their separation had nothing to do with cultural differences or inflated expectations whatsoever, and they just found out too late they didn't get along that well as human beings, as man and woman. Or maybe it was just like Kaori said, and she simply made a pragmatic choice to leave him because he didn't want to go back to America. The big question was whether Kaori knew about the money, either before she married him or after she'd left him. Given the tone she used when discussing her family and the fact that she'd pointed me in the right direction, I had to assume she wasn't part of the plot. Unless, like hotel detective Imanishi said, the murderer unconsciously wanted to get caught.

Whatever the case, given the financial purgatory Inoue Development was trapped in thanks to the Chayamachi land deal and the Emerald Greens golf course fiasco, it was no mystery why the Inoue family had been in such a rush to marry off Kaori. For them, none of the other documents even mattered after they'd seen a copy of the trust bequeathing eighteen million dollars to be doled out in million-dollar increments each year after Richard Gale's twenty-first birthday.

Whatever Kaori and the Inoues and Kusanagi and the Komoriuta-kai might have been guilty of, I no longer thought they were part of a plot to kill Richard Gale. Hotel detective Imanishi was right about that—no yakuza hit would come off this sloppy or this complicated. The pictures of Emiko and Gale at the Horse of a Different Color proved they were part of a plot just the same, but it was the pictures of the other women that gave the game away.

And there were loads of pictures with loads of girls, at least six before Emiko came along. Aside from the one hidden-camera postcoital threesome snapshot taken inside a cheap love hotel, most pics were innocent enough— Richard and some girl having a drink, Richard and some girl dancing in a nightclub, Richard and some girl chatting on the street. In each he still wore his wedding ring, but the women didn't seem to mind. No doubt they were paid not to. They were all part of a pattern engineered to show some future court that Gale was habitually unfaithful to Kaori, who was, after all, still legally his wife. They were taken to prove that Kaori deserved alimony, and lots of it. Whether or not anyone could prove he actually slept with these women didn't matter much, especially given that most family court mediators were conservative types— retirees, bored housewives who probably imagined their own husbands were up to no good and who were probably right. Detective Kusanagi knew his audience.

That's where I figured Emiko must've come in. The

Komoriuta-kai probably provided the women, girls who worked for them in strip clubs and soaplands, maybe one or two flat-out prostitutes. But Detective Kusanagi wanted to establish that this Richard Gale was no mere dabbler in imported sex workers, hardened bar girls, or dopey coeds, but a regular home wrecker. Emiko was a married woman nearly ten years his senior, a woman with a terminally ill husband. I couldn't be certain why the Komoriuta-kai chose Emiko, but I had a few ideas. Maybe they knew she was vulnerable, knew she was in no position to say no. Her husband owed them money, was in a coma, and she had nobody to turn to for help.

What they didn't know was that she'd screw up the entire plan by killing Richard Gale with a straight razor. And much as I'd been trying to cobble together some version where that hadn't happened, as much as I wanted to believe Emiko's loopy story about falling asleep and suddenly waking up in the PanCosmo stairwell, it was becoming clear that Emiko had to be the one who killed him. I didn't understand why, but I hoped she was still alive to tell me.

Across the room, the phone started making noise. I expected it was Mr. Oyamada again, wondering if we were still on for tonight. Instead the caller ID read BALDERTON_KENNETH. Outside the fog was lifting but still had a long way to go.

Chapter Twenty

Tower of the Sun

Hiya there howdy! Do you know how to ski? asked little
Gamma-san, the academy's beaming star-
burst mascot, from a dangling ad as the train
headed off the map, past the Yodogawa River
all the way up into the hills to Suita. Outside
the city center, the shopping arcades, office
towers, and apartment blocks gave way to
the smoke-spewing factories and grim ware-
houses that earned Osaka its reputation as a
huge industrial manufacturing center. No
quaint little lanes or tree-lined avenues in
sight, just heavily trafficked freeways and
networks of crisscrossing railroad tracks.
Getting outside the JR Osaka Loop line was
like venturing backstage, seeing all the rigs
and pulleys that made the downtown magic
possible. It wasn't pretty, but behind the cur-

tain, things rarely are. Better to keep the heavy machinery and the underpaid stagehands in places like Indonesia, rural China, Mexico—off in the wings where the well-heeled ticket holders couldn't get a glimpse of them.

As I watched the factories give way to rolling foothills covered with toy houses I was starting to wish I hadn't agreed to meet with Curry. There was too much waiting back in the city proper and coming here felt like I was fleeing, seizing on a convenient excuse to get the hell away from it all. Then again, all my cards had already been played. All I could do was sit around and wait for Kusanagi to stumble over his dead dog, discover the file was missing, and put in a call to Mr. Noguchi and his muscle boys of the Komoriuta-kai. It was no use trying to run around the city looking for Emiko. If she wasn't in their clutches already, the Komoriuta-kai had no better chance of finding her than I did.

Besides, this trip to Suita wasn't exactly a social call.

When Curry phoned, he'd been tense, out of breath. He didn't say much, only that he needed to talk to me, that it was important. It was about Richard Gale, he said. Some information he'd learned over the weekend that might be related to his death. That very definitely was related to his death. He said he didn't know what to do, wanted to talk to me before he went to the police. It wasn't the sort of thing he felt comfortable discussing over the phone. He sounded shaken, and it was tough to imagine anything shaking Kenneth Balderton short of an earthquake. Then again, everything that had happened on this trip was pretty tough to imagine, starting way back with somebody giving me an award.

I transferred at Senrichuo then took the monorail in, exiting by the Expoland amusement park. No colorful lights and cheery music at this hour of the morning, just skeletal roller-coaster tracks and a motionless Ferris wheel. Must've been more Ferris wheels per capita in Osaka than anywhere in the world.

I was to meet Curry inside Banpaku Kinen Park, site of the 1970 World's Fair. The exposition was a big deal for Osaka, the first full-fledged international event they'd hosted since World War II, just the kind of thing the Kinki Foundation was hoping would come along again any minute. Now that the city had lost its thirty-million-dollar bid to host the 2008 Olympics, looked like they'd have to keep waiting.

I found Curry standing alone near the massive Tower of the Sun sculpture just inside the entrance. The thing looked like a giant totem pole with two outstretched wings and a grumpy face in the middle, topped off by some kind of golden disc. Curry stood with legs shoulder-width apart, arms crossed over his chest, gut spilling over his jeans. His face was fraught with concentration as he studied the monument. I walked up and stood next to him.

"What you think of it, then?" Curry asked.

I shrugged.

"Supposedly it's a good one. Famous and all that."

"I like sculptures that look like people."

"Yeah," said Curry. "Sod it, care for a walk?"

We headed west along a gravel path bordered by rolling open lawns, the only grass I'd seen outside the Nanko Bird Sanctuary. At the edge of the park a few of the exposition's original space-age, ultramodern buildings remained, left-over beacons of a future already come and gone. Along the way we passed a few joggers and one or two families but not much of anybody else. Curry apologized for dragging me all the way up here, said it was the only place he could think of he was certain we wouldn't be overheard. He walked with his shoulders stooped, hands pocketed in a blue Chelsea F.C. warm-up jacket so big they probably could've squeezed the team's entire back four inside. He tried small-talking me for a while, asking about the conference and how I was getting on, but neither of us was in the mood.

"Did you go to the funeral, then?" he asked.

I nodded. "Me and the richer half of Osaka."

"Big turnout, then? Many foreigners?"

I shook my head. "A few. Nobody from his family. I hope you didn't bring me all the way up here because you feel guilty about missing the service. It's a nice park and everything, but—"

"I need advice," he said. "Figured I could trust you. Turns out I didn't exactly have the full story in regard to Dickie, God rest his bastard soul. For one thing, I found out he'd been separated from his wife for more than six months."

I already knew this, but Curry didn't need to know just how entangled in the whole mess I'd become. As far as he was concerned, I didn't know anything he hadn't told me back when I'd shared a harmless curiosity about the American who'd died next door.

"How'd you find out?" I asked.

"Coming round to that," he said. "This Sunday I went round to the pubs with a mate I hadn't seen in ages. Well, you can hardly call this dive the pubs, but at any rate. Mate of mine works for a big advert firm writing copy for the overseas markets. We got right pissed and the subject of Dickie Gale comes up. He starts telling me all about how Gale had been shagging everything in sight since leaving Kaori. Getting a bit worked up about it, saying how it wasn't right, him doing that without giving Kaori a proper divorce."

"This mate of yours a friend of Gale's?"

"Dead opposite," he said. "Anyway, 1 didn't understand why he gave a toss about it. 1 try to change the subject, give him a bit of stick about Leeds United, Harry Viduka being a fat Aussie bastard and such. But he won't let Richard Gale lie. He's obsessing, getting angrier with every pint. Finally, 1 ask him why it's any of his concern."

Curry took a deep breath, going momentarily silent. We were walking by a carp pond where a group of small children watched the fish turn lazily in the water. "The thing of it is," Curry said, voice dropped as if he were afraid the kids would hear. "The thing of it is, Gale wasn't the only one sullying his marriage vows. Turns out this mate of mine was seeing Kaori. In secret. Had been seeing her for a while, even before Kaori and Dickie called it a day. Says nobody knew about it. And it gets worse."

At the north entrance of the park, a taxi rolled through the gate, slowly moving past a thicket of trees and disappearing from view near a building that signs announced as the National Museum of Ethnology. We turned right, headed the same direction.

"This mate of mine says he and Kaori wanted to elope," Gale said. "Move to England. Only Richard Gale stood in the way, right? Because he and Kaori were still married. He said, well, he told me that he came up with a plan. A plan involving some right dodgy characters. Kaori didn't even know about it. He said she still had a soft spot for Richard, so he'd worked the whole thing out with her old man. Mr. Inoue paid for Gale to be set up, photographed with various women. Only Mr. Inoue didn't want anything linking him to the business, so he'd paid cash to my mate. Mate deposited the cash in his postal account, transferred it to some detective agency, detective paid the bad guys. 1 told my mate, stop right there, not another word. I don't want in on this, and walls have ears and such. But he's right pissed by now, no stopping him. He tells me he never wanted Gale snuffed, just out of the picture. But now everything is fucked, and he's worried they'll trace it back to him, find out he was involved. He's gotta leave the country, he and Kaori both."

"This mate of yours have a name?" I asked.

Just then the taxi rolled up, out of nowhere. I got a sick feeling even before I even glanced over my shoulder as it pulled up beside us. The taxi stopped and the doors sprang open.

"What's this about?" Curry started.

Out came the Tin Man and two of his friends. Someone had been stupid enough to give the Tin Man a gun and the Tin Man was stupid enough to point it at me in the middle of a park full of witnesses. Except as I looked around I noticed there wasn't anybody watching. The Tin Man's gun was silver, glinting under the sunlight just like his suit. I hoped he wasn't stupid enough to pull the trigger and knew he probably was.

"They said I'm supposed to pick you up," the Tin Man droned.

"The fuck are you?" Curry asked, trying to mask the tremor in his voice. "The fuck is he?" he asked me.

"He's here for me," I said, stepping toward the Tin Man. "Stay out of it and let me deal with him."

"Stay out of it?" said Curry. The Tin Man lowered his gun and motioned his cronies to step back. It was only then I realized it wasn't fear I was hearing at the edge of Curry's voice, though he must have been afraid, afraid so long it had transformed into something else entirely.

"Bit late for that, you stupid cunt," Curry said.

Then something large thudded against my head and the world reeled sideways. I could smell the grass and something cracked my head again, sharper and louder. Time elapsed and I felt myself being lifted off the ground, carried up into the sky. Then I didn't feel much of anything at all.

Chapter Twenty-one

Emerald Greens

*T*he taxi was traveling over a hilly, deserted dirt road
flanked by large elms and overgrown weeds.
Two men were flanking me, while the Tin
Man sat in the front seat. Apparently my
mate Curry hadn't come along for the ride. I
had no idea how long I'd been out. There was
no meter on the cab, and no license, either,
not much of a surprise given who I was sharing a ride with. I reached a hand to feel for
bumps on my head and one of the guys
jammed me under the ribs with the barrel of
a gun, just to let me know he had one. Wherever we were looked like an ideal place to
dump a corpse.

We passed an abandoned bulldozer resting at an angle to the road, halfway up an
embankment, its wheels sunk into mud that

had dried long ago. About a minute later we made a left at a large sign with faded lettering.

Inoue Development Welcomes You to the Future Home of

EMERALD GREENS
GOLF AND SPORTING CLUB

GRAND OPENING SPRING 1997

A single low building lay in the clearing ahead. Beyond it, an expanse of weeds and dead grass rippled in the wind. About the only guy I could imagine playing here was Heath-cliff from *Wuthering Heights,* and as far as I knew, he didn't like golf any more than I did. I briefly considered the possi-bility I'd died and gone to hell, but ruled that out on ac-count of I didn't see any of the people who promised they'd meet me here.

The dirt road came to an end in front of a low structure made of cheap concrete, half-rotten plywood over all the windows, uninspired graffiti on the walls. A silver Jaguar was parked out front, but it looked like a piece of scrap metal compared to the Toyota Century limousine next to it. The Century was nothing like the Toyotas you saw in America—only six hundred were produced annually, and a fair share went to the Japanese royal family. A few years back, Toyota had taken the radical step of exporting the luxury vehicles by making a grand total of eight available on the international market. Two went to oil princes in Dubai. I thought about memorizing the license plates but my brain wasn't up to it and I didn't think it would do much good anyway. Who was I going to report them to, Imanishi the hotel detective?

The driver pulled up next to the other cars, then killed

the engine and popped the side doors open, bringing in a rush of cool air. The Tin Man got out first, then the guy on my left. The guy on my right stuck the gun in my ribs again to let me know it was my turn.

"I'm a little light on the fare," I said. "One of you guys spot me a few hundred yen? I hear you like lending money."

Another dig with the gun to let me know how funny I was. Someone pulled back the white curtain in the limo parked next to us. I saw only a hand and the outline of a face and then the curtain was closed again. The taller weeds bowed with the breeze, greeting me as I stepped from the taxi into a bright, sunny day. My mouth was dry and my head felt like it was filled with wet cement.

We walked down a dirt path to the building, through a doorless entryway, then down a hall littered with newspapers, snuffed-out cigarettes, beer cans. We turned into a room on the left, Tin Man leading the way, me and my two escorts trailing. Thin slivers of light slanted in from cracks in the boarded-up windows, struggling a few feet before succumbing to the darkness. As my eyes adjusted, I could see a single folding chair in the center of the floor. Five men in sunglasses and dark suits were positioned around the perimeter of the room. Against one wall sat a small man in a large wheelchair. It was so dark I couldn't make out much more than his general shape, but I knew who he was just the same. Mr. Tadamitsu Noguchi, head of the Komoriuta-kai, leader of the most feared criminal organization in the Kansai. Somehow being face-to-face with unmitigated evil was kind of a letdown, maybe because I couldn't even see his face. One of the guys forced me into the folding chair then backed away.

"So tHis is the mAn," Noguchi said. His voice was being masked by some kind of electronic device that made him sound like a robot from some cheesy sci-fi movie. "The mAn wiTh the quEstiOns. The quEstion mAn. You hAve quEstiOns for us, qUesTion mAn?"

"Sure. Where's Emiko?"

"A quEstiOn from the quEstion mAn," said Noguchi, remaining perfectly still in his wheelchair. A pinprick of light reflected from the center of his neck, probably a tiny mike they'd clipped to him in order to run his voice through whatever ridiculous speech-altering device they were using. "EmIko is slEeping. She's deAd tiRed. Found heR wandeRing the streETs in a daZe. SleepwAlkiNg. WiThoUt slEep tHe mInd eaTs itsElf. UntIl alL thAt's lEft is bAd ideAs. MaNy prOblEms sOlved when peOple sleEp on thEm. Alas, we'Re a slEep-deprIved nAtion."

Around the room the Komoriuta-kai flunkies all acted like they'd drawn "rigor mortis" in a game of charades. The feeble light made their faces look ashen, unreal. Zombies in sunglasses. I didn't see the Scarecrow among them.

"FoRgIve our enTourAge," said Noguchi. "Not meAnt as a shOw of foRce. PrEcauTionAry meAsuRes. Not tHe bEst of tImes nOw. ENemiEs wAnt to foRce us iNto reTirEment. After all wE've dOne. HAd to briNg you hEre. Best to stAy away frOm OsaKa. This cluBhoUse sicKens us. This gOlf coUrse. ConfUsion and misUndeRstAnding. Such a waSte. But that's wHy we gO on. To pUt eveRythIng in oRder. That's why we'Re heRe. To mAke things good."

"Short of raising the dead, I don't think it's possible."

"Now thEre's an idEa," said Noguchi. "RaIsing the deAd. What does eveRyone thiNk of that idea?"

The perimeter zombies tried to suppress their giggles but couldn't. Even Noguchi started laughing, a grating digital wheeze that echoed off the walls. I didn't see what was so funny, and as I watched Noguchi's outline, I noticed he was still completely immobile. No heaving shoulders, no bouncing head. Something wasn't right about the whole setup.

"Alright, enoUgh," said Noguchi. "Have soMe respect."

The zombies instantly sobered.

"HeRe's how we sEe it," Noguchi said. "You oWe us oNe dog. One dOg and a ceRtain cAse file. But we cAn coMpromIse. You giVe us tHe file, we can foRget the dOg."

"I want to see Emiko."

"He waNts to see Emiko," echoed Noguchi. "SomEone arRange for him to see EMiko."

One of the perimeter zombies went to work on his cell phone.

"He's arraNging for you to sEe Emiko," Noguchi told me. "We'Re reasOnaBle. But we neEd thAt file. Put this whOle thiNg to bed. No neEd for any mOre killiNg. We'Re sorRy for whAt happEned. We coulDn't haVe known Emiko would do whAt she did."

"You're saying she killed him?"

"Too bAd. But we can't tell craZy people jUst by looKing."

"Why would she do it?"

"We cAn't read miNds."

"Why did you even have to use her?" I asked, even though I had my hunches about her role in the scheme. "You must have plenty of women to do your bidding. Why get a civilian involved?"

"TheRe's a saYing," said the voice. " 'A man's disSipaTion can alwAys be traCed to his wife's caRelessNess.' Emiko's husBand owed us moNey. We weRe told a marRied womAn was neEded. She seEmed perfect and we woulDn't have to pay heR. We gaVe Emiko a chance to maKe gOod. She made veRy bAd."

"You should've left her alone."

"She coulD've said no."

"Except you would've killed her husband."

"We doN't go arouNd killiNg," said Noguchi. "But heR husBand is a goNer. He's not coMing back. We'Re neVer getTing what's owed us. The best we could hope wAs that Emiko would do some woRk. Help offSet his nonpeRforming loAn. We couldn't haVe knoWn Emiko was siCk. Wait a minute, heRe she is nOw."

One of the zombies stepped forward and handed me his cell phone. Glowing on the display screen was a matchbox-sized image of Emiko. She was sitting, slumped on a couch I recognized from her apartment, her face unreadable. Her eyes were open but there was no way to tell whether she was alive or dead.

"TheRe she is," said Noguchi. "Now you'Ve seen Emiko."

I gazed at the image, let it burn into my mind. The picture could have been taken minutes or hours or days ago, but it was definitely her. I tossed the phone back to the zombie who'd given it to me. He missed it and it clattered to the ground. The zombie got on his hands and knees and groped for the phone, looking like a blind man in his stupid sunglasses.

"We neEd thAt file," said Noguchi. "So we can put everYthing to bEd. We've maDe good. Now it's your tuRn."

"Not good enough," I said. "I need to talk to Emiko, and not on the phone, either. I need to see her in person, see that she's alive."

"She's aliVe," said Noguchi.

"You'd better hope she is."

"She's sleePing."

"Because if she's dead, you're never getting that file."

"We don't go aRound killing peOple."

"Maybe you figure killing Emiko will insure this thing stays buried. Because if the police get to her, this whole alimony-extortion entrapment scheme you and the Inoues and Kusanagi and apparently my good pal Curry so harmoniously collaborated on might get exposed."

"Emiko is siCk. The police woN't belieVe a woRd."

"You're right," I said. "Unless she has evidence to back her up. Which is why the file is so important to you. The pictures, the articles, the documents—it's all laid out so nice and neat even some backwoods police box troll from the Mie Prefecture could put it together. I've left the file in a secure location. A trusted colleague of mine is under instructions to retrieve it if he doesn't hear from me by a certain time. Then the whole thing gets handed over to the cops. I haven't squealed yet, so you still have a chance to—how did you put it?—make good."

Noguchi went silent, thinking it through.

"You'Ve told no oNe?"

"Not yet," I said. "But the clock is ticking."

"AlriGht," he said. "SomeOne take hIm to see Emiko."

The Tin Man stepped from behind me, motioned me to my feet. A shaft of light caught his shiny suit, the reflection partially illuminating Noguchi's face. It wasn't pretty. His mouth was slack, drooped to one side like it was sliding off his face, while his eyes were wide open and staring off into nowhere. I don't know who I'd just been talking with, but it clearly wasn't Mr. Noguchi. He was little more than a ventriloquist's dummy. The wet spittle clinging to the edge of his mouth was all that kept me from thinking he was already a corpse. The Tin Man started toward the doorway and the light went with him, leaving Mr. Noguchi again masked in shadow.

he Tin Man walked a few paces behind me, telling me which way to turn as we moved down the hall. The two of us took a different route out of the building and wound up out back in an open field choked with weeds and yellowing grass that was probably once intended to be a fairway. The sunlight was blinding after being in the stale little room. I started around the corner, toward where the cars were parked, but the Tin Man told me to stop.

"We're supposed to go this way," he said. I turned around to see which way he meant. The Tin Man had his gun drawn and was pointing out into the empty field. In the distance a weeping willow moved slowly in the breeze.

"You sure?"

His bullet-shaped head jerked up and down and he waved the gun again, just to make sure it registered. The gun didn't worry me as much as the way he wouldn't meet my eyes. I patted down my pockets and discovered I'd been stripped of my wallet, and my cell phone. I didn't take it as a good sign.

We didn't walk far, maybe a hundred yards. I knew where to stop before he even told me. A rectangular patch of freshly turned dirt sat to my left, the earth still black and moist. I guessed this was their idea of taking me to see Emiko. In front of me was a newly dug hole, the same dimensions and maybe five feet deep. The Tin Man told me to get inside it.

I wondered where I'd miscalculated.

"Get in the hole," the Tin Man repeated when I didn't move. I could hardly hear him. His voice was frayed at the edges, half lost to the wind. I turned to face him. All around grass rippled in the breeze but the Tin Man's suit didn't budge. "They said you're supposed to get in the hole."

"That's a goddamn grave."

"No more talk," hissed the Tin Man. "Get in the hole! Get in the hole!" While he howled like some deranged golfer trying to will a ball into the cup I judged the distance between us. He'd get a shot off, no question, but I knew if I got in that hole I'd never get out again. The idea of dying on a golf course bugged me even more than the idea of dying itself. There's absurd and there's just plain ridiculous.

But my mind was racing too fast to allow my body to take the only chance I had left. Why were they willing to risk killing me without getting the file first? Why hadn't the file been enough to keep Emiko alive?

And then I saw the hole in my thinking, a hole big enough to bury us both. Just as Emiko's story without the file would mean nothing to the police, the file without Emiko attached was harmless. There were no direct links to the Komoriuta-kai in any of the documents. The girls Gale had slept with had no doubt been provided by the gang, but it's not as if they filled out invoices, issued receipts, punched time clocks. Even if the police were able to track down the women based on a handful of photographs, it would take a long time, and the Komoriuta-kai were smart enough to cover their tracks. Take away that Emiko had been visited by the Scarecrow, followed by the Tin Man, and coerced by Mr. Noguchi into sleeping with Richard Gale, and half the story was missing. Anyone coming across the file would take it for routine detective work. A premarriage investigation, a surveillance job when the marriage went sour. No direct evidence that Emiko had killed Gale. Nothing that proved he had even been set up—

not by Kusanagi, Mr. Inoue, the Komoriuta-kai, Curry, or anybody else.

"I'm supposed to fire one warning shot," the Tin Man said. "To show I'm serious. They told me to say you have one last chance to save your life. You're supposed to tell me where the file is."

File or no file, I was finished. They'd staged the meeting to find out how much I knew first and who else I'd told, information I'd gleefully volunteered with the slightest of promptings. File or no file, I was nothing but a liability now. I wondered what would have happened if I hadn't broken into Kusanagi's office, whether Emiko would still be alive. I wondered what was going through Emiko's mind when she killed Richard Gale in the first place, how someone like her could've gone crazy enough to cut a man's throat and slash his face to ribbons with his own razor blade. I wondered what the hell actually happened in Sapporo. I even wondered what happened in the final act of *The Whispering Goat,* but mostly I wondered how it all would've turned out if I'd have told Mr. Oyamada that I was worn out from my trip, needed some sleep, if I'd said maybe we could get drinks another time, offered him a rain check. Even if I lived, I'd never have all the answers.

"This is your last chance," said the Tin Man.

"Have a heart."

"Tell me where the file is."

I shook my head. "You're going to kill me either way."

The Tin Man didn't contradict me, I'll say that much for him. He even looked ashamed as he raised his arm above his head, pointed the pistol at the sky. The breeze had died out. The grass, the weeping willow, and everything else were absolutely still. The Tin Man tightened his face.

"I'm firing that warning shot now," he said.

There was a pop, then nothing but the far-off sounds of distant traffic. That would've been my best chance to rush him, try to make him miss the next shot, hope that I could wrestle the gun away before he got off a third, but in the next moment he'd already lowered the gun and trained it at my chest. His eyes were filling with tears and his face was twitching around so much I half-expected him to say it was going to hurt him more than it would hurt me. I felt my legs go weak but willed myself to remain standing. I bit down on my tongue to keep from crying out, tried to force my eyes to stay open. That was the hardest part, making myself watch until the very end. The Tin Man tightened his grip on the gun, his finger tensed on the trigger as he squinted his eyes.

Then there was a single crack and his eyes sprang open.

Before I could even wonder at the sound, I registered the funny look on the Tin Man's face. The top of his head had blossomed out, erupting in red. The gun went off with a loud pop but it was no longer trained on me and the bullet sank into the ground. The Tin Man's eyes rolled back. He dropped the gun and didn't so much collapse as implode, crumpling as if every bone in his body had simultaneously slipped out of joint.

I jumped back, nearly stumbling into the grave as I looked around to see who'd shot him. But my rescuer was nowhere in sight. The breeze resumed its dance with the willow tree. Blood issued silently from the hole in the top of the Tin Man's skull, trailing down his head, soaking into the earth.

I didn't waste any time. I grabbed the gun, shoved it in my waistband, then went through the dead man's pockets. I found my wallet, the PanCosmo cell. For good measure, I took his wallet, his phone, and a set of car keys, then rolled his body into a grave meant for mine. All of this I did only half-aware, still numbed by the event I'd witnessed. I knew the physical components at play—gravitational force, wind direction, the bullet's velocity—but I couldn't fathom how they'd combined into such a miraculous, one-off equation. But there was simply no other explanation. The Tin Man had just been killed by his own warning shot.

Chapter Twenty-two

The Average Person's Mouth

*T*he taxi and the Toyota Century were long gone, but the Jaguar was still there when 1 made it back. 1 hit the button on the key chain and the lights came on, throwing twin beams over the concrete building. No signs of life from within. Should've figured the silver Jaguar belonged to the Tin Man. He seemed to like all things shiny and expensive.

1 got in the car, slid the key in the ignition, then headed down the dirt road, anxious to put as much distance as possible between Emerald Greens and myself. 1 hit a two-lane blacktop and turned left. 1 had no idea where 1 was. 1 didn't care. Anywhere was better than where 1 should've been.

1 thought about Curry as 1 drove. 1 didn't understand why he'd let me get involved,

why he told me as much as he had about Kaori Inoue and Richard Gale, even sent me to the funeral, when he was a part of the whole setup. Maybe he'd contact with me as a way of keeping tabs, finding out how much I already knew, so if I got too close they could stick me in an unmarked grave at an unfinished golf course in the middle of nowhere. But now I knew why Kaori had volunteered so much information. She really hadn't known how Gale died. She must've had her suspicions given the warning she gave me about asking too many questions, but she wasn't part of the plot. She'd been telling the truth all along.

And I thought about Emiko. How she'd lied to me, pretended she hadn't even known Richard Gale was dead. She might have been trying to repress her memory of the whole night, might've suffered some kind of psychotic break, or some posttraumatic amnesia, or any number of fancy psychological maladies, but even she knew she killed him. She knew because she'd cleaned up after herself. I remembered the way her hair was wet that first night I'd found her lying in the stairwell. Remembered the way her lipstick looked freshly applied. There would have been an awful lot of blood. No one could hack up Richard the way they had without getting covered with it. She'd killed him. Then she'd taken a shower, put on makeup. She'd buttoned up her raincoat to cover the bloodstains on her dress. She'd taken the stairs because they were dark and there was less chance of passing anyone on the way down. Why she pretended to be sleeping, I couldn't say. But I kept remembering the way she looked at me that night, her eyes pulsing with fear, swimming in confusion. And the sadness. I hadn't imagined the sadness, I knew that much now. Since that first encounter I'd spent time looking into those eyes, looked deep and long until maybe I'd been blinded, made unable to see the facts for what they were. Emiko had killed Richard Gale and I'd helped her get away with it. Until the *yakuza* caught up to her, caught up to us both. Then I'd helped them kill her. By stealing the file and threatening to expose it all, I'd given them no other choice.

Just then the phone started ringing. But it wasn't my phone from the PanCosmo Hotel. The car was filled with some cutesy Morning Musume song the Tin Man had picked for a ringtone. I couldn't remember the words but it was a big hit, something about a young country girl who'd moved to big-city Tokyo and got her heart broken. No name on the caller ID screen, just a number and a text message.

ARE WE GOOD?

I waited for a red light, then typed a response.

WE'RE GOOD.

The dashboard clock read 4:34 P.M. and the winter light was beginning to flatten. I hit the send button and hoped the message bought me some time. My plan was to get back to the hotel, pack my bags, and get out of Osaka before they figured out I was still alive. The song chirped inside the car again and I picked up. Another text message.

THE FILE?!?

I thought for a moment before typing my response. They still wanted the file, even though both Emiko and I were presumably dead? Maybe it meant they were just trying to tie up all the loose ends, but maybe it meant something else entirely. Maybe it meant Emiko was still alive.

We don't go around killing people, the voice posing as Noguchi's had told me, and there was a grain of truth in it. Killing was risky, and the *yakuza* were still businessmen at their core, still naturally risk averse. Even someone as disconnected from the world as Emiko couldn't just disappear without anyone noticing. At the very least, the hospital staff would wonder why she'd suddenly stopped visiting her husband. Questions would be raised, neighbors interviewed. As long as Emiko didn't pose a threat, killing her was unnecessary, even reckless.

The only problem with this line of thinking was they'd decided to kill me *whether they got the file or not.* But even this made a certain sense. Emiko might have killed Richard Gale, but I still knew more about the plot that led up to his murder than she did, which meant I was the greater problem. She didn't know about Detective Kusanagi, Kaori Inoue, Curry. She couldn't see beyond her own role in the drama, didn't realize she was just a bit character in a larger plot, albeit a character whose wild improvisational turn had stolen the show. The only way she could harm the Komoriuta-kai was by confessing to the cops, and given that she'd lied to me, she obviously still had a capacity for self-preservation.

THE FILE?!?

I studied the two-word message, nearly rear-ending the car in front of me. I'd planned to leave the file for hotel dick Imanishi, let him puzzle over it until his brain exploded. I'd figured it contained nothing that could save me or anybody else now, but maybe I was mistaken. I'd been wrong just about every step of the way so far, was on a regular hot streak in that department. I typed in my response.

PANCOSMO HOTEL. ROOM 1142.

The reply came almost the moment I hit the send button.

WE'RE THERE. GET TO IMAZATO. PUT HER TO BED.

I pulled over the car and dug through my wallet until I found Imanishi's card. I dialed the number on the Pan-Cosmo cell phone and waited. I didn't even let Imanishi get in a greeting because once he started talking he was hard to stop. I told him to get the file out of the safe. I told him the men responsible for Richard Gale's death were on their way to the hotel, would be showing up in an hour, maybe earlier. There was no time to waste. I'd explain everything later, but right now he needed to call the Osaka police and make sure they were there waiting when the Komoriuta-kai showed up. I told him to take every precaution he deemed necessary because I doubted they would give themselves up without a fight.

"Permit me one question," Imanishi began. "These men—"

"No time," I said, and hung up. Two minutes later I ditched the car at the side of the road near the first train station I saw. I still had no idea where I was, but the trains would be faster than driving anyway. The route map was a tangle of color-coded lines and unfamiliar names, but all lines eventually led to Osaka the way all rivers flow into the ocean. I bought a ticket and made my way to the platform. Imanishi called twice while I waited, but I ignored him the first time and switched off the phone the second. If the train was on time, and the trains were always on time, I'd be in the Imazato neighborhood in about ninety minutes. Another five minutes, I'd be at Emiko's apartment. Everything would be over in less than two hours. Everything except that wrongheaded hot streak I was on.

As the sun went down on another unremarkable Tuesday evening, Imazato was a vision of idealized community. Men coming home from work, briefcases in hand, satisfaction of an honest day's work on their faces. Women carrying bags of fresh vegetables bought at charming corner grocers, hurrying home to cook warm meals for their families. Smiling schoolkids in their sailor uniforms and funny caps, dogs wagging their tails, sniffing the air as they trotted past family-owned restaurants. It looked like one great big happy village where all the old people were good-natured and wise, where all the men were hardworking and dependable, the women nurturing and kind, the children carefree and healthy. A village where everyone ate well and slept well and looked out for each other and nothing truly terrible ever happened.

I waited for someone to buzz themselves into Emiko's apartment complex, then came in behind them while the gate was still open, trying my best to look like an upstanding citizen. As I walked up the stairs to Emiko's apartment I could hear the sound of laughter on TVs, the gentle clanging of pots and pans. I smelled sizzling meats and bubbling soups. Only Emiko's unit was silent. Through the peephole I could see a light was on. I knocked on the door.

"Who is it?" replied a male voice inside.

I didn't know the Tin Man's name, so I had to improvise. "They said I'm supposed to come here," I said in a voice as deep and dumb as I could muster. "They said I'm supposed to come put her to bed."

"About fucking time," said the voice. "Door's unlocked."

I removed the gun from my waistband and walked inside.

A light shone from the bathroom down the hall. I heard drawers being opened and closed. The living room was dark but I could make out Emiko's form. She was lying on the floor, her back turned and curled like an embryo. She wasn't moving. I held the gun tight and rounded the corner.

A stick man with dirty yellow hair and an ugly brown suit was squatting on the floor, his back to me as he rummaged under the bathroom sink using only his left hand while he kept his right tucked snugly under his opposite armpit. There was a bad smell in the air. A smell like gasoline. The Scarecrow didn't even bother looking up at me as he spoke.

"What took you so long?" he asked.

"Is she dead?"

"I doubt it. Bitch bit my fucking hand." He withdrew his left hand from his armpit, waved it above his head without sparing a glance my way. A flap of discolored skin hung loose between his thumb and forefinger and blood was trailing down his wrist. "I'm telling you, this suicide thing isn't gonna work."

"Why not?"

"My fucking hand is why not." The Scarecrow tucked the injured appendage back under his armpit. He pulled out a bottle from under the shelf, saw it was hair gel, tossed it aside. "Blood is everywhere is why not. Signs of struggle. I had to choke her to make the pills go down, pin her to the floor until they took effect. There's gonna be bruising and she bit my hand and I don't even know if she swallowed enough pills to kill her. She's got my DNA on her fucking teeth. That sound like a suicide to you?"

"So what now?"

"Peroxide or Mercurochrome or some shit is what now." He grunted. "Have any idea how many bacteria live in the average person's mouth? This whole show is amateur hour, start to finish. Getting that demented woman involved. You know why she said she killed that guy?"

I grunted negative.

"Some nightmare she was having is why." The Scarecrow gave up on the search under the counter. I kept the gun trained on him as he rose, but he still didn't look up, instead resuming his panicked search in the corner, tearing through a shelf lined with bottles of shampoo, cleaning products, boxes of contact lens solution. "Claims she doesn't even remember doing it. Said she was dreaming about some guy with the face of a wolf, that she had to kill this wolf or some shit like that in the dream. Next thing she knew, here's this fucker with his face hacked up and she's holding a razor blade. You believe that shit? Goes to show you, even the normal-looking ones."

Scarecrow knocked over a bottle of men's cologne, cursed as it shattered on the floor. I tried to wrap my mind around what he'd just said, but my mind was stretched taffy thin as it was.

"You still got that gun?" he said.

I grunted positive.

"Shoot her."

"But they said—"

"You're right, too much noise. Strangle her. New boss will have to live with it. I'd do it myself but my fucking hand. We can cut her up in the shower. Find a couple suitcases or something, haul her out. I saw a golf bag in there we can use. Speaking of golf, what about that other guy?"

"They said I was supposed to kill him."

"Supposed to? What's 'supposed to' mean?"

"Means I had a little bad luck."

The Scarecrow finally looked up, registering the gun before he even realized he wasn't talking to his pal the Tin Man. He just sighed and clasped his hands on top of his scraggly dandelion head without even being asked. "Wonderful," he said. "The inmates have taken over the asylum."

I backed away and motioned him down the hall. I kept him two paces ahead of me until we reached the living room about three steps later. I flicked on the lights, told him to stand against the back wall. There were signs of struggle alright. The heated table was overturned and what was left of the pills were spilled across the hardwood floor. Emiko's eyes were closed. A sleeve of her white blouse was torn, one corner of her mouth was smeared with blood, and a small, purplish bruise was forming on the right side of her neck.

"What now?" said the Scarecrow. Blood from his hand was getting all over his hair, streaking it red. His lipless grin made me think of all those bacteria in the average person's mouth. I'd guess he had the average person beat. I turned my attention back to Emiko, watched the slow rise and fall of her chest. She was still alive.

"What kind of pills you give her?"

"Sleeping pills."

"How long ago she take them?"

"Maybe half an hour," he said.

I nodded. She still had time.

"Maybe an hour. Two hours, a minute ago. Last week."

"Stop talking."

I didn't know how much time she had left, but I knew I needed to wake her up, get her to a hospital. The problem was what to do with the Scarecrow, and the Scarecrow knew it. Something pulsed behind his eyes and his grin went wider as he sensed my indecision the way piranha register vibrations in the water.

"You don't have much time," he said.

"Shut up and let me think."

"I'm just saying," he said. "They're gonna find out you're not dead, you know. This is the first place they're gonna come looking."

"Not another word."

"Fine," he said. "But her breathing is getting shallow. She's starting to turn blue. That's no good. You know, now that I think about it, I'm pretty sure it was at least two hours ago I gave her the pills."

"Are you *trying* to get yourself shot?"

He shook his yellow head. "I'm just saying."

I took another glance at Emiko.

"Your phone," I told the Scarecrow. "Nice and slow."

He rolled his eyes and dug around awkwardly inside his jacket. My finger tensed on the trigger, ready to fire if he drew a gun or a knife or nail clippers or anything besides the cell phone. He removed the phone, held it extended in his left palm. I still didn't like the way he was looking at me, as if any second people were going to pop out from behind the furniture with party hats and noisemakers. I leveled the gun at his forehead, took his phone away, then moved a step back.

"What are you doing?" he asked.

"Calling an ambulance." I had the gun in one hand so I had to open the phone and dial with my thumb. Like trying to eat with one chopstick. I should've just let the Scarecrow dial, but I was afraid he'd try to put in a call to his cronies or test out some other bad idea. Guy looked like he had a brain bulging with bad ideas. I'd dialed the first two digits of the 1-1-9 emergency number when I saw a flash of movement.

The Scarecrow leaped forward, seizing the barrel end of the gun before I could move. It was a suicidally stupid gambit, but maybe he figured it was his only chance, figured I was going to kill him anyway. That's the problem with thugs—they assume everyone thinks like them, so they're always paranoid, always conjuring violence out of thin air. I had no intention of shooting him, but my intentions didn't matter. I held fast, tensing my grip as he yanked and pulled. The Scarecrow was still wearing that checkmate grin on his face as the bullet ripped through his throat, went out the back of his neck, and smashed into a porcelain statue of Winnie-the-Pooh on the bookcase.

Both hands went to his neck as he fell back against the bookcase. The gun clattered to the floor, skittered underneath the couch and went off again, firing into the wall. Blood gushed through the cracks of his fingers, poured over his hands, down his suit. I still had the phone in my hand. I dialed the final digit, put the phone to my ear. The Scarecrow coughed a wet spray. My stomach knotted and I had to look away to keep from getting sick. The dispatcher came on the line.

"May I have your location?"

I blanked.

"What seems to be the problem?"

The sound of the gun hadn't stirred Emiko. I didn't think anything would. The Scarecrow was all wheezes and burbles, his mouth opening and closing on nothing. There was no saving him. Emiko still had a chance, but it was going to cost her. There was too much to explain and I wasn't going down for this.

"Is this an emergency? You dialed the emergency number."

"Help," I said.

"What is the trouble, sir?" prompted the dispatcher.

"I've been shot."

"Sir? Where are you? I need your location."

"She shot me in the neck . . ."

"I need to know where you are."

"Imazato. She just fucking shot me."

I gagged and sputtered for the dispatcher then tossed the phone into the Scarecrow's lap without even bothering to hang up. He followed the phone with his eyes, then looked up at me, showing a faded version of that condescending smile. He'd given up trying to stop the blood with his hands, given up on everything. The whole apartment complex was completely silent. Good. That meant the neighbors had heard the gun go off, the shattered Winnie-the-Pooh, the Scarecrow hitting the floor, the gun going off again. With any luck, one of them would call 1-1-9, report shots fired. With any luck, the dispatcher would put two and two together, realize the calls came from the same building. I hoped they'd be able to save her but I wasn't going to wait around and find out. I left Emiko the way I should've left her all those nights ago. Sleeping on the floor, a small body curled in on itself.

Chapter Twenty-three

Escaping Osaka

*I*n the train I could feel eyes roving me like flies swarming a corpse. It was like one of those nightmares where you suddenly realize you're naked and you hope no one notices the exact moment everyone notices. Only in this case naked would've been better. Better than having blood on my clothes, flecks spotting my cheeks and forehead. Better than smelling of gunpowder and panic. Better than having a face that broadcast these thoughts to everyone on the train, made them as clear as the woman's sugary voice announcing each stop on the Sennichimae line.

But there was no blood and no one was staring. Not many people, anyway. Mostly just one junior high school kid, and he wasn't even staring so much as glancing up at me every three or four seconds until our eyes met, at which point his would sink again into his comic book. Maybe he wondered how a guy could sweat so much in January, but no one knew I'd killed anyone, framed anyone, fled from a crime scene. If anyone was looking at me, it was just because I was the only white guy on the train. I was getting the *gaijin* stare, a feature of life in Japan that ex-pats found by turns flattering or amusing or irritating or threatening, depending on their temperament and who was doing the staring. While I played eyeball tag with the kid I tried to push disturbing images of the Scarecrow from my mind by wondering how Richard Gale would've reacted to the attention he no doubt received in one form or another on an almost daily basis. Strangers speaking to him as they would to a child, expressing surprise, confusion, or even disapproval if he answered in Japanese. New acquaintances constantly asking if he liked Japanese food, being skeptical that he could truly enjoy sushi or soba, marveling that he knew how to work chopsticks. Well-intentioned neighborhood policemen giving him an escort when directions were all he'd asked for, waiters and salespeople avoiding him out of sheer embarrassment, terror-stricken at the possibility of misunderstanding. Children pointing, old women tugging at the hairs on his arm, and young women—well, I guess I already knew how he dealt with the attentions of young women.

From what Curry and Kaori and even Emiko had told me about Richard's desperately wrongheaded assimilation attempts, such reminders that he'd never really belong would've rankled him. He could read *kanji* and stomach natto paste and even marry into a prominent Osaka family, but his own skin would constantly betray him, expose him as an outsider.

For someone bent on immersion, the PanCosmo was a funny choice of residences. It was a sophisticated international five-star hotel, a sovereign zone where most employees spoke English, were used to dealing with all kinds of foreigners, did everything they could to drain the voltage from culture shock. He could live the entire six months there and never have to say so much as *domo arigato* or worry about the myriad of ways he could offend his neighbors without even trying. In a way, his being at the Pan-Cosmo made perfect sense. He wouldn't be the resident oddity, just another guest, albeit one whose long-term stay at such exorbitant rates probably merited more special treatment than he knew. At the PanCosmo, he could retreat a safe distance from the culture that both attracted and eluded him, give himself enough space to create the illusion of belonging.

Deluding himself also meant never asking why women were suddenly throwing themselves at him after he separated from Kaori. Given that he was twenty-three, maybe he just figured he was on one hell of a lucky streak and thought it best not to ask too many questions, just enjoy the ride while it lasted. But part of him had to know something was going on, and there were all sorts of ways he could have spun it. If he didn't like the idea that maybe women saw him as a curiosity, an exotic conquest, he could've reversed it, convinced himself that their sudden interest was a form of acceptance, a sign that he was finally overcoming the barriers, real and imagined, that kept so many lonely ex-pats from ever really integrating into society.

Could've been all or none of these, I'd never know. Hard to guess what a guy could be thinking when all you have to go on is one elevator ride, some pictures, and a few secondhand accounts. And how much could those accounts even be trusted, given that one came from an ex-wife, another from a rival who'd participated in an entrapment scheme, a third from the woman who'd killed him?

Just as I'd never get a grip on who Richard Gale really was, I realized his death was never going to make any sense, either. The closer I got to it, the further into unreality it receded. Ever since I'd walked into the PanCosmo Hotel, events seemed to piggyback on one another in violent free association, each generating its own distorted echo. I cut myself shaving and meet Richard in an elevator. Richard gets killed with a razor and I encounter his killer in a stairwell. A razor appears in a puppet play called *The Whispering Goat* and Richard's killer flees the theater. The puppeteer has a twin who was killed by a dog, I kill a dog with a razor. The puppet wears a blond wig, the woman who killed Richard wears a red wig, Richard's ex-wife wears a black wig. A man in a coma owes money to a man in a wheelchair. I call one gangster the Tin Man, Emiko calls another the Scarecrow. The Tin Man points a gun at Emiko's husband's head as a warning, the Tin Man later gets hit in the head with his own warning shot. Mr. Oyamada has a polyp in his throat, Richard gets his throat slashed, Mr. Noguchi speaks through a mike device attached to his neck, the Scarecrow gets shot through the neck. I help Emiko get away with murdering one man, then frame her in the death of another.

Every detail recurring in a series of funhouse-mirror reflections, every event replicated in layers, shot through with schizophrenic logic, merging and accelerating toward some inexorable conclusion. I had to get out of Osaka, escape while I still had a chance. I should've gone straight from Emerald Greens to the Kansai International Airport, but two hours ago I still thought I had some say in what happened next, could keep events from spiraling further out of control. The Scarecrow's death changed that. I hadn't wanted to shoot him and he got himself shot just the same. And there would be inconsistencies if the police took a close look. Emiko's prints weren't on the gun. The bullet trajectory would be off, the timing of Emiko's overdose questionable in relation to the timing of the gunshots. My prints would be on the gun and the Scarecrow's cell phone. At least one witness had seen me entering the building and someone probably saw me leaving. For all I knew, half the residents of the apartment complex were leaning out their windows, taking pictures with their cell phones as I fled. This kid on the train who kept staring at me might remember a jumpy-looking *gaijin* who boarded at Imazato and kept staring at him.

But it wasn't the police I was worried about. It was my own lack of control, my inability to extricate myself from a situation that had nothing to do with me. It was the way everything I did rippled with unseen consequences, sent hidden machinery into motion. *Stay out of it?* echoed Curry's voice in my head. *Bit late for that, you stupid cunt.*

Detective Imanishi and the police would have to figure everything out for themselves. They never would, but I didn't care. Mr. Oyamada and Master Toyomatsu and Tetsuo and Kiyoshi would have to come to grips with the Sapporo Incident all on their own. The Kinki Foundation could give my award to the runner-up. And Emiko . . .

In the end, I'd done all I could to save her life. That's what I kept telling myself. Had I not gone to Imazato, the Scarecrow would have killed her, one way or another. At least now she had a chance. Maybe if I'd never stolen the file from Kusanagi's she wouldn't have been in danger.

Maybe if I'd left her sleeping there in the stairwell that night, none of this would have happened. But she had killed a man after all. Nightmare or no nightmare, she'd drawn the blade across his throat, opened an eight-inch gash in his neck. She'd slashed again and again and hacked and cut and swung the blade until blood seeped from thirty-two separate wounds in his face. Then she'd taken a shower. She'd put on a raincoat and walked away.

And yet I still thought of her as a victim. I knew she'd killed Gale and I knew she'd lied to me about it, but some hitch in my thinking just wouldn't allow me to think of her as guilty. I'd like to believe it wasn't just because she was beautiful. Wasn't just because I felt sorry for her. Sorry that her husband was lying in a hospital bed locked in his own damaged brain, sorry for the way she'd slipped into a shadowy world most of us will never see. My relationship with Emiko may not have been deep and it may not have even been real, but I felt a connection. When the Scarecrow told me Emiko had killed Richard while in a nightmare, I could almost see it. Not her attacking Richard, but the nightmare itself. I could picture the old man trembling in bed, hear his whispered gibberish, see his wolfish grin. I saw the whole scene so clearly it was almost as if the dream were my own, as if it had been waiting there all along in some otherwise unreachable part of my subconscious.

The train rocked and squealed on its tracks as it plummeted underground into the darkness. A shudder ran through me and I had to grab a strap dangling overhead to keep from falling. The kid was staring at me now, no question, and I couldn't blame him. My face must've looked ghoulish in the dull green light as I suddenly realized I simply couldn't leave Osaka. Not now that I finally knew the answers, or at least where to look for them. Even as I lurched from the train at Namba station and ran through the underground tunnel to the Midosuji subway platform I could hardly believe what I was thinking. Maybe Tetsuo Oyamada had been right all along. Maybe it was just like the Nocturne Theater manifesto said: *the truth lies in the ambiguities of the subconscious.*

I was in Tennoji but may as well have been in Tennessee or Timbuktu for all I noticed of the scenery. I climbed back to the surface of the world and then made my way down the hill to the colony of love hotels bordering the park. For the last half an hour the rational part of my brain had been throwing a tantrum, kicking and screaming and telling me in no uncertain terms where I belonged was in the departure lounge of Kansai International, sipping on a cocktail in the airport bar and clutching a one-way ticket to anywhere else. By now that part of my mind had pretty much given up, resigned itself to sitting in the corner with a dour expression and awaiting its chance to say I told you so.

The lights were off at the Rainbo Leisure Hotel. A few middle-aged women wearing long winter coats and way too much lipstick were standing on the corner of Tannimachi-suji as I turned left at the bottom of the hill and headed up a slight incline. Other than that, there wasn't much foot traffic, which was good news. The Rainbo Leisure Hotel was still closed for repairs, and this time there was no construction crew milling around the lobby. The door was locked, and for once my YMCA membership card wasn't up to the task. But I wasn't giving up that easily. I looked up at the empty building, searching for a way in.

A garbage chute descended from a fifth-story window, stopping about eight feet above the ground. One of those chutes you see at construction sites, a series of interlinked hollow plastic cylinders held together by thin chains. No doubt a truck or Dumpster had been parked underneath it to catch all the plaster and shredded carpet, but it was gone now. I stood underneath the chute, gauged my chances. The thing looked sturdy enough, no question, but getting inside wouldn't be easy. There was no rim, no ridge or anything else to grab onto at the bottom, just smooth plastic. I stared at it a few more minutes then went around the corner.

I approached the two women standing on the sidewalk. They looked like housewives waiting for the bus except neither were clutching shopping bags and there was no bus stop nearby. They weren't what you'd call stylish, but neither did they look down-and-out, and in formless winter coats they were dressed less provocatively than your average high school girl. It was only the overdone lipstick that made me guess they were lower-rung prostitutes. Streetwalkers were a rarity in Japan, but I guess times really were changing.

"Sorry to bother you, ladies," I said.

They looked at each other, looked at me, nodded.

"I need a little help."

They looked at each other, looked at me, then turned and began slowly walking in the other direction. Where was that famous Osaka friendliness everyone told me about? I trailed after them, deciding on a different approach said to be successful in winning over the locals.

"Who wants to make some money?" I called.

They stopped. They turned around. One muttered something to the other in Chinese, so I guess they weren't really locals. They took two cautious steps my way. I reached into my wallet and they shook their heads as if to say, *Not here, not in public.* I explained I needed a woman who was strong, had a good back. A woman who wasn't afraid of getting her hands dirty. Maybe two women would be better, I said, because it was going to be a tough job. Hell, I didn't even know if I'd be able to fit inside. Not to worry, though, I added, one way or another it would be over in a matter of seconds. The confused looks they gave me meant they'd understood every word or none of them. I said I'd pay them each ten thousand yen for two minutes' work. They understood that perfectly. We headed around the corner.

It took a lot of gesturing and pointing, but moments later I was standing atop a teetering human pyramid of sorts, each of the women cupping one of my feet and straining under the weight as I hoisted myself up and into the chute. I was just able to grab the rim where the second-lowest plastic tube met the first to pull myself inside. It was a tight squeeze and the tube was slick with chalky dust. I called out a thanks to the women, who were already gone. The sound echoed inside the narrow tube. I started climbing.

I don't know how long it took, but by the time I popped out inside the fifth-story hallway of the Rainbo Leisure Hotel my arms ached and my mouth tasted like drywall. I tried brushing off the dust but only managed to create thick white clouds that settled right back on me. The hallway was all done up in yellow. Yellow carpet, yellow walls, yellow ceiling. I headed for the stairs, descended one flight, and exited on the green floor. I had to peep through doorknob hollows again to find Tetsuo's room, but this time he wasn't in it. He'd be at the Nocturne Theater about now, slipping into his black hood, readying to take the stage.

I walked inside, flipped the light switch. Nothing happened. Tsutenkaku Tower shone through the window, bringing in just enough light to see. Empty coffee cans clanged and rolled over the floor as I stumbled around until I found a candle. The room was still littered with books but there was only one I was interested in. I found it next to his futon. *Ambiguities of the Subconscious* announced the notebook cover. The entries were dated and every page was filled to the margins with cramped handwriting. I opened to a random page and read:

Dec 14—Dreamt my grandmother and grandfather were blind and spent their days in a basement, endlessly walking through a maze of curtains. I had to be careful because if they touched me I'd go blind, too. My grandfather was angry, said it was all Einstein's fault. I can hear my brother's voice somewhere in the curtains but I can't see him and worry that I'm going blind. I decide I have to leave the house. Next thing I'm in the National Bunraku Theater, in the hallway by the offices. Four shabbily dressed men are sitting in a sofa at the top of the stairs. They're laughing. I ask them what they want and they giggle some more, then suddenly stop and look ashamed. "There's a hole," one said. "Under the stairs. We swear we didn't know." More laughing.

Dec 15—Went out drinking. No dreams, but a very dry mouth.

December 16—I'm talking with K when a fish falls out of my mouth and lands on the table. We watch it flop around, its mouth gaping and eyes bulging, then K covers it with a tissue. Now K is no longer there and I'm outside. A mother and her two children are across the street

*waving at me. She and her kids interlace their fingers in
some strange sign and smile. One of the little kids, an
older boy, comes across the street and tells me, "It means
carpenters." He starts back across the street and is hit by
a huge truck. The woman and her remaining child enter
a building on the other side of the street. I have to catch
them, to tell them about the accident. I enter the building
and I'm in a huge movie theater, like the biggest theater
in the world. It's packed with thousands of people, the
auditorium seating pitched at an incredibly steep angle.
Onscreen is a black-and-white silent film of a woman
crying. I see K in the first row of the audience and try to
make my way toward her. Suddenly I'm onstage and it
turns into that dream again, the one where I'm trapped
in a giant glass bubble. I pound my fists and bang my
head again and again against the smooth glass walls but
I can't get out.*

I stopped reading and turned the pages until I'd found
the date I was looking for. Friday, January 11. The night I'd
arrived in Osaka. The night Emiko killed Richard Gale. The
candle flickered and I heard the sound of sirens. I waited
until I was sure it wasn't the cops responding to reports of
a man breaking into a hotel under remodeling. The sirens
receded down the street and I resumed reading.

*Jan 11—I'm in an old house in the woods. I'm looking for
somebody and I can't find them. I reach a doorway at
the end of the hall and push open the door. It's dark and
the room smells sour. There's an old man sitting in a
white bed. He's whispering something over and over to
himself. Then he sees me and his hands start to shake
and he tries to smile but I notice the old man has the*

muzzle of a dog and yellow pointy teeth. The Dog-faced Man keeps whispering and I start to back away but the door I came through is gone. He starts barking between whispers and white foam spews forth and the sound gets louder and the room gets smaller. The old man is trying to get out of the bed but he can't stop trembling and suddenly I understand I have to kill the Dog-faced Man or I'll never be able to leave the room. I look down and there's a knife in my hand. I move toward the old man and for a moment he stops trembling and the bark turns into a laugh and the sagging skin around his throat jiggles. I feel myself getting sick. I slash the knife across his throat. White slathering foam gushes from his doggy mouth and I slash and slash but his skin keeps writhing around his throat and he keeps laughing and I wake up on the floor sweating and teeth clenched.

I read it again, slower this time, lingering over every word, and then closed the notebook and blew out the candle to sit in the dark and listen to the voices stored in my head.

Master Toyomatsu was the first. *With Tetsuo, it was as if his subconscious were very near the surface. He had an uncanny ability to transfer it through the puppet into the hearts and minds of the audience, to affect them on an almost subconscious level. It's like an electrical current opens, passing through the puppet, connecting you with the audience. This deep connection is something you can't really control, but when it happens, it's incredibly powerful . . .*

And then Tetsuo, speaking to me a few days ago in this very room. *Imagery from* The Whispering Goat *is from this dream I keep having,* he says. *A recurring dream, I guess you'd call it. I wanted to call the play* The Dog-faced Man *but I got outvoted.*

Emiko spoke next, words she'd said that night inside the overlit café. *Through his actions onstage, the thoughts and emotions he transferred through the puppet, I believed I could see the inner him, experience the person behind the hooded black veil.*

And later, her voice inside the sad karaoke parlor, recounting a dream. *I come upon a door at the end of the hall. I open it and there's an old man sitting upright in bed, his hands trembling as he whispers words I can't understand. I look closer and realize the old man has a long snout and teeth like a wolf. I woke from this dream terribly frightened, but when I tried to figure out what so disturbed me, I was completely at a loss . . .*

And finally the Scarecrow, minutes before he died. *Claims she doesn't even remember doing it,* he tells me. *She said she was dreaming about some guy with the face of a wolf, that she had to kill this wolf . . .*

I left the notebook where I'd found it, rose and made my way out of the dim room, nearly tripping over a stack of books before I reached the door. Stumbling around in the dark, pretty much like I'd been doing from day one. I didn't want to think about what I'd just read because I'd start drawing conclusions and the only conclusions I could draw were ones I didn't want to believe. It was hard enough to swallow that Emiko killed Gale because she was acting out a nightmare, much less one that wasn't even her own.

There would be plenty of time to think on the plane. I headed down the stairs of the deserted love hotel. If there were no direct flights to America, my plan was to go to Tokyo for the night, find a cheap hotel, and try to get on a flight the next day. Noguchi's men would've made it to the

PanCosmo by now, though how it played out from there was anyone's guess. I figured as soon as I'd called Imanishi he'd probably decided to have a look at the file before the cops arrived, hoping to deliver the whole package as if he'd solved the crime all on his own. But once Imanishi studied the file, he'd have figured that his suspicions about Kaori Inoue were a little off the mark. Though he'd have no way of knowing Emiko's identity, he'd know from the photos that she was the red-haired woman caught on the video surveillance camera, the woman he suspected I'd met in the stairwell. He'd also realize that though the killing itself may have been amateurish, Richard Gale was the victim of a professional operation after all, and maybe I'd been right in guessing the Komoriuta-kai were involved. Knowing this, he'd have little choice but to go to the police. He couldn't hope to bust the whole operation on his own, and he had the integrity of the PanCosmo Hotel to think about, after all.

Of course, the cops would have plenty of questions for him. One question he wouldn't be able to answer was where the file came from. And once they found out the woman in Imazato who shot the Scarecrow was the same woman who appeared with Richard Gale in the pictures, the questions would multiply. I had to get away before the questions found their way to me.

I unlocked the door on the ground level, walked out into the cool night air. One of the Chinese women was still standing on the corner, smoking and watching the traffic go by. I realized I was still covered in dust and tried to brush myself off. I was patting down the back of my slacks when I realized something was missing. After all I'd been through I couldn't help but laugh, because it was either that or throw myself under a train. The woman heard me laughing, gave me an uneasy smile. I thought about trying to work another deal, paying her a hefty sum to accompany me in a cab back to my hotel. Then I'd give her my key and send her up to room 1142, have her retrieve my passport, the one I'd left sitting inside the night table drawer like some idiot tourist. But I knew it would never work. Detective Imanishi and the cops would be waiting, watching, and besides, plans just had a way of going wrong inside the Pan-Cosmo Hotel.

Any other night and it all would have been breathtaking. The thousands of bodies swirling in a mad ballet inside Namba station, the chorus of pachinko parlors and advertising jingles blaring from the mouths of animated characters on the video billboards outside, the *chindonya* drumming up business on a Dotombori street thick with the mingled smells of grilled meats and fried octopus, of steaming noodle broths and sweet bean cakes. The blazing canyons of light mirrored on the silent Dotombori River, the dense neon riot of Soemoncho, the musical laughter of the idle young in America-mura. Any other night and this ordinary winter Tuesday in Osaka might have felt like Christmas and New Year's and the Fourth of July all rolled together into a noisy festive mess. So much to see, so much to smell, to hear, to taste, to buy. On any other night it would have seemed ridiculous to me that a city with the boisterous, unrefined beauty of Osaka should have to actively sell itself to a world that should have been beating its door down, that the city should need organizations like the Kinki Foundation at all.

But even a city like Osaka feels different when you're trapped, stuck in a place you don't belong. The people in

Umeda or Namba aren't people anymore, just frenzied masses always headed in the wrong direction, and the narrow streets don't feel quaint but choked off, constricted, suffocating. The musical soundscape lapses into a shrill atonal cacophony pierced only by laughter at once empty and menacing, and the gaudy soft-core porn beckoning from every surface of the pink districts seems no longer harmlessly lurid but downright hellish. And the lights, the ceaseless blinking blazing searing lights everywhere, only make you think how sad and desperate this need for attention, how childlike and primitive our collective fear of the dark.

I wondered how the city looked to Kaori, who could afford anything it offered but only wanted to buy a way out. Or to Richard, a twenty-three-year-old misfit millionaire who'd come halfway around the globe determined to make a new life for himself, only to end up living inside a hotel room, jobless, and friendless. Or my pal Curry, who'd watched the expats come and go, who threatened to leave every year but never did because there was nothing waiting for him in England. Most of all, I wondered how Osaka felt to Emiko as she endlessly wandered these streets of a world she longer inhabited but couldn't escape.

I tried to see the city from all these vantage points as I walked north from Namba station, but I couldn't. I was locked in my own perceptions just like everyone else and I was sure this would be the last of Osaka I saw for a while even though I wasn't leaving. The days ahead would be spent in grim police stations, facing grim men, and answering the same grim questions over and over. I knew I'd be taken in the moment I set foot inside the PanCosmo Hotel, so there was no point in rushing back. No point in rushing anywhere anymore.

Almost without thinking, I found myself walking toward the Nocturne Theater. It seemed appropriate somehow. I'd never seen the final act of the play, never found out how it all ended. The onstage happenings and their similarities to Richard's murder now had an explanation, albeit one that needed a lot of explaining, but I still didn't really get the puppet drama itself. I thought about how Tetsuo had mentioned something about a speech in the third act, how it hinted at the meaning behind the metaphorical whispering goat. Part of me hoped it would help explain what happened in Richard's hotel room that night, show that Emiko hadn't acted out Tetsuo's dream itself so much as the play it was based on. Somehow that seemed a more acceptable level of insanity. But in truth, I didn't think unraveling some strange puppet-show symbolism was going to help me or anybody else now. It was just a way of forestalling the inevitable. A way to lose myself in the dark.

But I was too late. The police were already there before I even got close. As were fire trucks, ambulances. A crowd had gathered on the opposite bank of the Dotombori to watch the smoke pour from the busted-out windows and the flames lick the building's façade. All around, blackened, shriveled bits of paper fluttered through the air, falling to the ground like wounded birds.

Chapter Twenty-four

Concierge Tanaka

*T*hey didn't arrest me outside the hotel. The smartly dressed quintet of women bowed and smiled as programmed when I entered the lobby. Concierge Tanaka handed me the key card to my room as always, along with a copy of the evening newspaper. They didn't intercept me outside my room. They weren't inside my room, either. Neither was Detective Imanishi. Neither were the Komoriuta-kai. My PanCosmo cell phone was silent. No gruesome pixilated images, no text messages, no voice mail.

I went over to the safe, opened it, found the Inoue file still inside, apparently untouched. My passport was right where I'd left it. In the closet, the satchel case I'd taken from Kusanagi Investigations and Research was there, along with my bloody shirt and the razor I'd taken from Emiko's apartment. The schedule for the Kinki Foundation conference lay open faced on the writing table in the corner. "Building Bridges" was tonight's theme. Not bridges between cultures or bridges to the future, just actual, physical bridges. A lecture on the history of Kyoto's ancient Sanjo Bridge, a discussion of art and literature inspired by the arched Taikobashi Bridge, an overview of competing designs for the multimillion-dollar remodeling of the Ebisubashi Bridge, the bridge from which I'd tossed the Tin Man's cell phone into the water before hailing a cab back to the hotel.

I'd stayed watching the fire in America-mura longer than most. Even from the other side of the river you could feel the heat on your face. I saw bodies being carted out and loaded into stretchers, but from far away they all looked the same. Hardly anyone spoke as they watched. Of those that did, nobody seemed to know anything about how the fire started or whether they'd managed to rescue everyone.

I don't know what happened, why there was no one waiting at the PanCosmo to make my life worse, but I wasn't complaining. More than anything I wanted sleep, but there would be time for that on the plane. I turned on the TV, let it play while I packed. There were helicopter shots of the fire on the news and live interviews with reporters stationed in front of the burned-out building, but the details were just emerging. Firefighters believed the blaze started in a small theater in the basement. Several people were at a local hospital being treated for smoke inhalation. There was at least one confirmed fatality, but officials weren't releasing any names until the family had been notified. I decided to call Mr. Oyamada, tell him he should contact the authorities to see if his son was alright. I figured I owed him at least that much. But when I called I got his voice mail. I didn't leave a message.

Still no mention of a shooting in Imazato before I flipped off the TV five minutes later and headed out the door. I decided to take the file with me, ditch it somewhere once I got back to Cleveland. The satchel case with the shirt and bloody razor I left behind because I didn't want trouble at the airport. I was just shutting the door on room 1144 when something caught my eye. Actually, it was the room number itself. I was supposed to be in room 1142. The sign said 1144.

The room adjacent to the one I'd just walked out of was 1142. I tried my key card. It didn't work.

I went down the hall, counting the room numbers off.

1142, 1144, 1140, 1138, 1136, 1134.

At the elevator, I reversed and headed back.

1134, 1136, 1138, 1140, 1144, 1142.

Somebody had switched the brass room-number plates on the doors. I hadn't noticed when I entered because I was used to just going to the fifth room on the right-hand side, paying no attention to the numbers. I had no idea what to make of the switch but I was done solving mysteries. I picked up my suitcase and took the elevator back down to the lobby. I was done taking stairwells, too.

Concierge Tanaka was disappointed to learn I was checking out early, but he understood when I told him my mother back in the States had to undergo an emergency operation. I handed over my key card, the complimentary cell phone, and settled the bill. I made sure to stand right in front of the surveillance camera, just so there would be a visual record of my checking out should anything happen to me between the hotel and the airport. The room-number switch was still bothering me. Just before I left, I asked Concierge Tanaka if he'd seen the hotel detective recently.

Concierge Tanaka frowned. "We have no hotel detective."

"Sure you do," I said. "Guy named Imanishi."

I dug into my wallet, slipped Imanishi's card onto the front desk. Concierge Tanaka's frown deepened. He stared at the card for several moments and then said, "Oh, my." He picked up a phone behind the front desk and started dialing. I reached across and pushed the hang-up button on the cradle.

"What's going on?"

"I'm afraid there has been a misunderstanding," he stammered.

"Misunderstanding?"

He put the phone down and sucked air through his teeth. That sound again. "Mr. Imanishi *does* work here, of course. He's been executive director of the PanCosmo custodial staff for several years. But he sometimes, well, he aspires to other duties. Quite without our approval and much to our displeasure, I can assure you. I certainly hope in misrepresenting himself he hasn't caused you any difficulties during your stay here at—"

"You're saying he's a janitor?"

"The head janitor," Tanaka said. "We've warned him about this sort of behavior in the past. He hasn't had any episodes in quite some time. We so hoped these troubles were behind him. But with the recent excitement—"

"So he didn't used to be a cop?"

"No, nothing like that," muttered Tanaka. "He's been

here since we opened in 1989. As his uncle is one of the hotel's leading shareholders, over the years we've done everything we could to be accommodating, to tolerate his, well, his eccentricities. I'm terribly ashamed about all of this. On behalf of the entire staff, I beg that you will find the kindness in your heart to please forgive the PanCosmo Hotel for this most egregious—"

"How the fuck did he lose his ear?"

Of all the questions I had, for some reason that was the one that came out. Concierge Tanaka blanched. The swearing seemed to knock all the officiousness out of him. "Nobody really knows," Tanaka said in a low voice. "Not that he doesn't tell stories, mind you. In one, a member of a motorcycle gang cut it off during a knife fight when he was sixteen. In another, he lost it escaping North Korean spies who were trying to abduct him. They tried to grab him off the beach." He gave me a wan smile. "By the ear, apparently."

I closed my eyes and pressed a palm to my forehead to keep my skull from erupting. I'd had it almost right from the start. "Detective" Imanishi found out about the murder when one of his cleaning staff discovered the body. Instead of calling the cops right away, he'd decided to play detective and ransacked the crime scene before they got there. He'd had access to every room in the hotel, mine included, and copying the video surveillance tape wouldn't have proven difficult. The deeper he got into his "investigation," the less inclined he would be to involve the real authorities. He couldn't do it without incriminating himself and bringing his fantasy crashing down. Even when I called to warn him that the Komoriuta-kai were on their way, he still hadn't involved the police. He'd decided to take matters into his own hands. What happened after that I wasn't sure, but I knew the door-number switch had something to do with it. My guess is he tried to lay some sort of trap, maybe even attempted a citizen's arrest. I had a feeling it didn't work out quite as he'd planned. That I still had the file meant it hadn't worked out quite how the Komoriuta-kai had planned, either.

Concierge Tanaka glanced over his shoulder to see if we were being watched, then leaned halfway across the front desk. "If you'd like to register a formal complaint, I can get the manager," he said. "Between you and me, I don't think anything will come of it as far as Imanishi's employment status. But you might be able to get a voucher to use during your next visit. A free night or two might be worth the trouble."

I just sighed, told Concierge Tanaka there was no need to get the manager involved. He nodded and asked if I needed transportation to the airport. He was calling a cab for me when my conscience finally won the silent battle raging in my head ever since Imanishi had first walked into my room. I'd held out on him, even misled him, and if something happened it was partly my fault. I couldn't leave not knowing.

"Your cab will be arriving momentarily," said Tanaka.

"I'm an idiot," I told him.

"I'm sorry?"

"Nose-hair trimmer. I forgot my nose-hair trimmer."

"Oh?"

"Left it upstairs. And it was a gift. From my mother. A real nice, state-of-the-art piece of equipment. She finds out I left it in Japan, I hate to think what might happen. Can I have my room key again? I'll be right back. Tell the cab to wait."

"Certainly," said Tanaka. "You were in room eleven . . . ?"

"Eleven forty-four."

Concierge Tanaka nodded, then reached into the drawer. A cloud of doubt formed over his features and dissipated almost the same moment. He smiled and handed me the card key for room 1144. We bowed to each other and I had to keep from running as I headed back across the enormous lobby.

Just about everything that could be opened or disassembled had been. The rest they'd just plain destroyed. The back had been ripped off the television set, the beach-scene watercolors torn from the walls and slashed, the safe unlocked, the drawers yanked open. Someone had run a knife up the back of the upholstered chair, the table was overturned, plants had been unpotted and dirt dumped all over the carpet. They'd searched everywhere a file could be hidden and lots of places it couldn't have been. In the bedroom the pillows were shredded and white feathers covered the floor like freshly fallen snow. The bedside table was smashed to bits, the large mirror above spiderwebbed in two different places.

They obviously hadn't been worried about making noise, but everything was silent now except the shower they'd left running. Steam rolled out beneath the bathroom door. I approached slowly, listening to the hiss of the water, half-wishing I still had the gun as I pushed open the door. A rush of hot air billowed out and I was enveloped in a thick white cloud. For a moment I was unable to see a thing, but as the steam disappeared through the open door the room began emerging. No one was in the shower. I turned off the faucet, felt my shirt adhering to my skin. Then I noticed Imanishi's silver tape recorder sitting on the bathroom-sink counter. I noticed small drops of blood spotting the sink. I picked up the tape recorder and hit the play button. The whiny gears started turning.

You oWe us oNe dog, said the distorted voice. *One dOg, two footSoldieRs, and a ceRtain file. We'Re willinG to com-Promise. TheRe's a car ouTside. Bring tHe file. Your colleAguE needs slEep. He's fallinG to pieCes.*

Then a hiss and a click and the tape went silent. I hit the stop button, put the recorder down. The blood dribbled across the counter, down onto the floor. I followed the trail all the way to the toilet and lifted the lid. Inside something pink and seashell shaped rested at the bottom. I reached in and fished it out. It was Imanishi's ear, but it looked different from the last time I'd seen it and it took me a moment to figure out why. This ear wasn't the prosthetic one.

Chapter Twenty-five

Journey to Chayamachi

I dropped off the key with Concierge Tanaka and tried to pretend nothing was wrong, even as I felt Imanishi's severed ear press against my thigh. I'd wrapped it in tissue and stuffed it in my front pocket. Maybe they could still sew it back on, but this was an afterthought. Taking it just seemed better than leaving it somehow. Concierge Tanaka wished me a safe and pleasant journey. The quintet of women by the entrance bowed and smiled as I walked out the door. I considered asking all five of them if they wanted to get married, private investigator Kusanagi's warnings be damned. We'd live in Utah and raise an army of smiling, bowing children and send them out to conquer the world with good manners and impeccable oral hygiene.

There were plenty of taxis in the roundabout and I didn't know which one was mine until a cabbie stepped out and gave me a wave. Looking beyond him, I saw the black Toyota Century parked at the end of the line like sludge on the bottom of a clear blue lake. There were No Parking signs all over the place but nobody in their right mind would ever ask a Century to move. I wondered if they'd been here ever since I arrived, had watched me walk in, waited for me to find the tape recorder and the ear. I was so bent on looking for cops that I could've missed them. The cabbie popped his trunk, motioned me to hand him my suitcase. I ignored him and walked right on by. The doors of the limo popped open as I neared. I ducked inside and the doors closed behind me automatically.

Lace curtains covered the windows and the interior was warm and dark, a leather-upholstered cave on wheels. The heater must've been going full blast but you could barely hear it. Mr. Tadamitsu Noguchi was propped opposite me, his frail body leaning to the side, mouth slanted open, head angled toward the ceiling. Dark as it was, I could see his face more clearly now than at Emerald Greens. Prominent brow, a nose almost equine by Asian standards, wide cheekbones, and a chin like chiseled granite—all of it lost now under skin which hung bloodless and sagging from the once stately architecture of his face, a face bereft of symmetry and robbed of any expression save sluggish bewilderment. He was dolled up in a black suit and someone had put a pair of sunglasses on him. Nobody else was in the backseat and I couldn't see who was in the front because it was curtained off. I set my suitcase on the floor in front of me. There was so much legroom in the limo I wished I had more limbs. The car pulled away from the curb, headed down the roundabout. I saw my confused cabbie trying to peer inside as we passed.

"So much unnEccesSary killiNg," said the distorted voice. I saw the device clipped to Noguchi's collar, the one I'd noticed just for an instant at the golf course. I leaned across the gap separating us and took it between my thumb and forefingers.

"PleaSe don'T do thAt!" said the voice.

It wasn't a microphone, but a tiny wireless video camera no bigger than my pinky toe. Anyone who needed a camera that small was up to no good, but I'm sure the item was a hot seller in Osaka's electronic ghetto of Den-Den Town. At least the Komoriuta-kai had found a more novel use for it than spying on the girls' locker room.

"We don't liKe thAt," the voice said. "PleaSe stop."

I wobbled the camera around, giving the viewer dizzying shots of the interior of the limo before finally leaving it pointed straight up at Mr. Noguchi's face, a low angle on his nostril. Mr. Noguchi let out a weak groan and thin saliva strung glistening down onto his lapel. I took out the handkerchief in his front pocket, gave his chin a wipe and stuffed it back in. There was a tiny microphone on his wrist, clipped where his cuff links would have been.

"So who am I really talking to?" I asked. I figured whoever was in front must be the new *kuro maku,* the "black curtain" running the show from behind the scenes until the old man finished fretting and strutting his hour upon the stage.

"Who we aRe is not impoRtant," said the voice. I guess I agreed because it would have been easy enough just to yank back the partition and have a look, but I didn't bother. We rounded a turn and Mr. Noguchi's head slumped to the side, revealing a small speaker built into the headrest. I'd probably find the same thing on his giant wheelchair. In my sleep-deprived state, the whole setup didn't even seem that strange.

"Where is Imanishi?" I asked.

"Your collEague the cleAning mAn is wiTh us."

"I don't see him."

"He's heRe. Just lisTen."

The limo swerved hard right. I slid over in the seat, my hand slamming against the window as the limo swerved back the other way. I heard a muffled thump in the trunk and then silence. I guessed that was Imanishi. Mr. Noguchi's head had flopped onto his other shoulder now, and his sunglasses hung halfway down the bridge of his nose. His eyes were clouded, unreadable. No telling whether he was cognizant enough to feel humiliated, so I went ahead and felt humiliated for him.

"Okay, so he's back there," I said. "Is he alive?"

"We don't go arouNd killiNg peoPle," said the voice. "Not liKe you AmeRicaNs. ViolEnce the primaRy iMpulse. So imPatient for bloodsHed. We loSt two good mEn today. Not the bEst of tiMes."

"Condolences. Is Imanishi alive or not?"

"Yes. The cleaning man is veRy stubBorn. Like a bad stAin. We've tRied to be reAsonAble. EveRy step of the wAy. To comproMise. We'Re not asKing much. We just neEd the file."

"And then what?"

"Then we'Re good. We pUt it all to bEd."

I tried to think it through, but my mind was already shutting down, throwing the switches on all the higher functions. Thinking hadn't done me much good lately, anyway. Every time I'd figured I had it untangled I'd just created more knots. I felt myself getting drowsy in the heated confines, sinking into the car seat like it was a warm bath. I just wanted everything over and done with.

"I'll give you the file," I said. "One condition."

"We'Re all eaRs."

"Stop harassing Emiko." Even as I spoke it seemed a foolish demand—I didn't know if she was alive or dead, in jail or in a hospital or what. "Leave her alone. Same goes for her husband. From this day forward, his loans are off the books, paid in full. Once I give you this file, you're to leave my friend Imanishi alone, too. And me. I never want to see or hear from any of you people ever again."

"That's moRe than oNe condiTion."

"I'm not finished," I said. "I know you have friends in the police department. If Emiko lives through the fake suicide you set up, they're going to have questions for her. I want you to make sure she walks."

"That will be difFicult."

"I don't care."

Even at this hour we hit a snarl of traffic near the Yo-doyabashi Bridge and the limo came to a virtual halt. The car looked ridiculous surrounded by all the microvans, subcompacts, and K-cars, the colorful Daihatsu Copens, toy-box Nissan Cubes, and sleekly feminine Toyota WiLL Cyphas. Like a Black Angus in a parade of show ponies. Other drivers gave us a wide berth but that didn't help us get across the bridge any faster. I heard whispering up front, voices discussing something. Then the digital wheeze I was supposed to believe was Mr. Noguchi spoke.

"Do you haVe the file on yOur peRson?"

"Maybe."

"We thiNk you do," said the voice. "NothIng to stop us frOm taKing it. Now we cAn do whatEver we wish. Now it's youR turN to coMpromiSe. We've reconSideRed. Less dan-Ger if Emiko disAppeaRed. Less daNger if you both disap-pEared."

We were halfway across the bridge now, above an island engulfed by a split in the river. Ahead lay Sonezaki, site of the most famous lovers' suicide in the history of Bunraku. I thought about the woman at the puppet-head bar talking about the *michiyuki,* the journey the lovers make before dying at dawn. If Emiko and I were going to die, this was as close to a *michiyuki* as I would get. Riding in a gangster's limo with a paralyzed old man and an earless hotel janitor in the trunk. Except we weren't lovers and I wasn't going to die, and if I could help it, neither was Emiko nor anybody else.

"Maybe it would be less dangerous if we disappeared," I started. "But the Tin Man already tried that trick on me, and look where it got him. The Scarecrow didn't have much more luck with Emiko. Killing me is just going to create problems. For one, your friends in the local government aren't going to like two dead Americans in one week. Bad for tourism. Maybe they crack down on you for a while. And like you said, now isn't the best of times for that to happen. If what I read in the papers is correct, your gang is gonna have more than enough to worry about soon as the honorable waxwork here kicks the bucket." I jerked a thumb toward Mr. Noguchi. "Extra police scrutiny is something you don't need. Besides, you don't go around killing people, remember?"

No reply was forthcoming. They were letting me sweat it out, literally. The air in the car was heavy, hard to breathe. Probably even worse in the trunk. We made it across the bridge, past Sonezaki, through the dense thicket of Umeda. The stores were closed, the trains had stopped running, and there was hardly anyone on the streets. My eyes kept closing and it was all I could do to keep from nodding off. The scenery outside was rendered a series of ellipses, train stations, department stores, and sky-rises fading in and out until suddenly I noticed we'd stopped moving. We were on a deserted street, either side flanked by rows of one-story wooden houses with tiled roofs. I'd never been here before, but I knew well enough where we were. It was Chayamachi, the undeveloped part of the neighborhood that had been vacant going on ten years, the ghost town in the middle of Umeda that had triggered the downfall of Inoue Development. You could say we'd come to where it all started, but you could just as easily say it started in the ballroom of the PanCosmo Hotel, or in a hotel room in Sapporo. Or on some stretch of the Hanshin expressway where Emiko's husband got in a car accident, or at the Nocturne Theater the night Emiko came under Tetsuo's spell, or where CEO Martin Gale's plane crashed, or at the National Bunraku Theater where I'd interviewed Tetsuo years ago, or in some mountain resort town where Tetsuo had lost his twin brother. There was no single starting point, but I knew, one way or another, this was where it was all going to end.

The driver got out of the car, walked around to the back. I heard the trunk being opened and waited for gunshots. Instead all that came were muffled thumping noises and the sound of the trunk being closed again. The car rocked slightly with the impact and the driver came halfway around the vehicle. My window rolled down automatically. The driver's arm came partway through the window. A hand in a white cotton glove held a gun to my temple. Another moan from Mr. Noguchi, the faint noise escaping his mouth like it had traveled a great distance and overcome all kinds of obstacles only to emerge a strangled sigh.

"Is the file in yOur sUitCase?" the voice asked.

I was too tired to negotiate. "Yes."

"LeAve it and gEt out."

I leaned over and started to unlatch the suitcase.

"The whole thiNg. LeaVe it aNd get out."

The driver with the gun took a step back and the doors popped open. I slid out, hands in the air. He motioned me to walk a few paces and then turn around. I did as instructed. The air outside was refreshingly cool after being in the car and I could feel myself coming to life again. The driver kicked the back of my knees and forced me to kneel. I was facing an empty house, the wood already moldering, windows boarded up and no lights on anywhere.

I heard a dog barking somewhere in the distance.

A door opened and closed, and I heard the sound of the limo speeding away. I slowly rose and turned around. Executive Custodial Director Imanishi lay curled on the ground, hands taped behind his back, legs bound at the knees and ankles. Both his eyes were swollen purple, blood was crusted under one nostril, and they'd taped a whole tissue packet to the side of his head where his ear had been severed. He was alive though and urgently trying to tell me something, but there was tape over his mouth, too. I ran over to him, knelt down and tried to unravel it. He kept moaning. I yanked the tape loose.

"Did you record the license-plate number?" he asked, gasping for breath. "Tell me you remember the license number?" I looked over my shoulder, saw the limo's tail-lights receding in the distance. They made a left turn and were gone.

"It's over, Imanishi," I said.

"I counted the turns from the trunk so we could retrace the route if necessary. Though judging the intervals between was difficult because I couldn't see my watch. Through trial and error, if we repeat the pattern of right, right, left, right—"

"Imanishi, it's over."

But he paid no attention. With one fake ear and the other recently mutilated, he probably couldn't hear me at all. He kept babbling about rights and lefts, about justice and the struggle against evil and the integrity of the Pan-Cosmo Hotel as I undid the tape on his wrists, but his heart wasn't in it anymore. By the time I loosed the tape from his knees he'd lapsed into silence. He didn't ask me about the file or the woman in the stairwell or anything else as I helped him to his feet. The two of us stood there in the moonlight, avoiding each other's eyes, knowing we were lucky to be alive and feeling emotions neither of us wanted to share. I looked around at the crooked streets and wondered where the nearest hospital was.

Chapter Twenty-six

The Fire and the Firefly

Over the next few days, I spent a lot of time in hospitals.
Like everyone else I can't stand the places,
but after all the chaos of the last few days,
maybe I needed their veneer of orderliness,
the tranquillity of shiny floors, long empty
hallways, cloying soft music. Maybe I needed
the slow ballet of doctors with their eyes
glued to clipboards and nurses in white
shoes wheeling patients through the corri-
dors. Needed watching ordinary people arrive during visiting hours, bearing flowers
and fresh fruit, looking anxious and hopeful
or just tired. Needed to sit in waiting rooms,
thumbing through boring magazines, dozing
off and waking to find myself surrounded by
new faces. But late at night was when I
seemed to need the hospitals most. Walking

the darkened hallways, thinking of all the people sleeping behind the doors, their bodies prone and inert, minds dreaming unknown dreams.

The facility where Tetsuo Oyamada was being treated had a reputation as one of the finest hospitals in the Kansai, a fitting place for the son of the executive vice co-director in chief of the Kinki Foundation's Annual Conference Awards and Invitation Subcommittee. I spent a fair amount of time with Mr. Oyamada, but we never did get around to talking about the Sapporo Incident. There were bigger things on his mind now.

Tetsuo had been admitted the night of the Nocturne Theater fire, given emergency treatment for smoke inhalation and burns running from his neck down one side of his chest and arm. The doctors said it could have been much worse, that Tetsuo was lucky he hadn't been killed rushing back into the building, trying to rescue the one person still trapped inside. The fire had spread quickly, and if it had been a packed house there would certainly have been many more casualties. Of course, the house was never packed at the Nocturne Theater, and as it happened, the small crowd reacted about as calmly as you could hope for given the events of that night.

The fire started in the middle of the second act, during a part of the play where Tetsuo and his puppet Kimiko were waiting in the wings. Ichiro, the manpuppet slated to die by Kimiko's hand, was delivering his tired soliloquy when an audience member in the front row calmly stood up, lit a rag stuffed inside a jumbo beer bottle filled with gasoline, and hurled the bottle at the stage. Glass shattered on the front of the proscenium and flames shot every direction. As the shadows raced offstage and the audience scrambled to get out, the man removed another bottle from his backpack and tossed it stage right. Blue flames clambered up the curtains. Two more bottles followed, aimed at the rear of the room. As the theater became engulfed in flames and patrons stumbled through the gathering smoke toward the exit, the man sat back down with calm, unhurried motions, as if he were merely returning to his seat after an intermission. Then he removed a final bottle from his backpack, lit the fuse, and shattered the gasoline bomb at his feet.

Tetsuo hadn't even seen how the fire started, but when he heard what had happened he ran back into the theater to find the man still sitting there, eyes shut, arms crossed over his chest, as the circle of flames closed in on all sides. Tetsuo screamed himself hoarse and tried to break through the wall of fire but was rebuffed by the heat and the smoke, and eventually collapsed. By the time the firemen arrived to drag Tetsuo out, the flames had spread and grown so blindingly fierce that the firemen couldn't even see the form sitting in the front row, didn't even know anyone was there until the fire was extinguished and the smoke had cleared to reveal a small black body propped in a metal folding chair. The heat was so intense it had shrunken the man's very bones, and when one of the firefighters first saw him from across the room, they initially mistook the corpse for one of the Nocturne Theater's puppets. It took three days for dental records to confirm what Tetsuo had told the police, and what I suspected that night while I watched the fire from across the Dotombori River. A man named Kiyoshi Hasegawa had set the blaze. Police said the motive was revenge, though discretion prevented them from elaborating further.

There were no other casualties, and aside from Tetsuo no one suffered serious burns. Four other people were treated for smoke inhalation, however, and though most of them were released the same night, one patient was kept on a bit longer on account of his advanced age. Master Toyomatsu had not only been in the Nocturne Theater the night of the fire, but was a regular patron, according to Tetsuo. When I asked him how he could be sure, Tetsuo just smiled and said, "Funny thing about those black hoods— just because people can't see me, they always assume I can't see them, either."

According to Tetsuo, on nights the National Bunraku Theater had no performances scheduled, Master Toyomatsu would come to the Nocturne dressed in a baseball hat, dark glasses, and an old sweater. He'd always arrive just as the houselights were going down, would sit silently throughout the show, and then hurry away the moment the performance ended. The only person who was there more often, said Tetsuo, was a strange woman the puppeteers had all come to refer to as Hotaru. They called her Firefly for the way her eyes gleamed in the dark, the way her whole face seemed to radiate when the lights went down. Everyone thought she looked a little overzealous, and her absence on the night of the fire seemed eerie until they later read about what had happened in Imazato and saw her face on television.

Master Toyomatsu and Tetsuo shared the same room during their recovery. They must have eventually got to talking, because the final time I went to visit I bumped into Mr. Oyamada in the waiting room. There had been a promising development, he said. Master Toyomatsu was allowing Tetsuo to rejoin the National Bunraku Theater. After delivering the news, Mr. Oyamada beamed and shook my hand and even went so far as to clap me on the shoulder as he thanked me over and over, ignoring my protests that I had nothing to do with it.

When I visited that last time I found Tetsuo alone, Master Toyomatsu having been discharged earlier that morning. He was still heavily bandaged around his chest and right arm, but otherwise he seemed to be recovering well. Still, he wasn't quite the same Tetsuo I'd met in the barren Rainbo Leisure Hotel. No longer fidgeting with nervous energy, no longer speaking in manic sentences laced with words like "atavistic" and "metaphorical." Some of his books had been brought from the hotel, but as far as I could tell he hadn't bothered cracking any of them. His *Ambiguities of the Subconscious* journal was there too, wedged at the bottom of the stack. I asked him if he'd still been writing about his dreams. Tetsuo shook his head, eyes dropped to his lap as he spoke.

"I can't remember them since the fire," he said.

"It's probably because of the painkillers."

"Maybe," said Tetsuo. "But I think I'm finished with all that. I've decided to go back to the National Bunraku Theater. I'm half a mummy anyway," he said, glancing up at me with a weak smile. "Might as well go all the way."

But as we spoke, it became clear he was relieved to be returning to the National Bunraku Theater. Despite his mummy comment, he seemed to reverse his previous stance completely, saying that maybe Bunraku wasn't the most cutting-edge art form in the world, but that there was something to be said for not pandering to the latest trends. That Bunraku was a worthy art form precisely because it had so few ties to the modern world, and through its longevity had earned itself a different kind of freedom— the freedom to pursue artistic purity untethered by mass commercial appeal, a freedom enabling performers and audiences alike to experience moments of beauty and sadness that reached across the centuries.

Twisting a phrase from the Nocturne Theater's manifesto, he told me Japan was an old place and had seen so much already, had gone through enough changes during the previous century to last most countries a millennium. And wasn't this insatiable hunger for the new partly to blame for everyone's rootless confusion, partly to blame for what this country had become? And did anyone even stop to think about what this country, this world, had become?

At first I thought Master Toyomatsu must have given him an earful while they shared the room, brainwashed him with pro-Bunraku propaganda while he slept. But seeing Tetsuo's eyes narrow and his hands fretfully pick at his hospital gown as he pontificated, I realized Tetsuo was just getting better, becoming his old self again. Not the quiet thirteen-year-old kid with moppety locks, but the man that boy was growing into. A genius with his mouth closed, according to Kiyoshi, but otherwise a confused and strangely likable young man.

He went on to say the Nocturne Theater people were smart, but technically they couldn't hold a candle to the puppeteers at the National Bunraku Theater. Sure, they could do all the showy stuff, but the subtleties of the art form escaped them. And even if they eventually learned to operate with greater finesse, no one would appreciate it. It would be like giving gold coins to a cat because the audience at the Nocturne, to the extent there was one, only wanted darker and bleaker and weirder and bloodier. Spending time there made Tetsuo appreciate how many bright moments there actually were in the traditional dramas. Dance interludes, comical scenes, even a happy ending once in a while. Focusing so exclusively on the dark side day after day had started to affect his mind, he said, changing even the way he dreamed.

Your dreams weren't the only ones affected, I thought. But I was determined not to let him know how much damage his subconscious had unleashed, didn't see what good it would do to tell him that in striving to connect with his audience, he'd managed to transmit his dreams in a way that exploded all the high-minded metaphors for that magical something that passed between a performer and an audience, rendering them in nightmarishly literal terms. Even when I'd read about the dream he'd been having and saw how closely it corresponded with Emiko's, I'd resisted the only conclusion possible, thought surely there must've been a more rational explanation.

But the more I thought about it, the more I decided there wasn't. Realizing how easily I'd been able to picture the details of the dream, how I could all but see the Dog-faced Man when I closed my eyes, made me think that if I dwelled on it I'd lose my grip on reality, slip into that shadowy world Emiko had fallen into. I wasn't going to tell Tetsuo what I'd learned about the ambiguities of the subconscious, because if I voiced my thoughts they'd probably end up hospitalizing me too, in an entirely different kind of facility. But just before I left, I couldn't help asking Tetsuo about what happened in the third act of *The Whispering Goat.*

"They get the wrong guy," Tetsuo said. "You know how in scene one Kimiko and Hajime are planning to kill Kimiko's philandering husband? And then in scene two, you see Kimiko kill that guy in bed? Well, it turns out to be the wrong guy. They had it all set up with a dude who worked at the front desk of the hotel, but he accidentally slipped Kimiko the wrong room key. So she ends up killing the guy in room 142 instead of room 144."

I just nodded along and smiled as he told me how it all ended with Kimiko and her conspirator Hajime sitting in the same hotel from scene one, staring down at the razor and wondering what to do next. I didn't let my mind anchor on the details, refused to search for any distorted similarities between the play and the world waiting for me outside.

And I tried not to wonder if it could all happen again. If some other troubled audience member would one day start empathizing all out of proportion and find their dreams suddenly hijacked, their lives thrown violently out of order. I told myself it was a fluke, that it only happened because Emiko was halfway into the shadow world before she'd ever set foot inside the Nocturne Theater, that the violence which erupted inside the PanCosmo Hotel that night was the end result of a combination of factors not likely to be repeated. I refused to consider that Emiko wasn't the only one it had happened to, refused to entertain doubts raised by Kiyoshi Hasegawa and the Sapporo Incident. And I didn't want to think about what Master Toyomatsu said, either, about how Tetsuo's subconscious was still raw and uncalibrated, and how puppeteers are never really any good until they're fifty-five or sixty.

No, it was all just a fluke, I told myself. Tetsuo thanked me for visiting, and said if I really wanted to help kids learn what true art is, I should come back to Osaka and do another piece on the National Bunraku Theater. I said I'd keep it in mind, then wished him a speedy recovery. Maybe in another eight years, I'd be ready to write that follow-up article, but at the moment I had no desire to see a puppet show ever again.

The hospital where Imanishi had his ear sewn back on and was being treated for a broken wrist and two fractured ribs became another one of my haunts, though I spent more time in the waiting room there than in Imanishi's company. One of the nurses seemed to have it in for me and was always chasing me out of the room long before visiting hours were over, which I suppose was just as well. I couldn't decide how much I should tell Imanishi about the woman in the stairwell and the Inoues and the Komoriuta-kai. Before each visit I arrived at a new policy only to change my mind.

Sometimes I decided I'd at least tell him that esteemed guest Richard Gale was secretly a millionaire, that somebody found out and was trying to get money from him when the plan went horribly wrong. Surely, Imanishi deserved that much. Other times, I vowed I'd come clean on the whole thing, tell him every detail, leaving only Emiko's identity a secret. Funny that even after everything, I was still protecting the woman in the stairwell. Long after she needed my help, long after anything I could say or do would make any difference whatsoever.

I'd walk into Imanishi's room, say hello and take a seat by the window, expecting him to pull a little silver tape recorder from his hospital gown and start plying me with accusatory questions laced with hospitality. But for whatever reason, he never did. In fact, every time I tried to bring up Richard Gale, he'd suddenly decide he needed a glass of water or more medication, and would hit the call button to bring the nurse trundling into the room. He no longer seemed to have any interest in the Richard Gale case whatsoever. I suppose it was a good sign as far as his mental health was concerned, but it left us with little to talk about. When I showed up for my third visit, the nurse told me Imanishi was sleeping and was not to be disturbed. She wasn't a good liar, but getting turned away came as kind of a relief. Imanishi and I had pretty much nothing in common except the dead American and the PanCosmo Hotel, and neither one of us was much for small talk.

I never saw Imanishi again, either at the hospital or the PanCosmo, though Concierge Tanaka and I did have a brief conversation about him just before I checked out. While Imanishi was in the hospital, the management had raided his office and found not only the stolen surveillance tapes, the wig fibers, and the tape recorder, but also a stash of hidden camera equipment. Enough, Concierge Tanaka whispered, to spy on half the guests of the hotel. After the requisite consensus-building, the managers of the PanCosmo Hotel predictably decided not to dismiss Imanishi, but had instead granted him six months' paid absence to rest and recover at a facility in Nara. In the meantime, they were exploring the possibility of creating a special position for him in the back office, one in which he no longer had access to rooms and would be prevented from interacting with guests, but could put his detective skills to modest use as executive director of inventory control. I never did find out how he lost his first ear.

With Mr. Oyamada no longer worried about his son's future and Imanishi no longer trying to solve mysteries, the rest of my stay at the PanCosmo Hotel was pretty quiet. No calls, no unexpected knocks on the door. When not visiting the hospitals, I caught up on the news, buying three papers every day and reading them cover to cover. All of them had stories about Emiko, but the only story about Richard Gale

I could find was buried in the crime section of the local paper. The big news was that the official investigation surrounding Richard Gale's death seemed to be heating up. Acting on the surveillance footage of a red-haired woman recovered from Imanishi's makeshift crime lab, the cops had taken Kaori Inoue in for questioning. They'd made some phone calls across the Pacific and found out that Richard Gale was not your average *eikaiwa* teacher, not by a long shot. As the sole beneficiary of an eighteen-million-dollar inheritance, his wife clearly had a motive for killing her estranged, philandering millionaire spouse.

I doubted the cops would get much from Kaori. They'd go on questioning and releasing her and she'd play whatever part she needed to—the grieving widow, the wrongfully accused victim, the naïve young woman taken in by some exotic, charming foreigner. No cop I'd ever met would be able to match her cool gaze without going a little weak in the knees, and even in decline the Inoue name still had enough pull to make officials a little reluctant to tarnish it unnecessarily. Besides, if what Curry told me was true, she was innocent. According to him, he'd arranged it all without her knowledge. Still, it was as difficult for me to think of Kaori as innocent as it was for me to conceive of Emiko as guilty, complicated as the situation was. Complicated and difficult, my friends, until the very end.

The police would never solve Gale's murder. It might have been different if they'd collared Curry, but Curry was long gone. The first time I tried calling his office at Koiwazurai Entertainment they told me he was out for the day. The second time they said he'd gone missing, and asked who I was, how I was acquainted with Kenneth Balderton, if I knew anything about his sudden disappearance. The third time they just told me he was no longer an employee and transferred me to a guy named Bertie Lahr who was now handling all his translation work. I hung up before Bertie came on the line, wondering whether the Komoriuta-kai had decided their *gaijin* conspirator was too big a risk and offed him, or whether he'd simply panicked when Kaori was arrested and caught the first available flight to Heathrow. The second scenario seemed more likely. Curry liked to play the jolly fat man, the comically misunderstood stranger in a strange land, but when it came right down to it, he knew how to take care of himself as well as anyone.

When not reading, I slept. When not sleeping, I killed time attending Kinki Foundation activities—a boat cruise down the Okawa River, a seminar on the Fukui Prefecture's glassware production, an information session on applying for corporate subsidies in the Wakayama Prefecture. Given that the whole point of the conference seemed to be to promote the Kansai region in hopes of luring foreign businesses, I got the feeling the Kinki Foundation wasn't exactly thrilled with the sparse attendance. There were only a handful of people at most activities. I was usually the only non-Japanese in the room, and it wasn't like I was the chief executive of some multinational corporation or even a guy looking to relocate his yo-yo factory. But people carried on, as the people of Osaka do. Everyone was warm and friendly and skilled at hiding their disappointment. The city had seen better days, but it had seen much worse, too, and you got the feeling that Osakans were better able to handle the psychological impact of the terminal recession because, unlike those in Tokyo, they'd never tricked themselves into believing they were at the center of the universe, anyway. Aside from a certain janitor I'd met, most of them were too pragmatic to harbor grandiose delusions.

I spent my last morning in Osaka shopping for a suit to wear to the Kinki Foundation's annual conference awards banquet that night. After the Komoriuta-kai drove off with my suitcase, I'd had to buy a new one, along with another pair of pants, two white button-down shirts, socks, underwear. Most of them I picked up at stores on the lobby level of the PanCosmo, but I decided to go to the Takashimaya department store for the suit. There were hundreds of closer, bigger, and more stylish stores in Umeda, but for some reason I was drawn to Takashimaya. Maybe because the old-fashioned, unhip, and reassuringly aboveground building it occupied appealed to the Midwesterner in me, maybe because it wasn't jammed with people younger than I was, or maybe just because going there reminded me of Emiko.

While I picked through the racks I watched her ex-coworkers and wondered how many of them remembered her, how many of them had recognized her face on the news and wondered if there was anything they could've done, how many cursed themselves for not making more of an effort to keep in touch after she'd quit, wished they'd had some idea of what she'd been going through. But they had their own problems like everybody else, and when someone is so bent on withdrawing from the world, there's not much you can do to keep them from falling through the cracks. I ended up buying a conservative black suit made in Italy. It was a little tight in the shoulders and cost more than I should've spent, but what the hell. It's not every day someone gives you an award.

⊖

*I*n my room on the eleventh floor, I put on a clean white T-shirt and the same white button-down. I donned my new suit and checked myself in the mirror. The person staring back at me looked exhausted and slightly perplexed, but at least he had a new suit on. There was still two hours until the awards banquet started. I decided to go to the bar on the sixth floor to try to come up with some kind of short acceptance speech while I drank a couple of cold Kirin lagers and maybe caught the Channel Eight weathergirl on TV.

But when I opened my door to leave, the woman standing in front of me looked much like she must've when Richard first met her. The sight of Emiko's pale face hidden behind dark glasses and framed by the auburn-colored wig jarred me, but I suppose she had good reason to be in disguise now. Ever since the business in Imazato made the news, her existence had undergone another swift transformation. To her it must have seemed like she'd fallen asleep and woke up inside someone else's life all over again.

The Scarecrow, it turned out, wasn't on the best of terms with the National Police Agency, having previously served time for racketeering and weapons violations. He was already wanted on charges ranging from extortion to assault and battery stemming from an unrelated loan-shark scheme in Kobe when a certain brave, long-suffering housewife in Imazato shot him in self-defense after he'd drugged her and threatened to murder both the woman and her comatose husband.

I had no idea whether Emiko had improvised the story herself, if the cops had concocted it as a way of rewarding her for getting rid of the thorn in their sides, or if the

Komoriuta-kai had acted on my demands. Whatever the case, the press latched on to it right away. The tale of the "Housewife Vigilante," as she was dubbed in features and editorials all over the country, caught the imagination of a public increasingly sick of the usurious tactics being used by criminal loan-sharks and so-called legitimate creditors alike. Overnight, she became a symbol of resistance, an example of courage in the face of adversity. She hadn't simply accepted her sad fate in life like so many, but had stood up and said "enough," she wasn't going to take it anymore. She represented a uniquely Osakan no-nonsense approach to dealing with hardship, argued one local paper, while an overwrought Tokyo editorialist called her no less than the modern-day embodiment of Japan's ancient fighting spirit. Luckily for Emiko, the press was notoriously fickle, and the frenzy probably wouldn't last more than a couple of weeks if she kept a low profile.

For a few moments I just stood there holding the door, unable to say anything.

"You look like you've seen a ghost," she said.

In a way I felt I had. After I'd walked out of her apartment, I'd tried to avoid thinking about her. I was glad to know she was alive, but even as I saw her face on the television and read about her "heroism" in the newspapers, I'd convinced myself she wasn't quite real. And I certainly didn't expect her to show up at the PanCosmo Hotel. If I were Emiko, I would've never set foot in the place again. But she looked good, well rested, stronger somehow than she'd seemed before.

"Do you mind if I come inside?" she asked, eyes darting nervously down the hall. I motioned her in and she strode across the room, going to the window and pulling the curtains closed. "Sorry," she said, "but they're always watching me now. I've been a prisoner in my own apartment ever since I left the hospital."

"What about your walks?"

"Those days are over," she said. "I can't set foot outside without being chased by cameras. I think I managed to give them the slip this time thanks to my little disguise, but who can be sure? Anyway, I can't stay long. Have you got anything to drink? I could use something."

"Coffee, tea, water . . ."

"Maybe something a little stronger."

The room was dark now, lost in shadows, but I didn't bother turning on the lights. I fixed a couple of drinks from the minibar, a vodka tonic for her, Suntory on ice for me. When I turned around, she'd taken off her dark glasses. She peeled off her wig and shook her hair out. I started to say something, but she held up a hand to quiet me.

"I know you have lots of questions. Believe me, I have questions of my own. And maybe one day there will be time for all of our questions. But I can't talk anymore, can't even think right now. I've done nothing but talk and sit there listening to my own head for these last few days. And I didn't want to come back here, but I had to. I need this. Maybe it seems strange to you, but this is what I need."

Then she took off her coat. She didn't stop there.

Neither one of us stopped for a long time. And for once, I didn't feel much like talking or even thinking, either. There were lots of thoughts I maybe should've had, but everything happened too quickly. No chance to wonder if she knew I was the one who'd shot the Scarecrow, if this was her way of thanking me for saving her life or just for listening, if it was her way of trying to reconnect to the everyday world or her way of trying to escape it altogether. No chance to wonder if sleeping with someone as unhinged as Emiko was dangerous or just a bad idea, maybe a little unfair, maybe even a little sad. No chance to wonder if this was what I'd really wanted all along, if this was why I'd protected her for no good reason, or if this was just something that happened the way these things sometime happen. No chance to wonder about her comatose husband lying in a hospital bed somewhere, locked inside his own damaged brain, no chance to formulate all those questions I wanted to ask about dreams of the dog-faced man and what went through her mind when she woke up and discovered herself alone in a room just like this, covered with the blood of a stranger. No chance to ask whether her dreams were her own now, how she would fill her days without long walks and pass her nights without the Nocturne Theater, whether she'd given up on invisibility, what she planned to do next, if she really believed what she was doing here, now, with me, was actually going to help her. No chance to even decide she didn't know most of the answers any better than I did, and that what we know so often makes so little difference.

No words were exchanged the entire time and we hardly made a sound until the very end. And when it was over we both slept. Sometime later, I awoke to see her across the room, putting on her clothes. After getting dressed she came back toward the bed and stood over me, her pale white face emerging from the darkness.

And suddenly I thought about Richard Gale, how there were no resistance wounds on his body. That part had always bothered me because, no matter how drunk he was, he must have felt something. I'd always imagined the fatal wound was the first one, that she'd quietly walked to his side of the bed, leaned over and gently drawn the razor across his throat, almost like the death scene in the puppet show. That then there was a remorseful pause before the frenzy that followed, a moment where Richard woke to see Emiko hovering above him just as I did now, her skin the color of old pearls, her face softly luminous in the dark. A moment where he knew what was happening, where he weighed everything that had happened to him in the last several months and chose to surrender, to just close his eyes and await whatever would come next.

When I opened my eyes again Emiko was gone and the phone was ringing. The clock said it was 7:24. The Kinki Foundation's awards banquet started about twenty minutes ago and I figured the call was probably Mr. Oyamada, wondering where I was. I let it ring. When it stopped, I got out of bed. I slipped on my boxers and a fresh white T-shirt and poured out the untouched drinks still sitting on the corner tabletop. I picked up my suit lying in a wrinkled heap on the floor, pulled open the curtains, and made myself a fresh drink. A few minutes later, the phone rang again. Darkness spread over the city, the glass and steel high-rises beyond Osaka Castle twinkling to life even as their forms merged with the deepening shadows of the low winter sky. From here the city looked far away, impenetrably dense and complex, yet somehow immaterial, nothing but a convolution of shapes glimpsed in the act of vanishing. I let the phone ring one more time, then put on my new suit and headed downstairs.

Acknowledgments

Thanks first to John Williams for his keen editorial eye and hard work in whipping this book into shape. As always, I'm indebted to Dan Hooker for sticking by me and giving me encouragement throughout the entire series. I'm grateful to my parents for being my first and most loyal readers (among the innumerable other things I'm grateful to them for). I'm also thankful that my wife, Chee-Soo Kim, was patient and supportive enough not to kill me while I was writing this book, though she certainly had every right.

I owe a huge debt of gratitude to Yoshihito Terahara for his extraordinary kindness in introducing me to Osaka. You're a good guy, Mr. Terahara, and I hope this book doesn't get you into trouble. If it does, you can blame Shane Stiles for getting us together. Similar thanks (and simultaneous apologies) to Rie Maruo and especially Junko Matsumoto from the City of Osaka. I'd also like to thank Emi Watanabe, Keiko Miki, and particularly Asako Shiomi for their help.

The National Bunraku Theater is an experience that should not be missed if you're lucky enough to visit Osaka. I'd like to thank everyone there for allowing me a glimpse at this fascinating art form, and beg you'll forgive the many liberties I've taken in this novel. Many thanks to Akira

Igarashi and Yoshinobu Fujii, and above all to Keiko Kobayakawa for sharing her knowledge. Puppeteer Kiritake Ichisuke took time from his busy schedule to answer my questions, and for this I'm extremely grateful. I hope to see you perform again someday soon.

Of course, I wouldn't have understood much of what was being said without the interpretative skills of Ms. Ohigashi. *Domo arigato gozaimashita, Ohigashi-san!*

Thank you also to Shuzo Takahashi for showing me around the Hotel New Otani, and thanks to the staff at the Green Hill Hotel for making me feel welcomed.

Christian Greenaway and Shuko Matsuura, I'm glad to have met you both and you made my visit heaps of fun. Come visit Chicago—I owe you lots of drinks. Hats off to Chris for the *eikaiwa* thoughts, as well.

My biggest thank-you of all goes to Kozue Tanaka for her gracious hospitality while showing me around Osaka and patiently answering my silly questions for months afterward. The best part about working on this book was getting to know you a little, and I hope we will be friends for years to come.